KENNETH PANNEBECKER
READING, PA

D0952092

KENNETH PANNEBECKER
READING, PA

RAVEN

Also by William Kinsolving
Born With the Century

RAVEN

A Novel by

William Kinsolving

G.P. PUTNAM'S SONS
NEW YORK

Copyright © 1983 by William Kinsolving
All rights reserved. This book, or parts thereof,
must not be reproduced in any form without permission.
Published simultaneously in Canada by General Publishing Co.
Limited, Toronto.

Library of Congress Cataloging in Publication Data

Kinsolving, William.
Raven.

I. Title.
PS3561.I58R3   1982   813'.54   82-13238
ISBN 399-12755-0

Printed in the United States of America

For Caroline

1

The front came through right on time; Buck Faulkner felt the
north wind on his back. He and his crew had been in Maine for
five weeks. The weather had been foul, with fog and storms over
the Atlantic. For six days, they had been waiting for a change.
The previous night, Doctor Kimball, the director of the U.S.
Weather Bureau in New York had called, waking up the whole
boardinghouse. He had predicted a front would come down from
Canada in the afternoon and would sweep the storms away from
the East Coast. That the cold wind would clear Maine before it
would clear Long Island. At the same time, a fat high-pressure
system seemed to be forming around Greenland and would clear
the Atlantic.

Buck gazed across the beach to the shelter they had built for
the Belle Nuit. The plane's crew was working on her, tuning the
engine for the hundredth time, checking the fuel mixture, trying
to find a few extraneous ounces to pare off her. A dozen citizens
of Old Orchard were standing around the shelter, discussing
their favorite subject since the Belle Nuit's arrival: the fame that
the flight would bring to their town. The single representative of
the press, a pimply-faced stringer from *The Bangor Gazette*,
tried in vain to get a conversation started with one of the crew.
Buck smiled at how different it must be for Byrd, Chamberlain,
and Lindbergh down at Curtiss and Roosevelt fields. Each day

7

packs of newspaper reporters followed them from their fancy Long Island hotels to the airfield.

Jack Llewellyn, the head of Buck's crew, leaned out of the cockpit and gave a yell. Even at this distance, Buck saw his blue eyes light up and his wide smile snap across his face. The two men were the same age, nearly the same height, Buck being a little taller, but Jack Llewellyn making it almost even with a ramrod spine hardened through two years at West Point. He had resigned from the Military Academy to protest the Army's treatment of General Billy Mitchell. Mitchell, a great hero of World War I, had been court-martialed for criticizing his colleagues' lack of foresight in not developing an air force. Once out of the Academy, Jack regretted his idealism and hoped his connection with the flight of the Belle Nuit would help reinstate him with the Army.

Llewellyn spotted Buck and gave the circle-o high sign. The rest of the crew were watching: George Cruz, Little Albie, Hank the Guzzler, and Adam Starrett. They were ready to go. Buck smiled; Commander Byrd had his own private battalion, and even so, his plane had cracked up when taking off on a training flight in the mud.

Buck cupped his hands and shouted with the wind, "We'll leave in half an hour!" He turned from the beach and hurried toward their boardinghouse to get ready. That was the trouble with Roosevelt Field, he thought: grass runways turn to mud. As if emphasizing his point, he stamped on the hard sand of the Old Orchard beach. He glanced down its long flat length to its end, where it was cut off by a rock jetty that jutted across and sank into the sea.

Certainty gripped Buck with an erotic excitement. He knew he was right. The Old Orchard beach was one of the most eastward points in the United States. The flight to France would be shorter. The Canadian front would clear the weather three or four hours before it would reach Long Island, and then the daylight would be over. Those people down there wouldn't take off in the dark. Not even Chamberlain would do that. Commander Byrd's plane wasn't ready, in spite of the money behind him, and Lindbergh was too careful; he'd wait until dawn. The Belle Nuit would have a whole night's head start. As he looked up at the sky, Buck already could see a brightening.

8

The old frame boardinghouse was only a short distance from the beach. Buck went upstairs to his room. He changed out of his foul-weather gear into his flying outfit. The leather helmet and goggles were government issue. He had worn them when he flew nights for the Postal Service between Richmond and Atlanta and when he did barnstorming stunts for extra money.

His pants were an old pair of gray flannels he had worn superstitiously to all the exams he took during the two years he spent at Massachusetts Institute of Technology. In one pocket was a twenty-dollar bill in case he needed cash in France. His worn-down cowboy boots were from the same college period, an admitted affectation; he had purchased them in Los Angeles. Coming from the "Far West," as his fellow classmates had perceived him, he had been expected to appear in some sort of cowboy vesture. At the time, the boots had satisfied their expectation; for the present, Buck was certain that the French press would take particular notice of his feet.

A cracked mirror hung over the old bleached chest of drawers. Buck looked at himself. The leather helmet made his face appear even larger than usual; all his life, people had commented on the massive size of his head, his high forehead, and solid thrusting jaw line. His mouth was set hard; his nose was broad and straight.

He wished he were five inches shorter than his six-foot-three. He wished he were twenty pounds lighter, so the Belle Nuit could carry that much more fuel. He was too big to be a pilot, and he knew it. But he wasn't going to allow someone else to fly the Atlantic first just because he didn't fit.

Again, he sensed with certainty the frenzy of fame that awaited him. He was ready for it. At twenty-three, he had spent most of his life alone. He had come to suspect that being alone in a plane was preordained for him. Staring at his reflection, he wondered as he had innumerable times, who his mother and father were, and how they would feel if they learned of his astonishing accomplishment—the first man to fly the Atlantic solo.

There was a furtive knock on the door to his room. Buck recognized it. He said, "Come in."

His landlady came through the door and closed it behind her, leaning back against the same wall that had supported them

9

during their first silent urgent assignation. That tryst had occurred four days after Buck and his crew arrived. Soon after, her husband had been hired to guard the Belle Nuit through the long Maine nights.

"I just heard," she whispered. "You're going." She was holding a small, thick book with both hands against her breasts.

Buck nodded and went over to her.

"Is there time?" she asked.

He shook his head, took her in his arms and kissed her. As usual, she remained rigidly vulnerable, giving her sinewy body to him. Over three weeks of lovemaking, she had never taken off all her clothes and had always listened for the step in the hallway.

She pulled back from Buck and whispered, "I'll never see you again. I'll never forget you." With the grim acceptance of what she perceived as her bleak future, she said, "You'll be living a life for so many of us." Then, diffidently, she said, "Think of me—a few times." Her last words were said as if it were too much to ask.

"I will," he said, and he meant it.

She handed him the book. "Here. Carry it with you." It was an old Bible.

Buck kissed her again as he slipped the Bible inside his jacket and figured how he would get rid of it later. It was extraneous weight. His crew wasn't even allowing him to wear a belt. He thought of what the French press would say if he got out of the cockpit and his pants fell down.

"I have to go," he said.

As if her life of living ended, and one of remembering began, she solemnly pronounced, "Goodbye." She turned her plain face toward the window, which had just lit up with sunshine. For a second, Buck could see how she would look when she was very old. He reached out and turned her face back. There were tears in her flat blue eyes, but he made her smile through them with a familiar intimacy of his fingers curling through her straight brown hair. Then Buck hurried out and down the bare steep stairs.

On the rickety front porch, the woman's husband, the Belle Nuit's conscientious night watchman, was nailing a sign to the front balustrade. It read:

BUCK FAULKNER AND THE CREW
OF
THE BELLE NUIT
STAYED HERE PREPARING FOR THE
FIRST SOLO FLIGHT OF THE ATLANTIC
WHICH COMMENCED ON

And here the lettering was less professional:

May 19, 1927

Already a crowd had gathered in front of the house, and when they saw Buck, they gave a hearty cheer. The man had finished tacking up the sign and thought the response was for him. He acknowledged it with a shy bow, then he saw Buck and awkwardly reached out to shake hands. Surveying the sky, which was clearing rapidly, Buck shouted above the crowd, "To the beach!"

They surged through the village and welcomed their neighbors, who joined the noisy procession. Conditions looked good. Buck noted that the wind was dying down and figured he had a couple of hours of daylight.

Across the beach, he saw that his crew had moved the Belle Nuit out of the shelter. Several children broke ahead of Buck to help push the plane.

In the rush, they nearly knocked over the stringer from *The Bangor Gazette,* who was approaching to take Buck's picture. The boy knelt down on the sand and tried to snap a shot, but couldn't make his camera work and looked down at the mysterious black box disconsolately.

Buck stopped beside him and said, "Come on with me." The stringer jumped up and hurried along behind him. Buck was aware of the importance of recording the flight of the Belle Nuit. The general press was not interested in coming to a small village in Maine during a rainy spring, so he had to make do with what he had. He reached out and took the camera out of the stringer's hands.

"How long have you been working with this thing?" he asked.

" 'Bout a week. Doesn't work, though. I just carry it to get into places."

"Ever notice that the shutter has this safety catch here?"

Chagrined, the boy admitted, "No, sir."

11

"They should have told you about it. Do you have film in there?"

Sensing Buck's concern, the stringer became aware of his responsibility. "Yes, sir."

"The picture you take here"—they were twenty-five yards from the rock jetty—"will be printed in every newspaper in the world." As the boy's mouth fell open, Buck lined him up so that he would get an angle of the takeoff similar to the picture of the Wright brothers' first flight at Kill Devil Hill. "I'll clear the jetty by five feet. Take the picture as I'm going over. The sun's enough behind you, you'll get some good clouds." He turned abruptly and started back to the opposite end of the beach.

The stringer followed, dog-trotting to keep up with Buck's long stride.

"Sir, can I ask you some questions?"

"If you don't forget to get back down there."

"I won't. How long do you think it'll take to get to France?"

"About thirty-five hours if we're lucky; about four weeks if I'm not, and some boat happens to pick me up."

"What'll you do to stay awake?"

"Push."

"Push?"

"You don't think that plane flies by itself, do you?"

The boy gave a cracking laugh. "How will you spend the Orteig Prize?"

"It's already been spent getting this far. That's why I have to win it."

"To pay back the San Francisco syndicate who built the plane?" the stringer asked guilelessly. Glancing at him, Buck thought that the kid might be smarter than he looked.

"Them and a few others."

"What about the Frenchmen who tried last month? Do you worry about dying?" They both noticed some large black birds circling, probably blown to the coast by the storms.

"I worry about not living enough, that's all."

As they walked between the tread marks in the sand leading to the Belle Nuit, the stringer was losing his breath keeping up. "You'll change history, won't you?"

Buck shook his head, already checking the Belle Nuit. "No, I'm just fulfilling it. The future is flight. If I don't do it, one of

12

those fellows down on Long Island will." Several gulls took off in front of them and maneuvered out of their way.

"Then what's it mean?" the boy panted.

Buck halted so abruptly that the boy had to step back. "It means that the whole world will want to fly. Right now, people think of planes as toys, for races and stunts. After this they'll realize their dreams. It's something for America to look forward to."

"No, I meant, what's it mean to you personally? I read about Icarus a couple of days ago. Maybe we aren't supposed to fly; maybe crossing the Atlantic is kind of too close to the sun."

"Icarus?" Buck laughed. "Good Lord, is that the angle of your story? Let me give you some advice. Forget Icarus. Your readers want heroes, and I'm going to do my damnedest to be one. I want to do something that will make people proud, not just of me, but of themselves, because, by God, human beings can do anything! Can you remember all that?"

"I've got an infallible memory," the boy said with certainty.

"Then take your camera and get back down to the jetty."

"Thanks, Mr. Faulkner," he said as he turned to run. "And good luck!"

The Belle Nuit was rolling easily along, thrust forward by as many willing hands as would fit along the edges of the wings. The plane was ready; Buck was sure of that. He had never flown it at the fifty-four-hundred-pound weight, but he knew he had enough beach to get her up. He and Lindbergh had bought the same kind of motor, the Wright Whirlwind, and both planes had been constructed in California, Lindbergh's in San Diego, Buck's in Oakland. Buck's was more expensive; it cost him eleven thousand five hundred dollars. At that, it was infinitely cheaper than Byrd's monster of a Fokker, or Chamberlain's Bellanca.

Buck had designed the Belle Nuit himself, using more of what he had learned in the air than in the classroom at M.I.T. He knew enough to write the laws of aerodynamics in pencil so they could be erased and modified every hour. At the Institute, he had waded through Professor Hunsaker's store of aviation technology and observed the wind-tunnel tests on planes sent up from the manufacturers, Curtiss and Vought. However, barnstorming and night flying for the Postal Service was how he learned about design. He could feel a plane as he could feel his own body. As far as Buck was concerned, the Belle Nuit was nearly perfect.

The 220-horsepower Wright J5 air-cooled engine was what made the Atlantic flight possible. The drag caused by the nine radial cylinders was more than offset by the loss of weight of a liquid cooling system with its cylinder water-jackets, radiator, coolant pumps and plumbing. New instruments developed just that year gave the flight a better chance in bad weather and at night. For example, the Earth Inductor Compass was the first not affected by iron deposits on the ground or by the plane's vibration. Buck was particularly pleased with the Artificial Horizon, which gave an accurate reading of the plane's altitude.

The plane was painted black, to go with her name and to let in any heat the sun might offer over the Atlantic. The propeller and spinner were silver; the name and designations were in red-and-gold lettering, a dashing wrapper for a motor and the five fuel tanks, which blocked the pilot's view, crammed the cockpit into his lap, and took up every centimeter of available space.

Almost the entire population of Old Orchard surrounded the plane. Jack Llewellyn had traced a line in the sand. He asked, then finally commanded everyone to stay behind it. Reluctantly the crowd stepped back as Buck made his way to the plane. Standing next to it was his landlady holding an apple pie.

"It's the third one I cooked, waiting for this day. They say three's a charm."

Buck gave her a kiss on the cheek, which made her blush and the crowd cheer, then picked up a slice of the pie. He ate for a minute and then shouted, "Let's get the hell out of here."

As Jack Llewellyn held open the door to the cockpit, Buck shook hands with the rest of his crew. They had dreamed about the takeoff a hundred times. After the tension of the week of waiting, the familiarity of the routine was a relief. As the motor caught, Buck looked out of the side window at the wind sock on top of the shelter. It indicated a good strong head wind. He wanted to take advantage of it, and he opened the throttle. The R.P.M.s were just right. Buck's front view of the beach was limited by the slant of the fuselage at rest and a fuel tank in front of the instrument panel. He wouldn't be able to see the rock jetty until he was halfway down the beach and the tail skid lifted. Buck wasn't worried; he had walked the beach so many times that he knew it by heart.

"Don't try to lift her until you pass the halfway mark," Jack Llewellyn said unnecessarily, as Buck tested his ailerons and rudder. "You've got four thousand feet. Use them. If you get up and don't have control, touch down again and get it. Control means speed."

Buck smiled. He knew Jack wasn't admitting the things that really worried him: a soft spot of sand, a wheel strut torn off, a fuel tank ruptured, a fuel explosion. Jack also had walked the beach a lot.

When he noticed Buck's smile, Jack laughed and smacked him on the shoulder.

"Get out of here, will you?" he said. "I'm tired of sitting on your eggs." He hesitated, not content with the easy camaraderie. "This is more than fame and fortune, Buck. You're redeeming a man and his ideas—and a lot of other people who think he's right. . . ."

Buck laughed out loud. "Redemption be damned, Jack. In a few hours, we'll catch up with the future and we'll never let it go. Hey, that's inspiring! Tell that newspaper kid I said that, will you?" He laughed at himself and drew down his goggles.

"Just don't ascend above ten thousand feet, unless it's clear," Jack said, still worrying. "If you get ice in the venturi tubes, these fancy instruments won't be worth a hoot in hell . . . I'll meet your boat, unless you want to fly back." The prevailing winds over the Atlantic blow from west to east. Two weeks before, the great French flyer, Charles Nungesser, had tried to buck the winds in his 450-h.p. Levasseur biplane. He and a colleague had disappeared over the English Channel and were presumed dead.

"One way this time," Buck said, thinking it was fitting at that moment to remember the price his trip had already cost others. Jack Llewellyn jumped down and secured the door. To the side of the aircraft Buck could see, but not hear, the crowd yelling. Buck waved and signaled to George Cruz and Little Albie to pull the wheel chocks. As soon as they did, they joined Jack, Hank, and Adam Starrett on the struts. Buck edged the throttle for-

15

ward, and the Belle Nuit began to lumber forward. As the plane picked up speed, the crowd ran alongside, continuing to yell and wave.

Buck glimpsed the halfway mark, a post painted black and red, with an empty keg of bootleg hooch nailed to the top. In the next five seconds, the tail skid lifted off the ground and Buck could see where he was going. He pulled back on the stick, and after a heart-sinking moment, the wheels lifted off, then bounced back down on the sand.

Buck knew the Belle Nuit was going to make it. As he pulled back again on the stick and was airborne, he saw the photographer. The left wing dropped; he corrected it with the aileron, steadied it, and prepared to pull back on the stick. In fifteen seconds, they'd be over the jetty with room to spare.

Strangely, Buck actually saw the bird break from the others in the flock and glide in a long arc, down toward the Belle Nuit. With the plane so loaded, there was no possibility of maneuvering. Without the slightest deviation, the blackbird flew straight into the propeller. Buck heard the motor falter; blood and bone hit the windscreen. He pulled hard on the stick, but the plane sank enough for the right wheel to hit a rock of the jetty. Buck felt the strut tear out of the wing. He was able to keep the plane from nosing over, but it side-slipped badly. Hitting the water sideways, the fuselage tore in half; the weight of the Whirlwind motor pulled the cockpit down in the water.

Several whalers were floating nearby; some of the villagers had put out to watch the takeoff. Buck scrambled out of the cockpit and waited for one to row over to him. For the first time in his life, he was glad that he didn't have parents. He wished he didn't even have friends, or backers who had put their expectations on him. He saw the tail section of the Belle Nuit floating above the water. The red-and-gold letters "US-F" stood for "United States to France." On the jetty, the crowd watched their brush with fame sink in fifty feet of water.

The villagers who picked him up were mercifully quiet, asking only if he was all right. He wasn't, but he nodded and remained silent. Having lived with despair all his life, Buck never admitted it. He had lost his chance for quick fame.

When they reached the beach, no one spoke except the

stringer, who announced, "I got a terrific picture, just as the raven hit you. . . ."

In a motion that seemed dreamlike, Buck put his hands on the boy's camera, pulled it from him, and threw it into the sea.

As he handed the boy his wet twenty-dollar bill, Buck saw the townspeople and crew staring at him. They watched in embarrassed silence as he made his way up the beach. Only Jack Llewellyn was missing. Buck didn't see him again for twelve years.

2

By the time Buck walked into the offices of the Grumman
Company on Long Island in the fall of 1932, he had been fired by
five major airframe manufacturers. As usual, the problem had
been his impatience. Buck had resented the owners who interfered with his independent ideas on how to run their companies.
He had worked for United Aircraft, and lobbied in Washington
for Boeing, an activity that he loathed. He had managed to
return to California in time to put in six months with the
Loughead brothers just before their company, Lockheed, went
bankrupt. He had scraped together a little money to start a trunk
line in Georgia, and it was bought out from under him when
American Airways acquired its dominant position over the
South.

Whenever he had left a job, Buck made certain that the people
for whom he worked knew exactly what he thought of them. On
two occasions his thoughts were delivered in a fist fight, with the
result that he became nearly unemployable. Grumman, however, was a new company. Buck talked his way into the office of
a vice-president and offered himself at a sacrifice, plus commission.

"Thank you for the privilege, Mr. Faulkner," the vice-president said acerbically. "But our sales force is full."

"Really? Who's your man in Bolivia?"

The vice-president's demeanor clouded. "Bolivia?"

Buck stood up and leaned on the man's desk. "You mean you

don't have someone down there? You're missing a chance at selling a hundred aircraft."

"In Bolivia?" the vice-president asked, unbelieving.

"There's a war going on down there," Buck said, talking fast. "Did you know that? It's over a piece of hell in the Chaco desert, between Bolivia and Paraguay. For five hundred years, nobody cared about it, but this spring, damned if they didn't find oil on the worst part of it, the Boreal. War was declared about fifteen minutes later, and they're trying to fight it without one damn plane in the air."

"You seem to know a lot about Bolivia," the executive suggested.

"I lived there as a child; my father was a diplomat." Buck smiled casually. When one doesn't have a father, creating one is easy.

"Then you speak the lingo?" The executive was interested in spite of himself.

"Enough to sell your FF-1," Buck said, never doubting his ability to communicate, with or without language. "Listen to me," he continued, beginning to pace the vice-president's office, his size reducing the room's impressive proportions. "You have a good plane. An all-metal reconnaissance fighter built to land on a carrier is just what the U.S. Navy, your *one customer,* wants. But what do you do when they get enough and stop ordering? You find yourself another customer *fast,* a customer who needs planes now, a plane that can take off and land on a dime." Buck paused and walked over to lean close to the vice-president's face. "Or on *short desert airstrips—*get me?"

The vice-president blinked, then nodded.

A month later, in November, Buck was flying over Brazil in a slightly modified FF-1, following the Paraguay River north. He was glad to have the job, but still felt that the aircraft business was getting away from him before he had his chance with it. Ever since Lindbergh's landing at Le Bourget, the public had been galvanized by the possibilities of flight. Each month new records were established; aircraft companies had started and grown, airlines had organized.

Buck had worked for many of them, those who deserved a share of the new industry and those who didn't but took it anyway. One of Buck's heroes was Jack Northrop of Lockheed.

19

Without even a high-school diploma, he had become a genius in aerodynamic design. He had developed some of the fastest planes on record, including the Lindbergh Sirius; the Alpha, with its all-metal stressed-skin fuselage; and the Vega, which had circled the globe the year before. Buck wanted a man like Northrop to design planes for him. Otherwise Buck knew he'd stay a salesman for someone else, a prospect that depressed him whenever he thought of it.

When the Paraguay River turned toward the northeast, Buck banked west into a blinding sun. Soon he was over the Chaco Boreal, the rising thermal air rocking the FF-1 hard. Buck hadn't made up his mind which side of the conflict to sell to first, and his employers didn't care, as long as he had a solid commitment by Christmas. Rather than flip a coin, Buck decided to land in the first break in the pervasive *quebacho* trees, no matter which country it was in.

Buck had learned that Bolivia and Paraguay were old enemies. The nefarious Victorian arms dealer Basil Zaharoff had played the two countries against each other in 1894. Originally, Zaharoff had tried to sell arms to Paraguay, which at the time appeared to be winning. When they refused him a visa, he had gone to Bolivia and prompted the Bolivians to make an immediate peace, ceding whatever territory Paraguay claimed. Then for several months, Zaharoff had shipped more arms to Bolivia than South America had ever seen. Bolivia declared war again and won.

By the time Buck's plane landed in a clearing on the Bolivian side of the conflict, the two combatants had regained their equality in arms. The heat of the South American summer was intense and unremitting. He was welcomed with a fusillade from an astonished group of soldiers, none of whom had seen a plane before, much less heard its roar. Luckily, they were poor shots. When they managed to overcome their wonder, they led Buck to their commanding officer.

Their captain sat fanning himself outside his tent in a camp well back from the front lines. He listened torpidly as his men loudly described the wonder of what they had seen. Unwilling to display any amazement before his men, the officer addressed a long statement to Buck. Not understanding a word, Buck responded inscrutably with a wide motion of his arm in the direction of where he had left the plane. Finally the captain mounted his horse, a badly spavined gray, and rode to the clearing. After studying the plane for a while, the captain approached Buck with a long speech to which Buck nodded whenever there was a pause. When the captain dismounted and approached the aircraft, Buck realized he had agreed to take the captain for a ride.

The clearing was not the longest, and the solidity of the ground a dangerous unknown, yet a refusal could kill the sale. Nervously, Buck helped the captain into the reconnaissance seat and strapped him in.

The takeoff was complicated by an event that Buck had not anticipated. The spavined horse bolted at the roar of the motor and hauled two attendants in front of the aircraft as it moved down the clearing. Fortunately, the horse was stronger than it looked and dragged the men safely past. After the plane cleared the *quebacho* trees, Buck heard a rapid falsetto behind him. He turned to respond but the captain, eyes closed, was not speaking to Buck, but to God.

Within a week, the clearing was graded and the *quebacho* at both ends were cut down. The captain's superior officers began arriving each day by horse or staff car to examine the plane, and most of them demanded a flight. Buck realized quickly that status was involved, not to mention manhood. The captain was building his future career, and Buck was learning Spanish. Buck arranged to fly into Santa Cruz for fuel. On one trip a politician showed up at the airport, and Buck was able to start discussing business.

At first, there was talk of ordering twenty-five planes. After Buck mentioned money, the Bolivians still wanted fifteen. Within the next few weeks, more politicians arrived in Santa Cruz to review the war from the air. A week before Christmas, Buck was told that the Bolivian Minister of War was coming down from La Paz for a flight, after which he would sign an agreement to purchase twelve aircraft immediately with an option for another twelve in a year, should the war not be won by then. Buck wired the terms to Grumman and figured his commission. In a burst of enthusiasm, he painted Bolivian insignia over the American ones.

The Minister of War arrived at dawn with a retinue of bristling military officers. He had been educated in France and addressed Buck in French. When Buck replied with the one word of French he knew, *merci,* His Excellency assumed that his pilot shared his fluency.

Apparently, the Minister of War had flown before, and he relaxed as the plane leveled off. Buck was surprised when his passenger suddenly burst into a stream of agitated Spanish. Then Buck saw an aircraft with Paraguayan colors on the fuselage following them in a five-o'clock attack position.

The War Minister yelled what Buck thought was *"Caramba!"*

Buck rolled the FF-1 and put the plane through several routines he had learned in barnstorming. He dived, pulled out, rolled, looped-the-loop, made an Immelmann turn, and went into a dead spin, pulling out within a hundred feet of the desert floor. By then the Minister of War was retching between curses in his native tongue; still, the other plane remained at five o'clock, proving it could do anything the FF-1 could do and remain in a perfect attack position.

Buck realized then what the enemy was flying. He had seen the plane in an air show earlier that year going 215 miles an hour behind a Pratt and Whitney engine that produced 550 horsepower. It was a P-26, a single-seat fighter that Boeing was trying to sell to the Army as the standard pursuit plane of the decade. The version Buck had seen in the air show had not been armed. The one behind him was, yet it didn't do anything but follow.

Buck decided to level off. As soon as he did, the P-26 moved up and flew along just off the FF-1's port wing tip. When Buck looked over at the open cockpit, he saw that the pilot was an American and he was laughing his head off. Then with a wave, he banked the Boeing plane off and headed in the direction of Paraguay. Buck tried to follow, but the other plane was too fast.

The Minister of War had recovered by then, and witnessed the race. When it was lost, he signaled to Buck to land. Buck did as he was ordered, noting that his passenger remained awesomely silent. Within the hour, the Minister of War departed by staff car. No agreement was signed, and Buck sensed an immediate chill in the center of the Chaco Boreal.

For the next week, no one even requested a flight. Buck knew the Bolivians had contacted Boeing to compare prices, and had discovered that they would have to pay more for a plane like the

P-26. It was not until Christmas Eve when he spread his sleeping bag under the fuselage of the FF-1 that Buck remembered Zaharoff's technique of switching sides. His status among the Bolivian military had dissolved further to a stony silence; he was sleeping under the plane to make sure it wasn't pilfered. The Bolivian officers had not hidden their contempt for what they considered an inferior piece of goods, and the soldiers who patrolled the clearing had been regarding Buck with glowering hostility.

Buck had remained diplomatically friendly. Going over to the Paraguayans would be risky, particularly if they already were flying the P-26 and wanted to test it in a dogfight. His only other choice was to fly the FF-1 out of the area and back to Long Island, thus ending any future he might have in the aircraft business. He thought he could get a job trying to sell insurance or bonds, although not too many people were buying them that year.

As he turned over on the hard ground, Buck thought of his adoptive parents. His mother had died suddenly of an embolism when he was sixteen, and his father, a corporation lawyer, had never recovered from his wife's unexpected death. He pined away for several years providing Buck with anything he asked for. When Buck was at M.I.T. his father died.

Reaching above his head, Buck ran his hand over the belly of the fuselage. He remembered the first day he flew in an old Curtiss JN-2. He had been riding horseback at what was then DeMille Field in the San Fernando Valley and seen the plane about to land. Buck had cantered his horse to where the plane had taxied to a stop. He begged the pilot for a ride. It was 1915; Buck had been ten.

Mr. DeMille subsequently had given up flying for the movie business. Buck had never understood the choice. Once Mr. DeMille had flown, Buck wondered, how could he have done anything else? Buck had soloed, illegally, at twelve. He had felt something that he wasn't able to describe.

If he flew the FF-1 back to Grumman, Buck saw his uncertain future never ending. He thought of park pigeons who prefer strutting to flying. He thought of a wounded hawk able only to walk.

He stood up and prowled restlessly around the plane. The

Boreal was bearable in the middle of the night; Buck's guards slept heavily a hundred yards away under the *quebacho*. Buck glanced up at the crescent moon. Flying back to that kind of future wasn't worth the gas. Buck decided he'd just as soon risk his career on the barren Chaco Boreal.

The gamble was that he could make his FF-1 seem more attractive than the P-26 to the Paraguayans. He strolled quietly down the clearing away from his sleeping guards. In the bare light of the new moon, he walked the several miles to the Bolivian camp. An unofficial Christmas cease-fire had wound down the conflict; any edge of suspicion was dulled by the considerable amount of liquor the soldiers had consumed.

Buck made his way to the explosives shack, where ammunition was kept. The guard on duty was drinking beer from a large cache of bottles. Buck sat down beside him, expressing greetings as best he could and gesturing for a beer. The guard was therefore surprised to feel the neck of his bottle suddenly jammed to the back of his throat. His teeth went through the glass and after that, he felt nothing until morning.

Buck unlocked the door to the shack and quickly found dynamite, a crate of caps, and a coil of fuse. He took a short length of the fuse and, using his belt, bound ten sticks of dynamite together around a cap. Stuffing them into his jacket, he relocked the door and after pulling the glass out of the guard's mouth, propped him up as if he were asleep. Then Buck walked back to the clearing, greeting whomever he saw with Americano Yule tidings.

By the time he reached his plane, Buck had a half-hour of darkness left and nearly a full tank of gas if the guards didn't wake up in time to shoot a hole in it. Based on what he had seen of their marksmanship, he thought he was safe. He measured the length of fuse for a ten-second burn and secured it carefully to the dynamite cap in the center of the ten sticks of explosive.

When he could see the end of the clearing, Buck got into the cockpit quietly and lit a cigar. At first, the noise of the motor turning over did not arouse the guards. When it did, the reflex was one of confusion; by the time they began shooting, the FF-1 was out of range clearing the *quebacho*, and heading across the battle line.

Buck had left the Bolivian insignia on the plane in case the P-26 was out flying, which he doubted. His plan was to find the airstrip from which the Boeing had taken off. Its Pratt and Whitney engine was powerful, but the plane was heavy. The Paraguayans would have had to clear a long runway. Buck figured his chances of finding it were fairly good if his fuel held out.

Due to the hour and the holiday, everything was quiet. An occasional settlement of huts looked desolate and scorched. Buck lit another cigar from the stub of the first one. He would have relished the early-morning flight except for the odor of Bolivian tobacco, but he knew he would not be able to take both hands off the controls later to light a match.

After two hours, he started to worry about fuel. He thought he had covered most of the Chaco even as far south as Argentina. He decided that if he couldn't find the P-26, he'd follow the Pilcomayo River southeast toward Asunción, fly as far as the gas tanks allowed, ditch the plane, and float by raft into the capital. If that happened, he wouldn't tell Grumman about it, or anyone else.

Just then he saw the airstrip. It was unmistakable, with a dead wind sock above a shelter large enough to house the P-26. With no hesitation, Buck dived down and buzzed the field. He glimpsed tents, huts, and several vehicles beside the shelter, but no sign of life—it was, after all, Christmas morning. He also noticed that the airstrip itself had been carefully leveled and raked, a luxury his Bolivian hosts had not provided him.

By the time he banked back and buzzed the field again, there was considerable activity. Many of the soldiers threw themselves down on the ground to avoid strafing. Others were wheeling the P-26 out of the shelter; Buck knew he had to hurry. He rolled quickly, opening his cockpit as he flattened out over the desert. Grabbing the dynamite, he lit the fuse from his cigar.

The P-26 was at the end of the runway and starting to move. Buck came in at twenty feet, judged the wind and dropped the dynamite. As quickly as possible, he threw the cigar after it and pulled out. Looking back, he saw that the people on the ground were running in all directions and that the P-26 was gaining speed down the runway. The dynamite exploded, cutting the length of the airstrip in nearly equal halves, with a crater twenty feet wide. As he banked around, Buck saw the P-26 careen off to one side and stop.

Taking advantage of the hesitation, Buck brought the FF-1 in for a landing on the half of runway the P-26 had just used. The Grumman plane easily came to a stop before reaching the crater. Quickly he stood up and climbed out of his cockpit, his hands in the air and a smile on his face. A large contingent of soldiers in various stages of dress rushed from the huts and tents and fired haphazardly as they ran.

Buck tried yelling, *"Amigo! Amigo!"* but the soldiers ignored the sentiment. Fortunately, the P-26 taxied between Buck and the onrushing Paraguayans.

Buck kept his hands in the air and watched the other pilot jump gracefully to the ground. Laughing and slapping his knees, he arrived just ahead of the first mass of soldiers who were eager to shoot Buck, but couldn't because the other pilot was in the way. Buck recognized him, but didn't know from where. He wore U.S. Army surplus jodhpurs, shirt and boots, and damned if he didn't have a silk scarf, brilliantined hair and a carefully clipped black mustache just like every Hollywood stick jockey who had ever flown into a sunset.

"Smile! Fast!" he yelled at Buck. "Make like old friends! Gimme a glad hand! Quick!" He reached Buck and gave him a bear hug. Buck kept his hands up as the two men were quickly surrounded by the Paraguayans.

"Pretty fancy flying, pal. Bet you thought you'd impress everybody with it," he laughed, and said, through his smiling teeth, urgently: "Put your hands down, will ya?"

Buck did as he was told and began a hollow laugh. "I figured they'd be pleased that my plane took half the runway yours did."

"You figured wrong, pal: all they're impressed with is that you're a Bolivian bomber and deserve to die!" He put his arm around Buck's shoulder and laughed genuinely. Then he raised his other arm for quiet. Buck ruefully acknowledged that at least one pilot in the Chaco was still a star, and that he spoke his audience's language fluently.

At the same time, Buck saw several officers behind the circumference of soldiers. He watched their gestures, which indicated that they understood the significance of his landing. Before he had a chance to reach the officers in order to further explain the FF-1's many advantages, Buck was pushed in the direction of the tents by the American pilot.

"Just stroll easy like me and I'll save your balls for another day," the pilot said through his wise smile.

"I don't know if I can strut like that," Buck said.

"Don't even try. You're too damn big; you'd throw something out."

"Where have we met?" Buck asked.

"In that cat house in Memphis?"

"Never been to Memphis. What's your name?"

"Eddie Stockton." Buck was wrong. They hadn't met, but Buck had seen the pilot's picture ever since he was a child. Eddie Stockton had been an ace in World War I and had raced planes first for the Army, then for private companies. In the years when pilots were living legends, Eddie Stockton had been one of the most famous. He once said, "If the motor's good enough, I can fly an egg-beater." Dashing, devil-may-die-but-not-me, always ready with a quip for the press, he had bounced from company to company as a test pilot. Boeing had taken him on, but not as the chief test pilot. Instead, they had sent him to Paraguay to ferry the P-26.

Both Buck and Eddie saw the cloud of dust at the same time. An automobile of unfamiliar design careened across the runway toward the two planes. Whoever was driving paid little attention to what might be in the vehicle's path. As it went by, Buck saw that the driver, a thin American man with straw colored hair, was wearing a three-piece wool suit in the middle of the Chaco Boreal's broiling Christmas morning.

After the automobile had passed, the soldiers regrouped around the pilots. Ignoring their rifles, Eddie, still smiling, urged Buck toward the tents. Buck, however, was watching out of the corner of his eye as the man in the three-piece suit halted his vehicle next to the FF-1. He stepped over to the plane and laid down on his back in the dust under one of the landing gears. When he pulled out a wrench, Buck turned.

"Easy," Eddie Stockton said. "Just keep heading my way."

"That crazy son of a bitch is fooling with my plane. See you later."

Through gritted teeth, Stockton chanted, "You'll get your ass blown to smithereens."

Buck began walking, but then started to run. The Paraguayan soldiers around him began to bellow, but they dared not shoot for fear of hitting their fellow soldiers on the other side of the circle. Buck had to duck under several rifle butts that were swung in his direction, but he managed to reach the FF-1 and fall to his knees beside the figure lying in the dirt, tinkering with the landing gear.

Buck yelled, "What the hell do you think you're doing?"

The man glanced at Buck briefly, oblivious to any disturbance. "It's a good idea, retracting the landing gear like this up against the fuselage, but there's still drag. The wheels have to disappear completely and be covered. The fuselage has to be ab-so-lutely smooth." He spoke with an acute intensity. "Do you know about flush rivets?"

Buck did not reply, but knew in the instant that he had found his genius.

3

When Boeing sent Eddie Stockton and Skip Hendrickson, the man in the three-piece wool suit, to Paraguay to sell the P-26, the company overlooked a basic member of the expedition: a salesman. Eddie could fly anything and make it look good. He could outdrink his customers and seduce their daughters as well, but he couldn't close a deal. Skip Hendrickson did not indulge in Eddie's vices or any others as far as Buck could tell. Skip spent his spare time with a slide rule and a sketch pad, continuously noting, drawing, and theorizing about future airplane designs, but doing nothing to obtain contracts. Consequently, Buck realized that he might be the answer to a prayer, an unfamiliar role.

Boeing was part of a larger company, United Aircraft, which included United Airlines, Pratt and Whitney, and Hamilton Propellers. Buck, along with the rest of the aircraft business, regarded it as the sweetest monopoly in the world, one which was in the position to dictate the future of the industry. When United Airlines ordered sixty new passenger planes from Boeing, the in-house deal thereby prevented Boeing from supplying either TWA or American. Thus, the other two airlines were looking for someone else to build them a new passenger plane, one that could compete with United's Boeing 247. Buck hoped that the challenge might hook his genius.

"I think the 247 is Boeing's big mistake," Buck said to his two countrymen. "But I'm not going to tell them about it."

They were sitting at a table in the airstrip's largest hut. Made of adobe, and with a dirt floor, it was the coolest place within five hundred miles. The Paraguayan officers used it as their mess. Several days had passed since Eddie Stockton had extricated Buck and Skip Hendrickson from the incensed mob of Paraguayan soldiers. Since then, while the bomb crater was being repaired, Buck had flown several officers in the FF-1. He felt sure of a sale, particularly after seeing their reaction to the news that the Bolivians had ordered a dozen. He had also cabled Boeing in Seattle, informing them not only of his presence in Paraguay, but also of his influence in Bolivia, and had been hired at four times the salary he was making at Grumman.

"I'll drink to that," Eddie Stockton offered, and he knocked back a shot of a local blood-and-mud liquor, which Buck and Skip didn't touch. They stayed with the local beer.

"What's wrong with the 247?" Skip asked after his usual pause of consideration.

"It's a compromise. They're building a passenger plane with ten seats. They can't make money on that many tickets; they're still going to depend on mail and cargo. The 247 is going to waste everybody's time because it's hedging its bet on people. It's *people* who want to fly and it's people who'll make the profit margin. Mail and cargo will be secondary. People want time."

"You're right, pal," Eddie Stockton said fatalistically. "We're the only ones that know how little there is of that." He stared into his glass.

"How many passengers do you need," Skip Hendrickson asked, "to make a profit?"

"Let me borrow your slide rule and pad." In less than two minutes, Buck said, "Twenty-one passengers and a crew of four."

Skip reached for his pad and started sketching, letting Buck watch what he was doing. "Range?" he asked.

"Three hundred miles," Buck replied.

The three men sat silently for an hour. When Skip filled one page of the sketch pad, he tore it off and started on the next. The aircraft took shape with only a few significant alterations from his original outline of a two-motored, tapered-wing aircraft, with two rows of passengers, ten and eleven on each side of the aisle,

30

and in the aft section of the cabin, a galley and a restroom. Skip finished with a drawing of the aircraft in flight through woolpack clouds. He put the pad down, and the three men looked at it with silent appreciation.

"That's what we'll call her," Buck said intently. "Cumulus."

Skip ran his long fingers through his straight strawlike hair. "We will?" he asked, smiling doubtfully.

"Why not?" Buck replied. "If we build her, we have the right to name her."

"I don't think I can afford it. Can you?"

"No, but for this plane, I'll raise the money."

Skip believed him; Buck knew it.

"How much do you think it would take?" Skip asked.

Buck spread the pages of Skip's notebook in front of him. Slowly, he said, "I'd raise two million to start the company. We could build this plane from the ground up for a hundred and fifty thousand."

"Hey, pal, heard of the Depression?" Eddie laughed. "They aren't giving money away any more."

"I'll raise it," Buck said. "You want to come in with me?" He looked evenly at Skip, who again pushed his fingers through his hair, first on one side of his head, then the other. "If not," Buck continued, "I'll give you ten thousand dollars for these drawings." When one didn't have any money, it was easier to make offers.

"I'll come in with you," Skip said simply, "if you can give me some things I want."

"Such as?"

"I don't particularly like owning things. I'll want you to have control. I've found that business doesn't interest me very much. The success or failure of this one would be your responsibility. I've been in this line of work a long time. I've worked for everyone around; now I want to work for myself. If you can provide me with a company, I'll provide you with some good designs."

Buck smiled, saying, "You've been thinking about this, haven't you?"

"For some time," Skip responded. "Haven't you? Your figures seem to be pretty exact."

31

Buck nodded. "It's funny we had to come down here to meet each other."

"It's fate," Eddie Stockton interjected. "Besides, where else in hell are you going to find a test pilot like me?"

"To the Cumulus," Buck said as he raised his beer bottle. Skip reached over and touched his bottle to it.

"I'll drink to that," Eddie said, and knocked back another mouthful of the blood-and-mud liquor.

Over the next month Buck devised an entire air force for the Paraguayans based on the FF-1 and the P-26. They were so impressed with his ideas that they urged him to become their agent for any future arms they might need. At the same time, Buck took great pains to have the concept of Paraguayan air supremacy fed to his old friend, the Bolivian Minister of War. Using the American embassies in Asunción and La Paz, Buck had the Paraguayan sales figures translated into French and delivered to His Excellency. A response arrived quickly along with delighted cables from Grumman and Boeing which were delivered to the Chaco by American diplomatic courier each week.

Soon after, Buck had the pleasure of meeting the Bolivian Minister of War at a new airstrip, which had been raked and leveled to Buck's specifications. He and Eddie flew the two planes over the border to the secret site, and for sheer fun, put on an aerial show before they landed. After they taxied toward the automobiles at the end of the new airstrip, Buck was greeted effusively by His Excellency, who not only kissed him on both cheeks again, but hung an ostentatious medal around his neck.

Within an hour, Buck accepted signed orders for two dozen of both planes. If Bolivia got them first, a large bonus was promised. Again Buck was offered a lucrative arrangement to act as agent for other weapons, particularly any kind of tank he could find. Buck made no commitment, but on the flight back to Paraguay, he figured that such a deal would give him a credit rating of about a hundred thousand.

When they landed, Buck noticed a great deal of activity around the airstrip. Taxiing to the shelter, he saw Skip and another American uncharacteristically standing in the sun. They were surrounded by several officers wearing side arms. No one was looking friendly. Buck looked across at Eddie Stockton as the Paraguayan officers escorted Skip and the other American to them.

"This is John Slater from the Embassy in Asunción," Skip said. "Has some bad news."

The man from the Foreign Service shook their hands formally. He too wore a suit, but it was white linen. "President Roosevelt was sworn in four days ago, gentlemen."

Eddie Stockton laughed and said, "Thanks for the bulletin. You have the weather report as well?"

"He's embargoed the Chaco war," Slater said. "No arms of any kind may be sent to either country involved. The Paraguayans have just learned about it and are not happy. In spite of my official protest, they are not inclined to give up the two planes they have."

"How the hell do they expect to fly them?" Eddie Stockton spat out.

"They'll hire people. In fact, they wanted to hire you two, but Mr. Hendrickson and I took the liberty of discouraging them."

"Can we get out of here?" Buck asked.

"Yes, I can include you in my diplomatic immunity. Of course, such rules are theoretical at best; so, while they are still inclined to respect them, I'd suggest we all walk quietly over to my car which is behind the shelter. They're looking for excuses to keep you here to teach them to fly."

Both Buck and Eddie turned to look back at their planes. They were surrounded by twenty troops. Another twenty were stationed around the shelter.

"Where are we going?" Buck asked.

"To the Embassy in Asunción. From there—"

Buck interrupted. "That's too far and too hot, even driving all night through the Chaco. What's going to stop someone from bushwhacking us?"

The diplomat shrugged. "I suppose the specter of the Marines arriving to inflict punishment."

"I don't trust specters," Buck said. "I'd rather crash-land in Argentina. It's a hell of a lot closer than Asunción. Eddie, ask them for a case of beer for the trip."

Before Slater could argue, Eddie asked for the beer. The officers sullenly agreed and sent a soldier to get it. The four

Americans then walked to the diplomat's car. It was an old Packard with several spare gasoline containers strapped on to the running boards. The beer was put in the trunk. The Americans got in, and the car slowly drove away. As they passed the end of the airstrip, they looked back. The rest of the soldiers had rushed around the two planes. One of the Paraguayan officers was getting into the cockpit of the P-26.

"Goddamn, let me go back there," Eddie Stockton murmured.

Buck, who was sitting beside him in the back seat, put his hand on Eddie's shoulder and said quietly, "Later." They exchanged a look, and Eddie laughed.

They drove south until Buck was certain they were not being followed. Then he said, "Slater, stop the car."

The diplomat thought perhaps someone was ill and quickly obliged. Buck reached over, took the keys and started issuing orders.

"Skip, get up on top of the car and watch for anyone coming. Eddie, get the beer out and empty the bottles."

"All of them?"

"Pour them out; don't drink them. Slater, are those spare gas tanks full?"

"Yes, but I have to object to whatever you have in mind as being dangerous and unnecessary."

"You can't guarantee that. There's nothing stopping them from contacting their friends anywhere down the road between here and Asunción. Their government can blame whatever would happen to us on bandits. Show me the Marines or stay out of the way."

"You're underestimating the influence of the United States of America."

"You're right. I am. On the other hand, our President has just pulled the rug out and left us here to sweat. I'll just take care of myself, and you too if you want to join us. And I'll tell you something else. I don't like those bastards stealing our planes."

"I'll drink to that," yelled Eddie Stockton, and he finished off a beer.

"There are only three seats in those planes," Slater said.

"Someone can sit on your lap," Buck said as he took off his shirt and began to tear it into strips.

An hour before dawn, they were back at the airstrip. Silently, they synchronized their watches in the light of a carefully shielded match. Then Skip took one of the gas tanks from the running board and disappeared into the night. Buck and Eddie got out and reconnoitered. The two planes had been rolled to a ready position, half outside the shelter.

The two men returned to the car. Eddie picked up the case with half the beer bottles. They had been weighted with sand, filled with gasoline and stuffed closed with a piece of shirt. He, too, hurried off toward the airstrip.

Buck got into the back seat and checked the rest of the beer bottles that were propped on the floor of the Packard. Slater remained in the driver's seat gripping the wheel, looking straight ahead into the darkness. His suit was no longer the near white it had been, being spotted with gasoline and his own nervous sweat.

Fifteen minutes later, Buck lit another match to check the time. He sat up and reached over to tap Slater on the shoulder. Slater jumped slightly, nodded and started the car. Slowly they moved forward and followed the ruts in the road toward the end of the airstrip.

Across the field, an explosion shattered the quiet of the desert night and sprayed the surrounding *quebacho* with fire. That was Skip's gasoline can. From the car they could see several figures begin to run toward the flames.

"Go!" Buck shouted, and Slater jammed his foot on the accelerator. The Packard reached top speed. Buck lit the rags in the beer bottles, as he glimpsed more figures running across the runway. He began throwing them at anything that moved. At the same moment, Eddie Stockton ran down the landing strip, lighting and lobbing his beer bottles into each tent and hut, ending near the shelter where the vehicles were parked. He threw all the remaining bottles at the Paraguayan cars, which exploded just as the Packard drove up.

Eddie jumped onto the running board, and Slater drove the short distance to the two planes. According to their plan, Skip was already supposed to be there.

Buck and Eddie left the car and jumped into their planes. Slater jammed a branch between the spokes of the Packard's steering wheel to set it, pressed a cufflink into the horn to keep it

35

blowing, moved a rock onto the gas pedal, turned the headlights on, and popped the clutch. As the car lurched across the runway, Slater jumped out and ran to Buck's plane. The Packard received most of the Paraguayans' attention as the final three beer bottle bombs in the back seat went off, setting the car aflame. Twenty yards beyond the airstrip, the car, still lurching ahead, exploded.

Buck signaled for Eddie to get moving; he needed the runway. Eddie looked around for Skip, then gunned his plane down the airstrip. Just as Buck started to move, Skip appeared running out of the darkness. He ran to the wing, hauled himself up to the reconnaissance seat behind Buck and climbed in to sit on Slater's lap.

Buck was grateful that the FF-1 didn't need much runway. The Paraguayans had recovered from their surprise and began shooting. As Buck's speed increased, one group was running up the airstrip toward the plane. As the plane left the ground, a bullet cracked through the cockpit's windscreen.

When he leveled off, he turned to see if his passengers were all right. Skip sat as impassively as if his seat in Slater's lap were a Pullman chair. Slater looked sick, but otherwise in one piece. Ahead, Buck saw the P-26's running lights go on. He snapped the switches for his own, and immediately Eddie banked back to fly in tandem. In the dim light from the P-26's instrument panel, Buck could see Eddie's grin.

As dawn broke, they flew over La Esmeralda and crossed the Pilcomayo. They landed near Tartagal to get more fuel and make diplomatic connections with the American Embassy in Buenos Aires. Within a week, they reached the capital. Three days later, with Slater's help, Buck not only had managed to sell the two planes to the Argentines for cash, but had negotiated contracts for fifteen more of each of the aircraft. He urged Grumman and Boeing to fill the orders as quickly as possible, before President Roosevelt embargoed the rest of South America.

Buck took it upon himself to reserve the most pleasant accommodations available on the S.S. *Panagro* back to the United States. Slater came with them. Their escape from Paraguay had embarrassed Washington and jeopardized Slater's career so badly that he resigned from the Foreign Service. For most of the trip, he sat in sullen silence. Then Buck found out that Slater had a Yale law degree. Since there was no escape on the ship, Buck worked on Slater and finally convinced him to consider the aircraft business. By the time they disembarked in California, the four men had formed a company.

It was to be called The Hendrickson-Faulkner Aircraft Company. Buck had hesitated to have his name in the title. In spite of his success with the Argentine sales, his reputation still was not attractive in the business. On the other hand, Skip Hendrickson, who had worked for Jack Northrop, Don Douglas, Claude Ryan and Bill Boeing, was well known for his design capabilities and well liked for his imperturbable personality. Buck thought his own name might jeopardize the project, but Skip insisted. The company was going to be Buck's; the aircraft were going to be Skip's. With that settled, all they needed was money.

After his arrival in Los Angeles, Buck had no luck with the banks; they were still shaky from the Depression, and still worried about Roosevelt. He spent a month digging, and raised one hundred and twenty thousand dollars from two investment bankers and an entrepreneur who had discovered oil in his back yard near Inglewood. As Buck told the others, it wasn't enough.

"But I'm willing to start with that much," he said. "It's easier to raise money with part of something that exists than selling the whole of a good idea."

"Even if it's just a fuselage with feathers?" Eddie Stockton said, laughing.

At the time, John Slater was studying to take the California Bar exam. "Don't get me wrong," he said. "I don't want you to hold up for my convenience, but I think it would be devastating to start and, for one reason or another, not be able to finish. Where would you build it, anyway?"

"I talked to a man last week in the movie business who owns an old sound stage down near Carson. It hasn't been used for years, and he can't sell it to anyone. He says he'll rent it to me for a dollar a week, with a mutually agreed figure of sale. If we make it as a company, we buy it at his price. There's a lot of land around it that's available. . . ."

They sat disconsolately around a table in an old Mexican restaurant across the street from Union Station in downtown Los Angeles. Buck and Slater drank beer, Skip coffee, and Eddie tequila.

"I heard from a friend yesterday that Don Douglas is building a passenger plane," Skip said. "Calls it the DC-2."

The atmosphere became tense. Don Douglas was one of the major airframe manufacturers in the industry. His company in Long Beach had already proved itself. Since 1920, it had produced first-rate aircraft, including the World Cruiser, the first aircraft to circle the globe.

"Who's buying it?" Slater asked.

"American and Pan American. Both have ordered thirty planes."

Eddie Stockton gave a long whistle.

"How many seats does it have?" Buck asked, feeling sick and angry.

"Fourteen."

"Fourteen?" Buck shouted. He looked at each of the men around the table. "We've got to start. Right now. Don Douglas can read a slide rule as well as we can. It's not going to take him long to figure out what we already know: that he's building sixty money-losing machines." He laughed with delight. "Listen to me. Right now we don't have any competition. The 247 and the Lockheed Electra have ten seats, the DC-2 will have fourteen. That gives us maybe a year. Ours has twenty-one, and we can build it in four months. It'll take all those people six months to realize their mistake and another six to fix it, if they can. They might have to build a whole new airplane.

"A half an airplane won't fly," Slater said finally.

Buck leaned in on the table.

"I'll raise the rest of the money. I swear it. We've got to go ahead. We'll never have a chance like this again. Here's the address of the sound stage. We'll start hiring on Monday, 8 A.M. sharp. If you're not there, I'll know you're not with me. I'm going to build the Cumulus with or without you." He stood up, put the address and some money on the table, then walked out of the restaurant.

He hadn't gone twenty yards down the street when he heard Skip call after him. "Wait a minute, Buck."

Skip walked up to him and smiled. "Buck, I wonder if you're free this weekend. My family has an old fashioned Fourth of July picnic. Could you come out on Sunday?"

Buck stopped walking. "That's not what I expected to hear."

"Um? Oh. Well, Buck, of course, we'll be there Monday morning. If you say the company's starting, who's to say it isn't? Now, how about Sunday?"

Buck had not met Skip's family, but as he had been searching for money, he had run across the Hendrickson name more than once. He had learned that two Hendrickson brothers had arrived in California during the Gold Rush. They had not found any precious metal themselves, but they had made a good deal of money shipping gold from the fields to banks in the city. Their offspring had been successful in a cross section of California business, and the current generation headed a number of banks and law firms.

Skip had grown up tinkering. The family regarded him as an anomaly because he went to Cal Tech instead of law or business school. He had graduated with honors at twenty, married a girl he had known all his life, and they had settled in San Marino, where they raised their four children. When Skip was hired by Boeing, he and his family had moved to Seattle. A measure of his commitment to his and Buck's company had been his willingness to return with his family to San Marino on the speculation that the Cumulus would be built. At the picnic, however, Buck learned that the decision had been made easier by his family; they had hated Seattle.

"After being born and raised in Southern California sunshine," said Delilah Hendrickson, Skip's wife, "I felt we were living on the backside of Jupiter." Where Skip was unassuming, Delilah was caustically direct. She laughed and said, "No matter what else happens, I'll always be grateful that your crazy idea got us all out of Seattle."

"What's crazy about it?" Buck said, laughing as Delilah led him out the door.

The back yard was filled with people—the children involved in a noisy softball game, the older people drinking and chatting on the flagstone terrace. Everyone was involved in a game, a discussion, or an argument. Delilah stopped and looked at Buck directly.

"It takes a lot more than money to make an airplane fly, doesn't it? We have some doubts; that's why we all wanted to meet you."

"Who's 'we'?"

"The family," she said as if the answer were obvious. She guided Buck to a group of people beside the pool.

Between innings, Buck met Skip's brothers and sisters, as well as their children. Skip's father, a judge in San Francisco, was kept appropriately busy as umpire. Buck felt their honest hospitality, yet sensed an appraising distance. When introduced, Buck noted their recognition of him as someone about whom they had already found out a great deal. After having satisfied their curiosity, Buck had the impression that they would compare their observations later.

The situation was unnerving. Distracted by the practical matters of starting his business the next day without the money to finish one plane, Buck was not prepared to handle the intricacies of a family reunion in which he was so obviously an outsider. He wished he could leave, but he needed to speak to Skip about the sound stage.

He found himself wandering through the house on the pretext of finding a telephone. Bicycles, athletic equipment of all kinds, a stack of Flash Gordon Big Little Books, saddle shoes, boots and a wagon were deposited along the hall. He turned into a game room with a Ping-Pong table, a Zenith radio console, a Victrola with a stack of records beside it, and a Monopoly board. Buck examined a Jack Armstrong hovering-disc gun, models of planes and cars, and some comic books with unknown heroes. The door swung open and a young girl came running in at full speed. Intent on what she was looking for, she didn't see Buck until she was running out with an old softball, apparently needed in the backyard game.

"Oh." She smiled, embarrassed. "Hello."

"Hello." He was a little embarrassed himself and put down the comic book.

"Are you lost?" she said.

"Yes, I guess I am. I was on my way out." Distractedly, he looked toward the door.

"Already? There's going to be fireworks as soon as the sun goes down."

"So I heard. I wish I could stay, but—"

"You're Buck Faulkner, aren't you?"

"Yes."

"I'm Jennifer Hendrickson." She wore her blond hair parted

40

in the middle and held back by two barrettes. Her eyes were green, and she gazed at him with an amused, knowing look. She wore a light-blue sunsuit with a halter top. On her hip was a grass stain. Her face reflected some of her father's lean angularity, but her lips were fuller and her nose was more regally prominent.

"I think you've been hiding," she said with the forthrightness of her own security.

"Who would I be hiding from?"

"From all this *family*." She laughed, then abruptly hesitated and looked at Buck so seriously that he too laughed. He stopped, realizing why she had become so serious. Then he laughed again.

"I'm so sorry," she said, mortified.

Still smiling Buck said, "I suppose your father told everyone not to say anything about families in front of me."

She hesitated, then admitted it. "He told us you were adopted and even *they* had died." Feeling herself getting in even deeper, she smacked her own forehead with her hand and rolled her eyes up. "Boy, am I dumb."

"I doubt that." There was an awkward pause, then he asked, "Where are you going to school?"

She answered his question automatically, regarding it as the digression it was. "I'll be a freshman at Stanford this fall—when I heard about you, I thought about being adopted myself. I guess that's what everyone does."

"I doubt if you are. You look a lot like your father."

"I know. Can I ask you something?" He nodded. "Do you wonder who you look like, I mean, what your real parents were like?"

"My *real* parents were the people who raised me." He smiled at her worried look and dismissed it. "You mean my biological parents. Yes, I wonder."

"Any ideas? I bet your imagination got pretty crowded with them."

"A million. For a time I believed they were the Prince and Princess of Montenegro—"

"Where's that?"

"It never mattered." They both smiled, but her face reflected concern and purpose.

"Yes, I can understand that." She was no longer embarrassed by the subject and when she looked up, her smile had an edge of familiarity.

"Well, I guess if you and Daddy build this airplane, *we'll* have to adopt you."

He nodded and asked her to take him back to the picnic. In the future, Buck would say that he hardly remembered meeting her that day, but Jennifer insisted that on that day, she fell in love with him and never stopped.

4

First they rented the sound stage and set up a design section at one end of it. The building was old and constructed of wood; it creaked alarmingly when the Santa Ana winds blew in from the desert. The floor had a tendency to give way, and the hazardous areas were marked off with yellow paint after one of the engineers broke an ankle. The next day he returned in a cast.

The employees, pleased at finding a job during hard times and getting into a company on the ground floor, were inspired by Buck Faulkner's fervor and confidence. Buck did not just hire people; he converted them.

The first order of business for the carpenters and machinists was to make sure the sound stage would not collapse from the weight of the plane. While Skip directed the drafting, Buck designed a sprinkler system that could be activated in case of fire. He also hired a caterer who specialized in feeding movie companies on location; Buck wanted the Hendrickson-Faulkner workers to eat well. Skip had hoped to use some Pratt and Whitney radial engines, but because they were designated exclusively for Boeing, Buck was unable to secure any. Instead, he made down payments on two 600-horsepower Hispano-Suizas.

By the time the machinists began fashioning the wing's superstructure, the formers, chords and stringers, Buck had spent most of his money. Slater told him that he had about two weeks' pay left. Besides studying for the Bar exams at night, John was acting as contract negotiator and bookkeeper.

"We can pay them for two weeks, and beg two more out of them. After that . . ." He shrugged.

Buck was sitting on a cot. For several weeks, he had stayed at the sound stage overnight to go over blueprints and check and repair machinery. On their own time, two of the machinists had built a shower for him, and Skip would bring him an occasional change of clothes. Still, Buck looked more disheveled and fatigued than he wanted anyone to think he was.

"Four weeks," he said. "By that time, all we'll have is a skeleton."

"If we had the motors, I'm sure Eddie could fly it," Slater joked, but Buck didn't laugh. He had wasted too much time with prospective investors who expressed interest and then didn't answer his phone calls. His original backers would not increase their contributions, even when Buck told them that they might lose what they had already invested. Those who wished to risk substantial cash in the aircraft business preferred to do it with established companies. Those with "funny money" to plunge preferred the movie business. Finding venture capital had become impossible, and he resolved to do something for which he was ashamed even before he did it, not because it was wrong, but because he had to do it secretly.

In the weeks since the Independence Day picnic, Buck had been invited back to San Marino often. On the few occasions when he had left the sound stage and accepted the Hendricksons' hospitality, he became friendly with several members of the family. Skip was oblivious to their various accomplishments and tended to forget that he had an uncle and cousin who ran a prestigious investment-counseling service in Los Angeles. When Buck met them, they were congenial and communicative; when he called, they set an appointment that day for lunch. He told them on the phone that Skip did not know he was coming. They understood and promised that they would say nothing.

They met at the California Club, and as soon as they were seated in the dining room Buck sensed that his hosts had been expecting his call. They seemed to know why he was there, how much money he wanted and how quickly he wanted it.

"I get the feeling," Buck said finally, "that I'm replowing a

44

field you're already familiar with. I don't want to waste your time."

Both men immediately demurred. "Buck, we've been hoping you'd come," the uncle said. "When you called today, we were relieved; we couldn't figure out a sure way to call you without Skip hearing about it."

The cousin continued. "We're familiar with the difficulty of finding venture capital in Southern California at the moment. When Skip told us what he was up to, we knew right away that financing would be a problem. Since then, we've done some homework. Frankly, we're impressed that it took you so long to call us. You've stretched your money pretty far. We were getting worried, though."

"I'll confess," Buck said, "so was I."

"As far as we're concerned," the uncle went on, "the Cumulus project seems viable. We believe you'll find a market for it, though perhaps not with the major airlines. They're notably myopic about new companies. You've handled the situation with Skip with great perception, realizing his disinterest in finance. If he knew the family was involved, he'd be embarrassed, which would affect his work."

"Did I hear," Buck asked, "that his family *is* involved?"

The Hendricksons smiled and looked at each other. The uncle nodded assent to his son, who stated, "We will make one million dollars available to Hendrickson-Faulkner immediately. Our attorneys are drawing up papers for an anonymous corporation. In time, we would wish to be repaid with a margin of profit."

Buck sat quietly as the two Hendricksons glanced at each other again.

"Forgive my suspicion," Buck said, "but it's a chronic condition of my business. What else do you want?"

Without hesitation, the uncle replied, "The success of Hendrickson-Faulkner. That's all. Our money will go into a limited partnership, you and Skip will remain the general partners, and Buck, you will retain control."

Buck said nothing for a moment. "It's hard to believe. I keep looking for a catch."

"I can understand your feeling," the uncle said. "Trust us, Buck. Like any family, we're only seeing to the interests of one of us. Skip presented a real problem; you've allowed us to solve

45

it. Besides that, you seem to us to be a good businessman—in spite of certain incidents we heard about on occasion." He and his son laughed good-naturedly. "Buck, as far as the Hendricksons who know you are concerned, you're a member of the family."

"And one of them thinks of you a good deal more than that," the cousin laughed. "It seems Jennifer, Skip's eldest, has developed something of a crush on you."

Buck shrugged, going back to a point in the conversation that was bothering him. "What did you mean when you said you could understand my feeling?"

The uncle did not retreat from the question, but chose his words carefully. "You were wary of trusting us. Trust begins in a family, and it occurs to me that so far, the world hasn't presented you with many opportunities for trust. We hope you can experience it with the Hendricksons."

Buck felt a familiar anger. The presumptions and even the assumed compassion seemed almost smug. Buck forced a smile.

"I'm grateful for your support. As for 'trust,' I learned very early to trust only myself; I was the one person I could be sure of." He laughed quietly. "You *can't* begin to understand that. . . . Anyway, I'm glad you've decided to join me."

The two Hendricksons understood the implicit warning. The conversation shifted immediately into the intricacies of finance and marketing. By the end of the meal, the Cumulus was assured. As Buck drove back to the sound stage, he carefully planned how he would explain the sudden good fortune to Skip.

Abruptly, Buck remembered what the cousin had said about Skip's daughter, Jennifer. She had used the word "crowded" to describe his fantasies about his parents. He smiled; most people thought being adopted left a vacuum. It did, but what filled it were the arbitrary imaginings about parents, both glorious and grotesque. Buck had been impressed that she could sense the congestion. He remembered her green eyes and the light-blue sunsuit she had worn the day they met.

The two of them spoke each time Buck visited the Hendrickson home. He remembered that on one occasion, she had asked him when his birthday was. He had told her, and she had wondered if the date were the real day or the day he had come home with his adoptive parents. At the time he had laughed, but the memory soured. She was ten years younger than he; she couldn't understand. As he drove, he forgot about their conversation and considered automatic stall slots.

In spite of everyone's intense dedication over the next four months, the plane was not ready for testing until nearly Christmas. When she was finally finished, Buck discovered the wing span was too long to get out of the sound stage's door; in the excitement of the final push, no one had bothered to measure. The carpenters cut a six-foot horizontal space on one side of the door, and the Cumulus was towed out into the sunlight for the first time.

To describe the Cumulus on the ground, "sleek" was not a word anyone used. "Stumpy" was more appropriate. The Cumulus was built as a dray horse rather than as a thoroughbred, a dray horse that would never tire of working, but one that would never win a race or a beauty contest. It had a snub nose and a double tail unit. The cylindrical fuselage resembled what one worker had called "a pregnant cigar" and that description stuck. When the plane was taxied around the sound stage, Eddie Stockton insisted that she seemed eager to fly.

Late one night in December, the Cumulus was towed on a flat-bed truck over to the Long Beach Municipal Airport. Buck was concerned about Skip, who sat between him and the driver in the truck's cab. The two partners shared a bone-deep fatigue which in the last few weeks had been overcome only by nerves and obsession.

Catching Buck's worried glances, Skip said, "Remember what a flamingo looks like standing in the mud. But when it flies . . ." He was as unperturbed as ever. He looked back through the rear window at the Cumulus with affection. Eddie Stockton, riding in the cockpit, gave a thumbs-up sign.

Most of the crew had either followed the plane in their cars from the sound stage, or were waiting in the early-morning dark as the flat-bed truck turned into the airport. Some had brought their wives and children to share their excitement. The catering company had sent a coffee truck for the occasion. Feelings were high, and when one car in the procession started blowing its horn, the rest of the vehicles were quick to join in. Buck heard the chorus, jumped out of the truck's cab, and ran up to the motorcycle cops. He gave each of them ten dollars and told them to turn on their sirens. When he returned to his seat, he said to Skip, "Maybe we'll wake Don Douglas up."

With horns and sirens blaring, the motorcade moved slowly down a runway before the massive hangars and construction sheds of the Douglas Aircraft Company, the main tenant of the airport. Buck enjoyed the irony of his plane being tested in front of the company he would be rivaling. He hoped Don Douglas himself was up in his office watching through binoculars.

At the end of the runway the Cumulus was unloaded. The crew made certain of the work they were already sure of, moving over her in dead earnest. Just before dawn, John Slater arrived with a half-dozen representatives from the different airlines. Letting them watch a test flight was risky, but Skip and Buck were sure of their plane and wanted orders to fill. The reps from the big airlines barely deigned to show interest, but the others were enthusiastic the moment they saw the Cumulus.

Buck's landlord in the movie business had sent a camera car to record the maiden flight, reminding Buck of the *Bangor Gazette* stringer who took the picture of the Belle Nuit. Publicity was always important; so was history. Buck planned to send stills of the Cumulus all over the world. Looking back, he was glad he had thrown that kid's camera into the Atlantic.

The last car to arrive brought Skip's wife and daughter. Buck noted with appreciation the absence of the uncle and cousin, a measure of their trust. Delilah came over and kissed him for luck. "So you think this crazy idea is going to fly?" she said, laughing. She was a large woman who wore her jet-black hair parted in the middle and drawn back severely in a bun. It dramatized her wide green eyes, olive skin and fast-breaking smile. Buck had not noted the green eyes before, except in the daughter. He had grown fond of Delilah over the past months, and he appreciated her sharp humor.

"Of course it'll fly," Buck said. "Last week Skip had it tap-dancing."

Eddie Stockton came over and said, "I've got a date for lunch with Shirley Temple. You think we could get this fandango in gear?"

They walked over to the Cumulus and helped Eddie up to the cockpit. He shook everyone's hand accepting the attention as he had in the old days, when pilots were the stars of flying.

Buck, Skip and John Slater stood watching as the crew backed away, leaving two men standing below each motor, one with a fire extinguisher, the other ready to pull the chock blocks.

"It's like a birth, isn't it?" Buck heard Jennifer say, to which Delilah replied, "Not quite, dear." Others laughed, but Buck turned and gave Jennifer an appreciative nod. Behind her, he saw the camera car ready itself to speed down the runway beside the plane.

"Come on, Skip," Buck said and led his partner over to the car. They got in beside the driver and cameraman, who made room for their unexpected passengers just as the crowd of employees began to applaud and shout. Buck waved at them. Immediately the starboard engine slowly turned, coughed, then caught life. The second Hispano-Suiza took longer, but then doubled the roar. The engines' backwash kicked up a wide trail of dust behind the plane as the R.P.M.s wrapped up, then slowed. Eddie Stockton nodded through the cockpit and gave a thumbs-up sign. Buck pointed down to the far end of the runway, balled up his fist and made an uppercut toward the sky.

The chock blocks were pulled and the fire extinguishers cleared. The engines roared again, and the Cumulus shuddered as it began to move. Buck and Skip could see Eddie Stockton concentrating, urging the Cumulus on and, abruptly, up. The tail wheel lifted, and then, with a slight hesitation, the two wheels left the ground. She was airborne, retracting the landing gear smoothly into her belly, and rising through the still, clear air into the morning sky. Eddie banked her neatly and gained altitude.

Buck was standing in the camera car watching the plane as it circled around to approach the field again. For a moment he felt as if he were going to explode with excitement. Then he caught Skip's smile and quickly sat. His first cognizant thought was what Jennifer Hendrickson had said. The flight was as close to a birth as he could imagine. He remembered the crash of the Belle Nuit and how long the second chance had taken.

"Buck, take a look at this, will you?" Skip handed him a folded piece of sketch paper. As the camera car turned and headed back down the runway to prepare for the Cumulus's landing, Buck opened the paper and saw a drawing of a monoplane providing for a pilot and four passengers with a low cranked wing.

"I thought we'd call it the Stratus," Skip suggested, as if his presentation were the obvious way to spend time while watching the Cumulus's maiden flight.

"What is this?" Buck asked, amazed.

"You mentioned three weeks ago that there was a market for a personal executive plane. Said we would make a profit."

Buck watched his partner and saw the future. As the Cumulus roared back over the airfield, showing itself off for those who made it and those who would buy it, Skip said, "When the flamingo flies, it's beautiful. Of course, it'd fly better if it didn't have to drag its legs." Buck grinned, thinking that Skip could design a better bird than God's.

Later that day, Slater and Skip ceremoniously evicted Buck from his living quarters at the sound stage. Since he couldn't stand to live far away, he bought a small house nearby on twenty acres of land overlooking the Pacific near a village called Palos Verdes. From his front door, he could reach the field in twenty minutes. Even so, he spent little time at his house, and John Slater made certain there was a housekeeper and cook.

During the next three years, Hendrickson-Faulkner secured a place in the burgeoning aircraft industry. Even though it could have made them money, the major airlines did not order the Cumulus. Skip's uncle had been prescient about the reason: large companies recognized only big, well-established manufacturers. Nevertheless, the smaller trunk lines established a steady backlog of orders, enabling Buck to buy enough land to build their own airfield, and to construct enough hangars and sheds to build not only the Cumulus, but the Stratus as well.

Buck's prediction had been correct; Skip's design for a personal aircraft attracted the attention of every private buyer. By 1936, the company went public. Skip began designing a larger passenger plane with four engines, and incorporating a pressurized cabin to allow higher flight and, thus, greater speed. The new aircraft was named the Cirrus, and with it Buck prepared to take on Boeing's Stratoliner in selling to the major airlines. By then, Hendrickson-Faulkner had a reputation.

During those years, Buck became as close to Skip as he imagined brothers to be. Totally different in temperament and style, they surprised each other with the uncanny similarity of their ideas. Skip never stopped conceiving new designs, appearing one day with sketches of an autogiro, the next week with concepts based on reaction propulsion. Conversely, Buck would describe an aircraft that he believed might be successful. Within days, the first sketches would appear.

Skip seemed content with the relationship; he never questioned Buck's many decisions and never seemed to be surprised by the results, accepting them as the natural progress of the company. When Skip returned from a trip to England, where he had gone to investigate an experimental gas-turbine jet engine, Buck was waiting at the assembly shed to show off their first runway, which had been graded and surfaced while Skip was away. Skip just smiled and walked across it pulling out his new sketches to show Buck.

Buck was treated as part of the Hendrickson family. He was invited to their holiday celebrations, became the godfather of two children, and was an usher in three weddings. Buck was even included in family vacations to the Hendricksons' compound on Lake Tahoe. He went only once. He was uncomfortable, not with the Hendricksons, but with the idea of vacation. He returned to the field after four days.

The rest of Buck's social life took place in Hollywood. His name began appearing in the gossip columns as well as on the business page. One caption described Buck, who was shown escorting two actresses into a restaurant, as "flying through the stars." Neither of the actresses was a star nor much of an actress. Both, however, had established reputations.

Buck was comfortable with people in the movie business, and he enjoyed their company. Making aircraft and making movies provided the same almost adolescent exhilaration. Money beyond fantasy was attainable, and power, although provincial, was blatant.

At first Buck was uneasy that any kind of notoriety might hurt Hendrickson-Faulkner's reputation, but in fact, his exploits enhanced his prestige with his customers. The only place where such news caused Buck the slightest concern was with the Hendricksons. Skip was oblivious, but Delilah enjoyed herself.

"According to what I read in Mr. Hearst's paper, if you laid all those women end to end, they'd extend the length of your runway." The double-entendre was intended. "Buck, where do you find time to brush your teeth and build airplanes?" Buck shrugged innocently. In spite of his growing reputation, the Hendricksons continued to treat him as part of the family.

Late in 1937, Buck arrived at Skip's house for a dinner. When he walked through the front door, he was met by one of the largest gatherings he had seen there. They yelled, "Surprise!" and then sang, "Happy Birthday." Buck glimpsed Judge Hendrickson, the uncle and cousin who had backed him, and Skip, who had his arm around his daughter, Jennifer. She was smiling triumphantly. Buck had seldom if ever been speechless, but he remained so as his godchildren toddled up with a model of the Cumulus.

Delilah led him to a striped tent in the garden, while a small band struck up "There's a Goldmine in the Sky." On a center table stood a huge cake in the shape of the Cirrus, complete with propellers, which turned at the flick of an unobtrusive switch. The children loved it and begged to eat the motors. Buck could say only, "Don't show this to Eddie Stockton. He'll try to fly it out of here."

Throughout the meal, the family dropped by Buck's table with little presents. Others congratulated him on his business success. Some of the men sat down and asked Buck how he was keeping the unions out of the Hendrickson-Faulkner hangars. One cousin warned him that they were all Communists working for Joseph Stalin. Buck listened and adroitly turned the conversation. He wasn't too worried about the Communists. He had been to several Hollywood parties staged for various left-sounding causes. Even John Slater had hosted a benefit for the Abraham Lincoln Brigade, the American unit that was fighting alongside the Russians against Franco in Spain.

As for the unions, his opposition had nothing to do with politics. He just didn't like anyone coming into his hangars and telling him what to do. Besides, he had always treated his workers well; he thought of them as a family. Still, if they wanted to organize, Buck felt he could live with the union, though he kept that opinion to himself.

At the end of dinner, Skip walked out to the center of the dance floor with a glass of wine. He stood there, looking down at his feet as the surprised guests became silent. Skip never spoke in public. When the tent was quiet, he looked up and said, "This party is the best idea we've had in a long time." Everyone clapped, and Skip raised his hand for quiet again. "Credit where it's due. Jennifer suggested it and did most of the work." Again there was appreciative applause. Skip couldn't spot Jennifer in the crowd, but Buck saw her at a nearby table. Just before her father began speaking again, she glanced over at Buck, surprised but pleased to see him looking at her.

The last time they had spoken, she had told Buck that she was considering applying for law school, but first she was going to work and travel for a year. He smiled, remembering her sunsuit and the grass stain. She had grown up since then. Buck had met a young man she was dating at college. Apparently, nothing had come of it.

Skip was finishing his speech: "We came here to wish Buck a happy birthday. Seemed to me that something should be said about what he's done for us. Those of us who know him have been enriched by his ideas, his vision and most of all his friendship. We're lucky to be part of his life."

As everyone stood up to applaud, Skip hurried back to his seat. Across the tent, Buck sat feeling as if he were part of the audience rather than the center of attention. He knew he was expected to say something. Slowly he got up and walked toward the dance floor.

The band played a fanfare. Buck hesitated. It was only when he looked down and pretended that he was addressing a crowd of strangers that he was able to speak.

"I gave up on birthdays some time ago, but after this one, I think I'll enjoy growing older. . . . I also gave up on families some time ago, but after meeting the Hendricksons, anything's possible. The luck is all mine, Skip."

He raised his glass and as he drank it off, he had an idea. He turned and nodded to the band, which started to play. While the guests continued to clap, Buck walked over to Jennifer's table, reached out his hand and asked her to dance.

Jennifer's mouth opened slightly, not with surprise, but as if taking a breath before leaping across an abyss. Then her neck straightened and she took his hand. The band was playing "Red Sails in the Sunset." He and Jennifer went to the center of the dance floor, and he turned to take her in his arms. For the first time, Buck realized that she was in love with him.

"So I owe all this to you," he said cheerily.

"I hope you don't mind."

"Why would I mind?"

"I don't think you like surprises." She smiled.

"I liked this one."

"I'm glad, . . . but Buck, wasn't there a moment when you were a little irritated that all this could be planned without your knowing about it?"

He didn't answer, but whirled her around so that her full skirt billowed out behind her.

"You're a very good dancer," he said.

"Thank you."

"What?" he asked, referring to her tone.

She moved closer so that he couldn't see her face.

"Am I being laughed at?" he asked.

"No, just enjoyed."

"Really? I didn't know I was so entertaining."

"You are."

"How?"

Jennifer leaned back slightly so she could look at Buck. "I think you just realized my own little surprise, and I'm enjoying watching you dance around it."

They barely moved, only enough to keep time to the music. Buck was about to laugh off what she had said and to pretend not to understand. Instead, he nodded. His acceptance made her slightly embarrassed, and she dropped her head to his shoulder.

"Should we stop dancing?" he asked.

"No, not yet," she answered quickly. Other couples finally had joined them on the dance floor so they were no longer under the family's scrutiny.

"I'm at a disadvantage," Buck said. "You seem to have watched me closer than I have you."

She nodded. "For a long time."

Again she leaned back to look at him. "You don't have to say anything, Buck. I'd rather you didn't. You're too good at saying what people want to hear."

Her body barely brushed against his as they pivoted and glided to the music. "I'm going to Europe next week for six months," she said abruptly. "It's funny; I didn't want to go because of you. Now I wish I was leaving tonight."

"I'm not the man for you, Jennifer. I'm not good enough for you, and I don't think I have room in my life for—"

As if reading a rule she said, "Please don't reach conclusions on the dance floor."

The music ended. She stood before him, smiling up into his eyes. He noted her pale-blue China-silk dress. Her shoulders were bare and he realized his right hand had rested on her naked back as they had danced. "And please don't tell me how crowded your life is. Goodbye, Buck. I'll try not to write."

She turned and walked away. Buck didn't see her again that evening, nor during the week before she left for Europe. The next time they met was five months later when she returned unexpectedly from her trip. By then, the Hendrickson-Faulkner Aircraft Company was about to fall apart.

5

By 1938, more and more uniforms began showing up at the field. Buck saw the military market developing. He studied how Mussolini's bombers had checked the British fleet while Italy took Ethiopia, and how Hitler's Junkers had devastated Spain. The more Buck learned, the more certain he became that his planes would soon be going up against Messerschmitts, Junkers and Heinkels. War was coming. Buck was certain that the United States couldn't hesitate as it had done during World War I, and he was determined to be prepared with a bomber.

Buck wanted to call it the Thunderhead. It would have less range than the Boeing plane that Buck had heard about, but it would be able to carry more bombs. In a European war, load was as important as range. Although the Army Air Corps was already committed to Boeing, Buck was certain that, as the war approached, the country would need more bombers. The Thunderhead would be designed as another Hendrickson-Faulkner dray horse, with no frills other than its dependable, awesome power.

1938 was the opportune year for the company to have a military project in the works. Four years before, the military had instigated a competition for a bomber. Though not yet in a position to participate, Buck had attended the fly-off at Wright Field near Dayton. Glenn Martin had built the B-10, a medium bomber with two 750-h.p. Wright radial engines on an all-metal midwing. Don Douglas entered with a military version of the

DC-2 with a gun turret and glassed-in bombardier's position in the nose. The Boeing Company submitted their first four-engine bomber, the 299.

Buck had stood in the reviewing stand with several high-ranking Army officers. Every man present had been a pilot; some had gained considerable fame in the First World War. They had spoken of Hitler's Luftwaffe, as well as the Japanese invasion of Manchuria. In the context of such globe-girdling challenges, the Boeing plane with its massive range had presented them with exciting alternatives.

Unfortunately, during the fly-off, the 299 crashed. Ever since, the results of that crash had intrigued Buck. Subsequently, Don Douglas had been awarded the bomber contract, but several officers had returned to Washington and convinced their colleagues that Boeing should continue work on the long-range bomber. Consequently, Boeing built a prototype SB-15 with four Pratt and Whitney 1,000-h.p. radials. After study and refinement, the Army Air Corps had given the go-ahead for fourteen production models they were calling the "Flying Fortress."

They had made this decision despite the crash. Buck noted that a few determined men in the Army Air Corps had somehow saved the Boeing from being jettisoned. Such was the catalytic power of the coming war. He knew that Hendrickson-Faulkner, because they had been involved mainly in commercial aircraft, had not developed a line of influence to Washington. When war came, Buck knew military politics would be essential, and he hoped to make such connections with the Thunderhead.

The problem was Skip. Buck submitted to him a list of requisites that included four engines for longer range, gun blisters to house 20-mm. cannon for self-protection, and room for ten tons of bombs. Buck wanted a new plane rather than a military conversion of the Cirrus.

Skip listened as he always did when Buck handed over stats, made notes, studied the figures, and then, without comment, went off with his sketch pad. Each morning when Buck came into his office, he hoped to find some sketches on his desk; that was how he had first seen the designs of the Cirrus. But nothing happened. Buck controlled his impatience. He knew the Thunderhead was a difficult plane to design: the requirements often contradicted each other. Aside from the Boeing bomber, most four-motor aircraft that were practical at that time took off and landed on an unlimited length of water.

After a month of silence, Buck became anxious. He decided to break with tradition and drop in on the design section. He walked from his office, which was in the largest of the six construction hangars, down the runway to the old wooden sound stage. Skip and his engineers had insisted on staying there, monastically separated from the other workers, who looked upon them as a strange bunch of doodlers. Still, they never missed a deadline, even if it meant working weekends or all night; so, on his entrance, Buck was surprised to find the sound stage almost empty. Even Skip was not at his usual drawing board. When Buck asked where everyone was, the draftsmen shrugged. Buck decided to wait and wandered about glancing at the various designs.

What he saw had nothing to do with the Thunderhead. Most of the work was for a small single-engine turbine jet. The shoulder wing had a semipositive sweepback and seemed to call for laminated wood. There was no drawing of a bomber anywhere.

By the time Skip arrived with some fifteen members of his design team, Buck had given up trying to control his temper. Skip ignored his partner's scowl and hurried past toward his glass-enclosed office. "Come on in, Buck. I have something to show you."

Buck followed and said nothing until they were alone in the office. He was aware that they could still be seen by the design staff. "You've never done something like this behind my back."

"On the contrary, Buck, everything I've done has been behind your back. I'm sorry you walked in today. We planned a presentation next week."

"Of what? That jet I see on the drawing boards out there?"

Skip ran his fingers through his hair. "This plane will put us ten years ahead of anyone in the industry." He opened several drawers and pulled out rolls of blueprints. "We were over at the wind tunnel at Cal Tech. . . ."

Buck interrupted. "That's too far ahead. Nobody will buy it. It's a whole new science of flying. How long is it going to take you to test it and get one of those in the air? Two, three years? And then what about production? Another year? And what are they going to fight a war with in the meantime? Blueprints?"

"Just a minute, Buck."

"We don't have a minute. You've wasted I don't know how long on a theoretical exercise. Where's the Thunderhead?"

Skip disregarded the question as he unrolled a blueprint on his desk. "They're working on a gasoline turbine jet in England. They'll have something to fly next year in Germany, I've been told. Italy, too, . . ."

"Where's the Thunderhead?"

Skip looked up and blinked at Buck's anger. "It just doesn't interest me, Buck."

Buck almost reached over the desk to grab him, but didn't.

"What's that mean?" he said.

"Anyone can design that plane. There are half a dozen companies that can build it, and will, or some variation. What's the point? With this," he indicated the plans on his desk, "we can define the future of flight."

Reaching across the desk, Buck grabbed the top blueprint and balled it up in his hands. "And what the hell do you think is going to pay for us to get to that future? We don't have anything to sell to anyone, Skip. Hitler and the U.S. Army Air Corps aren't going to wait for you to get this damn thing in the air. And even if they did, we wouldn't last that long as a company."

Skip glanced quickly out of the glass of the office, embarrassed that their argument could be seen and probably heard. "You're so sure. What'll you do if a war doesn't come?"

"It's *always* come. It's a question of being ready. And we're *not* ready because of this." He threw the balled-up blueprint against the glass, startling the already apprehensive staff. "You've built yourself a little ivory tower in here, Skip. You can't see the rest of the world." He turned to look at his partner, "Or maybe you just don't want to. Well, this company can't afford your indulgence and stay in business."

Skip stood up and silently stared at him. He seemed to Buck to withdraw out of reach. Buck sensed his old panic of loss, and hated Skip for being able to inflict it on him after all these years. Fear replaced trust in an instant. Buck reacted as he always did. He became aggressive.

"You're spoiled, Skip. Everyone else spoiled you, and I've

59

spoiled you. You can't just sit in here building toys any more. I can't afford the luxury of your innocence." He tried to stop, but from past experience he knew he couldn't, so he got out as fast as possible.

"I expect some plans on my desk in a week. If they're not there, I'll find somebody else to design the Thunderhead."

As he walked out of the office, he confronted Skip's design team, who were clustered around the first row of drafting tables. "You better get your heads out of your collective turbine asshole and give me a bomber to build," he shouted.

Outside, Buck thought his rage would lessen, but it didn't. In Skip's last look, Buck recognized the superiority of security. In retrospect, the Hendricksons' affection seemed a patronizing sentimentality. At least they couldn't take the company away; he owned 51 percent of that. As he walked back down to his office he thought of what that 51 percent meant without Skip Hendrickson.

He stopped and looked down the length of runway. Two days before, Buck had negotiated with the banks to finance a second runway along the western border. He swore to himself that he wasn't going to lose his company.

During the week, he saw no one in the old sound stage. Buck forbade Slater even to negotiate. As far as they could tell, the design team, including Skip, showed up each day and were putting in long hours. Slater tried to convince Buck to soften his ultimatum, but Buck refused.

At the end of the week, Skip called. Not a trace of their previous argument was revealed in his voice. "Buck, I was wondering if you have a moment, could you come down here? We have something to show you."

The intensity of Buck's gratitude almost left him without words. "I'll be right down," he said, stopping only to pick up Slater. When the two men walked in they were surprised to find Skip's uncle and cousin, as well as a major in the Army Air Corps. To Buck, the face was familiar.

Skip introduced them.

"Major Llewellyn, my partner, Buck Faulkner."

"Hello, Buck." The same smile lighted his face. Jack Llewellyn enjoyed the surprise.

60

"What the hell are you doing here, Jack?" Buck said, trying to act as if he were pleased.

"Didn't know you two knew each other," Skip said and left them to go to the front of the room.

"We have a lot to catch up on, Buck. I'm military liaison over at Lockheed."

"Looks like you made it through West Point," Buck smiled, acknowledging the immaculate uniform and the gleaming gold of his rank.

"No, V.M.I.," Llewellyn said, his tone daring anyone to imply the school was secondary to any other, or his career being limited by his attendance there.

As Buck introduced Slater to the major, he experienced a sudden fear. Outsiders had never been included at such a presentation. As Skip waited at the front of the room looking down at his feet, Buck found a chair and sat with the other guests. The design section remained standing behind them as Skip began to speak, and Buck noticed that Eddie Stockton was with them.

"I want to welcome those of you who aren't familiar with our little 'inner sanctum.' The reason we've asked you here is to get your advice." He was speaking pointedly at Major Llewellyn and to his relatives. Behind him stood a huge illustration board, the first page of which read "Project X." One of Skip's draftsmen stood on either side to pull pages back over the top. When the title page was lifted, Buck saw a turbine-jet fighter climbing dramatically out of the clouds.

Skip began to speak, but Buck didn't hear the words. He waited, hoping the next page would be flipped over showing the Thunderhead. It didn't. The next page was a graph of the jet's speed and climb.

Without a word, Buck stood up and walked out through the groups of engineers gathered at the back of the sound stage. Skip said nothing as Buck left; no one else moved. At the door, Buck hesitated, but no words came to his mind. He thought that if he turned back and saw Skip he would shout some incomprehensible bitterness. He went out quickly.

By the time Slater had followed him back to the office, Buck had contacted five of the best designers in the aircraft business and offered them jobs at Hendrickson-Faulkner. Three had expressed enough interest to come down to the field. "We'll carry Skip for a while. Let him dabble while we go ahead with the Thunderhead."

Slater nodded. "That's a pretty impressive airplane Skip's designed. He says it'll go four hundred fifty miles an hour."

"That'll keep it ahead of the market for the next five or ten years. I'm in the business to sell what we build. How about you?" Being alone always had made ultimatums easier.

Slater didn't hesitate. "What do you want me to do?"

"Clear out the north end of Hangar Six. I'm putting the new design team in there."

"Should I tell Skip?"

"No, he'll hear." As Slater turned to leave, Buck added, "What did Llewellyn think of Skip's project?"

"Seemed interested."

"A shot of military encouragement. It's a cheap stimulant."

Three days later, Buck hired a designer from Consolidated and his first six engineers. Within the hour, Buck heard that Skip had left the field.

"Any messages?" Buck asked.

John Slater stood in the small office, looking deeply concerned. "Yes. He said that his understanding was that he designed the planes for this company and hired everyone who worked on design. He said if that was not the case, he was with the wrong company."

"He may be. He'll have to decide."

"Buck, it's inevitable that partners are going to disagree. But we can't lose him."

"If we have to, we must. He has the choice. We don't."

"My God, Buck, he's the company. Without him . . ." Instantly, Slater regretted his words.

"You're wrong." Buck spoke quietly, but dangerously.

"I know, I'm sorry." Slater mumbled.

"I know what Skip Hendrickson's worth, just as I know what every riveter in the hangars is worth. If they all left, if they folded up the hangars and rolled up the runways, there'd still be a company because *I'd* be here to put it back together again. If Skip leaves the company, that's his choice, but he's not taking the company with him."

"What should I tell him?"

"Nothing."

"What about his design section?"

"Are they down there?"

"Most of them, just sitting around."

"Move them in to Hangar Six. They'll work on the Thunderhead."

"What about the sound stage?"

"Lock it up. Work on the jet is over. No one goes in there. Tell the security guards."

Slater turned to go, then stopped. "You're making it impossible for him."

"He's doing that. I'm keeping us in business."

As an afterthought, Slater added, "His family owns a lot of stock."

"Offer to buy them out."

"With what?"

"I'll get the money."

Slater nodded. "Don't start to hate him, Buck. That's a part of family life you don't need. Family hate is worse than any other kind." Without waiting for a response, he left.

Half of Skip's team refused to shift to Hangar Six; they quit. The aircraft business was as prone to gossip as the movie business, and within days the partners' fight was common knowledge. Neither Skip nor Buck granted interviews, but several of Skip's designers offered the papers a black-and-white picture of Skip as the mistreated genius and Buck as the greedy businessman. Unexpectedly, Skip's turbine-jet project was not mentioned as the reason for the split. Buck learned why when a military courier arrived and informed everyone at the field that all work done in the sound stage had been classified top secret by the Department of the Army's War Plans Division.

Other messages arrived. The banks held up the loan for the new runway, and those that held credit for the company expressed concern over the company's future if Skip Hendrickson was not involved. The machinists' union, hearing the rumors and sensing weakness, began a work slowdown in order to gain shop steward representation.

Buck ignored the banks, but faced the unions head on. He went into the hangars and debated the union representatives in front of their constituents. He enjoyed the exercise; it released some of his bile. He wanted his workers to know his reasons and not have them misrepresented. The union people didn't like his technique of confrontation, and one particularly vituperative member shouted that Buck's current struggle was indicative of capitalism's downfall. Buck laughed at him, the first good laugh he had enjoyed in weeks, and the union man swung at him. He missed and Buck withdrew, still laughing. His employees seemed sympathetic, but as he left the hangar one of them, a woman, slapped his face. Buck let it go; he had made too good an impression with the others to be bothered.

Buck's strategy was to go on with business and wait for Skip to react. Buck was not inclined to negotiate, although he kept in touch with one of Skip's brothers, a lawyer. Buck would be happy to have Skip return and work on anything he wanted. The company, however, would build the planes that Buck said it would build. If Skip chose not to design them, someone else would.

The first intimation of Skip's decision came from Delilah. She telephoned, and for the first time since he had met her, she spoke hesitantly.

"Buck, something's happened to him. I've never seen Skip like this. He's so hurt. Can't you understand that? Well, no one's ever done anything like this to him. What I'm trying to say to you is that he doesn't want this to happen any more than you do."

"Doesn't want what to happen?" Buck asked.

She hesitated. "I can't tell you that, Buck. What I can tell you is that he loves you like a brother. We all do, and what's happening is a terrible waste." She hung up.

Within the hour, Eddie Stockton walked into the office. He never made appointments; he regarded access to Buck as his privilege. "For having saved Buck's ass in the Chaco."

"This damn thing with Skip. I have to tell you something, pal. I really do want to fly that rocket tube of his. I've flown everything else, and I figure it may be my last chance to get on the books. Can't stay young forever."

"You can, Eddie, and you're already on the books."

Eddie smiled. "I guess I just want to fly it."

"Maybe you will. It should be ready in about five years."

Eddie looked at Buck, then away. "Skip says he can build one in eighteen months. I have to believe him. I've been around him a hell of a long time. I want you to know he didn't ask me. I'm just going."

"Where?"

"I guess you'll be hearing about that. Goddamn, Buck, I wish he could build it here!" Realizing he had said more than he had intended, Eddie Stockton stuck out his hand.

Buck stood up and shook it. "Goodbye, Eddie."

Alarmed, Eddie said, "Wait a minute, Buck. I'll be seeing you around. Sure I will." He gave a reassuring smile. He needed to leave without embarrassment and Buck let him.

Later that day, Slater heard from Skip's lawyers. They wanted to start negotiation for Skip Hendrickson's withdrawal from the company. Buck told Slater that he wanted total and instant severance, and he was willing to make sacrifices to get it. The sooner the company was his, the sooner he could begin forgetting.

As he left the field that day, Buck accepted the probability that he would never see any of the Hendricksons again. He went to his house, yelled at the staff and told them all to get off the property. Then he started drinking gin. He hoped it would put him to sleep, but instead it only inflicted memories. He remembered the Chaco, Skip in his three-piece wool suit, the first time he met the family, his two godchildren. By the time he recalled his surprise birthday party, it was late and the gin was gone. He sat on his terrace and indulged in remembering his birthday party, Delilah's delight, the Hendricksons' appreciation of him, Skip's toast. As he remembered his dance with Jennifer, her car drove up and stopped in front of the house.

He watched as she hesitantly walked up to the front door. The lights were off, and she obviously was uncertain that she had the right address. She heard him get up and turned in alarm. "Jennifer," he said. He couldn't see her face distinctly, but it was obvious that she was crying. His arms were around her before he could stop himself. She clung to him, quickly raising her mouth to his.

They did not give themselves time to talk or think. He carried her into the house, her arms around his neck, and laid her down on the wide couch in the living room. When he kissed her, it was a mark of acquisition. He held her covetously. When her clothes became a barrier, she helped him remove them. As he continued kissing her, her short sudden cries agreed to his desire.

When Buck took off his clothes, she said with concern, "I haven't done this." He stopped her with a kiss. When they finally were together, she gasped with surprise. As her breathing became steadily deeper, she managed to say, "I love you . . . I've wanted so much . . . to say it out loud . . . I love you, Buck . . . I love you."

Buck tried to block out her words, kissing her breasts and holding her. He had always responded to the declaration of love with the anxiety that he was not capable of returning the emotion. As if sensing his thoughts, she grabbed his hair and pulled him down with her to the floor, driving herself onto him until her breath exploded in a high keening cry. For a moment, her pleasure glutted his mind.

He lay with her, feeling new edges of loss.

"Jennifer," he said. The sudden sound seemed too loud.

She shook her head. "Not yet. Just hold me, please."

He did, until she said, "I've probably made everything worse. I came to try . . ." She stopped.

"I thought you were in Europe."

"Mom wrote me about what was happening. I've been traveling for twelve days. The whole way I planned what I was going to say, how I was going to get you and Daddy back together, but I may never see you again."

She sat up, picking up her blouse and covering herself against the slight chill from the ocean breeze.

"I can't believe what's happened. I've never seen Daddy so angry."

"What does he do? Yell and scream? Kick the dog?"

"No. He locks himself in the study and sits."

"He'll live," Buck said. "I presume the family will set him up in his own company. He won't have time to sit around. . . ."

Objecting to his condescending tone, Jennifer said, "He loved you."

"So your mother said—'like a brother.' Maybe I don't know how to respond to that. What I do know is that as his partner, I couldn't let him ruin both of us. Partners shouldn't try to be brothers."

She didn't respond. Buck wished he could give her some sign of affection, but he knew he couldn't. So did she.

"I've honestly tried not to love you, Buck. I can't hurt my father, and you can't love me yet. *Yet,* hear that? That's hope for you! It keeps sneaking in." She attempted to laugh, then gave up. After a moment, she crawled over to lie in his arms. "Buck, I'll leave, I promise. But I need tonight. Let me stay."

Jennifer stayed until dawn.

6

"Buck, I want you to know that I deeply regret what's happened."

Jack Llewellyn's voice over the phone was unmodulated by the sympathy he expressed.

"I appreciate it, Jack." Buck responded carefully. "But if Skip and I are going our separate ways, better now than later."

"You're absolutely right. We've got a hell of a job to do. Better not to have any obstacles along the way. I just didn't want you to think that I or anyone in the Army Air Corps had encouraged Skip to move out. We had to classify his plane. Jet propulsion has a lot of possibilities, though down the runway a ways."

"I wish him luck with it. I hope the Army will help him out."

"The *Air Corps*," Llewellyn corrected, "will finance some research." His voice changed, indicating intimacy.

"He's moving over to Hawthorne, you know, next to Jack Northrop. Some of our people around here say that with those two geniuses in the same place, the air around there will get so rarefied that nothing will be able to fly." He chuckled at his own humor.

Buck didn't respond. He was anxious not to encourage any petty rivalry that Llewellyn could use. When Llewellyn noted the lack of reaction, he said, "Buck, I'll tell you what else they're saying around here, and in Washington as well. They're saying that you can build airplanes. Trouble is, you're not building anything we can get behind."

"Yes, we are. We're working on something . . ." Buck wasn't going to bluff; Llewellyn would have spotted it. When the news of Skip Hendrickson's departure was announced, 50 percent of the orders for the new Cirrus had been canceled. The banks tightened credit, and Buck was left holding a field, ten hangars, and a payroll, with nothing but tentative orders to keep the company together. The small personal plane, the Stratus, which had been so successful, had stopped selling as the economy worsened. Their original model, the Cumulus, had reached the end of its successful run when it was overtaken by the Douglas DC-3. It was apparent to even a casual observer that Faulkner Aircraft was a company without an airplane. ". . . a heavy bomber," Buck continued, sounding as positive as possible.

"The Thunderhead?" Jack Llewellyn asked, implying full knowledge of the project.

"We're not calling it that now."

Llewellyn chuckled, his lips again near to the mouthpiece. "No more clouds."

Buck repeated, "No, no more clouds. We're calling it the Falcon. When it's ready, it'll be the most useful heavy bomber flying. I'll put it up against anything that Boeing can fly at you."

"The 'Faulkner Falcon.' Not bad, Buck, not bad at all. I just wish it were ready now. I could probably get a few sold for you."

"I didn't know the Army—I mean, the Air Corps—was buying, Jack." Buck knew the Army Air Corps was as budget-bound as he was and wanted Llewellyn to know that they were both dragging the same kite on a windless day.

"We're not yet," Llewellyn said tersely. Buck smiled; for the first time he trusted the tone. "Our President is still leading us . . . like an ostrich," Llewellyn continued. "He wants to keep us out of it and grovel to the isolationists. But with his head in the sand, he presents a pretty vulnerable position. Adolph Hitler can recognize an ass waiting to be kicked. The rest of us have to be ready for F.D.R.'s sudden awakening." Llewellyn seemed about to criticize the government further, but he checked himself.

"In the meantime, Buck, the British know there's a war coming, and they're buying a lot of planes from anyone who has them. As a matter of fact, in a couple of weeks, I'll be looking after a British delegation. They're coming out here at Bob Gross's invitation to look at the Super Electra."

In 1933, Robert Gross had bought the bankrupt Lockheed Corporation for forty thousand dollars. In the subsequent five years, he had turned it into one of the giants of the industry. The Super Electra was the Lockheed Model 14. The previous July, Howard Hughes had circled the globe in that plane. Buck saw instantly a way to cash in on Lockheed's success.

"When exactly are they coming?" he asked quickly.

"Two weeks from tomorrow. Why?"

"How long are they staying?"

"Probably a week. Mr. Gross has planned quite a reception."

"Then so will I. Jack, I may be asking you a big favor in two weeks. I need a sale more than Bob Gross does."

"I'll look forward to hearing from you. Anything I can do now?"

"How difficult would it be to send me a few military police? I want to make an impression."

"They'll be there in three hours. Good luck, Buck. I wish I could get down there myself."

"I don't need luck. I need to fit eighteen months into eighteen days." He hung up and called the supervisor of Hangar Four, where the Cirrus prototypes were being assembled. Buck ordered the model that was furthest advanced to be towed out of the hangar, down the runway and into the old sound stage. When the supervisor objected, saying he didn't think the doors would take the wingspan, Buck told him to cut an opening. He then called the security guards and told them to open the sound stage and to clear it out.

Within an hour the Cirrus was waiting outside the sound stage as slots were tailored for its entrance. Soon after, trucks began to arrive. Workers unloaded a hundred cots and carried them into the building. An enormous catering truck drove directly into the sound stage. At the same time, Buck, his head designer and engineers walked through the hangars choosing a team of workers. An hour later, two hundred men assembled outside the sound stage as two new vehicles arrived simultaneously. One was a semi-tractor-trailer with its sides painted with the familiar logo of the Pathé Film Company. The other was an Army bus carrying twenty military police.

Buck made sure that his employees took note of the M.P.s. Then he led the selected group inside. Fifteen men got out of the film company's truck and brought in generators, arc welders, a forge and lighting equipment.

Buck let everyone settle down, then asked that the doors be secured. He looked at the Cirrus, motorless, with gaping patches of fuselage and wing, showing its skeletal innards. He remembered Jennifer's comparison of the Cumulus takeoff to birth. He smiled. Changing the Cirrus into the Falcon would be a more difficult transformation. It was a hell of a way to build an airplane, but the only way to save his company.

The men quickly quieted down and looked at him.

Buck glanced at his watch and began. "From this minute, each of you is on triple time for every hour you're here." He waited for their startled but pleased reaction to pass. "We'll be working on a secret project. Until it's finished, no one will leave the building except our cook. You'll have the best food money can buy, and the drinks will be on the house. We'll work in three shifts around the clock. There's one shower, so don't expect too many bubble baths. We'll be in here for eighteen days; your families will be notified. Each of you will be allowed to call out once every two days. If there's any reason why you can't stay, speak up now, because once we begin you're on for the duration." He paused. Everyone looked around to see who would leave; no one did.

"All right then," Buck cried. "We're going to build an airplane!"

They shouted their approval as Buck took off his coat and tie and rolled up his sleeves.

"We're going to build a bomber, a heavy bomber. It has to carry eight to ten thousand pounds and have a twenty-five-hundred-mile range. The Boeing plane can go up to thirty thousand feet. I want this one up there too. She'll have to defend herself, so we'll put armor inside her, and fifty-caliber machine guns wherever they're needed. The engines will be here in eleven days. I'll want her to fly in seventeen."

Several of the men whistled their surprise. "We're working

triple shifts," Buck went on, "so it's as if we had three times seventeen. Anyway, the air frame's half built already. If we can't finish this plane in fifty days, we're in a lot of trouble. Let me tell you something else: I'm not worried, because I've got two hundred of the best people in the business here. And I'm so damn certain of what we can do, I'll promise you right now that *I'm* going to fly whatever you give me at the end of seventeen days." The shouts became a roar as they accepted the challenge. Buck knew that many of them had helped him build the Cumulus. He raised his fist and made an uppercut toward the sky. Those who remembered the gesture cheered.

Buck went over to one of the men who had come in on the movie truck. Raising his arm for quiet, Buck said, "There's a catch. There's absolutely no way we could get hold of a lot of the armaments we need. Fifty-caliber cannons aren't available at the corner drugstore; there aren't any bomb racks at the local garage. I want to introduce you to Will Ackerman and his men. Will is what's called an art director for the movies. He helped build the machines for Charlie Chaplin's *Modern Times,* the pirate ships and guns in *Captain Blood,* and the planes that shot King Kong off the Empire State Building. He tells me they were all models, but a million moviegoers thought they were real, and that's good enough for me. In fact there's a rumor that Will Ackerman built Mae West's chest. Anything we can't get, he and his crew will make—which brings me to an important point: as long as the plane flies, the rest of the equipment doesn't have to function. The first people to see the demonstration will be English. They're very polite; they'll keep their hands off of things if they're told to. But every visual detail has to be perfect. The Falcon must look like the most formidable bomber in the world, and it must fly. Will can make sure of the first, and I hope to hell the rest of you will make sure of the second, since I have to fly it."

Again, the men laughed and clapped.

"One last thing before we get to work. I want to establish ease of service and repair as our new company's tradition. Customers know that when they buy a plane, they're not just paying the purchase price. They're going to have maintenance costs. The Messerschmitt-109 has an eleven-hundred-horsepower Daimler-Benz engine that can be changed in forty minutes. I'll want to do that with one of our engines as part of our presentation."

As the men turned to look at the Cirrus, Buck felt a surge of affection that he didn't trust and tried to joke about.

"We'll remember the next seventeen days for the rest of our lives. In fifty years, we'll run into each other with our wheelchairs and talk about how we built the Falcon. I hope you guys enjoy yourselves as much as I will. Now—*here we go!*"

Buck let the supervisors begin organizing the shifts. He walked from group to group, answering questions, making decisions, and arranging for machinery and other supplies to be delivered to the sound stage.

As he moved about, he noticed the old yellow circles on the floor. He remembered the days he had lived in the sound stage when they built the Cumulus. Abruptly he understood why he had taken the trouble to use the sound stage for the bomber. Buck had never honored any traditions; he thought he might like a few.

Glancing over at Skip's old glass-enclosed office, he decided to let the caterers use it.

During the first week, Buck found that most of the men worked at least twelve hours, some sixteen. Meals were the only constant, and the food lived up to Buck's promise. The bar was used sparingly, and usually to aid sleep. The shower was ignored until a "B.O." committee was formed, and Lifebuoy soap wrappers were pinned on sleeping offenders.

Buck set up the design section by the starboard wing, so that, as a problem arose, he could have the structural engineers work on it instantly. With Will Ackerman he decided how many gun blisters the plane should carry. As each decision was made, Buck directed the welders to cut the fuselage open. They chose ball turrets for the belly of the fuselage behind the bomb-bay doors; the chin was opened so the navigator could crawl up to double as bombardier. Above that position, in the nose, was another gun turret matched by one in the tail. In addition, two slots were cut on either side of the fuselage for side gunners. By the time the welders were through, Buck had directed the construction of a hundred feet of holes to be filled with Will's magical illusions.

Ackerman had acquired assorted cannons and guns from the studios' prop departments. When they weren't the right size, his

73

crew altered them on the spot. They painted rivets, screws and armor plate where there weren't any and performed miracles with Plexiglas.

Buck slept when he could, on an average of four hours out of twenty-four. Like his workers, he never left the sound stage. In his absence, John Slater ran the rest of the company.

Buck's cot was at an angle where he could see the plane. In spite of fatigue, Buck would often lie awake, watching the men work, considering the length of the horizontal stabilizer, deciding whether to use a plain split flap or a zap flap. He seldom remembered sleeping; he just went to the cot with one problem and woke up with the solution to another.

The night the five 1,200-horsepower Wright radials arrived, Buck had more problems than usual. He watched C crew attach one of the huge motors to the starboard wing. One of the workers lying on a cot nearby asked, "Worried?"

Buck glanced over at him, smiled and shook his head. He recognized the man as a riveter who took exceptional pride in his skill and speed.

"Just waiting for Christmas," Buck said, "a week from today."

The riveter nodded. "You don't have to worry about her. She's not going to be pretty, but she'll fly."

"How do you know?"

"I can feel it. Can't you?"

"At the moment, I just feel numb."

"Naw, you can feel it. I've worked for all the ones who know it in their bones. Jack Northrop, Lee Atwood, Kelly Johnson. Hell, even Don Douglas. He doesn't care that much about aerodynamics; he just figures what an airplane needs. You do that. Now, Skip Hendrickson, he had ideas that could get a garbage can to the moon. But ideas ain't feelings. That's the big difference. You can't just figure it all out on paper and in a wind tunnel. Anyway, she's going to fly. She's got the best damn riveting job going."

Buck wondered whether that difference had carried into his and Skip's friendship. Lying on his cot, Buck tried to deny the suspicion, yet it spread quickly to the rest of the Hendricksons and, through the feeling of betrayal, made their affection seem like manipulation. They were out of his life. The family had gone with Skip when he left.

Buck had no time for bitterness. He rolled over on the cot, thinking of Jennifer. She had loved him, as he had never been loved. He remembered her face on the morning that she had left him. Burnt out with loss, her green eyes had searched for what wasn't there. Even as she was trying to leave, her hands had held on to him. Yet, he couldn't say what she so obviously had wanted to hear: "I love you," or simply, "Stay." Then it became clear that she could do nothing else but leave. He fell asleep, still not understanding why he hadn't been able to respond to her.

Over the next few days Buck's reference to the day the plane was to fly as "Christmas" spread through the sound stage. "Five days to Christmas," was how one shift greeted another. Fatigue was setting in, but so was anticipation and excitement. The Falcon was coming alive. The "hundred feet of holes" of its fuselage had become a smooth column bristling with armament and glistening with faired Plexiglas.

Inside the aircraft, the electrical and hydraulic engineers had laid miles of cable and plumbing leading to and from the cockpit's instrument panel. For heightened visual effect, Will Ackerman added several blinking dials which approximated those required for British radio equipment. In the bombardier's section, he installed a bright-red attachment for the Norden bombsight. They had no idea what the sight looked like or how it worked, since the Norden project was a closely guarded military secret. If anyone asked about the red attachment, however, Buck could imply that the Falcon was getting the bombsight as soon as it was available. Although the fourteen 50-caliber cannons did not work, they looked deadly in the turrets and the side slots.

On "two days to Christmas" the painters began. Buck had decided not to apply a camouflage pattern, but to make the plane look as menacing as possible. He chose battleship gray, with no designation numbers, except on the vertical stabilizer, where he wrote "XB-33," the letters standing for "experimental bomber," and the number representing his age. Along the fuselage was a single stripe of red. Just under that was painted the profile of a falcon.

Faulkner Aviation had previously retained a firm of private detectives to advise them on plant security. Now Slater instructed them to find out where the British trade mission was staying and what they were doing. It became evident that Bob Gross of Lockheed was taking good care of them. The group was put up at the Riviera Country Club. In the mornings, they were shown around the Lockheed plant and specifically a wooden mock-up of the Super Electra which had been redesigned as a reconnaissance bomber. In the afternoon they played golf, and in the evening the Lockheed limousines picked them up and took them to parties at some of the glamorous homes in Bel Air and Beverly Hills. The schedule fit in perfectly with Buck's plan.

"Christmas Day" came, and Buck gave each man who had worked in the sound stage a wrapped present. Buck distributed the boxes personally and watched while they were opened to reveal a new razor, shaving soap, and a battleship-gray zippered flight suit. The flight suits had been made up in the costume shops of Pathé Films. Each man's name was stitched in red over the left breast. On the back was embroidered the profile of a falcon.

At 4:45 P.M., fifteen minutes after the rest of the Faulkner employees got off work, the military police slid open the sound stage's doors for the first time in seventeen days. The other workers had gathered outside. As a truck towed the Falcon out, they began to applaud. That day's test would be private. The next day, Buck hoped to show off for the British.

Buck climbed up into the fuselage and took the pilot's seat in the cockpit. For an hour, he tested the engines and taxied back and forth on the runway. Finally, he told his controller that he was going to take off. He was pleased to see all the men had stayed to watch. Buck revved the engines up to full power.

Without warning, the inboard engine fell off the starboard wing. Chunks of its shattered propeller shot in all directions. A piece flew through the cockpit, grazing Buck's temple. Fortunately, there was no explosion, but the ruptured fuel lines were pouring gasoline all over the wing and spilling it on the runway.

Buck cut the other motors, hurried back in the fuselage and dropped to the ground. By then, the fire equipment arrived and proceeded to wash down the gasoline. Slater ran up and pulled out his handkerchief for Buck's wound as the mechanics who were responsible for it began examining the fallen engine.

As tempers flared, Buck pushed his way through the crowd and yelled for quiet.

"All right, listen to me! Don't waste your energy blaming each other; we're working tonight. I want to tell you something: I could fly this plane on these engines if I had to, but we don't have time. We have to put in the spare engine by tomorrow and Will Ackerman will make this one look like new for our demonstration. So, don't worry. Now let's take the Falcon back to the sound stage. And listen! Don't dare get those outfits dirty." He smiled, breaking the tension. "I don't want you looking like a bunch of grease monkeys tomorrow."

"What about you?" someone shouted.

Buck looked down at the blood that had dripped on his shoulder. "It seems to go with the Falcon's colors," he said.

As he walked back to the sound stage, he said to Slater, "Go on ahead and get Major Llewellyn on the phone. I'm sure he's already heard the news."

John Slater looked surprised.

Still wiping blood from his forehead, Buck said, "You think these M.P.s are here *not* to notice anything?"

As the Falcon was towed through the sound stage's doors, the phone on Buck's desk rang. It was Jack Llewellyn. Buck didn't give him a chance to ask questions.

"Major, I'm happy to announce that I have the best heavy bomber in the world down here, and I think your group of Englishmen ought to have a look at her. We just had one of those mishaps that happen on a test, but we'll be ready by tomorrow afternoon."

"With three or four engines, Buck?" Llewellyn asked caustically.

"Four, of course, Jack," Buck said innocently.

"I heard you lost one." The Major sounded angry.

" 'Lost?' No, not at all. We have it right here. That's part of our demonstration. I wanted it to be a surprise, but that was the engine we plan to change. We'll do it in forty-five minutes—take it right off and put the other on."

"I heard it fell off."

"No, no. It just came off prematurely. Now Jack, tomorrow

evening Bob Gross is having a big shindig for the British at seven. His cars are set to pick them up at six-thirty. Would it be possible to arrange for the delegation to be ready at, say five-thirty? I'll have our limousines arrive at that time, and I'll promise to have them back in time for the Lockheed party."

There was another pause.

"I'm not sure, Buck. I don't want to be embarrassed showing a plane that doesn't quite get off the ground. I've taken that chance on you before."

Buck heard the old anger, but didn't respond to it.

"Jack, you'll be taking just as big a chance if you don't show it to them. I promise you, they'll see the Falcon, even if I have to fly it over to Burbank. If you don't tell them about it, they might wonder if you know what's going on outside Lockheed. You know the Falcon's going to sell. I hope you'll be in on it, Jack. I owe it to you."

"Spare me the altruistic horseshit, Buck. The British will be ready at five, and that bird better fly." He hung up.

Most of the men inside the sound stage could only watch as the crew mounted the new engine and repaired the wing mount. The engine that had fallen was hammered back into shape and Will's men fashioned a prop out of wood. It would be used after the flight to demonstrate how fast an engine could be replaced on the Falcon.

By morning, the spare engine was gently lowered into place. The Plexiglas in the cockpit had been fixed. As the mechanics finished, they hesitated and looked around for Buck. He was watching, drinking coffee.

"You wanna check this, Buck?" one of them asked nervously.

"It's all yours," Buck said and went on drinking his coffee. "But if this one falls off, the Falcon and I will come looking for you."

Buck knew that if the flight didn't go well, if the British didn't give him an order, the company would fold. His cash reserves had been used up in the last seventeen days.

Early in the afternoon, Buck tested the engine inside the sound stage. It barely quivered in its mount. He tested each of the other engines, then cut them off. There was nothing left to do but wait. The time passed slowly. Those who had resisted the bar gave in and ordered drinks.

Finally, the phone rang, and Buck heard Slater announce that the limousines had arrived and were proceeding down the runway to the sound stage, where Buck's other employees had gathered again to watch.

"Well," said Buck looking at the crew, who had changed back into their jump suits, "here we go." The massive doors slid open, and the plane was towed back into the sunlight. The British delegation, dressed for the evening, remained reserved as Buck escorted them into the plane. Several of them were wearing gloves. As Buck had predicted, they touched nothing. When Major Llewellyn saw the rig for the Norden bombsight, he winked, then escorted the delegation off the plane, leaving Buck in the cockpit.

Buck contacted his control tower; John Slater was there and answered with surprising passion: "Fly the hell out of it, Buck."

He did just that. The takeoff was long and smooth into an appropriately brilliant sunset. His first fly-over was at two hundred feet; his second was at a hundred feet, but with one engine cut out. He was tempted to go again with only two engines, but knew the Falcon had done more than enough. When he taxied up to the reviewing stand, the noise from the crowd quickly drowned out the engines. The crew approached and began replacing an engine. Buck sat in the cockpit watching the changeover; when the men broke their own record the rest of the workers cheered.

Buck got out of the plane and shook their hands. Then Llewellyn walked him over to the British delegation. Their reserve had dissolved.

Two weeks later, the details of the British order were finalized. They agreed to purchase one hundred Falcons for eighteen million dollars. Bank credit flowered, and the company bought a twenty-acre parcel of land that abutted their property to the south. Soon the payroll had tripled and still there weren't enough workers, nor enough hangar space. Construction spilled out on the runway and continued in the clear California weather.

Forty-eight hours after Hitler and Stalin signed their nonaggression pact, Buck heard from the British again. The order for Falcon bombers was tripled for another forty million dollars. The next day, a group of U.S. Army Air Corps officers arrived at the newly named Faulkner Field. Jack Llewellyn was among them, having recently been promoted to full colonel. The military officers made it clear that they were looking for a night-fighter and wanted Faulkner Aircraft to develop and build it for them. Colonel Llewellyn said little during the meeting, but it was clear that the plane would be his project.

"Why don't we call it the Raven?" he said, smiling cryptically.

A week later, on September 1, 1939, Germany invaded Poland. For a year, Buck worked so hard expanding the assembly line for the Falcon and designing the Raven, he became oblivious to almost everything outside of the company. Then, early in December 1940, he received two phone calls which rudely reminded him of the past and present outside Faulkner Field.

The first was from John Slater, who had difficulty controlling his voice. "Skip's experimental jet just crashed. They were testing it up at Muroc Dry Lake. Eddie Stockton is dead."

The second call came before Buck had a chance to react to the first. His secretary announced that the White House was on the line.

When he picked up the phone, a woman asked, "Mr. Faulkner?"

"Yes."

"Is the line clear, Mr. Faulkner?"

Realizing the necessity of some kind of security, Buck replied, "I'm sure there's no one listening in."

"Mr. Faulkner, seven members of your executive staff are or were members of the Communist Party. I can document their involvement."

"Who is this?"

"It's not the White House, but you'd better listen. I also can tell you who your mother and father are, your biological mother and father."

7

Buck stood at the front of the church with John Slater, Skip Hendrickson and others who were acting as pallbearers. Buck hadn't seen Eddie Stockton since the day they had shaken hands and Eddie had said, "I'll be seeing you around. Sure I will." Buck wished that they had seen each other again. Their goodbye had been about business, not friendship, and that too seemed a loss.

The coffin had been wheeled to the front of the center aisle. As the service was read, Buck looked at Skip, who refused to meet his eye. Buck was shocked at the change in his former partner. His skin was pallid, his lips compressed into a stringy line. His eyes were surrounded by circles of exhaustion.

Like a newscaster, the clergyman read the service with pauses that substituted for passion. Buck tried to remember Eddie and mourn him, but the words spoken three days before by the woman on the telephone resounded in his mind with all the emotion the clergyman lacked.

". . . You can call it anything you want: blackmail or paying for information. Your ethical definitions don't mean anything to me, but I need a lot of cash. And if I don't get it, you don't learn who your parents were, and the Dies Committee gets a list of your executives with a copy of their membership cards. I doubt if your friends in the Army Air Corps will be happy to have Commies building their airplanes." She had laughed. It was low, hard and nasty.

"How did you get your information?" Buck had asked. "Why should I believe you?"

"Ask John Slater if you can't believe me, you bastard!"

Buck glanced at Slater, who was standing between him and Eddie Stockton's casket. Buck hadn't mentioned the conversation to John or anyone else. He had believed the woman and agreed to meet her.

"I've been watching your house for a week," she had said. "I've been over every step of your land. I'm going to watch for three more days to make sure you don't try anything, no wire recorders, no setups. You try that, I'm gone. Thursday night, get rid of your 'servants' "—she had said the word with disgust— "and sit out in your back yard. If I'm satisfied you haven't planned a trap, I'll show up. I'm not bringing anything original with me, only copies, so don't think capturing or killing me will do you any good. And listen: I'm good at this, so don't mess around."

As Buck and the other pallbearers grasped the brass handles to wheel the casket down the aisle, Buck saw Jennifer. She had changed her hair style, something shorter but no less attractive. She was singing the closing hymn, until her green eyes met his. Then, her mouth stopped moving and she watched him approach.

She was standing next to her mother, on the aisle. Buck hadn't seen her for more than a year. He didn't remember her as being quite so lovely. With his free arm he reached out and touched her hand. For a split second before he moved by her, she grasped his fingers.

Delilah missed the gesture, but Skip didn't. As the eight men put the casket into the back of the hearse, Skip stared furiously at Buck.

"Don't ever touch her again!" Skip blurted. "You've already ruined enough. Do you understand that?"

"Skip, this isn't the time." Slater whispered as the congregation began coming out of the church.

Skip ignored him, speaking to Buck as if some long-imprisoned pressure were being released. "He'd be alive if we could have stayed. But no, we had to start a new company; we had to run it, because you were so eager to get into the war. Don't *ever* touch her again."

Delilah and Jennifer appeared at the church doors.

"Nobody's blaming you for this, Skip," Buck said, "but don't you blame me."

Delilah reached Skip's side and took his arm. "Come on," she urged, with a look at Buck that pleaded for understanding.

"Well if it's not *our* fault, whose is it?" Skip blurted, the dilemma momentarily defusing his anger.

Buck looked at him a moment, and said, "No one's, Skip." Then he shook his head and started to walk toward his car. He decided to let them bury Eddie without him; funerals were for the living, a ceremony for grief. Besides, he didn't want to cause Skip any more stress. Looking for Jennifer, he turned toward the congregation which had gathered on the steps. She stood at the top, hesitating to make a move which might indicate a choice between Buck and her father.

Buck went back to his office, tried to work, but gave up. He went home, hoping that the woman might appear early.

She didn't. He had to wait for dark. Knowing she was somewhere watching him, Buck walked his property for the first time since he had purchased it. He was surprised by its size and was caught off guard by the majestic views of the Pacific and the lush stands of citrus. Looking down at the beach, Buck considered the problems of constructing steps to allow access. Walking back to the house, he thought of putting in a tennis court at the edge of the avocado grove. He remembered that Jennifer was a good player. He looked at the house, white adobe with red tile roof, overgrown with bougainvillea. For the first time, Buck thought it might be too small.

Sitting on the terrace he designed another wing, with bedrooms and baths. Abruptly he realized that, as he pictured the new rooms, Jennifer appeared in each one.

"Mr. Faulkner, turn out the floodlights." The woman's hard voice came from the avocado grove. Buck got up and snapped the lights out. A half-moon lighted the terrace enough for Buck to see her approach. She was short, in her early forties, and walked with heavy, purposeful steps. She wore rubber-soled shoes, trousers and a plain sweater. Her dark hair was cut short and brushed back. She carried a binocular case in one hand; in the other was an envelope, which she dropped on the glass-topped table.

When Buck approached, he scrutinized the woman's angry, large-featured face. She was breathing heavily and Buck could see her teeth were rotten. He remembered the teeth.

"We've met, haven't we?" he asked.

She smiled bitterly. "I slapped your face once."

Buck remembered an incident at the field. "You worked for me?"

"Once upon a time. All right, listen. I've brought you two executives' names, copies of their membership applications in the Party, and a list of some of their activities on our behalf. I mean—" she corrected herself abruptly— "on behalf of the Communist Party. I've also brought an adoption record. It has your father's name on it, but not your mother's. They weren't married. You can verify it, because it has the Faulkners of Pasadena listed as adoptive parents and the dates are right. If you want your mother's name, it's going to cost you more."

Buck nodded and took a seat on a garden chaise away from the table on which the envelope lay.

The woman remained standing awkwardly.

"Look, aren't you going to read that stuff?" she asked.

"Not until I hear the rest of the terms."

"I want twenty-five thousand dollars. I want it in cash and I want it in forty-eight hours. Then I'll give you the rest of what I got. Otherwise, the Dies Committee gets the list of employees."

Buck paused, then shook his head. "It won't work."

"Why the hell not?"

"Because, like any blackmail, it doesn't guarantee that you won't come back for more."

"Listen, you pig-sucking son of a bitch, you can depend on me to disappear."

"You blackmail me, and then ask me to depend on you? I can't do that. The twenty-five thousand is easy, if you can figure out a way to guarantee you won't show up again."

She picked up the envelope. "I'm not here to guarantee you anything. I'd as soon see you rot."

"I'm not here to give out money for the rest of your life."

"You just lost your family." She turned and started to walk away.

"I've never had a family so you're losing more than I am."

"What am I losing?"

84

"Whatever you need to buy with twenty-five thousand dollars. I might be able to supply it, if you can give me some kind of guarantee—"

She stood for a moment, then spat out, "All right, here's your damn guarantee. The F.B.I. is after me for something that could get me the chair. You can check on that. Once I get out of the country, I'm not about to come back just to cause you trouble."

"I can't check unless I know your name."

Her fingernails gouged at the leather cover of her binocular case.

"I've got a lot of them. The one the G-men are after is Connie Mannheim."

She turned away, having said more than she planned. Sensing her despair, Buck spoke quickly.

"That would help until you ran out of money. The F.B.I. doesn't give up easily. It can be expensive hiding from them, even in a foreign country. You could blackmail me by mail." She started to object, but Buck cut her off. "I think I have a better idea."

"What?" she said.

"Will you sit down and listen without spitting and cursing?"

"Listen, I learned how to talk in the fields, not in Pasadena." She grabbed a chair and pulled it out. "Go on." She sat down.

"Look, you do have something I want. But unless I'm satisfied with our arrangement, I'll let it go. Faulkner Aircraft can do without seven executives, and I've done without parents all my life. The deal will work only if it's final and you can't come back later with further demands. The sides have to be equal."

"What the hell does that mean?"

"You'll have to tell me about yourself, something that you don't want me to talk about." He saw her tense and went on. "I can arrange a new identity for you, and security, as well as a job. That's worth a lot. It's better than running from country to country. You'll know I won't betray you, because if I did you'd betray my executives. In return, I have to have some guarantee you won't betray me or my employees. If you give me an equally powerful hold over you, I think we could work out an arrangement. A tense one, but one that both of us could live with. It'd be worth it. You'd have a future; I'd have a past. Otherwise—" he paused and looked directly at her— "you can take your envelope back and do whatever you want with it. I'll survive, and so will my company, but if what you say about the F.B.I. is true, your chances aren't as good as mine."

"What if I know more?"

"I'm sure I'll pay for it, one way or another. But let's make one deal at a time."

She stood up, grabbed up the envelope, looked at it, then walked over to Buck and dropped it in his lap.

"Of all people to trust!" She began to pace the terrace in front of him. "No, this isn't any trust. I still think you're a capitalist pig, making money on the lives of the people who work for you. Look at this place. You think any of your workers live like this?"

"Miss Mannheim, we'll discuss politics sometime, but this isn't the right moment."

" 'Miss Mannheim.' Cut that out. My name's Connie. Look, the F.B.I. wants me as a spy. They can fry me for treason."

When she didn't go on, Buck prodded her. "Are you a spy?"

She continued pacing. "I was a member of the Party; we did what they told us."

" 'We'?"

"Listen, you people can't understand. You have to start when you're six years old, working in the fields sixteen hours a day for half the year and then starve the other half. Try living out of the back of a truck that doesn't run. You'll go along with anyone who offers a bit of hope. Well the Party offered me hope when I was twenty and so desperate for food I was spreading my legs in the culverts. The Party kept me from being a whore; I suppose I still owe it that."

"You joined the Communist Party?"

"In 1926. They taught me to read and to think, . . . their way, of course. They took me out of the fields and got me a job in the hangars, first down at Consolidated, then at Douglas, Lockheed, and for a time with Hendrickson-Faulkner." She laughed quietly. "After I smacked you, George thought I better move, so I went over to North American until—"

She stopped pacing and turned to face him. "Is that enough for you?"

Buck stood up. Holding the envelope in one hand and tapping it lightly on the fist of the other, he walked over and looked down at her. "Connie, if this is going to work, we both have to accept each other. The more I know, the less likely I am to make mistakes in setting up your new identity."

She looked away, still angry, then slouched forward in resignation. "For Christ's sake, what else do you want?"

"What did you do as a spy? How did you find out about my parents? Who was 'George'?"

"None of your business! Oh, God," she said, and Buck saw her clench her fists with anger. Then she held up her leather case, and handed it to Buck. He could feel that it did not contain binoculars. "Listen, I could use a drink," she said.

"It's inside. What would you like?" he said as he put the case on the table. He presumed it contained a gun.

"Gin."

When Buck returned, Connie Mannheim was sitting at the glass-topped table staring into the dark. She took the glass as soon as he put it down and swallowed half of the liquor.

"There was a group of us. In the early thirties, a man from the G.P.U. came over from Russia and set us up. Now it's the N.K.V.D. They're just like the F.B.I., except they go all over the world. Our job was to get industrial information and send it to Moscow. It was during the first Five Year Plan; the Party wanted everything it could get to push industrialization. We gave them plans for capital equipment, assembly processes, as well as designs for the planes themselves. We were the best group they had in the United States. They told George that. We could do anything, and we did. Then we began to hear about the purges and the massacre of those peasants who refused to join collectives, five million of them. Then Bukharin was executed. He published a newspaper in New York, with Trotsky! And they killed him. I tried to stop supplying information, but they wouldn't let me. I was told they'd kill me if I stopped working for them. We were all told that. Then Stalin made his deal with Hitler. That was it. Not only was it the ultimate betrayal of communism, it made us traitors. We went underground, running every other week from one stinking hotel room to another. It's been like that for more than a year . . ."

She paused as her head sank forward into her hand. "Three weeks ago, they got him."

"George?" Buck said.

"Yeah. He made enough noise, so I didn't walk into the trap. I watched them drag him out of our hotel and drive away. See, the F.B.I. is only one of my worries. The Party is big on punishing anyone who tries to leave, and George and I threatened to talk."

She sat up abruptly in her chair. "He was a good man. All he'd wanted to do was farm his land, but the banks in Kansas took it away and he joined the Party. He and I were in the same group. He helped me learn to read. Stalin's betrayal wrecked him. I had to drag him into hiding. He didn't care any more. Now they got him, so it doesn't matter." She bowed her head further, and Buck expected her to cry. Instead, she looked up at him.

"It was him that decided to find out about your parents. You laughed at him once at a union meeting. He got mad and said we'd find out about your parents as insurance."

"How did he get it? Those records are sealed."

She laughed contemptuously. "I told you, we were good at what we did. If we broke into guarded military facilities, you don't think getting into some snap-locked room in the Los Angeles County Court House would be different. And who the hell goes in there to check to see if anything's missing? I want some more gin."

As he stood up, Buck asked, "Aside from my seven executives, do you know other members of the Party?"

"A lot of them."

"Just in the aircraft business, or—"

"All over California. But I ain't giving out any names."

"No, of course not." He started inside to refill her glass, but she stopped him.

"Wait a minute. Forget it. I don't want any more."

Buck sat down across from her. "Is there anything else I should know?"

Her head snapped up. "What do you mean?"

From her response, Buck knew there was more. "As I said, I need to know."

"Listen, I haven't heard what your ideas are. I've told you enough."

Buck reached into his pocket and pulled out five hundred-dollar bills, which he handed across the table. Connie Mannheim took them and spread them out like a hand of poker.

"You son of a bitch," she said quietly, "you knew it'd go this way, didn't you?"

Buck shrugged, and nodded at the binocular case. "We both came prepared."

"What's your plan?" she asked, putting the money in her trousers.

"The five hundred dollars should last you for a time. Tomorrow I'll start getting you new identity papers, driver's license, Mr. Roosevelt's social-security card, and a birth certificate. Within a week, we'll give you a car and rent a house for you away from the Los Angeles area. As soon as you move in, we'll make sure you find a job. In the meantime, you should dye your hair and buy clothes that change your appearance. Dark glasses will help. I don't know where you're living now, but I have to assume you're reasonably safe."

"Ha!" she retorted. "You don't know the N.K.V.D. They could be under the table."

"Yes, but it seems to me that they might have accomplished their purpose with George."

After a moment, she nodded. "But you never know."

"No, but your chances of anonymity are better here than, say, Brazil."

"You got all the answers," she said bitterly.

"Except who my parents are."

The envelope was still on the table between them, unopened. Connie Mannheim stared at it, then at Buck, hunched in her chair like a cornered animal.

"Look, I'll go along with you. I'll tell you who your parents are, but not the names of the Communists on your payroll. I got to have something in case you run out on me. I need some more money right now, another thousand bucks, and I'll need some time before I start working."

"Why?"

"It's none of your goddam business."

"If I'm paying for it, it is."

"It's all money to you sons of bitches, isn't it? Millions of people out of work and you know what's going to save the capitalist system? A war, and you're the luckiest bastard of the lot, aren't you?"

89

"I'm not interested in your economic theories, Connie. I've just offered you a safe future, and you're already asking for more money. If we have a deal, I want to know what my expenses are."

"I've got to get my teeth fixed. I've had bad teeth ever since I was a kid, and in the last couple of months they've been killing me."

"You don't need a thousand dollars for that. What's it for, Connie? You have to tell me the truth."

"Goddammit, you don't own me—"

"I own anything I pay for."

She grabbed the envelope and stood up. "Then forget it!"

At the same moment, Buck grabbed the binocular case and said, "All right." He opened the case and took out the small pistol. He didn't point it at her, but watched her as the implication of his possession became clear to her. He could shoot her, with no more explanation needed than that she had come as a thief and a spy. They both stared at each other. If he helped her hide from the F.B.I., he could be arrested as a traitor; if he killed her, he would never learn about his mother. They had made their pact.

Connie sat down again and began to talk.

"Your father," she said, as she slid the envelope across the table in his direction, "was a fisherman in a village in northern California called Princeton. His name was Herbert Johnson; he died two years ago at age sixty of a heart attack. Your mother is a woman named Nellie Jamison. She was a waitress most of her life in a place called Half-Moon Bay down the road from Princeton. Your father was married to someone else and had four children; your mother never married. I suppose they had a fling. Your mother came down to Los Angeles to give birth and put you up for adoption. I'll give you all the papers—"

Buck stood motionless. "Is she still alive?"

"The last we heard, she was in a state-run convalescent home near Vacaville. She was a lot older than your father. She's almost seventy now."

Connie misunderstood Buck's silence, thinking he was waiting for more information, when actually he was transfixed at hearing facts he had wanted all his life.

"All right," she went on, "I need the thousand because I think

I'm pregnant. I want to go down to Tijuana to get an abortion."

Without thinking, he reached out to grab her, and he shouted, "No! Don't do that." The gun dropped on the table shattering the glass top. Connie jumped up and didn't stop running until she was halfway into the avocado grove. Then, she turned to see whether he was coming after her. She watched nervously as he picked up the pistol and threw it as far as he could into the dark. Then he turned toward the avocado grove and yelled, "Connie! Connie! Come on back. We have to talk some more."

After a moment, she returned to the terrace.

8

Buck didn't know whether Jennifer was at home, but he figured the chances were good. Since she had come down from school for Eddie Stockton's funeral on Thursday, she probably would stay for the weekend. As he sped along the road to San Marino in the early-morning dark, he smiled to himself. He knew that, if she weren't at home, he would probably continue driving north until he reached her.

Jennifer was attending Stanford Law School. Six months before, Buck had seen a photo of her at the Spinsters' Ball on the social page of the *Los Angeles Times*. Her escort seemed dazed with adoration. Buck had clipped the picture, excluding the young swain. He had kept it in his desk for several days and gazed at it once or twice. Then he had thrown it away.

That night, after Connie Mannheim left, Buck couldn't get Jennifer out of his mind. Whether it was the shock of learning about his parents or the impact of their meeting at the funeral, he knew he had to find her.

For several hours, he had been trying to distract himself by incorporating a wing profile. The wing, sent out by Jack Llewellyn from the National Advisory Committee for Aeronautics, had a sharper leading edge. Its thickest portion would be moved back as far as possible beyond the halfway point of the chord. From that point, the wing surface would "dish in" toward the trailing edge. The air would pass over it in a laminar flow, reducing drag to one half that of the conventional airfoil. Buck was aiming at an air speed of four hundred miles an hour for the Raven.

The distraction didn't work. At four-thirty in the morning, he started the long drive to San Marino. He felt oddly adolescent giving in to such an impulse. He could have waited a few hours; for that matter, he could have seen Jennifer at any time during the previous year.

As he sat in his car, waiting as the dawn highlighted the outline of the Hendrickson house, Buck thought about his mother and father. He had no inclination to identify himself to any of his newfound family. He would find out everything he wanted to know through private detectives. As the front door of the Hendrickson house opened, he felt increasingly bitter.

With an angry frown on her face, Delilah came out and hurried down the curved flagstone path. She wore a bathrobe over her nightgown.

"What are you doing here, Buck?"

"I came to see Jennifer."

Her expression changed to fear. "Don't do this, Buck. Just don't do this. Skip's having a hard time—"

"Delilah, I didn't come to cause you or Skip any grief, but I have to see Jennifer."

"Why?" she asked.

"I love her."

"Liar!" cried Delilah. "You're using her to get at Skip."

Buck shook his head sadly. "It has nothing to do with that."

"Don't kid yourself, Buck. Go away, just go away. You're taking advantage of her just to punish Skip. He's had enough punishment, too much." Her voice broke as the front door opened again.

Jennifer hesitated on the steps. She had dressed hurriedly in slacks, loafers and a sweater. Glancing briefly at her mother, she walked in a direct path across the lawn to Buck's car.

"Honey," Delilah pleaded, "don't do this. It'll kill your father."

"No it won't," Jennifer replied, without taking her eyes from Buck. "I just promised him I'd come back."

"When?"

"Mother, I said I'll be back."

Buck opened the car door and she slid across to the passenger side, looking straight ahead. Buck heard the front door open again, but did not wait to see who it was. As the car moved down the street, Buck glanced in the rear-view mirror and saw Delilah stopping Skip from running after the car. Buck didn't want to see more. He kept his eyes on the road until he turned the corner.

Jennifer didn't look back, either. When Buck reached over and took her hand, she shuddered, but said nothing.

"I love you," he said.

"I knew yesterday."

"I've probably loved you for a long time, but for whatever reason, I didn't have the wit to realize it, much less tell you."

They came to a stop sign, and he turned to look at her.

"Are you all right?" Buck asked.

"Yes. I feel like I've walked off a cliff, but I haven't started to fall yet. So tell me quickly: what are we going to do?"

"I don't know the details, but we're going to be together for the rest of our lives."

"Oh," she said, opening her arms. They kissed, sinking down in the seat. Jennifer writhed closer in his arms and as Buck clung to her the back of his head cracked against the dashboard.

"Buck," she said in alarm.

"It's all right," he said. "If Henry Ford had wanted people to make love in his cars, he would have provided a mattress, which isn't a bad idea."

She laughed and said, "No nifty inventions in the middle of the street, please. This *is* San Marino, you know."

A car came up behind them and honked. Jennifer covered her face with her hands as Buck signaled the other car to go around, which it did, its horn blaring. By then Jennifer was laughing so hard, she didn't even try to sit up as Buck started the car and drove on.

When they came to the main road into Los Angeles, he pulled over to the shoulder and stopped.

"Two other mattresses come to mind," he said. "One is at a seedy little motel in Huntington Beach with a nice view of the water. The other's at my house."

"Huntington Beach sounds rather sordid," said Jennifer, "I'd guess you've been there before."

"You're right. And it's surely not San Marino."

"You're terrible!" She reached over and they hugged each other.

"Will you marry me?" he asked.

"Of course," she replied.

"When?"

She hesitated. "Let's go get some breakfast. Then we can talk."

"I just felt the whole Hendrickson family climb in the back seat."

She nodded.

"Let them go, Jennifer. We'll have a family of our own. That's all we'll need."

She smiled. "Nothing ever happens the way I think it will. I always imagined we'd have a huge wedding with everyone there. Buck, even if I wanted to, I couldn't just let my family go. I've thought about this ever since you and Daddy split up." She smiled at him. "Even when I was trying desperately to fall in love with someone else, I was still figuring out what would happen when I married you."

"The ardent young man at the Spinsters' Ball?" Buck asked.

Jennifer smiled. "I was hoping you'd see that picture. I thought I looked very . . . sophisticated."

"You did, and more than that."

"But I didn't hear from you." She looked at him curiously. "It's so ironic. I hoped that when you saw that picture, you wouldn't be able to resist calling. Then yesterday, when I knew I'd see you at Uncle Eddie's funeral, I was absolutely certain I was over you. Then you reached out and touched me and I knew that, schoolgirl fantasy or not, you and I were going to be married. That's when I started thinking about my family."

"Let me tell you my idea," Buck interrupted. "I want to court you for two weeks, enough time to show my 'respect,' then we'll fly across the border to Nevada and get married."

She leaned over and kissed him. "I read in the paper that once upon a time you flew some starlet down to Mexico for breakfast."

"That was *my* schoolboy fantasy."

She laughed. "Oh, I see: trying to keep up with Howard Hughes? Well, I'll tell you what I think as you drive me to the local hash house."

Buck laughed and started the car.

"After breakfast," Jennifer said, "I'll go home and tell the family that we're going to be married. By next week, I should know whether or not they'll join us at the wedding, and they may. The family's very strong when it comes to its own members. And they're very fond of me. If they do come around, and that will depend on Daddy, we'll have a regular wedding in several months, and you can court me all you want. If not"— her tone changed to one of determination—"we'll take out a marriage license, wait two weeks, invite them all, and get married even if no one comes." She frowned. "I'm afraid that's what will happen."

They drove up to a diner and sat for a moment before going in.

"They'll wait for us to fail, Buck. But we won't, and I know that with time they'll give in. Even Daddy. I'm absolutely certain of that."

Buck wasn't so certain, nor was he sure that he wanted the Hendricksons back in his life. He said nothing about them as he and Jennifer had their breakfast.

The courtship was, as predicted, a brief one. Upon hearing Jennifer's intention, Skip went into his study and closed the door. He seldom came out while she was in the house. Delilah on the other hand argued endlessly, begging her daughter not to marry Buck. Jennifer listened patiently and answered with calm persistence. Her mother gradually ran out of arguments and joined her husband in expressing only silent hurt.

The rest of the Hendrickson family took their cue from Skip. When Jennifer told them of her plans, they smiled and wished her happiness. Her father, however, began avoiding her in the hallways and turning away from her when she tried to talk with him. The morning she finally left, her father stayed in his study. Jennifer's last words to her mother were, "I hope you and Daddy will come to my wedding."

"You know we can't," Delilah said, and she hugged Jennifer desperately.

"Well, I'll send you and Daddy the time and place, in case you change your minds," Jennifer said, as she got in the car. She drove to Beverly Hills, where she had borrowed an apartment from a friend who was in Europe.

They decided to get married on December 28, in the Episcopal Church in Pasadena, which Jennifer had attended since she was a child. Buck asked John Slater to be his best man. Because Jennifer did not wish to obligate any member of her family, or have a friend as a substitute, she did not have a maid of honor. She told Buck that no matter how clearly she knew the contrary, she still hoped that at the last moment, the Hendricksons would come to her wedding.

Buck observed Jennifer's emotional struggles with her family from a distance. Since Connie Mannheim's visit, his curiosity about his own family had diminished daily, even as reports came in from the private detectives, even as medical bulletins arrived from the exclusive nursing home in San Mateo, where Buck had anonymously arranged to have his mother admitted. Now he no longer cared. They had never been a part of his life; he didn't want them as family the way Jennifer wanted hers. Under the circumstances, Buck considered himself lucky.

He was distracted by only one problem. Buck had promised to see that Connie Mannheim had enough money, not only to hide, but to give birth and support her child. She had agreed to have the baby, but subsequently she had vacillated, saying that her own security would be jeopardized and that she was going to Tijuana as she had originally planned. Buck promised more money and made it clear to her exactly what he could do if she had an abortion.

They met at a small Mexican restaurant in Culver City. After they ordered, Buck handed her, as promised, another five hundred dollars, a driver's license, a Social Security card and a birth certificate, all bearing the name of Helen Rassmussea, born in Medford, Oregon, in 1898.

"You got the year right," Connie said by way of thanks.

"My people are very thorough. The real Helen Rasmussea died in infancy, so stay away from Oregon."

She nodded. "I ain't going anywhere."

"We're renting you a house in a town called Saugus. It's about forty miles north of Los Angeles. When the time comes, you'll get money to buy a car. Then we'll find you a job. There's another small town nearby called Newhall."

A waitress brought a beer for Buck and tequila for Connie. As soon as the waitress left, Connie took a swallow of her drink and blurted, "Who the hell's *we?* I don't want a lot of people knowing about this, you know."

"Don't worry. A company like mine has hundreds of security problems. You're just one of them. You'll be lost in the shuffle. I'll see to that."

She nervously turned to watch the front door of the restaurant. She had dyed her hair, her teeth were cleaner, but the decay on them was still in evidence. Her new clothing was ill-fitting but effective enough as a disguise.

"So I just gotta keep trusting you. Listen, you bastard, I'm going along with you. But if anything happens to me, I'll fix you. I've made arrangements," she said threateningly.

"You have no reason to distrust me, Connie. What's wrong?"

Again she looked at the front door.

"I don't want to have this kid. I don't want the responsibility. What if something happens to you? I can't run, carrying a kid under my arm."

"Having a child will help your new identity. Besides, you'll have company the rest of your life."

She jabbed a finger toward his face. "That's *just* what I *don't* want."

"You might learn to like it."

"Oh yeah? Tell me all about it, Mr. Expert. What happens if we aren't so successful and the N.K.V.D. comes out to Saugus one night and takes me off, too?"

"What about George? Wouldn't having his child give his life some kind of meaning?"

"You son of a bitch, don't give me that sentimental crap. George and I had one thing in common: the Party. It wasn't any big romance, and I don't have to have a baby to prove anything about me or about George. So what's the big deal with you? Now that you got a mama, you want everybody to be a better one than she was?" She laughed and reached for her glass of tequila.

With one hand, Buck grabbed her arm under the table. With the other, he slapped the shot glass which flew back against the padded booth. Buck squeezed her other arm hard enough to keep her sitting down.

"I'm not interested in any of your theories," he said, smiling slightly for the benefit of anyone who might be watching. "You deliver your child or our deal ends, and both of us will take the consequences. But I'll make sure yours are worse than mine." He let go of her arm.

She didn't grimace from the pain, although her lips tightened menacingly against her rotting teeth. "Alright, if you want the kid so much, you take it. If you don't want it, give it to somebody else. But *I* don't want it."

Their waitress came up tentatively. Buck smiled and said, "We had an accident. Bring her another tequila, please."

The waitress returned with the drink and Connie Mannheim swallowed some of it. Buck saw that she was scared. "Connie, I still don't think you understand our deal. You see the couple in the booth by the window? He's wearing a blue sport shirt; she's wearing a beige dress. They work for me, and they're going to be looking after you."

"I'll be rid of them in about ten minutes," Connie said. "I told you I'm good at what I do."

"They're better, and less conspicuous. They also have instructions to protect you from whoever comes after you. If I were you, I'd cooperate with them."

"So they're going to know who I am?" she asked angrily.

"None of the details. As a matter of fact, they think you're spying on Nazis for us."

Connie Mannheim gazed at the couple, then swallowed the rest of her drink. When she put the glass down, she looked up at Buck, a worried expression on her tough face.

"Why are you doing all this?"

"I'm protecting my investment."

"Oh," she said, smiling craftily, "you talked to your two Commies."

"No. I haven't mentioned your information to anyone. The two names you gave me, John Slater and George Fishburn, are both vice-presidents, so I figure the other five names you have are down the executive ladder. It doesn't matter. I'm sure all of them have long since given up any connection to the Communist Party. If any of them are still supplying information to the Russians, I'm confident our own security will catch them. As I've said before, my company can survive even if all seven were arrested. My interest in you is the future. There are already a lot of Congressmen getting attention for pointing out Communists. If I ever need you, you're my expert. You can tell me who is and who isn't, not only at Faulkner Aircraft, but everywhere else in town. And as an expert, you could testify, if you had to, that my company is clear of such foreign influence."

"I'm not testifying, or telling you anything more," she said fiercely.

"Probably, you'll never have to. Just like buying any insurance policy, we both hope it never has to be used. But you're worth the premium. Now all I have to do is find a reformed Nazi for the same purpose."

"Very funny. But take my advice: don't get a pregnant one."

Buck smiled. "Alright, I won't. And don't forget: the deal's off if you do anything to harm your baby."

"Yeah, I know, you want the kid to have a chance at this lousy life. What the hell are you trying to prove?"

"Nothing that I know of, but I'm not paying for any abortions."

She gripped the edge of the table, hissing her words.

"Okay, but where can I have the baby where there won't be any records? The day they got George, I'd told him I thought I was pregnant. If the N.K.V.D. got that out of him, they'll be checking around. Don't you see—?"

"I would think a doctor in Mexico could be convinced to attend you and overlook filing any papers. We'll find you a house near Tijuana when the time comes."

"A kid with no birth certificate."

"Right, but with chances. And you'll have one, too."

"What's that?"

"To keep your child or not. You may surprise yourself."

Connie Mannheim looked at Buck and smiled contemptuously.

"Don't bet on me making up for your mother. She had her reasons; I have mine."

Their food arrived. They ate silently.

That morning, Buck had learned from Jack Llewellyn that ten of the first Falcon bombers to reach the British Isles had dropped their bombs over Rottenburg and Kassel. War was an inevitability, yet here he sat trying to convince a woman to have her unwanted child. Buck smiled to himself. He presumed his efforts indicated nothing more than his recently confirmed belief in himself, if not the rest of the world.

9

Wearing a white dress, a mantilla over her hair, Jennifer stood at the back of the empty church. When the organist began playing, she hesitated a moment, then proceeded up the aisle alone, her head held high, her eyes firmly fixed on Buck. When she joined him at the steps in front of the chancel, she smiled. The service was read. On cue, John Slater supplied the ring, and Jennifer strongly affirmed her vows.

It was only when they turned to walk down the aisle to Mendelssohn's triumphant music that she faltered briefly at the sight of empty pews. Then she took Buck's arm, and the bride and groom hurried down the aisle and out of the church.

A limousine drove them from Pasadena to Palos Verdes. They had decided not to have any kind of party, and a honeymoon was impossible because of Buck's heavy production schedule. As they rode along, holding hands, Buck finally said, "We'll never let this day go by again without a big celebration."

She kissed him, then laid her cheek on his shoulder. "A year from now, we'll have so much to celebrate," she said.

"Really? Such as."

"A year of success. A home. Maybe a family."

"Are you telling me something?"

"Only that I plan to have your child as quickly as possible."

"I see," Buck said, sliding open the window to the chauffeur. "Carl, hurry," he said and slid it closed again. Jennifer laughed.

* * *

101

Most of Jennifer's predictions were accurate. Within days, she had contacted an architect to begin work on expanding the house. The first week in January she transferred her credits to the law school at U.C.L.A., and several weeks after that, she informed Buck that he would become a father in late September.

At the same time, the pressure of Buck's work intensified. Making planes for the government was different from supplying the commercial firms. The government wanted to supervise everything. Only days after Jennifer had told him about the baby, Llewellyn was on the phone.

"Congratulations, Buck. I just heard the happy news."

"Thanks, Colonel."

"But why the big secret?"

"No secret, just dignity, Jack. . . . And why did my secretary say you were calling from Washington? Aren't you sending out your impossible aircraft proposals from Wright Field any more?"

"No, I'm digging the foundation for an office building in a swamp on the Potomac. All the services are going to move here. I'm just getting in first, Buck, putting my initials in the wet cement."

"Jack, will it fly?"

"If I have anything to say about it. And speaking of that, what's holding up our night fighter?"

"Tufts of silk."

For most of the previous two weeks, Buck and his aerodynamics engineers had been in the wind tunnel at the California Institute of Technology testing the laminar airfoil that Buck had designed for the Raven. In order to facilitate mass production, the tips of the wing were to be squared off. During the early tests, the wing had withstood a force equal to a transonic speed, and its shape had a drag factor of nearly 60 percent less than any airfoil previously tested.

In subsequent tests, however, when tufts of silk were attached to the airfoils' surfaces, making turbulence visible, the squared tips of the wings demonstrated violent stalling characteristics. Because Buck's mathematical calculations held firm when the team checked them, they decided that the Cal Tech tunnel was too small. They had then asked Boeing in Seattle for the use of their facility. Boeing graciously offered it, but with the stipulation that they be allowed to observe Faulkner's tests. Buck didn't mind, and the tests validated his calculations. He had ordered the airfoil into production the previous day.

"Don't worry," Buck said to Jack Llewellyn. "We'll have the prototype right on schedule. The Air Corps can depend on it."

"I have some news for you. Your order just went up. The original hundred and sixty has been increased to four-fifty. You'll get the official word from General Arnold's office, but I thought you'd like to know how well I'm looking after you."

"As always, Jack, I'm grateful for your attention," Buck said. "But I like to think the plane itself had something to do with it, not to mention the war."

"Of course, Buck. You're right. But you'd be amazed with how things work around here. Every little bit of interest and influence counts, and the war won't go on forever." He chuckled. "But you should know, Buck, I will."

They both laughed.

"Maybe if the Belle Nuit had made it," Buck said, "the world would have been saved from your strange audacity."

"Strange? What's so strange about it? All I want to do is serve my country and help you sell some of your puddle-jumping planes to the government," Jack said with fervor.

"Look, I'm glad you're recruiting members for the Faulkner Fan Club, but after this is over, maybe you'd like to buy some civilian clothes and come out here and build airplanes."

"Thanks, Buck, but after this is over, I'll be wearing a different uniform and building an Air Corps, without these unfortunates who call themselves 'The Army.' "

"You think so? I can't see the Navy allowing a new service. Look how they sit on the Marines."

Jack Llewellyn sighed. "Listen, Buck, the Army plods, the Navy lists, the Marines wallow; the Air Corps, however, will fly."

Buck laughed and said, "Make sure they build that office building big enough, Jack, or all of you will be so busy shooting at each other, you won't have time for the Germans."

When Buck hung up, he found himself suddenly apprehensive. He called in John Slater.

"For the duration," Buck told Slater, "we have to work for the military. But just as soon as the fighting is over, I'll want a product to sell that doesn't need a bomb rack."

Slater nodded enthusiastically. "There are some young engineers I've been watching. This should be right up their alley. As a matter of fact, T.W.A. is sniffing around, talking about building the biggest airliner yet. We could start with that."

Buck thought a moment, then shook his head. "Find out what they're looking for as a guideline, but don't commit us to anything. The only group crazier than the military is Howard Hughes running an airline."

"If you know him, it might help us—"

"Nobody knows Howard Hughes, and anyone who says he does is a liar. When we needed some publicity, Skip and I talked to him once about his flying the Cumulus. He said he would if we'd let him try for a North-Pole-to-South-Pole record. When we told him we didn't want to risk losing the plane, he went into one of the strangest rages I've ever seen. He didn't explode, he imploded. His eyes sank back, his voice rose to a soprano scream, his whole body started to shake. Skip and I got out of there, thinking he might reach some kind of explosive point and lay waste the whole block!" He laughed, and went on. "I'll tell you this: during the war, the military will walk all over Howard Hughes, but when it's over, they're going to latch on to each other and feed each other's lunacy. I want Faulkner to have other alternatives."

"I'll do my best," John Slater said and looked down at the floor. He hesitated and then looked at Buck. "I want to tell you something. I was a member of the Communist Party for about two years, 1935 and 1936. It was a mistake and I regret it, but it might cause you some trouble with some of these itchy Congressmen. I've wanted you to know I'll leave the company the moment I become a problem."

"I appreciate your telling me. Did you ever do anything that they could interpret as against the interests of the United States?"

"No, no spying or sabotage," he said, smiling caustically. "I was just another sap who honestly believed."

"Well, let me know if anyone bothers you," said Buck.

After John left, Buck wished his dealings with the other Party member he knew were as easy. Even with extensive security, Connie Mannheim remained not only indecisive about having her child, but increasingly suspicious. She would call him at odd hours from a pay phone near her house.

"Listen, there's this car been following me for two days. What are your people doing about it?"

Buck tried to contain his irritation. "Connie, it's probably our car. No one's after you."

"So what's going on, then? Maybe they're lying to you. Maybe you're trying to drive me nuts."

"Maybe you're drinking too much. I'm telling you, you're safe. Don't call me again. That's really dangerous. People watch me all the time."

"Goddammit, what am I supposed to do out here in this desert except drink?"

"After you have the baby, you can get a job."

"I'm getting rid of this thing!"

Buck didn't respond. Connie listened to the silence on the line, then started to cough. "You scum-sucking pig, what am I going to do with this kid? I could feel it moving today. Before today, it would have been easy."

"Don't call again," Buck said.

"Wait a minute. I'll make a deal with you. If I have this kid will you call off your watchdogs?"

"It's fine with me. I don't think anyone cares about finding you any more. But you change your mind a lot, Connie. You came to me for protection."

"I came to you for money. I can take care of myself. The kind of people you have out here make my skin crawl. I don't want them around."

"Agreed. Do you want help with the adoption?"

She hesitated. "No. I don't trust you with that kind of information. I'll take care of it." Then she laughed. "Don't be surprised if you find a basket full of trouble on your front doorstep."

She hung up.

Buck wondered whether someone had worked on his mother as hard as he was working on Connie Mannheim to let her baby live. He found himself identifying with Connie's child and becoming even more determined to defend it against its mother. His concern, however, stopped at the child's birth, although he knew Connie well enough to accept that he eventually would assume some degree of responsibility for her child.

Buck had taken her call in his study. When he returned to the bedroom, Jennifer was standing in front of her full-length mirror, her robe open around her swelled breasts and protruding stomach. When she heard Buck, she turned her head to smile at him. At the same time she touched her stomach.

"I've been having deep thoughts," she said.

"Be careful. They may confuse the child."

"Yes, they might. They confuse me. I've never been so confused with the future." She turned to look again into the mirror. "I've always been so involved with the present. But now," she put both hands over her belly, "it's only this child and me. I feel as though we're giving each other birth. When it happens, the future begins. There hardly seems to be any present, and all of my past seems so unimportant."

Buck stood behind her, looking into the mirror. "I agree, although I'm far from impartial."

She glanced up and caught his eyes in the mirror. "I'm so glad I'm having your baby."

"You're giving us all a future. For thirty-five years all I've had was a present filled with airplanes. Now," he smiled, "everything's possible; we have all the choices." He remembered that he had mentioned choices to Connie Mannheim.

"Put your hands on us," Jennifer said.

Buck reached around in front of her and put his hands on her stomach.

She sighed, and let her head fall back on his shoulder. "I have a confession to make. During that terrible year when we didn't see each other, I remembered our one night together, and especially your hands on me." She looked at them in the mirror and put her own hands over them. She smiled. "They distracted me from my studies. Oh, I wanted you so much."

"More than now?"

"No."

They watched themselves in the mirror for a time, then Buck lifted her up and carried her to their bed, where they made love slowly and blissfully fell asleep.

The months passed, with Jennifer's sensual and radiant pregnancy contrasting with Connie Mannheim's tempestuous one. In his office at Faulkner Field, Buck received reports from Saugus. Connie Mannheim's telephone calls became fewer, and in them, her attitude indicated an angry resignation to having the baby, but at the same time, she stated her adamant refusal to allow a doctor to attend the birth. Buck was too busy to argue the point and told his security people to make sure they had a doctor on call in case she needed one. When Connie Mannheim crossed the Mexican border and took up residence in the house that had been rented near Tijuana, Buck was considerably relieved.

Every waking hour of his time was devoted to meeting the accelerated British demand for thirty-five bombers a month, as well as creating the assembly line for the Raven. The Faulkner Aircraft plant expanded to employ twelve thousand workers by the summer of 1941. The size of the shop space and construction sheds doubled to more than eight hundred thousand square feet. Buck decided not to waste time on prototype development for the night fighter. He took the first production model and began running tests.

The night before the first test flight it rained. From his friends in the movie business, Buck had learned that rain on the day of an opening was good luck. In the morning, he drove over to the hangar where the Raven was being checked out, and wished the test pilot luck. Then he drove to the chase plane from which he planned to observe the first flight of the Raven. The chase plane took off, and from the observation seat Buck watched the night fighter taxi to the end of the runway.

A spray of rain rose behind the aircraft when the pilot performed a power check of the engine. As the test plane began to move, the chase plane came in at a hundred feet on a parallel run. The Raven went straight down the runway center line with little rudder control and lifted into the air. As it increased its climb angle and left Faulkner Field behind, Buck sat back and felt the first sense of relaxation he had experienced in months.

Over the next two weeks, test flights continued, establishing engine and systems operation. Buck watched each one and checked the statistics against his own projections. When the results matched or bettered Buck's expectations, he scheduled an air-speed calibration test flight. He had designed the Raven to be one of the fastest-production fighter aircraft in the world. Buck wanted the Army Air Corps, as well as the rest of the world, to know about it.

During that frenetic period, Connie Mannheim gave birth to a son. The security man called one morning to say that after a long labor Connie had finally asked for the prearranged doctor. The birth had gone smoothly, mother and son apparently were doing well, and no papers had been recorded. The doctor, however, had offered one piece of notable information: Connie Mannheim had given birth before, probably when she was very young.

With rueful admiration, Buck realized again that Connie Mannheim would never tell him everything. Then he left orders for his security team to return Connie to Saugus as soon as she and the infant were able to travel. From then on, Connie Mannheim would be, as agreed, without Buck's protection. Not once in all the months since she had come to Buck had anyone tried to contact her, much less harm her.

The day of the speed-calibration tests was hazy and calm. At exactly 7:00 A.M., Buck gave the test pilot the go-ahead. After the control tower gave clearance, the Raven took off into the misty September morning. In ten and a half minutes, the aircraft climbed to twenty thousand feet. Over the test frequency, Buck heard the pilot as he rapidly went through handling checks. When the pilot finished, Buck said, "Feel like a little excitement?"

The radio crackled as the test pilot laughed and said, "Turn your machines on. I'll be right down."

They heard the plane before they saw it, as the Raven plummeted down in a full-throttle dive to a heart-stopping altitude before pulling out and flashing across the test strip at 513 miles per hour.

The ninety men who had worked for weeks in wind tunnels to make silk motionless cheered.

"Stop grandstanding in our plane," Buck said to the pilot. "Let's see what she'll do without gravity."

After several speed runs across the field, the calibration technicians reported an air speed of 394 miles per hour. Buck ordered the test pilot up to twelve thousand feet, the critical altitude of the engine, above which power began to drop off at full throttle. After six level speed runs with military power settings on the engine, the technicians converted the aircraft instrument readings on an altitude correction chart. They reported a true air speed in level flight of 407 miles per hour. Buck had what he wanted.

Without waiting for the Raven to land, he called Jack Llewellyn.

"Colonel, you can send one of your Air Corps stick jockeys out here to compile the pilot's handbook for the Raven. He can enter a 400-plus mile-per-hour level air speed at 12,000 feet."

"I just heard. Congratulations, Buck. It sounds like you have a hell of a night fighter."

"What do you mean, you just heard? I just walked off the field."

"Just part of my job, Buck. I believe it was 407 miles per hour to be exact."

"Now you're showing off," Buck said, laughing, but not really amused.

"Buck, I believe in your plane and in Faulkner Aircraft. I'm going to get a lot of brass out there for the acceptance ceremony. You've done a hell of a job, and I'm going to make sure the Air Force knows about it. You've also helped to make me look good. I've been tapped for General Arnold's staff. You'll have a friend in high places, Buck. A good Air Force friend."

Buck paused before offering congratulations. "Be careful, Jack. They say shooting stars burn out, particularly one-star generals."

"Or they set the world on fire. How's October 2, for the acceptance ceremony?"

"We'll start painting her black tomorrow. I'll need some serial numbers to put on her."

"I'll see to it personally."

Buck paused, again wary. "And what's this Air 'Force'? Isn't 'Corps' being used any more?"

"By the Army," said Jack, his mouth close to the phone. "Some of us think 'Force' is a better word for a war and for a separate service. I'll see you on the second."

* * *

Two days later, Jennifer called Buck at the field to tell him her labor had begun.

"Now, I have it all worked out. Carl will drive me in to the Medical Center, and Sally is cooking you a good meal. I want you to come to the hospital as a well-fed father."

"As always, I'll do as I'm told. Are you all right?"

"I'm quite excited. When the contractions started, they made me giggle. Not for long, I expect."

"I love you, Jennifer."

"I can't wait for everyone to hear about our baby. Oh!" she cried suddenly, "dear me—" Then she laughed and gasped, "Buck, I love you. I think I'd better go."

"I'll meet you there as soon as I can."

"Don't hurry. I doubt if I'll deliver as fast as four hundred and—what was it?"

"Four hundred and seven miles an hour!" he declared.

She laughed again, said, "Ouch! I love you," and she hung up.

Yes, Buck thought, everyone would hear. He knew Jennifer was hoping that when her family learned about the baby they would welcome her back to the fold. Buck, however, was less sanguine.

Since the crash of the experimental turbine jet, Skip Hendrickson's company had been struggling. Private financing, even with the Hendricksons' considerable support, became impossible, and the military was occupied with more conventional needs. Once failure tainted an airplane company, buyers tended to move away. Buck had learned that a contract for another experimental jet had been awarded to the Bell Company. According to the rumors making their way through the industry, Skip Hendrickson was inclined to blame his former partner for his failure.

At the hospital Buck stayed with Jennifer as long as he was allowed, and then he waited with several other fathers in an egregious little room labeled above its door as "Pops' Corner." An hour later he learned that he had a son. Contrary to hospital rules, he spent ten minutes with Jennifer in her room. She had been given a general anesthetic, but it had worn off enough so that her eyes opened, blinked and focused on Buck. She smiled as if she had forgotten what had happened, then quickly remembered and said, "Oh, tell me, what is it?"

110

"We have a son," Buck told her and kissed the hand he was holding.

"Oh . . . how, how . . . wonder . . . oh." She couldn't keep her eyes open. "Tell everyone . . ." she said, and fell asleep again. Back in his office, Buck called all over town to friends and associates in the aircraft industry. He was certain the news would reach the Hendricksons.

Jennifer spent six days in the hospital to recover her strength. Buck visited as often as he could. On the second day he just missed running into Delilah and Skip in the corridor.

When he went into Jennifer's room, Buck saw clearly what her parents' visit had meant to her. She was radiant, holding her baby in her arms, smiling up at Buck with a sure triumph over the months of waiting.

"Did you see them?" she asked

"From a distance."

She nodded and said, "We'll see them again soon."

"Good," Buck said, still doubtful, but happy for Jennifer.

When Jennifer and the baby returned to Palos Verdes, the nursery was complete, there were flowers in every room, and a genuine English nanny had arrived. Jennifer insisted that they still keep their privacy at night, so the woman left with the cook after supper.

Luckily the baby didn't fuss the first evening home. Buck and Jennifer lay in bed and discussed plans for the baptism. They had decided to call the boy "John," a name that had no precedent in the Hendrickson family and sounded fine with Faulkner. Jennifer discussed the ceremony animatedly, certain that her family and friends would come to see her child.

The baby slept quietly in an antique cradle at Jennifer's side of the bed. The night was cool enough for a fire, and as they watched the flames, they laughed over all their plans for the boy: tennis, piano, riding, flying and French.

Abruptly, they became aroused and although the possibilities were limited, they managed to enjoy themselves. Aware that the time before the next feeding was approaching, they urged one another to fall asleep. In each other's arms, they dozed and drifted off.

The next sound Buck heard was not the baby's cry but Jennifer's scream.

"He's not breathing! He's not breathing!" Jennifer repeated as she shook the baby. Buck watched as the head rolled back lifelessly, the eyes opening on white. Jennifer cried out again. Buck picked the baby up from the crib. Its uncovered arms were as cold as stone. Buck held the tiny head to his ear, listening for breath. There was none. He lay the child on the bed, stripped it and put his ear on the baby's chest. There was no heartbeat. Kneeling beside the bed, he opened the child's mouth and breathed into it. As he did so, he glimpsed Jennifer watching with a look of horror. Finally, after many minutes, Buck straightened up and shook his head.

"No!" Jennifer shouted, and she picked the body up from the bed. Cradling the child to her chest, she rushed to an uphol-stered chair in front of the fireplace and sat down, rocking the child spasmodically. Buck reached out to take the body, but Jennifer arched away. "Take your hands away from him."

Buck watched as she turned, continuing with her frenzied rocking. His first thought was of Connie Mannheim's son.

10

In the waning moonlight, the desert hills beyond the San Fernando Valley looked desolate. The road twisted through them, making Buck's progress torturously slow. When he finally reached Saugus he discovered that the road on which Connie Mannheim lived formed the town's only intersection. He drove further into the desert, looking for her mailbox.

As he turned into the rutted driveway leading to Connie's cabin, Buck wished there were a reason to explain why his son was dead. When he stopped the car, however, he accepted that there was none, just as there had been none to explain the rest of his life. He would go on doing whatever had to be done.

The cabin had screened windows and canvas roll-up blinds. Buck saw an outhouse in back and, nearby, a lean-to for storage. A light was burning in one room, and Buck could hear a radio. Before he got out of the car, he looked at his watch. It was two-thirty. He walked slowly up to the front door and knocked. There was no answer, but the door was ajar, so he opened the screen and went in.

From where he stood, Buck could see a couch covered with a tucked-in faded green bedspread, two stuffed chairs with unraveling antimacassars on their arms, and the radio sitting on a cardboard crate. On the speckled-green linoleum floor were a worn piece of purple carpet and four empty tequila bottles. A pile of magazines lay in one corner, a stack of books was in another.

"Don't move or you're dead." She came in the door behind him.

"It's me, Connie."

"I don't care who you are, you move a muscle and you're a dead man."

Buck felt a gun jab into his back, and Connie's hand go over him, professionally searching for a weapon. When she was finished, she said, "Welcome to Shangri-la. What the hell are you doing out here?"

"I've decided to take you up on your offer. Can I turn around?"

"Which offer? Sit down at the end of the couch."

Buck did as he was told, noting that Connie was holding a .38-caliber snub-nosed revolver.

"Buying a gun can get you a lot of attention," he said.

"I'm taking care of myself. I'm not used to callers at two-thirty in the morning, but I keep ready." She carefully snapped on the revolver's safety and placed the gun between the seat cushion and the arm of one of the chairs for easy reach. Buck saw that she knew how to handle the weapon. As she sat down in the chair and faced him, he could see that her face was lined with exhaustion. She was wearing her old outfit of gym shoes, slacks, and an old sweater, all of which looked soiled. She stared at Buck for a moment, then laughed. Buck saw that at least her teeth had been perfectly filled.

"You've come for the kid," she said.

"Yes," Buck replied.

"Kind of sudden. Kind of late." Abruptly she leaned forward. "Your baby born yet?"

"Our son was six days old. He died several hours ago."

Connie Mannheim gasped. For a moment, her face revealed a semblance of compassion. Then she laughed, a harsh throaty sound. "Isn't it ridiculous that it was your kid instead of mine?"

"Where is he?" Buck asked, disregarding her speculation.

"In there," she answered, nodding in the direction of the lighted doorway. "He can't stand the dark." She sat in her chair, nervously nodding her head back and forth. The motion reminded him of Jennifer rocking in front of the fire with the lifeless body of their child in her arms. He stood up anxiously and said, "I'll take him now."

Connie pulled out the revolver again and pointed it at his head. "What's it worth to you?"

He was too tense to contain his anger. "You don't want him."

"What if I'm learning to like him? He's my child, after all."

"That shouldn't bother you; you've done this before." The instant he said it, he regretted it. Connie didn't move, only blinked, then snapped off the revolver's safety. "You son of a bitch, I ought to just blow your scummy head off. Goddamn you. How did you find out about her? You can't leave anything alone, can you?" She began to pace. "Have you contacted her? Does she know about me?"

"No," he answered, aware that if he was careful, he would learn more.

Connie smiled vindictively. "Oh. I get it. Part of the deal. You keep her out of it, if I keep out of my baby's life, now that you want him. You're a pig, you know."

"Connie, when you were in trouble, why didn't you go to her, your own flesh and blood? She might have been easier on you than I was." He was stringing together her inferences. In the next room, the baby began to cry.

"Because she doesn't have what you have—money!" Connie shouted, then looked away. "Besides, she has a decent life up there, a good husband, a lawyer—Jesus!" She shook her head with sad envy. "And a house in Hillsborough." She laughed bitterly. "I'm not anxious to spoil any more lives than mine, *and* yours if I have to."

Finding a lawyer in Hillsborough with a wife who had been an adopted child was possible; but Buck pressed a little more. "I have no desire to involve either one of them. But if she's anything like me, she might want to know who you are."

"She's nothing like you. Not every adopted kid wants to know so much. She was born in a culvert by a lettuce field. I was fifteen. Nobody cared much about what happened in the fields as long as we kept picking. I gave her up as soon as I could walk. I found out what happened to her the same time I found out about you. The Samuelsons raised her right, gave her everything. She didn't need me to turn up to spoil things." Buck watched her sit down in the stuffed armchair and put the gun back in its place. He knew with the year of birth and her maiden name he could locate the daughter.

115

"All right, take him," she said. "I haven't had any sleep for six weeks."

"Connie, this is a real adoption. No visiting, no communication. Just like your daughter."

Connie looked up at him, as close to defeat as he had ever seen her. "I know. Take him. I wasn't meant to have babies." She stood up and plodded into the kitchen saying, "I'll fix a bottle for the trip."

As he turned the corner into the lighted room, Buck glimpsed the mess of bottles, nipples, powdered formula, and laundry piled on the paint-chipped counters of the kitchen. On one side of Connie's single, unmade bed, he moved past another pile of dirty diapers in a bucket. On the other side was an orange crate stacked on top of several cardboard boxes. Inside the crate, the baby was lying on a soiled pillow, wailing. He stopped when Buck stood over him, blocking the light from the naked bulb hanging from the ceiling. For a moment, the only sound was that of bugs banging into the screens. Then the baby started to cry again. Buck picked him up and grabbed a clean diaper from a basket of laundry near the door.

Connie stood in the kitchen with a bottle of tequila, which she was drinking when Buck appeared. She handed him the formula and stared at him with loathing and despair.

"You think we'll get away with this?" she asked. "Or do you think it'll ruin us both?"

Buck had more than what he came for and hurried out to his car without answering. He drove several miles before stopping to feed the baby, which he did with awkward haste. He threw the filthy diaper into some brush beside the road and wrapped the fresh one around the infant. Surprisingly, the baby slept the rest of the way back to Palos Verdes.

They arrived at his home at ten minutes after five. There was only silence when Buck opened the door. He had no idea what he would find. He had considered calling someone to stay with Jennifer, but there was no one he could trust. Finally, he had decided to trust Jennifer herself. No matter how horrifying the shock of her baby's death, no matter how desperate the loss, he believed she would survive until he returned. Yet, as he had driven to Saugus and back, the specter of her self-destruction had appeared in endless variety. When he had left her, her face

116

seemed frozen into madness. As he climbed the stairs to the second floor, Buck accepted that what he was doing was madness as well.

The bedroom door was open; he walked in slowly, dreading what he might see. Nothing had changed; Jennifer was still sitting in the chair, holding the dead baby. She was motionless and did not react when he said, "I'm back." The baby boy in Buck's arms was startled and began to cry. When Jennifer heard him, her back straightened as if in a spasm. She did not look around. Buck walked over to their bed and laid the baby on it. Returning quickly to Jennifer's chair, he knelt in front of her, looking up into her contorted face.

She listened to the baby's cries without turning her face. When Buck reached out his hands for the body, she gave it to him. Then, without looking at Buck or the body, she stood up and went over to the bed. Holding the lifeless child in his arms, Buck watched silently until Jennifer reached down and picked up the crying infant, thus sealing their agreement and accepting its price.

In the dining room, Buck took a lace tablecloth out of a drawer of the sideboard and gently wrapped the tiny body in it. Going outside through the garage, he grabbed a shovel and walked toward the avocado grove. Dawn had begun. Even though there were no near neighbors, Buck nervously scanned the surrounding hills, remembering Connie Mannheim's observations. When he was sufficiently hidden by the trees, he placed the body beside a tree and began to dig. Finally, he lifted the tiny corpse and placed it down in the grave.

Buck hesitated before putting the first shovelful of dirt on top of the bundle of white lace. He tried to pray, but couldn't find the words. He gave up, but as he gently shoveled the dirt into the hole, he suddenly began to sob. The sensation startled him at first; he had never cried in his life. His tears did not stop until the grave was filled and he had covered it with brush and leaves.

He returned to the house through the kitchen and saw that Jennifer had been there heating a bottle. It was six-thirty; the cook would arrive at seven. As he climbed the stairs, he began planning how he would deal with servants, friends, anyone who had seen the baby in the hospital.

Jennifer stood beside the cradle, rocking it back and forth.

117

She did not turn around when Buck came in. He joined her at the cradle, and they stood silently looking down at the baby who lay quietly on his back staring up at them. When Buck glanced over at Jennifer, he hoped she would smile, but instead all she said was, "Cancel the baptism."

"I'll take care of everything."

Slowly she turned to him, her face contorted with sadness.

"Don't tell me anything," she said.

Buck reached out to embrace her, but she stepped away, staring at his soiled hands. Then she turned back to the child. He left the room with the terrible apprehension that their lives together were twisted out of recognition, and that the affinity gained so urgently after so many years was lost.

They told the nanny and the cook that Jennifer had decided to care for the baby in greater privacy at least for the first few weeks, and the women seemed to accept the explanations. They were used to the vagaries of the rich. Callers were told that Jennifer was exhausted, and the few appointments they had were canceled.

When Buck spoke with the rector, he didn't cancel the baptism; instead, he delayed it without specifying another date, again vaguely claiming exhaustion and schedule complications. The clergyman understood.

As the day passed, Buck waited for Delilah's call with a definite apprehension, not only because she had observed the child in the hospital, but also because of her acute powers of perception. He couldn't afford to chance her visit. The trick was to put her on the defensive. Anger might blind her.

As he expected, she called before the day ended.

"Hello Buck? It's Delilah," she said with genuine friendliness.

"Yes," he said coldly.

She heard the tone and decided to ignore it. "How's the new father?"

"Delilah, we're all exhausted. What can I do for you?"

She paused, then asked, "Is my daughter there?" with a warning tone.

"She's asleep. Can I help you?"

"Buck, you sound like an executive secretary. Can't we talk

118

like human beings? Remember, we were friends longer than we've been—distant."

"I would have liked to talk like human beings before now, Delilah, at our wedding for instance, or in the hospital a few days ago when you and Skip came sneaking in behind my back."

" 'Sneaking?' That's absolutely ridiculous. We hoped we'd run into you. Skip said that."

"It would have been fairly easy to arrange. And now I suppose you want to find out when I won't be home so you can sneak over here as well."

"Buck, you're crazy. The baby's our first grandchild. I hoped we could all get back together—"

"My son isn't going to be a battleground on which I have to fight you for my wife."

With the rage that Buck had anticipated, Delilah said, "I can't believe what you're saying. Are you telling me we can't see our grandchild?"

"Delilah, knowing you, I'm sure you'll find a way. Let me ask a favor for Jennifer. She's tired. Give her some time before you start your manipulations."

Shocked by such an accusation, Delilah replied, "I don't need to manipulate. She was happy to see us in the hospital."

"I won't speak for Jennifer, but I'm sure it occurs to her that while you were willing to come see your grandchild, you weren't willing to attend your daughter's wedding."

Delilah was quiet for a moment, then said, "Why are you starting this, Buck?"

"I didn't start it. All I did was fall in love with your daughter."

"You're still trying to hurt Skip."

Buck had accomplished the diversion he wanted, so he said, "Good-bye, Delilah," and hung up. He had no doubt that sooner or later, Jennifer would see her parents, but by that time the deception should be undetectable.

Newborn babies change rapidly in a number of weeks. To Buck's knowledge, no one had taken any photographs in the hospital. The dead baby had been born with only a wisp of hair, whereas Connie Mannheim's son already had a thick black thatch. Other than that, Buck couldn't discern a distinguishable difference.

For the next week, Jennifer managed to hide her grief. Buck kept to as normal a schedule as possible, accepting congratulations from all over the country. Gifts began to arrive at the house, one of which almost caused Jennifer to break. The package was addressed to "Master John Faulkner."

Night was the worst, when they were alone with the truth and each other. They both helped with the baby, and both found their affection growing despite the convoluted emotions that bound the three of them together. After several days the child rewarded them with what seemed an occasional smile of recognition. They accepted it, and accepted him; between Buck and Jennifer, however, a barrier grew. They seldom spoke, and lying in their bed at night, they touched only by mistake. One night, when Buck spontaneously reached over and attempted to take Jennifer in his arms, her body went rigid. When he kissed her, he could feel her jaw clench.

"What is it?" he whispered.

She didn't answer right away. Instead, she pulled herself out of his arms and stood with her back to him.

"Please . . . don't do that," she said.

"Why not?"

Slowly, she turned around, her eyes filled with tears. "I'm sorry. I can't stand your hands on me." She remained standing sobbing quietly.

Buck moved back to his side of the bed. "I'm sorry too," he said. "I love you."

At the field, Buck tried to relieve his own despair. He concentrated on preparations for the transfer ceremony. Jack Llewellyn had lived up to his word. With a planeload of Army brass, General "Hap" Arnold, the chief of staff for the air, was flying in for the occasion. Buck planned a surprise fly-over and air show for the benefit of his guests and his employees.

Daily, Buck went into the shop where the first five night fighters were being painted. On the fuselage and wing, the military insignia of a light-blue circle around a white star was outlined. On the tail were the Air Corps's serial numbers running from 41075 through 41080, the "41" standing for the fiscal year of the aircraft's order. At the last minute, Buck ordered the words "Air Force" painted on the nose.

The night before the ceremony, Buck suggested to Jennifer that she attend and bring the baby.

"We have to remember that as far as we know, no one suspects anything, but if we keep the baby out of sight, people will start to wonder. If you and he appear in public, it will dispel any suspicion. And remember, no one attending the ceremony saw the baby up close in the hospital."

Jennifer did not look at him as she paced nervously around the bedroom. "What about photographers?"

"They'll document this child. You can dress him to prevent a careful portrait, some kind of bonnet, a blanket around the face."

"John Slater came to the hospital."

"I remember. The baby was in the nursery. I showed him to John myself. There were five rows of babies behind the window. John won't remember one from another."

She stopped pacing and turned to him. "I can't."

"Of course you can. Everyone will be delighted—"

"With what?" she interrupted desperately. "With what?" She shook her head and covered her eyes with a hand.

Buck went to the crib and picked the infant up in his arms.

"With our son," he answered simply.

She turned abruptly. "Yours," she said, then covered her eyes again, repeating, "Yours."

"Look at him," Buck said angrily. "Look at him." As she did so, the child began to squirm and gurgle. "How he came here makes no difference. He's ours, and he needs us just as much as we need him."

She nodded, as tears fell from her eyes. Shaken by his anger, she slowly walked over to Buck and took the baby.

"I'm sorry. I'm sorry," she said.

"You don't need to be. You don't have to apologize to him, or to me, or to anyone."

She looked at him longingly. "I let my baby die. We made love while my baby died."

Buck felt such an intense conflict between anger and pity, that he didn't think he could take a chance on continuing the conversation. He asked simply, "Will you go tomorrow?"

121

"*Of course!*" she blurted and began to cry. The baby twisted around in her arms to look at Buck as he turned and left the room.

The next day, Buck got up early to make sure that everything at Faulkner Field was ready for the ceremony. A reviewing stand stood before Hangar 40, as well as a platform for photographers and newsreel cameramen.

As he was driven back to Palos Verdes to get Jennifer, Buck recalled that it was the day on which John would have been baptized. He hoped that Jennifer would not remember.

When he arrived at the house, she was just coming down the stairs, carrying the baby. She was wearing a bright-yellow dress with a tailored tweed coat and cloche hat to match. Buck could not remember the last time she had looked so striking. She did not look at him as she went out to the car. Buck followed and joined her in the back seat.

The baby, wearing a floppy hat, rested in Jennifer's arms. She remained silent throughout the drive. The only motion Buck noticed was her hand compulsively running back and forth over the folds of the baby's blanket.

They arrived at the reviewing stand well before the ceremony. Buck gently urged Jennifer over to a group of technicians who happily congratulated her on the baby. When they returned to the reviewing stand, Buck felt that Jennifer had relaxed slightly.

Just then, a line of olive-drab military cars sped down the main runway and pulled up in front of the reviewing stand. As the band began to play, Colonel Jack Llewellyn jumped out of the first car, and, saluting, held the door for General Arnold. Conversation was difficult in all the confusion of introductions and finding seats, but Jennifer managed to respond with her usual charm. As they took their seats, with General Arnold on Jennifer's right and Buck on her left, with Jack Llewellyn leaning over from behind, Buck thought they would make it. Jennifer barely took notice of the photographers, although she did keep the baby's face well hidden.

The public-address system announced the fly-over was beginning. Buck had invited other airframe manufacturers to take part in the air show, and each of them had sent over one plane. From a holding pattern over the Pacific to the west, each of them came in at two hundred feet. The first was a Lockheed P-38, next a four-engine Liberator bomber from Consolidated, followed by the Republic P-47 Thunderbolt, then two planes from North American, a P-51 fighter they were calling the Mustang, and their bomber, the B-25 Mitchell. Douglas sent the SBD-4 Dauntless carrier-based plane, and Vultee supplied the show with their A-31 Vengeance dive bomber.

Following the parade, Buck was ready to introduce the Raven. After a suitable pause, four black night fighters screamed down from fifteen thousand feet. In a procession of full power dives, they roared across the field in quick succession at more than five hundred miles per hour. In sight of the field, they rolled and returned in tight formation at two hundred feet. The display brought the military to their feet as the presentational P-20 was wheeled out of Hangar 40 and parked in front of the reviewing stand.

General Arnold reached over and shook Buck's hand, as he said to Jennifer, "You must be very proud, Mrs. Faulkner. This is a great day for the Air Force, and I think, for your son. What's his name again?"

"Raven," she said without hesitation.

General Arnold was delighted but surprised. "You honor us," he said. "I didn't know," and turned a mildly irritated glance at Jack Llewellyn for allowing the oversight.

Colonel Llewellyn looked at Buck. "I thought his name was John."

"No," Jennifer replied. "We've decided to call him Raven." Smiling hopelessly, she looked at Buck and said, "He couldn't be called anything else, could he?"

11

The P-20 Raven was rushed into service, and it quickly distinguished itself. Late in 1942 in England, the first Raven ace was decorated. By then, the renamed Army Air Force had made a permanent order for the fighter and was introducing it into every theater of the war. At the same time, Faulkner Aircraft was asked to take over a government-owned facility in Texas outside of Amarillo and, in association with Boeing, help build more Flying Fortresses.

Faulkner Aircraft went on triple shifts. Buck flew endlessly on military cargo planes between Faulkner Field, Seattle, Amarillo and Washington; Jennifer seemed almost unaware of his absence. When he was home she presented only the facade of her former self, as if by refusing to discuss the increasingly tenuous structure of their lives together, it would not be shaken. She neglected to return to law school, and gradually she stopped going to see friends. She rationalized the dissolution of her social and academic life with the demands of being a mother. The Hendricksons, however, were a more insistent problem.

On one occasion, when Buck was out of town, Jennifer took the baby to San Marino. On Buck's return, she refused to discuss the visit. From her few comments, Buck gathered that it had been a disaster. The following week in Washington, Buck was startled by a furious call from Skip. Enraged, Skip accused him of everything from the conceit of naming the child after his plane, to imprisoning Jennifer and her child in order to keep her away from her family. When Skip started in on Eddie's death, Buck hung up. The last thing he heard was Skip shouting he would kill him.

The threat didn't worry Buck, but he was concerned about Skip's state of mind. Buck knew that the Hendrickson Company had been subcontracted to do research on jet propulsion for the Air Force. The arrangement had kept Skip's group together, but the results would benefit another manufacturer's airplane. Skip was rumored to be performing in a highly erratic manner.

When Buck returned home, he refused to let Jennifer avoid his questions.

"I'm sorry Daddy called you," she said with a rigid smile. "He's having a very hard time."

"Did you tell your father I was keeping you a prisoner?" Buck demanded.

"No." She laughed vacantly. "He must have decided on that."

"Why?"

"I don't know."

"There must have been some provocation. Jennifer, you—"

"I don't know," she interrupted. "I suppose I didn't stay as long as they wanted."

"You'd have to move back there to do that."

"If I'd stayed any longer, they would have known," she cried suddenly. "They'd have *seen*."

"Seen what?"

"That he isn't their grandchild—"

"That's insane." Buck looked down at the infant in his arms who stared back with sudden curiosity at the sharp sound of his voice. Buck stood up and took the child across the hall to the nursery. Putting him in the new crib, Buck stayed until the baby settled down. When he returned to the bedroom, it was empty.

"Jennifer?" Her clothes were carefully laid over a chair. Buck went into the bathroom.

"Where are you hiding now?" he demanded.

"I'm getting ready to go to bed." He found her in front of the mirror wiping cold cream off her face.

Buck moved behind her so she would see him in the mirror.

She glanced down at the sink. "Look at me," he commanded. She tried. "Never mention where Raven came from. Not in front of him. Never again." Buck's voice lowered. "No matter how old he is. Is that clear?"

She refused to raise her eyes. Buck gripped her shoulder. "Is that clear?"

"Yes."

"And your parents are not mind readers. So don't be tempted to reveal it to them in hopes of getting their sympathy and forgiveness. They could never understand. Never."

"Oh, *never!*" she mimicked. "Only *you* can understand. Only *you* have suffered enough to know what *he* might suffer. You're his defender against me and my family. *You* gave him this life after all, so you have to protect him from the horrible truth. And maybe if he never knows, *we'll* be able to forget it. Oh thank you, Buck, thank you thank you, thank—"

"Stop it!" He had grabbed her shoulders and turned her around, banging his elbow against the marble wall of the shower.

Her gown fell off one shoulder as she shook her head. "I'll never forget it. You know why I ran away from my family? Because I couldn't stand to hear them say, 'Grandson, Grandson!' All I could think of was the lie. What did *you* do with *my* baby? Where is his poor rotting body?"

Buck slapped her. As if released, she slapped him back once, twice, a third time.

He deflected her arm and her fist hit a cabinet. She cried out in pain. Holding her knuckles which had begun to bleed, she said, "*I* love Raven, but *you* love the lie. Because it makes him so much yours."

As she caught her breath, they stood looking at each other. Then she turned toward the mirror and said, "No matter what happens, I thank God you got Raven, no matter how you did it."

Buck took her in his arms; she did not resist, but she did not respond. He held her for several minutes, until she said, "I'm not going to fight you, Buck. I don't have the strength for that, too."

"You won't have to. I love you."

Apprehensively, he made love to her that night. Afterward, as they lay on opposite sides of the bed, Jennifer said in a harsh

126

pragmatic tone, "You'd better sleep with somebody else, Buck. There's not enough of me left for you."

By then, he already had.

Connie Mannheim's daughter was named Cass Owen. She lived in Hillsborough and worked for the Red Cross. Her husband, Jim Owen, had practiced law for two years before joining the Army the day after Pearl Harbor. He was a commissioned officer stationed in England.

The information had been gathered by the Faulkner security section. Included with it was a picture of Mrs. Owen, and Buck studied it carefully. The only resemblance to Connie Mannheim was a feral alertness in the eyes. In the picture, Mrs. Owen appeared in a tennis outfit. According to her statistics, she was nearly four inches taller than Connie and infinitely more graceful. The picture was that of a very attractive woman.

In order to meet her, Buck asked an old acquaintance in San Francisco to include her at a dinner party. The dinner was at The Burlingame Country Club. Cass Owen sat on Buck's right. At first, they talked about the war; then Mrs. Owen surprised him.

"You're adopted, aren't you?" she said. "So am I."

"How do you know that?" he asked.

"I read newspapers and—" she laughed—"I remember trivia."

At a table full of strangers, they began to speak as confidantes. From nothing more than her attitude, Buck sensed her marriage was as tenuous as his.

He said, "Can I see you again?"

Without looking at him, she nodded slightly and said, "I gather from what you've told me, you love your wife, and I love my husband." Her brown eyes were steady and direct.

In rapid succession, Buck thought of Jennifer when she had said, "I can't stand your hands on me," and then of the small white bundle in the grave he had filled. To wipe out the images he repeated the question. "When can I see you again?" He no longer cared that she was Connie Mannheim's daughter.

"Do you know Hillsborough?" Cass Owen asked.

"I'm good at finding my way."

"I'll leave my address at the front desk when I go."

Buck already knew her address. "I'll find you."

She smiled faintly, accepting the risk.

Later, Buck found the Owen house and parked his car three doors away at the corner. He sat for a moment, remembering the numerous assignations he had had with married women before his own marriage. Secrecy had lost its exhilaration; his anticipation was dulled by the sense of betrayal he felt toward Jennifer. He realized he was indifferent to the idea of an affair. Yet, he got out of the car and went to the front door.

He didn't have to ring; Cass was waiting for him and opened the door. Her hair was wet from a shower; she wore a robe and bedroom slippers. There were no overtures. As soon as the door closed behind him, she opened her robe. In the hallway, they stood clinging together. Her body moved against him until his hands went under her robe and shifted her from side to side. She lifted one leg between his, digging her nails into his back.

"Come with me," she whispered. She led him into a dark room. In the light from the hall, Buck watched her slip out of her robe. Her skin seemed iridescent.

He undressed quickly. Naked, he watched her, wishing his needs were as simple as wanting a woman. Slipping between her legs, he tried to let sex make him forget everything else. He felt her body begin to grow tense and arched up to look at her. As her frenzied conclusion brought him to his own, he was shocked to see such loneliness in her eyes.

She pulled away and opened a silver box on a table beside her, took out a cigarette and lit it.

"I suppose you have to leave," she stated in a brittle tone.

"You do?"

"Responsibility to the war effort," she said with an attempt at sarcasm. Then, more sadly, "Your wife—"

Buck reached over and took her hand.

"Let's not punish ourselves, or each other, tonight."

She looked over at him quickly, her expression softening.

"You'll spend the night?"

"Yes."

She hesitated, then leaned down the couch to embrace him. "These days the least one can do is get through the nights, one at a time." She sat back to smoke and smiled as she exhaled.

"Being left does things to women like me, but it's a bad excuse. Buck, I'm getting cold. Can we talk in bed?"

They went upstairs to a guest room and, with only a few more words, fell asleep. Several hours later, Cass woke with a cry. For a moment, Buck thought she was Jennifer. He pulled her into his arms, and she fell back to sleep, but he didn't.

In the morning, as he stood at the door, Buck said, "Thanks for the hospitality. I'm glad I stayed."

"For surviving another night," she said, "it beat liquor or self-abuse."

He laughed. "How do you know?"

She looked at him quizzically and laughed. "I've tried them both."

"I'll expect you to be right here when I come back."

She smiled. "I won't expect you." She moved into his arms. "But you can surprise me." She gave him a final kiss. "I just don't want to ever expect you."

Over the next several months, Buck surprised Cass Owen often. When choosing a flight back to the West Coast from Washington, or Amarillo, Buck picked San Francisco as often as Los Angeles.

The day that Jennifer learned from her gynecologist that she was pregnant again, Buck was in Hillsborough. On the same day, Skip Hendrickson ran his car off a cliff in the San Bernardino mountains. Five hours later, a rescue party managed to pull his body out of the canyon.

When Jennifer tried to reach Buck, she couldn't find him. John Slater placed numerous calls unsuccessfully. Finally, he called Jack Llewellyn on the slim chance the general had an idea where Buck might be. Jack had more than an idea. He called Buck directly at Cass's and tersely gave Buck the news. Buck did not ask how Jack had found him. He got out of bed and left immediately for Los Angeles.

12

When Buck arrived at Palos Verdes, Jennifer was lying on their bed with a letter in her hand. Without a word, she gave it to him. The envelope was from a hotel. Above Skip's minuscule script was printed "Indio! The Date Capital of the World."

March 8, 1943

Dear Buck,

I don't pretend my hate of you is rational. You took my daughter. In one way or another, you've imprisoned her, for you'll have to admit, she is not herself. You are the new prototype, the one who will triumph because war is your success.

I suppose what is happening to me is called 'going mad'. I find that I have no resistance to the smallest emotion, which makes a big emotion unendurable. Yet there's a hypnotic clarity about this, as if I'm caught in a trance looking at something that will burn my eyes out, not to mention my 'soul', and yet I cannot look away. Here in this strange hotel filled with motifs of camels and Arabs, my love of my daughter and my hate of you shouldn't be leaking out of the walls. But it does.

I was reading the papers about the Battle of the Bismarck Sea, a real air battle apparently; fifteen thousand Japs were drowned. They're here, too. Pretty crowded room. Sanity = resistance to what numbers and words mean.

By the way, it doesn't escape me that my hate of you is a diversion for hating myself. I contributed a good deal to this apocalyptic progression.

Buck, do you remember what it was like to build an airplane just to see it fly?

There was no signature.

Buck refolded the letter and put it back in its envelope.

He looked at Jennifer. Her glassy stare was caused by tranquilizers. Before he could speak, she said, "You don't have to say anything."

"Yes, I do. I didn't destroy him; neither did you. Skip chose to destroy himself. That's what this means. Nothing more."

Jennifer did not respond. An hour later, he saw her getting into their limousine. The baby and nanny were already in the back seat. Buck ran out. Jennifer paused and reluctantly stepped out of the car.

"Where are you going, Jennifer?"

"I want to be with Mother." Their eyes met.

"Of course. You could have told me that."

"Buck," she interrupted, "don't come to the funeral."

He nodded. An awkward silence followed. Finally, he said, "I'll stay away. From here too. This is your home—and Raven's."

"Thank you." She had tears in her eyes, but she hurried back to the car and didn't look at him again as the car drove away.

For the next seven months, Buck never went home. Whenever he had free time he spent it in Hillsborough. When John Slater told him about Jennifer's pregnancy, Buck at first wanted to see her, but he couldn't overcome his bitterness. She hadn't even contacted him to tell him that they were having a child.

Buck immersed himself in business. The war was being won and there was an overwhelming pressure for more planes, more trainers for the Raven, more updated Falcon bombers for the Air Force, more wing sections for the Flying Fortress from the Amarillo plant. The Navy had proposed a seaborne torpedo bomber that could double as a tactical-support aircraft.

Early in October of 1943, Buck finally decided to go home. As his car drove through the gates, he noticed that a construction crew had begun work on the communications center being built in the avocado grove. The center not only would enable Buck to be in contact with his own organization, but would make all his communications secure.

As his car pulled up to the front door, Buck saw Raven sitting on the steps to the patio with a woman. Dressed in her usual rubber-soled shoes, sweater and trousers, Connie Mannheim was helping the little boy build a tower out of blocks. They were both laughing as parts of their construction toppled.

"Carl," Buck alerted his driver, "when I get out, come with me. I'll take Raven inside. When I do, get that woman in the car and wait for me. If she resists, carry her."

To qualify as Buck's driver, Carl had been trained as a bodyguard and a chauffeur. When Connie saw the two men approaching, she stood up defensively.

Buck did not look at her, but reached down and picked up his son. Raven recognized him and, smiling excitedly, said "Dadda!"

Connie Mannheim laughed. Buck turned so that Raven could no longer see her and carried the child into the kitchen. Behind him, Buck heard a scuffle as Connie was taken to the car.

Inside, Buck faced Jennifer, who had been talking with the nanny and the cook. "Why was Raven left alone?" he demanded.

Alarmed to see him, Jennifer gasped, "He wasn't alone. A nice woman with the construction people offered to—"

"*Never* leave him alone again," Buck said furiously. "*Never.*"

Immediately, Jennifer knew who the woman was. She cried out and began to shake.

Buck gave the boy to the nanny and hurried back outside. Carl was holding Connie in the back seat of the car. When Buck climbed in, she kicked at him and began to yell. Carl put his hand over her mouth.

"If you don't stop struggling," Buck shouted, "I'll turn you over to the police."

Connie stared at him a moment, then her eyes moved to Carl. Slowly, she nodded her compliance. Carl hesitated, then released her.

"I'll talk with her," Buck said. The driver got out, but stood next to the closed door.

Buck faced her from the jump seat. "Are you drunk or just insane?"

"I wanted to see my child. Most people think that's natural."

"Don't try blackmail, Connie. I've been too careful. You could never prove anything, and who would believe anything you said from a jail cell as a convicted spy?"

"I wanted to see him, that's all. Your wife didn't mind. I wasn't going to say anything to her—"

"If you come here again, I'll see that you're arrested. As of now, I'm cutting your finances in half. I will increase them again only if you cooperate. In the meantime, my security guards are going to photograph you so you'll be recognized by them."

"Recognized as what?" She spat out the words.

"As a former employee," he answered coolly, "who had delusions." He knocked on the window, and the driver quickly opened the door. "Carl, take this woman to the gate and have her photographed. Then take one of the guards with you and drive her wherever she wants to go."

She grabbed for Buck, and as Carl reached in to restrain her, she yelled, "Don't think about killing me, because I swear I'll get you first."

"Hold her, Carl. I'll get you some help." As Buck went inside, he wondered how soon Connie would become desperate enough to find her way to Hillsborough in order to confront her daughter. He was met in the front hall by the nanny, who was holding Raven.

"Mr. Faulkner, sir, Mrs. Faulkner has begun labor. I think you must summon an ambulance. She is hemorrhaging."

As Carl and a security guard drove out with Connie Mannheim, the ambulance arrived at the gate. Jennifer was lifted from the kitchen floor and placed on a stretcher. On the ride to the hospital, Buck held Jennifer's hand as she repeated over and over, "I knew she'd come, one day, I knew she'd come." Eventually, she was overwhelmed with pain. When they arrived at the emergency entrance, Jennifer was wheeled into an operating room. After a hasty examination, the obstetrician came out and informed Buck that the only chance of saving both mother and child was a Caesarean section. "If there's any doubt," Buck choked out, "save the mother."

The doctor responded by hurrying back into the delivery room. Within minutes, Buck heard a baby's wail, and soon after, a nurse came out to inform him that he had a son.

"How's my wife?" he asked, sensing her reserve.

"So far so good. I'll let you know."

For the next hour and a half Buck waited. Jennifer's own doctor arrived and hurried in to observe the proceedings. Buck paced the hallway. He wondered whether the baby would die, whether Jennifer would die. He thought of Raven on the terrace steps laughing with Connie Mannheim.

Finally, the doors opened and Jennifer was wheeled out. Glucose ran into her arm through an intravenous tube. Her hair had been covered with a surgical cap. Her face was drawn and ashen.

Afraid she was dying, Buck looked at the surgeon.

"She had a rough time. But she'll be okay," the doctor assured him. "She wasn't helping us much in there."

Buck looked at him questioningly, but the surgeon offered no more. Jennifer was taken to her room and transferred into the bed.

For six hours, Buck sat in the room as the nursing staff monitored Jennifer's vital signs. He was handed a note informing him that John Slater was in the lobby if he was needed. The nurses attending Jennifer tried to reassure Buck. One of them suggested that he go home and rest, but he waited, sitting quietly in a chair against the wall.

When Jennifer finally woke, it was with a cry of pain. Buck was at her side, but when she recognized him, she turned away.

"Mrs. Faulkner," the nurse said, "you have a healthy baby boy."

Jennifer stared at her a moment then glanced at Buck. "Have you seen him?" she asked.

When Buck shook his head, she turned back to the nurse. "Bring him to me."

"I'm afraid it's against hospital policy."

Jennifer's face set. "Bring him this instant." She tried to sit up, but the movement caused such pain she fell back, turning to Buck. "Please . . ."

134

"Who do I have to see?" he asked.

The nurses looked at each other. One of them answered, "The resident in charge." Buck left the room. Within ten minutes, he returned with the resident and a pediatric nurse who carried the baby. When Jennifer saw them come in, she said, "Help me . . . help me turn."

In spite of the intense pain it caused her, she turned on her side. The baby was laid on the bed, and Jennifer uncovered her breast. As the baby and mother struggled to make contact, Buck glimpsed at the massive surgical dressing over Jennifer's stomach. By the time the baby was suckling successfully, Jennifer was biting her lip in pain. Still, she waited until the baby was finished.

After the infant was taken back to the nursery, the nurse helped Jennifer to turn slowly on her back. Barely conscious, she reached out for Buck's arm and said, "I *must* nurse the baby. They *must* bring him to me."

"I'll make sure of it." For a moment, Buck held Jennifer's hand. He wanted her back. He'd do whatever had to be done to get her.

Jennifer remained in the hospital for three weeks. They named the boy Daniel, and finally went back to Palos Verdes together. Jennifer remained distant, but her silence no longer irritated Buck. Without being asked, he lived separately in the guest wing. He was determined to make her trust him again.

To that end, the first trip he made after Jennifer returned home was to Hillsborough. As usual, he did not call first; Cass was accustomed to his unexpected visits. Because they were sure that Llewellyn had some surveillance on the Owen house, they kept their greetings wordless and never stayed there. They usually drove north across the Golden Gate Bridge to the Alta Mira Hotel in Sausalito. In the car Cass asked, "What's wrong?"

When Buck didn't answer, she laughed bitterly. "So the little wartime romance is over. It didn't even last as long as the war."

"Cass, we knew what we were doing. We knew it would end."

"Sure, we knew everything, except that I was going to fall in love with you." Buck glanced over at her, but she didn't look at him. "It's been such a luxury," she went on, "loving someone who knew me—really knew me." She sat silently a moment,

135

then asked, "Don't I even get tonight?"

He shook his head. "I'm sorry."

"Then *why* did you come up here? It would have been a lot easier if you had just telephoned."

"I couldn't do that to you."

Buck heard Cass take a deep breath. "You can take me home now."

"Cass, one of us had to do this, sooner or later. I'm sorry Jim didn't come home first."

"That's the problem, Buck, I'm afraid it wouldn't have made a damn bit of difference. Right now, I dread his coming home." She opened her purse for a handkerchief to wipe her eyes.

Buck pulled the car over to the side of the road and stopped. They were on Skyline Drive in the hills running south from San Francisco; they looked down on the street lights patterning the length of the peninsula.

"The affection doesn't just stop," he said. "We took a chance because we needed each other. If we can end well, we can keep what we've had. I want you to—"

He was interrupted by the sound of sirens rising up from the towns below. As they watched, the lights went out in seconds.

Buck and Cass sat quietly, waiting for the all-clear to sound. When she began to cry, Buck slid over and held her. The sirens wailed again. Cass shuddered, then pushed herself out of the embrace. As the lights went on again, she stared out the window.

Buck drove her home. She opened the car door, and without looking back, walked away. Buck watched her as she fumbled in her purse for her keys, dropped them on the front step, and finally opened the door.

Throughout the rest of the war, Buck received five letters from Cass Owen. Each time she apologized for writing. The letters, addressed to his office and marked "Personal," were of love and memories, which Buck answered kindly but concisely. The only phone call was brief, factual and urgent.

"I need your help, Buck. Jim's wounded. I just got word that he was found in France, near Troyes. It happened behind the German lines. Jim's mother was a German immigrant; he grew up speaking the language. I suppose he parachuted behind the lines after Normandy to sabotage the Nazis' retreat. Can you help? He's wounded badly."

"What can I do?"

"Make sure he gets to a hospital, a good doctor—"

"I'll do my best."

"Do you have a pencil?"

"Yes."

She quickly rattled off Jim's serial number.

"Thank you, Buck," she said, and she hung up.

Buck got a message through to Jack Llewellyn at the Supreme Headquarters of the Allied Expeditionary Forces in London. Buck imagined the smirk on Llewellyn's face as he read a request to help Buck's lover's husband. In spite of the general's apparent discretion concerning Mrs. Owen, Buck knew that some day he'd use the affair. Jack Llewellyn's reply, arriving as a top priority message through the War Department, assured Buck of his debt. It read: "Message acknowledged. Favor granted. Interest accruing."

13

America was finished with war. Two days after peace was declared, the Army and Air Force canceled seventy thousand contracts totaling fifteen billion dollars.

In five months, Faulkner Aircraft's employment plummeted from twenty-five thousand to eight thousand. The Falcon and Raven production lines were closed down; the Navy torpedo-bomber was drastically curtailed. Fortunately for the company, Buck was able to get orders for a commercial airliner, the Heron, which John Slater's group had developed on paper during the war. Buck also initiated government interest in a jet fighter that the design group from the Hendrickson Company had developed.

When Skip's will had been read, Jennifer inherited a large portion of her father's stock. The other Hendrickson heirs agreed to sell out to her, and Buck did not hesitate in incorporating Skip's company into Faulkner Aircraft. He had convinced the Hendrickson employees to join him, promising them a free hand and suggesting they investigate two experimental Messerschmitt jets, the Me-163 and the Me-262. The planes had appeared briefly in 1944 and had flown in excess of five hundred miles an hour. Buck promised the Hendrickson design team that at the end of the war he would get the German research. Whatever they thought of Buck, the engineers wanted that research and believed that he could get it.

To that end, Buck scheduled an extended trip to Europe. His

clearance came through early in 1946. When he told Jennifer of his plans, she responded as usual, with a silent nod. Then she surprised him.

"I'm going away, too," she said without looking at him.

"Oh? Where?"

Without malice, she replied, "I don't want you to know."

"I see," Buck said. "What about the boys?"

"They'll stay with their grandmother until you or I return, whoever comes home first. That ought to stimulate us both." She smiled, then shook her head, frowning. "I suppose I don't owe you an explanation, but I feel I do. It's very important that I do this on my own. I'm not doing anything foolish. Think of it as a retreat; I am retreating from the front lines, in hopes I can come up on them from a different angle." For the first time, she looked at him. "Buck," she said unaffectedly, "this is the last chance I have of ever getting back."

"If you need to reach me—"

"Yes, the avocado grove," she interrupted flatly.

"When will you be going?" Buck asked.

"Right now, I think; I've procrastinated long enough. Could we say goodbye, then would you call the nanny to come help me pack up the children?"

They had not embraced since long before their son Dan was born. Buck had remained attentive, waiting for an opportunity to break through Jennifer's repelling distance. No such opportunity had occurred. Awkwardly, they stood facing each other across their bedroom. Buck could see what Jennifer's struggle was costing her; her eyes were drawn, and her face was slack and gaunt.

"I don't like not knowing where you are," Buck said.

Jennifer remained untouched. "You haven't known where I am for years. Neither have I."

"I can't imagine coming back here and not finding you."

She nodded. "I'll try to remember that." Abruptly, she glared at him. "But Buck, it may have to be that way."

He didn't answer; he saw that the thought caused her as much distress as it did him.

"Goodbye, Buck."

He left the room and was driven to the field. He couldn't wait to leave for Europe; he rescheduled the trip to begin within the week.

Three hours before his departure, John Slater burst into his office. "Fishburn just jumped out of the window of his office downtown." Then Slater crumpled into the chair across from Buck's desk.

For a moment Buck couldn't speak. As treasurer of Faulkner Aircraft, George Fishburn had proven himself one of its most dedicated employees. During Faulkner's rapid growth, he had been indispensable. He had a wife and three children; he had only more professional success to anticipate. Buck canceled his flight to Washington and ordered his car.

"Let's get over to his house," he said to Slater.

"Wait!" Slater ordered with uncharacteristic insistence. "You have to know something. Fishburn was a member of the Communist Party," he hesitated, "as I was." He looked at Buck to see his reaction. When there was none, he went on. "Last month, he and I both received blackmail threats."

Buck sat down slowly; a nausea began in his stomach. "Go on," he managed to say.

"Somebody has a lot of information: documents, Party membership, a lot. They asked each of us for fifty thousand dollars. We found the messages in envelopes stuck under the windshields of our cars in the parking lot. We'll have to tell security. I went to talk to Fishburn. We've known each other for years, and we fought our way out of the Party together. I decided not to pay and see what would happen. I tried to convince him to do the same. But he kept talking about his family and all the consequences. So he paid. He dropped off his cash in a locker in Union Station. Three days ago, he got another letter, demanding another twenty thousand . . . I've been trying to talk him out of it for three days." Slater paused, then said, "There's one more thing. I'm resigning, Buck, as of now."

"No, you're not!" said Buck, standing up. "I need you too much. If this company can't stand by its employees, it's not much of a company."

"Buck, don't kid yourself. It's going to get very rough. There's a lot of in-fighting in Washington. J. Edgar Hoover's in a frenzy; he wants the F.B.I. to go international and means to show off his abilities by rounding up Communists, or ex-Communists, or anyone who eats borscht. He'll make it impossible for you. You'll never get another military contract, and the commercial airlines will be convinced that giving you a contract is unpatriotic."

"We'll take care of that when we have to. Meanwhile you still work here. Come on."

A half hour later, their limousine stopped in front of the Fishburns' home. It was surrounded by reporters and photographers. Buck was about to tell the driver to go on, when he saw that one of the journalists was holding an envelope against the window glass. Aside from a name and address, it read: "Indio! The date capital of the world." Buck opened his door and let the man in.

"Sam Priest," he said, introducing himself. "Mr. Faulkner, we've met."

Buck said, "Who're you with?"

"International News Service. Science writer. I cover the aircraft business. May I suggest we drive around the block while we talk?"

"You have three minutes," Buck said. "Carl, drive on."

Sam Priest handed Buck the envelope from Indio. With a flat smile and narrow lips through which his tongue flicked out occasionally to moisten the corners of his mouth, the man's face was reptilian. His eyes were set too close together and to counteract their ocular effect, he wore out-sized horn-rimmed glasses.

"It was a long time ago, Mr. Faulkner. I was trying to get my first story, and you were trying to be a hero." When he made an attempt at levity, his tone was modulated down to a suggestive base. "You threw my camera toward France."

"Old Orchard," Buck said.

"The Belle Nuit, a beautiful plane downed by a raven," he said, watching Buck carefully.

Buck nodded and perused the letter. Quickly, he realized it rambled through the same accusations Skip had made in the letter sent to Buck. Instead of the query about building planes with which Skip had ended his letter to Buck, the second letter concluded with, " . . . I suppose everyone wants to leave a message. This is mine."

Skip's signature followed.

141

"Why do you think he sent this to you?" Buck asked.

"I'd like to think he had read my terse, effective prose. I've gained something of a reputation in the trade as a Faulkner watcher, an inclination born on that windy beach in Maine. Mr. Hendrickson had a message; perhaps he thought I would give it a wide exposure. I haven't, though. Please accept this letter with my compliments. I've made no copies."

Buck watched him and asked, "Why not?"

"Because recently it occurred to me that in the future, the press and the aircraft business are going to become increasingly entwined. I know the press intimately; I also know a great deal about the aircraft industry. I can serve on either side of the fence, but I believe the grass on your side, as well as the money, is greener."

"I already have a public-relations department."

"Yes, I know them all. They do a good job, but not a creative one, which at this particular moment you need. Mr. Faulkner, may I be candid?"

"What have you been, up to now?"

"Only charming and, I presume, impressive. The truth is, we of the press are all in the entertainment business. I can handle the audience that's waiting at the Fishburns'. By the way, they've heard that Mr. Fishburn was a Communist . . ."

"You're on for seventy-two hours. How do we get in to pay our respects?" The limousine had circled the block and was approaching the house again.

Sam said, "Walk straight to the front door. Say nothing. I'll handle the scavengers."

Buck and John spoke to Mrs. Fishburn and offered their sympathy. During their visit, Sam Priest had slanted the story to imply that Fishburn had worked himself to death out of patriotism and devotion to the cause of peace. After Buck and John left, Sam remained behind dealing with what he hoped were his former colleagues.

Later that night, Buck drove alone to Saugus on the chance he would find Connie Mannheim, but as he anticipated, the cabin was deserted. On the way home he considered what he would have to do to silence her. By the time he arrived at his house, it was four in the morning and he had no answers. As he wandered around the empty rooms, he missed Jennifer and the boys. He fell asleep in a chair by the living room fireplace .

The next day, in his office, he received a phone call from "Inga Hoffman."

"Guess who?" Connie Mannheim said without humor when the call went through.

"Where are you?" asked Buck.

"In Yuma. Seems the local gendarmes think I was driving under the influence. This is my one phone call; they're very law-abiding. They aren't even listening."

"Well, 'Inga,' what are you doing in Yuma?"

"Listen, scum-sucker, no games or I talk. You get me out of here, or—"

"Or what, Inga?"

She was silent.

"Anything you say, Inga, will cause you a lot more trouble than it would me. The sentence for drunk driving is much shorter than for treason. So I'd stay Inga Hoffman as long as you can. I hear the F.B.I. is deeply interested in Communists again; at least George Fishburn thought so."

"I heard about him. That's why I got the hell out."

"Listen, with fifty thousand in cash, you can afford your own bail."

"I can't get to the money. I buried most of it and spent the rest on phony identification and the car. I'm getting old. Listen, get me out of here. I'll give it back, what's left of it."

"And get some more from John Slater, or the others? No, you stay right there. Did you know that Fishburn had a wife and three children?"

"Yeah. Their tough luck. Not mine. When I get out of here, I'll get my boy—" She hung up.

Buck remained in Southern California to attend the Fishburn funeral. In three days, Sam Priest delivered on his promise. No mention of Fishburn's Communist background reached the papers. The service was attended by both military and political dignitaries. An hour after the funeral, Buck's plane took off from Faulkner Field.

Both Slater and Priest accompanied him to London. Jack Llewellyn offered Buck a bed in his flat on North Audley Street, a block north of Supreme Headquarters. Buck took advantage of the invitation; quarters were hard to find. On his first night

143

there they had a chance to discuss Buck's wartime surveillance. General Llewellyn was prepared.

"I've tried to find out as much as I could about your F.B.I. file, Buck. They are a fanatically secretive agency; but I can assure you that their interest in you was only routine until it crossed with the routine surveillance of the wife of an Army undercover agent. The Bureau reasoned the woman was in a key position to gain information, from you and from her husband. Your surveillance was then intensified. I was informed because of my friendship with you, and I demanded access to their reports. I didn't get them, only an occasional bulletin. Mr. Hoover is known to keep such information to himself."

Buck had gotten over his anger long ago. The completion of the adobe hut in the avocado grove had made him certain not only of his communications, but relatively sure of his immunity from surveillance. "Well, Jack, it seems like dirty business to me, peeping-tom thrills in the name of patriotism." He made sure the implication included the general.

"Buck, I don't give a damn if you have an affair or not, but if the woman turns out to be a spy, I figured I could let you know before the F.B.I. did. They can be rather dramatic; they like publicity. As a matter of fact, it cost me quite a bit with the Bureau when I called you at Mrs. Owen's house. I broke their cover."

"So you did me a favor," Buck said, smiling.

"Of course I did." Jack returned the smile and raised his glass. "What else? I don't regard your sex life as my primary source of amusement." He drank off his highball.

"What about her husband?" Buck asked. "What happened to him?"

Jack raised his eyebrows. "You haven't heard? Ah, I see. The affair has ended. I didn't know. The F.B.I. has excluded me from their mailing list. Another drink?"

"No, thanks."

As he spoke, Jack helped himself from a well-stocked bar in one corner of the small drawing room.

"Well, it seems Captain Owen speaks perfect German. For most of the war, he trained saboteurs outside London, who were parachuted into occupied France. When he heard about the plans for the Normandy invasion, he insisted on going in himself. Very patriotic, evidently. *Very* idealistic." Llewellyn let the inference hang in the air.

Buck put his glass down. "Since I'll be paying interest on the favor, I'd like to know what it was that you did for him."

The general leaned forward, his elbows on his knees. "Buck, friendship is made of trust, and by now, I think I've proven that you can trust me. So don't mistake my little jokes as anything more than what they are. Whatever we do for each other isn't about debts. It's simply the way we work together for both our benefits." He smiled. Buck did not respond.

Jack sat back and went on. "Owen was dropped behind the German lines in eastern France with a demolition team to blow up the bridges crossing the Marne to cut off the German retreat. From what I've heard, they were extremely successful. Unfortunately, Owen's group tried to filter through the front lines to meet up with the Allies and were caught in a crossfire. Captain Owen was shot up pretty badly. When I located him, he was in a Third Army field hospital. I had him transferred under orders from Supreme Headquarters, which was lucky for him. His leg was about two minutes this side of gangrene. He recovered in Paris, and before the end of the war, General Donovan had him in Germany working with the O.S.S. He's still working for this Central Intelligence Group that Truman's come up with—" Jack suddenly looked uncharacteristically self-conscious.

"Why do I get the feeling," Buck said, "that Captain Owen and I are going to meet?"

Jack smiled guilelessly. "You don't have to meet him, Buck. It's just that he's been working on the Nuremberg Trial investigations so he has access to the Messerschmitt plant and all their research. Buck, I want you to build that jet."

Buck wanted to build it too. The Faulkner proposal had been accepted by the Air Force; money for prototype development had been secured. The preliminary plans had already been drawn, and Buck knew he couldn't let a personal matter stand in the way. At the same time, he wondered if Captain Owen had learned about his wife's affair.

A week later, Buck was on board an Air Force transport bound for Munich. He carried identification papers from Supreme Headquarters that gave him virtual freedom to traverse any guard line established in Germany.

The Munich springtime was wet and cold. Buck felt it as soon as he climbed down from the C-47 onto the tarmac. As Jack had promised, a jeep pulled up to the plane. In spite of expecting Jim Owen, Buck was surprised to find him sitting on the back seat. They used the awkward position of the seats to avoid shaking hands, but a quick glance told Buck that Captain Owen knew about the affair.

Neither man spoke as they drove into the city through military checkpoints. In the fading dusk, Buck could see the obliterated landscape. He imagined his own trial in some American version of Nuremberg if the Germans had won. He shook his head. He believed the Nazis had deserved whatever they got, but the devastated city made him remember Skip's letter.

The jeep pulled into an enclosed courtyard. Searchlights played on the entrance of the building, and their papers were scrutinized by two guards. Not until then did Buck see that the captain's large and heavy suitcase was handcuffed to his wrist.

An Air Force major showed them to a conference room. He took out a key, unlocked Owen's handcuffs, and together the two officers lifted the suitcase onto a long table. Without further discussion, the major left the room. Buck noticed that Owen was wearing a side arm.

"Before we get to the suitcase," Buck said quietly, "we have something else to discuss."

"Yes," Captain Owen replied, "I owe you thanks for saving my life." He took out a pack of Lucky Strike cigarettes. "Mind?"

Buck shook his head. Owen seemed too young to be a saboteur, a spy, or a hero, too young to be Cass's husband. His face, a long narrow one, displayed his intelligence, but none of his emotions. His brown hair was in a meticulous military crew cut. Handling the cigarette, his long fingers looked like a pianist's. His uniform was too large; Buck presumed that Jim Owen hadn't recovered the weight he had lost when he was wounded.

"I meant Cass," Buck said.

Owen exhaled smoke and said, "My wife happens to be the most painfully honest person I know, with herself and with others. When I got back to London, I got a long letter from her telling me what you'd done for me, and also, what you'd done for her." He smiled bitterly. "I suppose you want to apologize.

146

Forget it. I don't want to hear. All over Europe I've seen what people are going through. My wife's having an affair while I'm getting my ass shot off doesn't seem like much by comparison."

"All right," Buck responded. "No apologies; no excuses."

Jim Owen shrugged and smoked. "Just one thing," he said. "If you think saving my life makes us even, forget it. I know what that cost you: a phone call and a favor."

"If I could do anything else—" Buck began.

"You can!" Owen interrupted sharply. "Leave Cass alone. Don't answer any more letters. She's still in love with you." He had smoked his cigarette down so far that it burned his lips. He took the butt out of his mouth and ground it out in the Spam can that was serving as an ashtray. He turned to the suitcase. "Let's get on with this. I'm not an engineer, but I brought you everything I could find. Look them over; I'll get photographic equipment to microfilm anything you want. You can stay here all night, but this stuff is carefully watched, so I have to get it back by tomorrow morning."

"I thought I was ahead of my competition."

Jim Owen looked at Buck with contempt. "A month after Berlin fell, the Russians came after this. We caught them with their hands in the till, which was lucky, because everywhere else in Europe they're so far ahead of us it's ridiculous. Joe Stalin hasn't told his people that the war's over yet. So you better get at it."

Owen went to the door and knocked. Buck hadn't realized that it had been locked, but an armed M.P. opened it, let Captain Owen out, then locked it again. Buck began immediately to sort the blueprints, drawings, logs and notebooks. Putting those to be photographed in a pile at the end of the table, he made notes as he went. When Owen returned with the microfilm camera, Buck began a quick study of the documents.

He wanted the first Faulkner jet to perform comfortably at the speed of sound, seven hundred sixty-two miles per hour at sea level. The jets already in the experimental stage in England and the United States tended to roll as they approached the elusive sonic speed.

Some members of Buck's design team insisted that thinning the wings was the way to solve the problem. Buck favored the swept-back wing, and what he saw in the German drawings validated this inclination. The research pointed to a thirty-five-degree swept-back angle. Under such air pressure, the controls could no longer be handled manually. They would have to use hydraulic power.

In the middle of his note taking, Buck remembered something Jack had said. He paused and studied Jim Owen at the other end of the room.

"Captain Owen, about those Russians—"

"Which Russians?"

"You said something about investigating some Reds who came for these plans. What happened to them?"

Owen considered answering the question, then shrugged. "It's no secret. There were six of them; two spoke German. They knew exactly what they wanted and where to look for it. I suppose they captured as many German pilots as we did. Anyway, they got as far as the design rooms. That's where we picked them up."

"Where are they now?"

"I can't tell you that."

"All right, what will happen to them? They aren't spies exactly."

The captain walked down the table to where Buck was sitting. "Don't kid yourself that we're not at war with the Russians."

Owen spoke with a passion that had been absent in his discussion of Cass. Buck remembered Jack Llewellyn's description: "Very idealistic."

Owen continued. "The Russians we captured are definitely spies. We'll hold them and eventually trade them for our people who get caught in the Russian sector, those that aren't shot or tortured. It isn't exactly even. The politicians in Washington can't decide how much authority to give us. Besides that, we seem to need about ten of their spies to trade for one of ours."

Owen went back to the end of the table and continued to photograph the stack of documents that Buck had selected.

"Captain," Buck said, "I may be able to help you. I know where you can locate a Russian agent to be used in your trading. She's in Yuma, Arizona. It might benefit your group rather than the F.B.I. to find her. She was trained by the N.K.V.D., then she threatened to talk. I would think that now the Russians might want to get hold of her. . . ."

14

The euphoria of peace quickly dissipated into international anxiety. In March, Winston Churchill described the "iron curtain which has fallen across Europe, from the Baltic to the Adriatic." Three weeks later, Russia stated its ambition to keep its troops in Iran and to establish a Soviet-Iranian oil company. Barely half a year after Japan's surrender, the West was developing new arms for the cold war.

Everywhere he went, Buck was feted as the builder of the Raven, making it easier for him to establish a European sales force and attract future customers for Faulkner Aircraft. In England Buck found himself a celebrity. R.A.F. pilots wanted to shake his hand; the Falcon bomber had carried many of them back at fifty feet over the English Channel while the Raven fought off pursuing Nazi fighters.

Buck saw that Great Britain had its own aircraft industry, but the rest of Europe had no plants, no designs and no workers. More important, they had no capital with which to begin development. In the aftermath of war, such expenditure had a low priority. Buck saw an enormous market.

After spending ten days in London, he and his party returned to the United States on an Army transport, courtesy of Jack Llewellyn. They stopped off in Washington long enough for

General Llewellyn to escort Buck through the Pentagon and introduce him to the top brass. The tour ended in Jack's spartan office.

"I like to think," he said expansively, "this place is the last impenetrable castle in the world. From here, we'll be able to watch over the earth."

"Don't you think Mr. Truman perceives the White House as the castle?"

Jack's smile turned malicious. "Like Mongol khans and feudal lords, we have an advantage: we last. Presidents only survive a term, or two if they're lucky. Even Roosevelt had to worry about reelection. We don't. We're here to stay, with one purpose."

"Which is?" Buck asked.

"Why Buck, to defend the nation, of course. But watch closely. Without any amendments, the government's going to have four branches: the judiciary, the executive, the legislative and the military. From right here, we'll control Congress with the budget, we'll run the President by running foreign affairs, and we have our own courts. This is *the* castle."

Buck smiled. "And, of course, the new Air Force will be in the throne room."

"Well, modesty prevents such a prediction, but I'd bet on us if I were you, Buck."

"I do, Jack, I do. Who needs Faulkner airplanes more than the Air Force?"

Jack nodded. "The war proved that as long as one plane is in the air, ships and tanks and troops are obsolete, just as General Mitchell said in 1927. The future of war is ours, Buck. All ours."

"I'd just as soon build airliners."

"I'll remember your inclination, Buck, but you better come up with that jet fighter. I took too many chances getting you the Messerschmitt plans. Of course, so did you," he said, again smiling with a hint of intimidation.

"As soon as I get to Faulkner Field, I'm looking at drawings."

The two men watched each other. Buck didn't want Faulkner Aircraft dependent in any way on Jack Llewellyn. The nation's military future was being shaped by ambition like Llewellyn's, and that thought made Buck apprehensive.

150

By the time Buck's plane touched down at Faulkner Field, he had been traveling for nearly four months. During that time, Buck had heard nothing from Jennifer. Once a week he had called Delilah Hendrickson's house to ask about his sons. Delilah would not speak to him; instead, the nanny had assured him that the boys were flourishing, in spite of missing their parents. They too had received no word from their mother.

Buck dreaded the thought of returning to an empty house. As the car drove to the front entrance, he was delighted to see Raven running down the terrace steps to greet him. Buck got out and lifted the boy high in the air. At the top of the steps Jennifer waited holding Dan in her arms. Buck walked slowly toward her.

"Hello, Buck," she said, smiling.

"Hello, my love. I've missed you."

She nodded, understanding what he meant. Carrying the boys, they walked across the terrace and sat down. Carl appeared with Buck's presents for the children, and the cook came out to ask if Buck was hungry. He was, and she hurried away to prepare something for him.

As the boys tore off the wrapping paper and began to play with their new toys, Buck said to Jennifer, "I have a gift for you, but I want to present it privately."

She smiled, and as she watched the boys, she said, "I love you, Buck. I plan to love you for the rest of my life."

He didn't speak. She continued purposefully. "Let me tell you some of my plans. I'm going back to finish law school."

"I'm delighted," he said watching her closely.

"Good. Because when I pass the Bar exam, I'll expect a seat on Faulkner Aircraft's board of directors."

She watched his surprise. Before he could respond, Jennifer explained. "I plan to be a part of your life, Buck. I also plan to be very useful to the corporation." She turned away and watched the boys a moment. Buck sensed she was having more difficulty with what she wanted to say next. She lifted her head slightly to a familiar angle of determination.

"I want to be on the board because of my father. Don't misunderstand; I don't want to represent his interests. I certainly have no idea of trying to make something up to him. The fact is that he contributed a great deal to Faulkner Aircraft. His company came to Faulkner Aircraft because of me. That's my responsibility and I want to assume it."

She watched Buck for a reaction. As usual in business matters, his face revealed nothing. "I've been in a sanitarium, Buck," she said quietly. "I thought I'd lost my mind, just as Daddy thought he'd lost his. Every day I met with a psychiatrist. I finally learned how much I was punishing myself for the imagined harm I caused my father. That punishment involved you as much as it did me. It won't be easy repairing our relationship. You may not want to take the chance."

"I've been waiting for the chance for months."

"I know," she said. "I was afraid that you'd given up."

He reached for her hand. "There's nothing else?" he asked.

She turned to him. "I want you to tell me"—she anticipated Buck's reaction by naming the subject which always had been censored between them—"how you found Raven, and about that woman who came here the day before Dan was born."

Buck watched her without moving. "Aren't we going a little too fast?"

"No," she responded conclusively. "Silence divided us for too long."

Jennifer called the nanny and asked her to take the boys inside. With surprising difficulty, Buck began to tell of the night their baby died. He recounted as many details as he had allowed himself to remember, telling Jennifer of Connie Mannheim, Raven's birth in Tijuana, and the long night drive to Saugus and back. Buck explained what had recently happened in Yuma to "Inga Hoffman," and his plans to be rid of her. When Captain Owen came up in the conversation, Buck decided to reveal his affair, along with the fact that both the F.B.I. and Jack Llewellyn knew the details. Her reaction startled him.

"I knew too, Buck."

Amazed, he asked, "How long have you known?"

She looked at him impatiently. "Buck, I have a great many relatives in San Francisco, none of whom like you. Sausalito isn't exactly foreign to them, and the Alta Mira has the best bar in town."

"I'm sorry. I thought I'd spared you that," he said.

"One way or another. I sent you to her." She reached over

and took his hand. "I knew I had you back when Dan was born. Whatever happened between us in the hospital gave me enough courage to go to that sanitarium."

They were silent until she said, "Buck, you're sending that woman in Yuma to her death."

Startled by the sudden accusation, he said, "You can't know that; neither can I. I don't know what Captain Owen's going to do with her; he told me he wouldn't tell me, even if I wanted to know. I only want her out of our lives. Right now she has every intention of stealing Raven. She sent George Fishburn to his death, and would have sent any number of others to theirs."

"She's Raven's mother!"

"No she's not! You are."

Jennifer glared at him a moment. "Buck, is your mother still alive?"

"What do you mean?"

"You just told me the Mannheim woman said your mother was still alive. Where is she?"

"She was moved to a private nursing home in San Mateo."

"Have you seen her?"

Buck didn't want to go on with the subject. "Once," he said.

"Of course you did," Jennifer said firmly. "Don't you see? You can't send this woman to her death."

"It meant *nothing* to see her! She wasn't my mother. She gave birth to me, and she resented doing that. I felt *nothing* when I saw her. Nothing!"

Emphasizing her words, Jennifer asked, "Then why did you go?"

"Because I hoped—"

"Yes!"

"But she meant nothing to me."

"It's Connie Mannheim who should mean nothing to you. You're confusing two mothers, yours and Raven's. You can't punish yours by destroying his."

Buck felt as if someone had hit him. Jennifer watched him with concern.

"Buck, you can't make up for your life with Raven's. He'd only suffer for it, and so would Dan." Her voice lowered. "Your favoring Raven is already too obvious."

"To whom?" Buck said with an effort.

"To me, and to Dan. He's only three years old, but he sees who's the favorite."

"I'll try to be more careful."

"I think you should remember that they're both our sons."

"Yes," he said, avoiding her eyes.

"Buck—" she waited until he faced her—"you *cannot* destroy that woman."

Buck's throat constricted. Finally, he said, "We decided never to tell Raven. There's no need for him to know anything. We made that decision. We have to live with it."

She looked at him incredulously. "I know that some day Raven may want to meet his mother," she stated insistently.

Buck stood up and said, "All right. I'll call Captain Owen." He started toward the house.

Jennifer started to follow him. "Buck, I have to tell you, I almost didn't come back."

He stopped and looked at her. "Why?" he said.

"Sometimes, I never wanted to see you again. I blamed you for everything, my father's death, my failure at law school, even the death of the baby. I was very angry, but slowly I realized how much I love you. So I came back. Nothing can keep me from being a part of you, whether I like it or not."

Buck held her until she said, "Go and make your call to Captain Owen."

The Faulkner technicians at the communications center in the avocado grove finally located Owen in Hillsborough. When Buck picked up the phone, he thought he was speaking to the Captain in Germany. "Captain Owen, this is Buck Faulkner."

There was a pause. "How ironic."

"Why?"

"Cass isn't here."

Buck realized the mistake. "I'm sorry. I didn't know—"

"Don't worry about it," Owen said. "You'll be happy to know that Cass and I are 'together' as they say. In fact, she's pregnant. But don't worry, your letters from the war are still safe in a Chinese vase on top of the bookcase."

"You've read them?" Buck said.

"I didn't bother. Why did you call?"

"To ask you to forget about Inga Hoffman. The situation is different than I thought—"

154

"It's too late. I'll give your love to Cass." He hung up.

When Buck told Jennifer about the call, she went to her own room and closed the door. They never talked about Raven's mother again for many years.

Buck learned that "Inga Hoffman" had been taken from the Yuma County Jail by two men who were ostensibly from the Los Angeles County Sheriff's office. They presented California extradition papers concerning alleged theft. Soon after, at the F.B.I. field office in Los Angeles, an envelope arrived containing documents concerning six executives of Faulkner Aircraft. An investigation began.

Buck anticipated the F.B.I.'s actions. He had Sam Priest orchestrate a press conference in which the six publicly admitted their past associations with the Communist Party and volunteered to cooperate with the House Un-American Activities Committee. John Slater ended the press conference with a ringing denunciation of Communism, based on his own experience and revelation.

In spite of being undercut, the F.B.I. continued an intensive probe into the lives of the six executives. Faulkner Aircraft covered their legal expenses, as Buck had promised. The F.B.I. discovered that the six men had received identical blackmail threats many months before.

The Bureau eventually traced the documents that they had received to a diner in Saugus, California. A waitress there had been given a hundred dollars to hold an envelope with instructions that if her friend, "Helen Rassmussea" did not phone her for a week, the waitress should mail it to the F.B.I. Four days later, the F.B.I. fingerprint file tied Connie Mannheim to Inga Hoffman and discovered her disappearance from the Yuma County Jail.

Buck apprised the F.B.I. of his professional relationship with Connie Mannheim back to the days when she was an employee at Faulkner-Hendrickson. He was prepared to defend the fact that he had sent her money during the war, but astonishingly, the Bureau presumed her financial support came from the Kremlin and did not look further.

Special agents searched the cabin in Saugus. Although a baby bottle was found among the paraphernalia that cluttered the drawers and cupboards, the item did not seem significant.

The two men who had taken her from the Yuma County Jail were not, of course, from the Los Angeles Sheriff's office. The F.B.I. suspected the N.K.G.B. They never were able to learn the truth, but because they expressed such a keen interest, Connie Mannheim became more interesting to the Russians, and therefore increasingly valuable to Captain Jim Owen.

15

Jim Owen smoked his cigarette in an upholstered swivel chair. He stared at the Chinese vase that stood on the top shelf of a bookcase. On each of his previous visits, as soon as Cass left him alone in the living room, Jim had reached up to make sure Buck Faulkner's letters were still in place. That day, he discovered that the vase was empty.

A dozen years before, he had been sitting in the same chair when Buck Faulkner had called asking him to forget the woman in Yuma. Jim smiled bitterly. At the time, he hadn't understood Buck's change of heart, but it became clear soon enough. Several weeks after Buck's phone call, Jim was sitting in the back of a truck with Connie Mannheim. That night, she and ten Russians were to be traded through the Brandenburg Gate in Berlin.

Jim Owen and two heavily armed soldiers stayed in the truck. Outside, O.S.S. officers assured the security of the exchange.

"I got to talk to you," Connie whispered urgently to Jim. He was in civilian clothes and obviously the only person with potential authority. He tried to ignore her. "You come over here, goddamn you," she bellowed, "or the Russians are going to know some things you don't."

Jim exchanged places with one of the Russians.

She spoke quickly. "Listen, I got a lot of things to tell you, if you give me a chance. You know who Buck Faulkner is? Head

157

of Faulkner Aircraft? Well listen, he's been supporting me for *years*."

Jim's attention was caught, but he knew never to display interest when information is being betrayed.

"You know why?" Connie continued. "Because I know a lot of his executives were Commies. And you know why else? Because his own baby died, his first one, and he took *mine*. My kid is Raven Faulkner! What do you think about that?"

Jim Owen said, "So what? We don't have anything against Buck Faulkner. Tell the Russians. Maybe they'll believe you."

He started to get up, but she grabbed his arm. One of the soldiers saw her lunge and quickly aimed his automatic rifle at her head. Jim signaled for the gun to be lowered and told Connie Mannheim to let go. She didn't.

"Listen, I know where a lot of Commies are. I'll give you lists of them. You'll be a hero."

He didn't react but only stared back at her. In spite of his interest, he knew he couldn't stop her from being traded to the Russians. When Connie Mannheim realized that her chances of escaping were hopeless, her mood suddenly shifted. She asked Owen to do her a favor. She had buried forty thousand dollars in cash by a hillside piling of the pier at Scripps Institute of Oceanography in La Jolla, California. She told Jim Owen how to find it and asked him to split it between her two children.

"I never gave them anything. They don't know I exist, and I don't want them to, so just give it to them, anonymously. Will you do that? Okay?"

"I can't make those kinds of commitments. If the money's stolen, I'd have to return it."

"I don't have any choice but to take a chance on you, so what the hell. As I said, one child is Raven Faulkner, the other is a woman named Mrs. James Owen. She lives in Hillsborough, California."

Jim Owen could hardly breathe. Hurriedly, he asked, "Why are you telling me this?"

"Because I know where I'm going, and I know you're the last son of a bitch who might listen. Ever since you people snatched me out of Yuma, I didn't know where I was, or where I was going. Cars, planes, and blindfolds. But tonight, a truckload of Russkies."

The guards suddenly ordered everyone out of the truck.

"You remember her name?" Connie asked.

Jim Owen nodded.

"What is it? Tell it back to me," she demanded.

He could hardly speak. "Mrs. James Owen, Hillsborough, California."

She nodded and got out of the truck. "And Raven Faulkner," she called.

Connie Mannheim was led through the Brandenburg Gate checkpoint. As he watched the woman disappear behind the searchlights in the Russian sector, Jim Owen concluded that probably only one man knew how the entire puzzle fit. That man was Buck Faulkner. Owen vowed to uncover the whole story and to use it one day against Buck.

On his first leave, Jim went to the third north piling under the Scripps pier. The money was rotting in an old beer cooler. Any doubt left in his mind about the staggering coincidence that Connie Mannheim had confessed ceased. The forty thousand dollars was more than enough proof.

After that, Jim's career progressed from Berlin to Athens to Beirut and finally to Tehran. Yet the time and distance did little to assuage his hate of Buck Faulkner. He was able to piece together most of the puzzle, and even figured out that the cash he had dug up was what was left from George Fishburn's blackmail money. He did not, however, return it.

Jim had never told Cass that Buck knew who her biological mother was, nor that he had sent her to her probable death. As his marriage had deteriorated, Jim nurtured his hate of Buck Faulkner and found it boundless. He lit another cigarette off the butt of the previous one and stared at the empty vase. Had she moved the letters to a safer place? Or had she thrown them away, ready at last to try and renew their marriage.

"Coffee?" he heard her call from the kitchen. In the fashion of California architecture, the areas of the house were divided by counters, bookshelves, plants, a free-standing fireplace—anything but walls. Jim hated the style; he preferred solid walls and private rooms.

"No, thanks," he replied.

Cass came in with a steaming mug and concentrated on not spilling it as she sat.

"We have to talk about Melanie," she said, not looking up.

"Our ritual," he replied.

She sat back and looked out the window toward the bamboo-shaded garden. "I wish you'd let me know before you just arrive like this. You have the advantage. You can prepare yourself. I can't."

"From now on, I will."

She looked at him for the first time since he had walked in an hour ago. "What does that mean?"

"I resigned."

In astonishment, she asked, "What are we going to do?"

"What do you mean?"

"We have a daughter; she's about to start high school. Should I get a better job?"

"I didn't know you had a job."

"I'm a part-time speech therapist. It helps with the bills, but it's not enough to send Melanie to a good school. Jim, what are we going to do?"

He took an envelope out of his pocket and placed it on the coffee table.

"Don't worry," he said.

"What is it?"

"Open it and see."

She picked up the envelope and pulled out a stack of money, most of it in thousand-dollar bills.

"What is this?" she asked suspiciously.

"It's twenty thousand dollars, plus some interest."

"Where did it come from?"

"I can't tell you that."

"Of course not." She threw the money down on the coffee table. "Just a bonus for murder or some other nastiness in the name of the government."

"Don't overdramatize my job. Besides, it's over. Let's just say that the money is more yours than mine. It should cover Melanie's schooling through college."

Cass stared at the bills, then sipped her coffee. "So what are your plans?" she asked warily.

"Have any suggestions?" Instantly, Jim knew he had made a tactical mistake.

"How could I?" she said deliberately avoiding his real meaning. "I don't know exactly what it is you do. I never have."

"You did once."

"When?" she asked contemptuously.

"When we were first married, before the war." She denied the memory and turned away. He continued, his hopes dwindling. "Before you met Buck Faulkner."

She didn't respond for a moment. "Are you ever going to let that go?"

"Are you?"

"Yes! Of course," she yelled at him. "It's forgotten, dead. The only time I think about him is when you bring it up."

"Really?"

"Yes, really! I don't need his memory like you seem to. I think you're dependent on him, Jim. You came back from the war needing to hate. Every time I'm on the point of forgiving myself, you come back and set me up again."

"If that's the way you feel," Jim said flatly, "why haven't you divorced me?"

"I wanted my daughter to have a father, even though he appears only once or twice a year, and disappears again to God knows where. She can think of you as a brave man, a hero working for his country, or whatever she wants."

"Is that all I am here, a father?" he asked.

"What else?" she began, then stopped, realizing the obvious.

He stood up so abruptly that she drew back, ready to protect herself. She watched him walk to the bookcase, reach up and with his long, tobacco-stained fingers, grasp the Chinese vase.

"Oh, God," Cass said, with more fatigue than alarm. "So that's what all this is about."

"What do you mean?"

"You found the letters."

"I've known about them since I came back from London."

She stared at him, incredulous, then laughed. "I'll bet you have. I bet every time you came home, you went right to the Chinese vase. That's *so sick*! Did you read them?"

He smiled bitterly. "Buck asked me the same thing."

She glared at him. "Oh, I see. You discuss me with Buck. How long has that been going on?"

161

"I don't talk to Faulkner. We've had to work on various projects together, but we don't talk. I just mentioned the letters to him once, a long time ago."

"You 'mentioned' them to him, but never to me. You just let that vase sit on the shelf like an icon of betrayal. You never gave me a chance, did you?"

"Was there a chance?"

She stood up, shaking with anger. "Why do you think I begged you to come back after the war? Why do you think I had *our child*? You never wanted me to love; you wanted Buck Faulkner to hate." She glanced down. "I'd forgotten those damn letters were even there!" She grabbed the vase from him, and threw it on the parquet floor. She stooped down, intending to grab the letters and tear them up. For a moment, she fingered over the shards of porcelain, then looked up at Jim.

He saw her confusion and believed it. "A cleaning woman?" he suggested.

She shook her head. "That luxury ended long ago. With Melanie's private school—" Then she gasped. For the first time in years, they exchanged a look of intimacy.

"Oh, no," she said.

"From one generation to the next, like cancer."

"Stop enjoying yourself," she snapped. "I don't want you to mention them to her. I'll wait for her to ask me about them."

"What if she doesn't?"

"Then it'll mean she's forgotten, too!" Cass blurted, as she got down on her hands and knees to pick up the pieces.

Jim watched her for a moment, then went into the kitchen to get a broom. Her reactions were all true, he was sure, but the fact remained that she had kept the letters. At the kitchen closet, he began to shake. He gripped the plastic door handle and twisted it until it broke. The pain in his hand helped him to retain control. He vowed that he would not succumb to the stress that had led so many C.I.A. agents to alcoholism, breakdown or suicide. Jim swore to himself that one day he would make Buck Faulkner crawl. He opened the closet door, and took out a broom and dustpan.

By the time Melanie came running into the house, the atmosphere was no more tense than it usually was when her father was home.

"Hello, Daddy," she said, with excitement and caution playing equally in her voice. She was for a moment a beautiful twelve-year-old girl filled with anticipation for presents. "How long are you going to stay?"

"Until tonight."

She went to kiss her mother. Jim remembered that at first, she had cried when he didn't stay. He couldn't remember exactly when she stopped doing that.

"Hi, Mom." Then abruptly she uttered, "Jesus H. Christ." She was staring at the money on the coffee table, which in the argument over the vase, her parents had overlooked.

"Melanie," Cass chided. She had not heard her daughter curse before.

"What's that?" Melanie demanded, ignoring her mother. She picked up the stack of bills and fanned them out.

"Melanie," Cass said insistently, "let me have that."

The girl did as she was told, but looked at her father suggestively. "Did you bring it, Daddy?"

"Yes, for your mother. The things I brought for you are in your room."

Surprisingly, Melanie did not jump up and run into her bedroom. With an unpleasantly calculating smile, she watched her father.

"I can't tell you, and you'll never guess," Jim said trying to make a joke.

"I bet I could!" She responded with such daring certainty that both her parents were startled.

"Well, don't even try," Cass hastened to say as she put the cash envelope into a drawer of her desk. "It doesn't concern you."

"I bet it does. I bet you're going to use it to send me off to boarding school."

"We want you to have the best, Melanie," Cass said.

"I don't *want* the best," she answered with abrupt petulance. "I want to go to school with my friends, here, with boys—" Her eyes halted on the space where the Chinese vase had been. With a split-second adjustment which her father could only admire, she turned to him with a bright, innocent smile, and said, "I want to see my presents!" She kissed him and then left the room as quickly as she could.

When Melanie found her mother's packet of letters, she had been looking for money. Her habit since childhood had been to rummage through her mother's clothes and handbags for occasional change. As she grew older, however, she was satisfied only with paper bills. Her mother never had noticed the loss, or, if she had, she never mentioned it.

Money had become increasingly important to Melanie. Compared to the girls with whom she attended classes, she was poor. Although the school required uniforms, Melanie knew that her friends' clothes were made by hand. She knew, because her mother bought them secondhand through the school's auxiliary clothing program. Once an upper-form girl recognized an old blazer by its lining, and teased Melanie until she cried.

Her mother had explained that her father worked "for the government," and to have such an important responsibility took great sacrifice, but Melanie had never understood why her father thought it was worth it. He never seemed happy; if he was making such a big sacrifice for something, it seemed to Melanie that he should at least be happy about it. If he wasn't, she wondered why he didn't come home and be an executive. She knew it was because he didn't want to live with her mother or her. When she found the letters in the Chinese vase, she realized her mother had reasons of her own.

As love letters, Melanie thought they weren't so hot. They did, however, refer to a love affair during World War II, one that "couldn't possibly last," but one that they "had wanted and needed" at the time.

The letters had only the man's first-name signature, but in one, Faulkner Field was mentioned. Melanie had never heard of Buck Faulkner, but soon after her discovery, she went to a library. Within a few hours, she had found out about the letters' author. One of the facts she had discovered was that Buck, like her mother, had been adopted. Immediately, she decided that someday the Faulkners would provide the wealth Melanie saw her friends enjoy.

From that day on, the Faulkner family of Palos Verdes, California, and Faulkner Aircraft, or Faulkner Aerospace, as it became, were Melanie's greatest obsession and deepest secret. She saved articles, pictures and items in newspapers and magazines which described Buck, Jennifer and the two boys. Naturally she believed the twenty thousand was Faulkner money. By the time she was a senior in high school, her research had revealed that the older Faulkner son was a student at New York University. The other one had entered the University of Southern California.

16

When Raven arrived in New York, he introduced himself simply as "Ray Faulkner." His connection to Buck Faulkner or the aerospace company was seldom realized. He had come to N.Y.U. because he thought he'd like Manhattan, and because the school did not have a football team. His grades had been consistently high, in spite of the time he spent with a convivial group of friends drinking beer, going to theater and movies, and working for various pacifist efforts. The future, however, seemed murky. He had decided to be a conscientious objector against the draft, which meant the probability of spending three years in prison. The obligation interfered with any long-range plans.

Before he met her, Ray noticed Melanie. Although a freshman, she appeared in two of his elective classes. Melanie wore cashmere sweaters and was the first woman Ray had seen who did not wear a bra. Peripherally, he noticed her long auburn hair, her long shapely legs and, as the days went by, her friendly inviting smile.

After several weeks passed, Melanie and her roommate walked into the bar where Ray and his friends regularly drank beer and ate hamburgers. He saw the two women and waited as Melanie walked across the room and rewarded him with her smile. He watched while she took off her parka, revealing a white silk blouse plunging to a heart-stopping depth. Then he went over to her booth to introduce himself.

Melanie's roommate left to go study; Ray's friends decided to go to a midnight movie. Ray and Melanie had been pressed together in the crowded booth and as they talked about professors and books, they couldn't help but touch, at first casually and then purposefully as Melanie laid her hand gently on Ray's thigh.

The climb to Ray's apartment was memorable only in that it allowed Ray to watch Melanie's firm, trim ass undulate up four flights of stairs. When he touched it, Melanie took his hand and said, "Come on, let's just get there."

Inside, they locked mouths and bodies together. Melanie groaned nicely and asked, "Where's the bathroom? I'll be just a second."

Ray and his friends had always laughed that whatever chivalry was left in the sixties involved the man assuming the responsibility for birth control.

"I'll take care of it," he volunteered.

As she wriggled out of her panty hose, she smiled at him slyly and said, "Making it with a Trojan is like wearing a raincoat in the shower. I'll be right back. Do you have any candles?" Naked, except for her purse, she disappeared into the bathroom.

As Ray carried candles into the bedroom and lit them, he tried for once in his life not to ask any questions, but he failed: Who was Melanie Owen of Hillsborough, California? Why was this so easy? He tried not to care, but he was uneasy about anything that came as readily as Melanie did out of the bathroom.

"I'm not going to fuck you with your clothes on," she said, and sprawled belly down on the bed, arching her back to look at him over her perfectly tanned ass. Turning on her side, she propped her head with her hand to watch him undress. Languidly, she stretched her legs and moved her thighs one over the other.

Before another question could form in his mind, Ray was out of his clothes. At first, he realized that Melanie was clearly performing, almost showing off her astounding techniques of lovemaking in order to give him pleasure. She succeeded in pleasing Ray and presumably herself, considering all her indications of delirium, but he still felt suspicious.

During the silence that followed, Ray finally let the questions he had slip out of his mind. Curiosity in the presence of such

167

basic uncomplicated carnal pleasure would be what his brother always accused him of: "intellectual beating off." Dan would be proud of him.

Within a month, Melanie left her dorm and moved in with Ray. He followed his decision to enjoy it and not ask questions. Melanie liked his friends; they went to movies and plays together, and although Ray's future remained undefined and Melanie's grades suffered, they seemed to be having a good time together.

The only activities that obviously bored Melanie were Ray's political interests. She didn't really care about pacifism and thought going to jail was stupid if a person could avoid it. When Ray and his friends began to discuss the cost of the twenty-two orbits of the Mercury 9 space capsule as a ridiculous priority for the country, she shrugged. When they urgently organized a demonstration to protest President Kennedy's first authorization for United States helicopters to fly strafing missions in South Vietnam, Melanie went shopping. As she covered the stores up Fifth Avenue and across Fifty-Seventh to Bloomingdale's, she pictured herself in the Faulkner house in Palos Verdes. She imagined leaning against the huge mantelpiece in the living room, which she had seen pictured in an architectural magazine. Perhaps she and Ray would fly out in one of the new Faulkner Aerospace private jets.

Neither Melanie nor Ray mentioned their living together to their respective parents. Melanie had an arrangement with another student who had an apartment. For a small fee, the girl took messages from Melanie's mother when she called. An unspoken agreement was reached about the phone in Ray's apartment: when it rang, he would always answer it. Usually, it was for him anyway, because that spring he was helping to organize a civil-rights demonstration at the Lincoln Memorial. He also spent a lot of time getting advice about his final appearance before the draft board.

When Ray's parents called, Melanie noticed that his phone voice became tense and he tore at his hangnails with his teeth until there were cuts on most of his fingers. She busied herself in order to appear oblivious to their conversations, but in fact she strained to hear every word. She was particularly frustrated that

168

Ray had only one phone in the apartment. At home, she had become quite good at listening in on an extension.

They had occasional arguments, usually about money that was missing from Ray's wallet. The amount was never great, usually a five- or ten-dollar bill. Yet, unlike Melanie's mother, Ray always noticed that it was gone and figured that she must have taken it.

More out of habit than anything else, Melanie denied that she knew anything about it. She didn't really need it; taking money was a habit. Ray tried to convince her that he didn't care about the money and offered to give her some. He just didn't want her to lie about it. She never admitted taking his money, however, and the issue remained unresolved.

The theft was an irritation to Ray. He admitted to himself an altruistic motivation to try to break Melanie of her pilfering habits. More than that, however, the fact that he was living with a luscious kleptomaniac threw the grand, ordered life style of Buck and Jennifer Faulkner into an interesting perspective. For that alone, Melanie was worth more than she could ever steal.

Bloomingdale's, however, did not agree. Melanie was arrested there one day for stuffing a regimental necktie into her parka pocket and walking out the door. She called Ray from the precinct house, and he managed to get her out on bail. As it was Melanie's first offense, the store eventually dropped its charges. The experience, Ray hoped, would have a remedial effect on her habit.

It did not. A week later, she gave him a necktie in the same regimental colors as the one used previously as "exhibit A."

Ray seldom wore neckties. He looked at Melanie, who returned his gaze with a smirk of stubborn pride.

"You bought it," he suggested hopefully.

"If you want to think that," she said, "go ahead. I don't care." She started to go into the kitchen.

"What the hell's that supposed to mean, Melanie? You know, they aren't so nice with second offenders."

She turned back, no longer smiling. "What they don't know, doesn't matter. You think anyone at that store gives a good goddamn about that tie? The important thing is that *I* know, and *you* know, that I went back in there and got it."

Ray thought of not asking about her bizarre reasoning, but gave in. "Why's that so important, for Christ's sake? You could go to jail, for a goddam necktie."

She walked over to him and put her arms around his neck. "Maybe we'll be roommates." She kissed him and flicked her tongue between his lips. "You may not want it, but that tie is worth more to me than your love-the-world pacifism is to you."

"What's that little sarcasm mean, 'love-the-world pacifism'? That's *worth* going to jail for. You think stealing a necktie is?"

She turned away and shrugged. "No, but *I* don't plan to get caught. *You're* asking for it. It's different, Ray."

"That's really stupid."

Melanie didn't move, but Ray could tell from her voice that she was angrier than he had ever seen her. "Don't ever call me stupid. I know you're smarter than I am, but you don't know everything." She turned back to him. The mean contortion of anger on her face shocked him. "Your fucking high ideal cuts off your view, so you don't see a lot. I *know* what I want, and if I can't get it any other way, I'll walk in and take it. That's the truth." She smiled, still angry. "Do you know what *you* want? Hell, no, except a perfect world—something like your mother and father have. Well, their world ain't so perfect. It's just—" she walked out of the room into the kitchen as she said—"rich."

"What the hell are you talking about?" Ray said as he followed her. "That's just what I don't want. As usual, you missed the point."

"As usual, I missed the point." She spoke viciously. "Well, smartass, *your* father and *my* mother had an affair for a couple of years." She watched him as the shock settled in. "You see the point? *No* perfect worlds, Ray, so you better open your eyes and take what you can get."

She had never intended telling him, but she didn't regret it a bit.

Ray knew she was a liar and a thief, but this time he believed her and realized the complexity of her deception ever since they had met. He couldn't help admiring her for her cleverness. She told him the details of what she knew about Buck Faulkner's affair. He cut off her story by taking her to bed.

". . . Do you think you might be a coward?" That was the

170

retired Air Force general. The other three members of the Manhattan Draft Board, all wearing civilian clothes, were a retired Navy captain, a retired Marine colonel, and a Lithuanian-American whose parents had emigrated in the twenties. They looked at Ray obliquely, except for the Air Force general, the chairman, who was smiling like a gargoyle. With increasing irritation, Ray answered his questions.

"No one can predict what he'll do in a set of unknown circumstances."

Contemptuously, the general looked off into the distance. He had received his star on his retirement, Ray thought, probably because he looked like a general: wavy gray hair, a clipped mustache, and iron-gray eyes. Moreover, he had been smart enough to make the rank without having attended one of the service academies. Ray knew from long experience what careful diplomacy it took to rise through the feudal structure of the military.

High-ranking officers had passed through the Faulkner home longer than Ray could remember. Their motorcycle escorts and chauffeured cars with pennants of rank fluttering on the front fenders had been impressive and exciting. As Ray grew older, however, he had seen the guests' friendliness turn into a nervous devotion. He became aware of the complex system of patronage that took place between the military and the aerospace industry.

The retired Air Force general who was asking the questions would have loved those parties.

"You mean 'unknown circumstances' such as war?" the general asked sarcastically, again smiling.

"Yes," Ray answered. "I've thought about how I'd *try* to act in war. That's why I'm here."

The Air Force general stopped smiling and shifted in his chair. The small room was stuffy with cigarette smoke; the air-conditioning in the Federal Office Building had not been ordered into summer service yet.

"Well, Mr. Faulkner, you seem to have some slick answers. I wish the rest of the world were as fortunate. Since war's so easy for you, let me—"

"War isn't easy for me," Ray corrected disgustedly.

"Let me finish. You've got some answers about war, but only for yourself. Take a more personal example. What would you do if two Russians walked up and started to rape your mother?"

Ray glanced around the hearing room to see if anyone else recognized the idiotic nature of the question. No one moved.

"With the respect your question and my mother deserve," Ray began, "let me say that I'd use what I've learned about nonviolent resistance to save the lives of the Russians."

The only laughter came from the secretary.

"Mr. Faulkner, why do you mention 'respect'?" the general asked. "A soldier has respect. But a conscientious objector usually calls me a killer. Don't you?" The other Board members came to attention and watched Ray. The former Marine Corps colonel shifted uneasily in his chair.

"Don't you, Mr. Faulkner?" the retired general repeated.

"I've never called you a killer," Ray said calmly. "On occasion I've called you a couple of other things—"

Several members of the Board laughed. The general ignored them and changed the subject.

"I had the honor to fly for your father once."

Ray felt the familiar shot of adrenaline. He began to sweat as the general continued.

"The Air Force put on a little air show of appreciation for him just after the war out at Edwards Air Force Base, really a desert then, called Muroc Dry Lake, nothing like what it is now."

"Which war was that, General?" the retired Navy man asked.

"*The* War, Captain," the general snapped off smartly. Then his look became one of genuine emotion.

"Mr. Faulkner, I flew a Raven in the War. Fifty-seven missions. On eight of them I should have gone down in the English Channel. The reason I got back was the plane that Buck Faulkner built. The Raven P-20 Night Fighter—for which *you* are named." He paused. "Your father's a great man. Do you have any idea of what these sophomoric convictions of yours are doing to him? Do you deserve the honor of your name?"

Ray was aware of his heart beating faster; he knew he was close to blowing up. The Navy man seemed to be scowling at the line of questioning, but he wasn't going to interrupt; he didn't have the rank. Military custom was respected to the grave, even in civilian clothes.

"General," Ray began, "my father and I have argued about this for years. Let me assure you, he disagrees with me totally. I

172

may not be the son he wished me to be, but, what the hell, he has another son, and he's never asked me to change my name— either one. I think your question is personal, inappropriate, and pure sentimental crap."

The general reacted angrily to the profanity as much as to the accusation. "Your father has spent his life making America strong. And you're going to spend your life trying to weaken us."

Raven shook his head and jabbed his finger toward his inquisitor. "You're concerned with winning wars. That ambition *requires* wars to win and a 'strong America!' I'm concerned with trying to stop wars—which would take a stronger America. My father," Ray shrugged, "he's just in the business."

The Air Force general leaned forward and folded his hands on the table. "What stops war these days is power, Mr. Faulkner. Nonviolence is regarded by the whole world as weakness. What makes this country great enough to indulge you in your ideal is *not* its citizens escaping their obligations, but rather—"

"I'm not trying to escape anything!" Ray had worked on controlling anger with the American Friends Service Committee. It wasn't helping much. "I'm on my way to three years in jail, which is a stupid waste of everyone's time. I'll meet my obligation, if you give me I-0 status, so that I can work in a hospital, as a civilian, and not waste the taxpayer's money in jail."

The general raised his arm in a gesture of sarcastic exasperation. "Your concern for the taxpayer is noted, but why not be a corpsman, I-A-0 status, helping men who are wounded in battle?"

Ray looked down at his hands. He had torn a cuticle until it bled. He folded his hands tightly in his lap.

"I've explained that, General. By wearing a uniform and going into battle, I'm supporting the war. By patching up guys and sending them back in, either to get killed or to kill, they become my surrogates."

"Are you afraid to get killed or to kill?" The general flicked a piece of lint off his shoulder.

"Sure, and your question is beside the point. I don't know what I'd do if someone tried to kill me. Bravery or valor or heroism doesn't preclude fear, does it? But let me tell you that I

173

sure as hell 'fear' jail a lot more than anything I'd get in the Army."

The general began to answer, then apparently decided he had had enough. "That will be all, Mr. Faulkner. You'll hear from us, as usual. I wish we could change your mind."

Ray stood up and turned to leave.

"Mr. Faulkner, excuse me." The only civilian on the Board leaned forward and said, "One word before you go. We see hundreds of young men, each with his own set of principles, some embraced as recently as the day before from a TV revival hour." He spoke slowly, searching for the words to communicate his concern. "I would hope only that you continue examining your ideals. I am not urging you to change, do not misunderstand, but the world is seldom as clear as it seems. It seems to me, Mr. Faulkner, that prison is not the place for your struggle."

The man had seldom spoken in the hearings. Ray wondered if a civilian sermon was the Board's technique of washing their hands of their decision. He doubted it; the man seemed too earnest, and the others seemed too bored with him.

"Thanks. I'll try to stay curious. I don't look forward to prison, but maybe it's part of the struggle. Remember Gandhi. And Thoreau."

"Remember Hitler," the Air Force general suggested, as he closed the file before him and placed it on a stack to his left. He opened another from the stack on his right and said, "Miss Squires, bring in our next claimant, please."

Awkwardly Ray and the stenographer walked out of the hearing room together. As he held the door for her, he glimpsed the next conscientious objector who wore a cloak and clutched a foot-long plastic crucifix to his breast.

The lucky bastard, Ray thought. He's crazy and he's got faith. They'll make him a general.

Ray went out of the building and walked to the subway. He looked at his dim reflection as he rode uptown to the Fourteenth Street station. The hearing, as usual, had not gone well.

The subway doors opened. Ray got off the end of the train and went toward the Twelfth Street exit.

"Hey, uh, mister." Ray turned and saw a guy with matted blond hair and watery blue eyes. He was dirty and wore a pea jacket. He had been on Ray's subway car. The weather was too warm for a pea jacket.

"Hey, man. I'm in some trouble, you know? Could you help me out?"

Drugs were his trouble. Ray decided not to respond. The two of them stood near the stairs to the street. Ray turned to climb them. Awkwardly, the guy pulled a hunting knife out of the pea jacket; the bone handle caught on his jacket lining.

"Gimme your goddam money, man." He shoved Ray against the banister rail. No one was coming. "I'll cut right through that fuckin' necktie, man."

"Okay. Take it easy." Ray tried a joke. "Do you take American Express?" The only answer was a thrust of the knife. Ray grabbed at it with his right hand and shoved it away from his stomach. He lost his balance and fell, pulling the guy down. In the same moment that he heard the puncture of the knife going into the guy's chest, the dead weight fell on him. He looked straight into the watery blue eyes as they stopped seeing.

Someone had heard; there was a yell. Ray pushed the guy off and got up. He glanced at the knife and remembered that one like it had been Dan's favorite Christmas present when they were kids. Ray reached out to touch the junkie's face. People were coming. He had killed someone. He ran.

A woman on the street looked at him and gasped. A black man put an arm around him and said, "It's over there, over there," and tried to lead him across the street to the emergency room of St. Vincent's Hospital. Ray lurched away from the man and ran east on Twelfth Street. After turning the corner, he realized that his tie and jacket were spattered with blood, and his hand was bleeding steadily. Ray watched a police car turn on Eleventh Street, then he took off his coat, shirt and the tie, and kicked them down a sewer. The wound didn't seem to hurt, though a wide flap of skin was loose across his palm. Wrapping his handkerchief around his hand, he put it in his pants pocket and looked to see if anyone was watching him. Of course not, he thought, not in New York. He'd have to cut off his head before anyone would notice.

He hurried down Sixth Avenue and turned on West Tenth, passing the Jefferson Market Library where he studied, and then Sutter's Bakery, where he and Melanie often had coffee and

175

croissants before hustling to their classes. Feeling dizzy, he noticed his pant leg was staining red. At the corner of Perry Street, he reached his building. In the small, dark vestibule between doors, he took off his T-shirt and wrapped it around his hand. Grabbing for his keys, he hoped he wouldn't run into any of his neighbors.

On the third-floor landing, Ray had to stop and put his head down between his knees. When the dizziness passed, he slowly went up the final flight and let himself into the apartment. Inside, he locked the two bolts and slipped the chain. Leaning against the door, he held his hand above his head to stop the bleeding. The T-shirt was saturated.

Ray pushed open the door that led into the kitchen. He put his hand in the sink and turned on the cold water. From the window, he could see up Greenwich Avenue to the Seventh Avenue intersection. An ambulance had just backed into the emergency entrance at St. Vincent's. It would be a short visit; they'd pronounce the guy dead and ship him to the morgue. Ray was clutching ice cubes and holding his hand above his head. His legs started to shake. Reaching down under the counter to the small refrigerator, he took out a carton of milk. As he drank, he watched as blood from his handkerchief and T-shirt drained down the sink. Holding the ice pack in the cut hand, he went back into the living room.

He squatted down on a stack of cushions and cradled his wounded hand in his lap so that the melting ice wouldn't drip on them. He thought about his ten years of battling with "D.O.D." over the principles of pacifism and the nonviolent training he had undergone for the past three years. To most people around Buck Faulkner, "D.O.D." meant the Department of Defense. To Dan and Ray, it had always meant "Dear Old Dad."

When he had declared himself a pacifist, his mother had stayed above the family "fury," as she called it. She had been "interested" in what she referred to as Ray's "beat-generation philosophy." Her expectations for him, of course, did not include his becoming a conscientious objector. To her, Raven's action was an intellectual baiting of his father.

In the nonviolence workshops he had attended, Ray had been trained to offer no resistance if he was physically attacked. He had been so sure of what he'd do if "it" ever really happened.

Instead, he had grabbed the knife, and pulled the guy down on top of it.

Ray remembered the blade being jammed against his shoulder as the guy shoved him back against the banister rail. Ray had seen the guy's arm pull back to stab him. What he had felt, he realized for the first time, was a spasm of rage.

Rewrapping his hand with the dish-towel ice pack, Ray considered whether he was a coward. He shook his head, thinking it wasn't really the time for any more "intellectual indulgence." Under fire, he sure as hell hadn't been so hot at using his principle. One of Buck Faulkner's favorite maxims was, "Whether a success or a failure, the intention makes the man." He suspected that he might be the son his father had wanted after all. That afternoon, however, Ray doubted his own logic as much as he had ever doubted his father's maxims. Again, he wished he hadn't heard about his father's affair.

The top front door lock clicked open. Ray sprang up and went back into the kitchen. The second lock clicked as he pulled a carving knife from a drawer and dripped blood from his hand on the blade. As the front door opened and was caught by the chain, Ray put half a loaf of uncut bread on the counter.

"Ray? Hi. It's me."

"Okay. Be right there."

The wound started to bleed freely again. With his hand in the air, Ray went to the front door.

Melanie laughed as he unchained the door, and said, *"Guess* what I found for tomorrow night? Little white gloves to go with my basic black and pearls. Your mother will love me." She kissed him, then saw his hand. "Ray! What happened?"

"You know how you've tried to stop me from gnawing at my fingers? I decided to just be done with it and cut the damn things off."

She did not laugh. "What happened, Ray?"

"I was cutting some bread . . ."

He had never lied to her before, and he did it poorly. Melanie realized he wasn't telling the truth, but knew better than to point it out.

"Ray, we have to go to the hospital."

"I've cut myself worse shaving."

"Ray—"

"Okay, but let's go to the Health Service."

"St. Vincent's is just—"

"N.Y.U. has a better sewing machine than St. Vincent's." His voice warned her not to argue with him. She shrugged and said, "You better put on a shirt."

As they walked down Greenwich Avenue, the ambulance from St. Vincent's drove by. Ray stumbled.

"Just a second. Just wait," he ordered.

She put an arm around him for support. The ambulance disappeared crossing Eighth Street.

"What is it?"

Ray turned with an intention of telling her, but thought better of it.

"Nothing. Let's go get this thing sewed up."

What was he supposed to have done, he asked himself—let the guy stab him? Ray believed with absolute certainty that if he hadn't grabbed for the guy's throat, he would've been another New York mugging statistic. The press might have picked it up, but not because of his being a pacifist. Ray knew his death would have been noted only because of his father. Again, he accepted the fact that he was no longer a pacifist; that he was Buck Faulkner's son.

17

Jennifer Faulkner's limousine crossed the Triborough Bridge, and proceeded down F.D.R. Drive.

"John, call the hotel, please."

"Yes, Mrs. Faulkner." The chauffeur picked up the car phone as traffic on the Drive slowed the limousine. The manager of the Carlyle Hotel would meet her at the curb and escort her to a waiting elevator. She did not like going into lobbies alone.

Jennifer went over her mental list for the rest of her day. Her secretary, Mrs. Syms, having flown from Washington with the baggage, would have hung up Jennifer's clothes, put Jennifer's own sheets on the bed, her towels in the bathroom, and organized her phone messages. Jennifer would spend twenty minutes on calls, then call Buck. It would then be three o'clock in California. He'd be at the field. She reminded herself to tell Buck about her meeting that morning at the Office of International Logistics Negotiations with the Pentagon sales people. She would explain their news carefully; more than anyone else, Jennifer was aware of Buck's growing frustration with the Pentagon.

She thought back to her decision to return to him. She remembered her time in the sanitarium and mused about what her life might have been without Buck Faulkner. She saw herself practicing law, with lots of time for privacy and spontaneity. She also saw herself alone; she couldn't imagine another husband.

She knew how effective she had become on the board of

directors; even those who had objected to her appointment because she was a woman were impressed. They knew that Jennifer Faulkner had made Buck rethink his strategy concerning the Pentagon. During the fifties, the Pentagon subtly but unmistakably began to dictate to the aircraft business. Buck could barely tolerate the Pentagon's spoon-feeding of contracts that began after the Korean War. He felt his independence was gradually being eroded. Time had proved that he was right.

Jennifer recognized his distress and tried to assuage it. Yet when she succeeded, she felt no sense of accomplishment, only an emotional exhaustion and renewed doubt. Sometimes she wondered whether the business had any morality, and she wondered how far Buck would go if pushed.

She had become stronger; she knew that some would say harder, but at least she was respected. Love was no longer what she thought it would be when she was a girl, but her love of Buck, in spite of everything, persisted. Sometimes it seemed beyond reason, as if it resided in a place shielded from scrutiny, certainly her own.

The limousine turned off F.D.R. Drive on Ninety-sixth Street and went west toward Park. In an hour, she'd try to reach Dan at his fraternity house. Since it was Saturday afternoon, he'd probably be out on the beach.

Raven and his girl friend would arrive at seven-thirty. Jennifer presumed that she was merely another one of Raven's mysterious exercises in romance. He had always liked surprise in his life; Jennifer had wondered whether it was a trait inherited from his biological parents or was a way to withdraw from the family and emphasize his separate identity.

One night when he was fourteen, he had announced, "I'm a pacifist, and you're a warmonger, Father." Their argument had spanned close to a decade, and Jennifer could not see any resolution in sight. Raven concluded every argument with the statement, "That's all a rationalization. Your business depends on war."

When Raven announced that he was going to N.Y.U. rather than Cal Tech or M.I.T., his mother reluctantly supported the decision, but when he declared himself a conscientious objector, she was almost as upset as Buck. She felt that Raven was publicly repudiating his father, and though she was sympathetic

180

to his reasoning, her ultimate loyalty was to Buck. He was the one emotional aspect that was immune to the cold appraisal of what she had become convinced was her fine mind.

As the limousine sped down Park Avenue to make the light, Jennifer smoothed her skirt and touched her hair in preparation for her arrival at the hotel. She stopped herself abruptly; the gestures were nervous ones which she worked to control. When they arrived at the entrance of the Carlyle, the hotel's manager greeted her, and a bellhop was there to carry her briefcase.

In the suite, Jennifer recognized every piece of furniture. She was admiring the fresh flowers when she was startled by Buck's laugh.

"I've been warned," he said appearing at the door, "that Jennifer Faulkner's back in town."

"What are you doing here?" Jennifer asked, moving into his arms.

"After I spoke to you yesterday, I got word from Jack Llewellyn that the Luftwaffe's delegation might need some final urging. I flew in last night and closed the deal this morning. They want the new fighter before everyone else, of course, but they ordered two hundred of them. I'm sure for that sale, the Pentagon will pat me on the head."

Jennifer smiled. "I'm so glad you're here. Raven will be so surprised."

"Do we know anything about the young lady?" Buck asked.

"Of course not. Another mystery. I have to do my phoning." She called out, "Mrs. Syms?"

Mrs. Syms came in with her clipboard and sat down beside the desk. Buck took Jennifer's hand, and for a moment they ignored her. Over the years they had developed an intimate shorthand.

That evening when Raven arrived, Jennifer welcomed the couple at the door.

"Hello," she said, taking Melanie's hand graciously. "I'm Jennifer Faulkner." She paid little attention to the girl, except to notice that she was very pretty. "Hello, my darling," she said as she kissed Raven. "I have a surprise for you."

Melanie had already seen the surprise. As she glimpsed Buck, she was unable to suppress a gasp. Buck, misinterpreting it as a reaction to his celebrity, smiled warmly.

"Jesus Christ, what are you doing here?" Raven said.

"What a way to greet your father," said Jennifer. She looked at the girl, smiling. "Please believe me, Miss—?"

Melanie was not ready to speak. Raven mumbled, "Owen. Melanie Owen."

Buck and the girl stared at each other as Jennifer continued, "Believe me, Melanie, I taught him better manners. Owen?"

Melanie was transfixed. Jennifer looked to Raven for an answer. "Yes, Mom. Owen," he said. Jennifer didn't respond. She decided that Raven had found the girl as a further method of embarrassing his father and for the moment decided to hide her fury. She turned to Melanie and said without inflection, "Do you like Champagne?"

Melanie barely managed to say, "Yes, Mrs. Faulkner." Raven went to pour the wine, but first he shook hands with his father. Buck didn't bother to disguise the fact that he recognized Melanie's name, and he glared at his son.

For a moment, Buck was shaken by the complications that the girl's appearance might present. Resolutely, he began to deal with the situation. He concluded that both the girl and Raven knew of his involvement with Cass Owen, and that any effort to subvert that fact would only make things worse.

Buck walked over to the couch and as Raven arrived with a Champagne cocktail for Melanie, Buck said casually, "And how are your mother and father?" Jennifer caught his eye long enough for her to understand the change of strategy.

Melanie's hand trembled as she took the glass from Raven. "I didn't know you'd be here," she said hurriedly, referring to Buck.

"No, of course you didn't," Jennifer said sympathetically, "but you did know that I'd be here."

Melanie looked at her, confused by the solicitous tone. "We didn't think you knew."

Jennifer slowly turned to look at Raven. " 'We'?" she repeated in a tone suggesting conspiracy.

"No one's guilty of springing any secrets," Raven said finally. "I didn't know who Melanie was—I mean, how she was connected to you when I met her. She had no intention of telling me. These things come out, almost by accident, like tonight. Maybe it's better that way. Maybe it's best that we all know everything." Raven suddenly considered telling Melanie and his parents about what had happened in the subway, but Jennifer interrupted the thought.

"I disagree," she said. "It's often best that we *don't* know everything. There's a great deal about everyone's life that is nobody else's concern." She glanced at Buck, who nodded agreement with the direction she was taking.

"The incident concerning Melanie's mother," Jennifer continued in a gentle tone, "took place nearly twenty years ago. I don't know or really care how either of you heard about it, but since it is neither forbidden nor particularly interesting, I suggest we let the matter drop."

She watched Raven and smiled matter-of-factly, then turned to Melanie, who was looking down into her lap, where her hands, still in their white gloves, were gripping her evening bag.

Attempting to be blasé, Melanie turned to Buck and said, "It must be pretty nice if that's all it means to you. . . . You asked me how my parents were. I think my mother's still in love with you, and my father knows it. I think he hates you. I suppose you could say, you've wrecked our lives." She smiled in a way that Raven recognized as pure audacity. "But thanks for the twenty thousand."

Melanie mentioned the money in hopes of securing an admission and establishing an intimacy between her and Buck to the exclusion of Raven and Jennifer. The idea didn't work.

"I'm not sure about your analysis of your parents," Buck responded, "but whatever 'twenty thousand' means, I promise you it doesn't involve me."

"Yes, you remember, for school," Melanie said with a provocative smirk.

"Sorry." Buck said. "I don't know what you're talking about."

Melanie saw that she was wrong, and tried to laugh her way out of it. "Oh, well, I guess I got that screwed up. Sorry." She reached for her Champagne.

Jennifer said quietly, "What else do you 'guess you got screwed up,' Melanie?"

"Wait a minute, Mom," Raven said. "You don't need to cross-examine Melanie."

"If I were going to do that," Jennifer replied, smiling at him, "you'd never even notice. I simply thought that while we're

183

here together, we could help Melanie clear up whatever other misconceptions she might have."

Melanie watched Jennifer and returned her smile. "Thank you. I may have a couple. One is that I thought there might be a few regrets about the affair." She looked at Buck.

"There were many," Buck said. "Your mother knew that, Melanie. The relationship your mother and I had caused us more grief than joy. I'd hoped enough time had passed so that its effect on others would have faded. I haven't heard from your mother since then, so I could only guess—"

"You wrote five letters to her," said Melanie quickly and looked around to see who was surprised. Only Raven was.

Buck closed his eyes and shook his head sadly. "She kept them."

"What else did she have? Nothing." Melanie responded angrily and put down her empty glass. "I'll tell you another misconception. I've wanted to meet you for a long time. I thought I'd like you, but—" she shrugged and smiled first at Buck, then turned to Jennifer—"I don't. So I think I'll go. I'm sure you'll all find something to talk about. Maybe it'll be me." She laughed and stood up.

"Melanie—" Raven began.

Melanie shrugged. "I'm not really hungry. The stores are open late; I have some shopping. I'll see you back at the apartment." She saw that she finally had said something that surprised Jennifer. "Oh yes, Mrs. Faulkner. We live together." She laughed and started for the door.

"How thrilling for you," Jennifer said as she watched Raven follow Melanie to the door. Jennifer looked at Buck. She could see that he was more affected than she was. She reached out and touched his knee and he put his hand over hers. Then Raven came back and stood awkwardly looking down at them.

Jennifer reached her other hand up to him, urging him to sit on the couch beside her. "Darling—"

"She's crazier than I thought," said Raven, ignoring his mother's gesture, "but I guess she has a right to be."

"Perhaps," Buck qualified carefully. "But I hope she hasn't used you to express her anger."

"Not until tonight."

"Raven," Jennifer said softly, "you have to consider the possibility that she's been using you ever since she met you."

"I've considered it, but couldn't you have been a little more sympathetic? She and her parents are still hurting."

Buck shook his head sadly. "If what she says is true, our sympathy can't help them. I've had to work with her father occasionally. He's hanging on to that anger, why I don't know."

"She told me he was with the C.I.A."

"He was. He left the Agency, angrily, I heard. He works as a Middle East consultant now, out of Tehran and Paris. I should also tell you that on several occasions he's been useful to Faulkner Aerospace."

Jennifer glanced at Buck, surprised.

"Good lord," Raven replied. "Why him? There must have been someone else you could have hired."

Buck shook his head. "He's very good at what he does. I've never let personal matters interfere with business. More important, Jim Owen took the assignments with no hesitation."

"I guess he's a businessman, too," Raven scoffed.

"I suppose so," Buck replied. Then he stood up and went to the bar to pour himself some more Champagne. "Needless to say, we didn't discuss his marriage. I haven't seen him for some time."

Shaking his head, Raven said, "I just find it hard to believe that you had an affair." He laughed nervously. "What the hell happened?"

Before Buck could respond, Jennifer said, "Raven, those were terribly difficult times for us. I left your father, for one thing. Your grandfather had died, and my family blamed it on your father. Your father was under enormous pressure. I've never told you this, but I went to a sanitarium for nearly four months. You stayed at your grandmother's. Do you remember that?" Raven shook his head. "I never told you, because it didn't matter. Your father and I have long since passed it by. Now, unfortunately, maybe it does."

Raven turned to his father. Each stared at the other with an inclination to tell his own secret. The tension between them was strong enough to alarm Jennifer. Not knowing what Raven intended, and not wishing Buck, in the emotion of the moment,

185

to reveal anything more, she cleared her throat and stated, "I presume that Dan knows nothing of the Owens, Raven. We'd prefer he didn't."

Once again included where his brother was not, Raven nodded and said, "It's your secret." He then sat down on the couch next to his mother. "Can you stand one more surprise?"

"Oh Lord," Jennifer said, smiling at Buck as he returned with the Champagne bottle to refill her glass. "Is it a good one or a bad one?"

"You'll love it," Raven answered. "I'm not so sure I think much of it."

"Then by all means, surprise us again," Buck said. "By now, we're ready for anything."

"I went to Times Square this afternoon and enlisted."

There was a motionless pause, then Buck said, "I was wrong. We weren't ready for that."

"Tell us what happened," Jennifer suggested.

Raven looked at her sharply. "What do you mean?"

His reaction caught Jennifer's attention. "Raven, we've lived with your pacifism for a half dozen years. You can't blame us for being curious how—"

Raven interrupted, "I'm not sure if any one thing did it. It's just that, well, I guess I realized my name is Raven Faulkner, and I might as well stop fighting it. Pacifism's too important to be used as a weapon in a family rebellion, which I suppose all this stuff was."

"Don't undersell yourself," Buck said, "about your conviction or about changing your mind. Your mother and I are proud of you for one no less than the other."

Jennifer took Raven's hand and asked, "What happens now?"

"I made a deal with them, that I wouldn't have to report until after I graduate. I suppose I'll have a physical in a couple of weeks."

"Are you sure you want the Army? I'm sure there'd be a place for you in the Navy or Air Force."

Raven laughed. "Oh I'm sure of that, too. You'd call Uncle Jack and by next month I'd be commanding an aircraft carrier. Father, promise me: don't pull any strings. Let me do this on my own. When I get out, I'll probably ask you for a job. Then you can use your influence all you want. You'll probably have to. I'm

186

not sure how Faulkner Aerospace can use an undergraduate degree in philosophy and English."

Buck laughed, finally allowing himself to express his happiness. But as far as Jennifer was concerned, one subject remained in need of further clarification. "Raven, about this girl," she began.

"Mom, you are the *most* tenacious lawyer." He leaned over and kissed her affectionately. "Melanie and I are 'just good friends.' Or we were. Who knows where we are now? Whatever, I doubt if the Army will let me take her with me. And I doubt if Melanie will wait for my return, don't you?"

His tone meant more to Jennifer than his words, but she suspected that the girl was not finished with them, no matter how humiliated she might have been that night. Without knowing it, Melanie was a pivot on which the whole of the Connie Mannheim story could turn. Jennifer was aware that if Melanie ever became aware of her position, she would become a serious threat. Jennifer wondered whether Jim Owen knew that his daughter had been living with Raven Faulkner. Shaking off her mood, she said, "Come along. It's time to eat. Surprise gives me a ravenous appetite."

At dinner Raven watched his father carefully de-bone a trout and lay the skeletal spine neatly on the side of his plate. If Raven's mother sometimes manipulated with charm, his father manipulated with temptation. Raven considered Buck's methods more subtle and more ominous. He listened warily as his father spun out Raven's future.

"I'll want you to know every aspect of Faulkner Aerospace. You'll start on the line, experience the pride of putting a plane together. It's hard work. You'll get to know and appreciate the workers. Then I'll want you in design, not only to learn how a plane stays up, but what kind of plane we'll be building in ten years. After that, you'll manage a section. By then, I presume, you'll be finished with whatever business and engineering courses you need."

"When did I do that?"

"At night."

Raven and Jennifer looked at each other as Buck went on. "After that, I'll send you on a tour of our offices around the world."

187

"You think you can trust me to represent you?"

"I'll take my chances. If you misbehave, I'll send your mother after you. When you get back from that trip, I'll expect you to know every marketplace we've got, and the kind of plane they're looking for down the road. You'll take that information and work in research at Ajo. I'm not going to make a scientist out of you, but I'll want you to be able to tell our people what you're going to need and to get them started. From there you'll go to Washington and find out where the money comes from, how to get it, and incidentally, how to give it out."

Raven had been eating as his father spoke. As he paused to sip his wine, Raven smiled. "How long is all that going to take?" he asked.

"About two years, depending on how hard you work."

"A challenge?" Raven scoffed. "What a corny device." Yet Raven immediately wanted to accomplish it all faster than his father suggested. "What then?"

"You start selling airplanes. That's when I enter your education full time."

"The old professor himself," Raven laughed.

"There's nothing certain about this business," Buck continued, "except that humankind wants to fly. We have to fight for every piddling order from any two-bit airline or two-bit country that can afford to buy. Then *we* find them their financing. We have to sweat every penny out of the Pentagon for research and development; we have to sweet-talk every politician, prince and potentate in the world who can make a sale happen. And then we build the best planes in the air, going as close to bankruptcy as our banks will let us, knowing damn well we have to sell more planes than have been ordered just to break even. Usually at that point, we have a strike or a recession, someone crashes one of our planes, which taints all our other models with death, or the defense budget gets cut and the Pentagon passes it on to us, or the President comes out in favor of submarines and our stockholders scream that we should retool for naval work. That's when you learn how to drink sand and sell airplanes."

He finished off another glass of wine, relishing every detail of the struggles he described.

Raven nodded and said, "And whatever the planes are used for and who uses them doesn't matter."

Buck put his glass down slowly and glanced at Raven.

"Are we now to have another sermon on morality?"

"No. I've been curious about how I was going to get over some things. You just gave me a glimpse of how it's done. The sale ends responsibility, doesn't it?"

Jennifer stated, "There are more laws controlling the end-use of an American airplane than there are for any other product in this country, *including* nuclear research."

"Raven, remember the chicken farmer," Buck suggested. "He takes thirty dozen eggs to market a day. At the market, the first ten dozen eggs are bought quickly by an angry man, who hurls them at a neighbor. Another ten dozen are bought by an old mad woman, who eats them all and dies. The final ten dozen are bought by various people, who scramble them the next morning for breakfast. Should the chicken farmer be arrested? Should the chickens be destroyed for producing a dangerous object? Of course not. The world needs chickens and eggs, and if I may say so, airplanes."

"My father, the chicken farmer," Raven joked, and his parents both laughed.

"My son, the prodigal," Buck said, "returned."

18

If you have four hundred horsepower under the hood, Dan thought, you should use it. Taking the Corvette to eighty miles an hour, he glanced over at his passenger, an Armenian who had come down from Fresno with a full scholarship, carrying his clothes in a potato sack.

"Mardigian, how come you know so much about pussy?"

Al Mardigian spread his arms expansively over the back of the seat. "Armenians can smell desire."

Dan smiled. "Really? How do you get anything else done?"

"That's only one desire," Mardigian replied and looked back at the freeway. "We can smell all kinds."

I'll bet you can, Dan thought, and he smiled.

"Mardigian, shall we go fast?"

"Always."

"Turn on the pig picker."

Mardigian reached under the dashboard and flipped a switch. A high-pitched pure tone poured from the radio speakers. Made at the Mole Hill, the device had been secretly installed by an ambitious young manager at Faulkner Field. Dan pressed the accelerator. The Corvette shot ahead at a hundred miles an hour. Al Mardigian smiled.

Dan knew why the Faulkner manager had done him the favor. After all, Dan was the boss's son; the manager was making a little investment in the future.

Not much of an investment any more.

The accelerator went down. The Corvette's speed increased to a hundred and ten, then to a hundred and twenty.

Flat feet. Raven had taken his army physical and been rejected because he had flat feet. Dan shook his head disgustedly, thinking how quickly his brother had passed from a conscientious objector to an employee of Faulkner Aerospace, without even the diversion of the U.S. Army.

The radar device began to waver its pure tones from high to low frequencies. Dan hit the brakes and was down to seventy, the speed limit, by the time they passed the California Highway Patrol car behind the overhead abutment. He and Mardigian laughed.

"If they ever get these things on the market," Dan said, "they'll put police forces all over the country out of business."

"No, they'll still get bribes," Mardigian replied, as the Corvette curved around the Freeway exit and went down to Highway 1 in Santa Monica. "At least I hope they do. Armenians bribe policemen on five continents."

A few minutes later, Mardigian tapped Dan on the shoulder and pointed. Flying along out over the ocean was a Bell Jetranger helicopter. It banked inland toward Dan's car until he and Mardigian could see arms waving. They waved, too, and the helicopter returned to its course in the direction of Point Doom.

"You're going to love it out here, Mardigian."

Dan's friend, Prince Harij, had asked whether Dan could give Mardigian a ride out to the party. At first Dan had been surprised. The Arabs whom Dan knew usually had time only for the wealthy and privileged.

"You been out here before, Mardigian?"

"No, never."

Dan had been to the Prince's beach house only once, for a religious feast, but the party he and Mardigian were to attend thankfully had nothing to do with religion. It was a birthday celebration for another Arab classmate, Sheik Ali Buson Halifa.

Dan turned off Highway 1. He drove down a curving canyon road, which slowly straightened and elevated to a cliff along the beach. A mile down the road, they came to a tall, thick oleander hedge. As the Corvette slowed down to turn at the gate, Dan and Mardigian could hear the whistle-ping of the helicopter rotors idling nearby.

An Arab in Levis and T-shirt opened the iron gate. The driveway led to a gleaming-white wood-and-glass "bungalow" overlooking the sea. Rolls-Royces and Ferraris were parked around the courtyard. Dan smiled to himself; not one Mercedes. He pulled in behind a yellow Ferrari, which he presumed had about sixteen coats of hand-rubbed lacquer.

As they walked up to the front door, Dan wondered whether Mardigian could really smell desire. Dan wasn't sure what his desire was at that moment, but he was sure it was intense.

The front door was covered in gilt with a line of Arabic script. As they approached, the door was opened by an Arab in a white kaftan, who smiled mischievously. The house, an old movie star's retreat, had been purchased by Prince Harij when he arrived to attend the University of Southern California. Originally a Beverly Hills designer's idea of a Cape Cod cottage, it had been gutted and turned into a white fantasia with billowing floor-to-ceiling drapes, wall-to-wall carpets, silk wall coverings, chrome appointments, and white leather furniture. In deference to the building's previous style, Prince Harij had named his estate "Moby Dick."

Dan and Mardigian strolled through the living room. Most of the party had gathered on a wide deck overlooking the beach. The guests were dressed in the California manner of casually explicit sex and money. There were numerous Arab men, but no Arab women.

The whistle-ping of the helicopter was slowing down. Forgetting Mardigian, Dan walked over to see what was going on. He noticed at one end of the deck a lamb being spit-roasted, and at the other, a lavish buffet.

Down on the beach, about fifty yards away, Prince Harij was standing with a group of friends, watching six cheerleaders with U.S.C. pom-poms perform an intricate routine. They were stark naked.

Dan knew they weren't real cheerleaders, but they were doing a good imitation. He saw that their cheerleading outfits, which must have been discarded earlier in their routine, were lying all over the sand.

The Arabs watched with appreciative bemusement. Prince Harij and the Sheik occasionally glanced up at the guests on the deck, recognized someone and waved. As a finale, the cheerleaders constructed a human pyramid on their hands and knees, then collapsed, shrieking and laughing, in the sand.

On the deck, the guests applauded and shouted their approval, but Dan was watching the Arabs on the beach. The Sheik and Prince Harij turned to each other, laughed, then started to walk toward the funicular that would bring them up to the house. They never looked back at the girls, who went running around the beach trying to sort out their outfits.

Dan was impressed by the Arab's cool. All his life he and his friends had lived with the famous Fitzgerald quote: "The rich are different than you and me." Dan remembered the day one of his richest friends had said to him, "Goddammit, what's *different* than you and me, man, are these Arab *mothers!*"

Across the deck, Dan saw some of his fraternity brothers coming on to a starlet. He wondered where the cheerleaders came from, and whether they'd be staying for the party. He glanced down at the beach and saw the six girls waiting to ride up in the funicular. They were no more than high-school age. Then it occurred to Dan why Mardigian had been invited to the party. He probably had trucked them in from Fresno.

Prince Harij and the Sheik had arrived on the deck, and the Prince was introducing a few selected friends to his guest of honor. None of the other guests approached the pair, so Dan resolved to wait his turn. He had learned something about diplomacy at home.

The Arabs greeted the Sheik with a salaam; with Westerners, he shook hands. Dan watched as one girl, in pants and diaphanous blouse, curtsied to the Sheik, obviously to bobble her breasts at him. The Sheik appeared not to notice.

At the same moment, Prince Harij saw Dan, smiled, and whispered briefly to the Sheik. Sheik Ali Buson Halifa glanced up, the courteous smile on his face changing to one of interest as Prince Harij escorted Dan over to the Sheik.

"Ah, Dan, how good of you to come. I want you to meet my friend. Have you met him before on campus?" The Prince spoke with the mixed precision of having learned English as a child from English tutors.

"No, and I'm afraid I didn't bring a birthday present."

The Prince laughed. "Of course you did. You brought yourself. Come."

The introduction was brief. The Sheik held out his hand to be grasped rather than shaken, then turned back to his friends.

Dan felt dismissed and walked away across the deck.

"Congratulations." Mardigian had appeared at Dan's side.

"What for?"

"They honored you."

Dan chuckled. "Really? I'd say they just dumped all over me, holding his hand out like I should kiss it."

"No, you were summoned."

"What the hell's that mean?"

"No one else was asked to approach. The Prince and the Sheik went to whoever pleased them. But the Prince was sent to get you."

Dan knew enough diplomacy to know that a little wiggle could be of importance in some other culture.

"Why me?" he asked.

Mardigian shrugged. "Maybe you'll find out, later."

"How come you know so much about Arabs?"

"My grandmother lived in Syria and Iraq, my grandfather in Persia. Then they came to America."

Dan chuckled. "And they chose to go to *Fresno*?"

"Fresno is a long way from the Turks." Under the smile Mardigian's words were bitter, but Dan wasn't interested in politics. He smiled suggestively. "Mardigian, did you get those girls here?"

Mardigian shrugged modestly.

"You little pimp, I knew it was you." Dan laid an arm on Mardigian's shoulder, a gesture he often used to impress smaller men. Since high school, Dan had developed his forearms with hand grips and weights. He had worked on the rest of his body as well, but he specialized on the forearms, because in high-school football, he used the flat side of his arm to smash into somebody's face while blocking. At college, Dan had no intention of playing ball, but he wanted his forearms to look big in the pushed-up sleeves of his sweaters. His slablike arm dropping on someone's shoulder gave an intimidating suggestion, and Dan enjoyed that.

Mardigian smiled as Dan grabbed his neck affectionately and pulled him along to the buffet table. "Ain't going to get too many

194

converts to Islam around here," Dan said, looking at the fruit punches. "Next time, we'll bring a flask."

As the sun set, torches were lit around the deck. The lamb was carved, and dancing began.

The cheerleaders were a continuing success. One of the girls went plunging into a knot of Arabs, hugging herself with her arms under her breasts, cocking her pelvis from one hip to the other, drawing attention to her long legs.

Dan had as good a time as possible, considering that it was a party without beer. He talked football with some classmates and put a hundred dollars on the next day's game. He ate a lot of caviar and lamb with more fruit juice, and he danced with several girls. Then the cheerleader with the especially long legs walked over and said, "Hi."

"Hi," he said, looking at her face for the first time. She was pretty, he thought, with big dewy eyes like Loretta Young, and cheeks as round and defined as her buttocks. Her hair was short and blond.

"You're Dan Faulkner, aren't you?" she asked.

"How'd you know?"

"I've heard about you."

"All the way up in Fresno?"

"How'd you know I was from Fresno?" She put her hands on her hips.

"Probably the same way you know about me."

"Some Arab guys over there told me about you."

"What did they tell you?"

"Oh, just some things."

"Well, did you like them?"

"Oh. Sure, I guess."

As she looked down self-consciously at her breasts Dan dropped his arm on her shoulder.

"What are you looking at?" Dan asked as he moved his face in close to hers.

Her head snapped up. "Nothing."

"*Wrong,*" said Dan, indicating her breasts. "These are a few of my favorite things."

She laughed breathlessly, shaking her head. "You're too much."

"How do you know?"

"Too much, too fast. Do you want to dance? It'll give me a chance to catch up."

He grasped the back of her neck with his hand and led her to the dance area. The only light was from the torches; the music was Elvis Presley. Dan was an enthusiastic dancer, and for his size, he moved with considerable grace.

"I'll tell you a secret if you promise not to tell anyone else," she said after a while.

"Okay."

"I lost my panties down on the beach."

Dan quickly turned so that the cheerleader's back was toward the edge of the deck, assuring privacy. Ever since he was a kid, women had come on to him. He ran his hand down her back and slipped it underneath her brief skirt. He held one bare cheek and slipped his other hand down to grab the second, rocking her back and forth on his hip. The cheerleader put her arms around his neck and began taking quick, short breaths as she arched her back.

"Dan, my friend." Prince Harij was standing beside them with another Arab, waiting for Dan's attention. Breathing hard, Dan and the cheerleader disentangled themselves.

"Sheik Ali and I have something we'd like to talk to you about. Would you join us?"

"Let's go," Dan said, and without looking back, left the cheerleader.

The Arab led the way into the house, through the living room and into a candle-lit study. The tables were glass on chrome pedestals; the floor was white granite. As they entered, the Prince spoke to Dan of the pleasures of beach life. Dan barely listened as they sat on a long curved couch. Then he heard Mardigian's familiar voice. The Armenian was talking with careful deference to the Sheik. The Sheik looked over, and Prince Harij and Dan moved over to the center curve of the couch where they could talk.

For a while they talked about football, about surfing, about the best surfboards. Dan knew a man who hand-made surfboards in Santa Barbara. The Sheik knew a man who made them by hand in Capetown. The Sheik spoke about shooting quail in South Carolina, and Dan told of shooting dove in Arizona. The houseboy standing behind the couch poured tea. Very pleasant, Dan thought, but it wasn't why they had asked him in.

"Dan, there is something we've been trying to find out," the Prince said at last, "and we're convinced you're the person who can help us." The Sheik concentrated on his tea, but the other Arabs were watching Dan intently.

"What's that?"

"Airplanes."

Dan felt annoyed. The Arabs obviously wanted a Faulkner Execujet or two and didn't want to wait the necessary two years for their order.

Bored, Dan replied, "Listen, I'd like to help, but I don't have too much pull over at Faulkner Aerospace."

"Yes, we know," Prince Harij said, smiling sympathetically.

Dan didn't like the reply or its tone.

"But Dan, we are not necessarily interested in Faulkner planes," Prince Harij continued. "We would never consider asking you to influence your father's company."

"We all have fathers," the Sheik chuckled knowingly.

"We *sure* do," the Prince said, proud of the colloquial phrase. "Dan, our fathers want airplanes, too, but so far they have been unsuccessful in getting what they want. If possible, we would like to impress them with what we have learned in America, make them proud that our schooling has been successful." The remark brought laughter from the other Arabs.

Dan watched without smiling. "How many planes are we talking about?"

"Between twenty and thirty," Prince Harij said.

Holy shit, Dan thought. "What kind of aircraft are you looking for?"

Prince Harij paused a moment, then answered, "Tactical fighters, providing an emphasis on counterinsurgency, and secondarily, interception, with an ordnance capacity to fulfill its various missions, including, if possible, miniguns, white phosphorus bombs, cluster canisters, and rocket pods. Missiles, either air-intercept or air-to-ground, are a consideration, but not primary, in this *first* order . . ."

The Prince spoke the last phrase very carefully. Dan heard it, and knew the Prince had done his homework.

"Sounds to me like you ought to be talking to the Pentagon.

197

Those guys are so hot to sell, for the right money, they'll give you Air Force One."

The Sheik answered quickly but precisely. "That is why we wish to discuss our needs with you, because we do not wish to deal with the Pentagon. Too much attention would be directed at such a sale, and too much time wasted working through their bureaucracy."

"Dan, we wish to buy American planes, but not from America," Prince Harij continued. "If our fathers want to buy them from us, we will oblige. If not, then we will sell them elsewhere. We hope you can help us."

"Well, thanks a lot, but damned if I see how," Dan said. "It's hard to move twenty or thirty planes around without making a lot of noise, even if you can find them."

Prince Harij smiled and said, "We've found them, Dan." He turned to Mardigian. "Haven't we, Al?"

Mardigian looked up for the first time and shrugged modestly.

Dan was astonished that Mardigian was already in on the deal. He thought Al was the procurer of little bimbos, not big deals.

"Tell Dan what you've found."

Mardigian continued to look submissively at the floor. "When the German Bundesluftwaffe first rearmed itself in the fifties," he began, "they bought among other things, four hundred and seventy-two F-86 Sabre Jets, most of them built in Canada under license from North American Aviation. Since then, the Germans have been replacing them with newer aircraft, and they're eager to sell some of the old jets. I believe we could get twenty or thirty planes from them."

"Who's 'we'?" Dan asked. He was angry. Mardigian had never mentioned airplanes to him. Still Mardigian didn't look up. The unpleasant silence was broken quickly by Prince Harij.

" 'We' is all of us, Dan, but only if you're agreeable. If you're not, we'll try to find another way. We could go through established arms brokers such as Merex in Bonn, or Interarms, but we would prefer you and Al to handle the deal, if you choose to." Dan was still looking at Mardigian. The Prince continued, "It could prove to be quite lucrative, perhaps an alternative to working for your father—should you wish such a choice."

Dan's head jerked around; he saw the Prince was playing no

games. The Arabs were the sons of powerful fathers and they knew the costs of independence.

"What kind of money are we talking about?" Dan asked. He saw Sheik Ali Buson smile as he drank his tea.

"The unit price of the F-86K Sabre Jet in 1959 was two hundred and thirty-two thousand dollars," said Prince Harij. "You would be sold aircraft that are probably eight to ten years older. Al says that Germany will sell them for seventy-five thousand each. We will pay you one hundred thousand each for the first twenty, and a hundred ten thousand each for the next ten if you can get them. We, of course, will sell them to our fathers for twice that. There would be a profit to your company of, let me see—"

"Five hundred thousand for twenty units," Mardigian offered, "eight hundred fifty thousand for the thirty."

"What company?" Dan almost yelled at Mardigian, who finally looked directly at him and smiled.

"Dan, I've set up a holding corporation in Liechtenstein with offices in Bonn and Zurich, all just on paper of course. The incorporation papers still have the name of the president blank. I am named as the executive vice-president. There is no way I can do this alone. I know that. When you've had time to think about it, you'll know that you *could* do it alone." Mardigian smiled carefully. "But by then, I hope I'll be invaluable to you."

The Arabs laughed and turned to look at Dan. He was about to tell them all to go fuck themselves. They got me out here to use me, just like Mardigian's dumb cheerleaders! he thought, but he was curious. There was a lot of money at stake.

"What about pilots?" he asked.

Prince Harij answered. "The United States will train any friendly country's pilots for a price under the International Military Education and Training Program. There will be no problem with pilots or components or technological training, particularly if we have American aircraft."

"And what about end-use papers?" asked Dan, surprised by how much the Arabs knew. "Anything military with 'Made in USA' on it is tied up by a little law called the Foreign Assistance Act."

"Dan, this is where we need you," Prince Harij said, lounging

199

back in the couch. "We have the money to buy the planes, Al has the strategy to do it, but we need you to bring it off. End-use papers go to the State Department, the Office of Munitions Control, *not* the Pentagon. The State Department has never been able to enforce punishment, and they are less influential with the Congress than the Department of Defense. Besides, we have Canada and Germany between us and the original transaction with the U.S. government. I'm sure that the State Department would very much enjoy having a friend named Faulkner who might be able to help them in the future, just as the Pentagon has your father. They would probably do you the favor."

"I don't like using his name," Dan interrupted.

Prince Harij didn't hesitate. "It's your name as much as his. And Dan, do not mistake this as an insult directed at your father or yourself, but only as a family truth. Perhaps the name is more completely yours than his."

Only one person outside of his own family, Dan remembered, had ever referred to Buck Faulkner's being adopted, and Dan had beaten him senseless. The truth of what the Prince said, however, pleased Dan inordinately.

"You see, Dan," Prince Harij continued, "much of this business depends on influence. You know that. And your father knows that. Influence is not only money, but knowing who will take it, and where it best should go. Such contacts can take a lifetime to establish. But a certain name, or a title, can bring about instant recognition and results. The West Germans would find it difficult to sell to Al Mardigian. It will be easier for them to sell to the son of a man whose planes flew into Berlin in 1948, and who has supplied their Airforce for so many years. Dan, our fathers give us our names, but we owe them nothing for using it. Who knows? Perhaps we will use it better, if it is Allah's wish."

Carefully, Dan said, "How are we going to start this thing?"

"It's already started. We've put fifty thousand dollars into a numbered account in Zurich as a loan to your company against future commissions. Contracts have been drawn with several blanks. When the money is needed for purchase, it will be forwarded immediately by our banks in London and Bahrain. All that's required is for you to make your decision, Dan."

For a moment, there was silence. Then Dan smiled; the Arabs smiled, and Dan stood up and shook hands with the Prince.

"Thanks for the party. Sheik Ali, happy birthday. I'm pleased to meet you. Forgive us if we leave. Mardigian and I have some blanks to fill in."

Dan dropped his arm around Mardigian's neck and led him out of the study to the front door.

As the Arab in the white kaftan opened the door for them, Dan squeezed Mardigian's neck hard.

"Listen, Al, don't ever set me up like this again. I'm not one of your cunts. *I'll* use my name but don't *you* ever do it."

Mardigian was hurting but managed to nod. Dan let him go, and they walked down the driveway to the Corvette.

"Dan, I think we can get the Sabres from the Germans for fifty thousand each." Dan turned to look at Mardigian, who smiled modestly and shrugged.

"You little pimp," Dan laughed. The profits would be double.

19

"It's strange to interview a legend," the journalist said, as he started a new reel on his tape recorder.

"A legend sounds like a dead man," Buck replied. "I'm just a businessman. The rest comes from the publicity department." He looked across the room to Sam Priest, who sat in suede splendor, feigning boredom and not missing a word.

" '*Just* a businessman'?" the journalist prodded. "You also have to be a diplomat, an economist, and even a spook. Your network has to rival the C.I.A."

Buck sat back in his chair and took a deep breath. Was it really worth the trouble of telling his story once again? Just to get on the cover of a magazine? Yes, at the moment it was. Congressmen read the magazine, or at least they looked at the pictures.

Over his marble-topped desk, which another journalist had likened to a landing deck, Buck paused. Raven watched from a couch off to the side. Buck wanted Raven to know every facet of the business, and dealing with the press was an important one. Buck believed in treating journalists like customers: just give them what they want. The trick was to make them want what he had to give.

The journalist continued. "Wouldn't you say the relationship between the Pentagon and the aerospace industry has become rather chummy? I refer not only to the increasing number of retired senior officers on your payroll, but to the Deputy Assistant Secretary of Defense with his international sales team."

"Why should I criticize anyone who helps me sell a plane, either here or abroad?"

"The United States is arming the world—"

"If we didn't, someone else would. The world wants to be armed, and it's better for us to do the job than anyone else, both economically and defensively. We create a lot of jobs selling airplanes; it helps immeasurably with the balance of payments."

"Then you admit that our defense policy is based on more than defense? Something like an extension of the American empire?"

Buck scoffed. " 'American empire?' Who's the emperor?"

"American business."

"Nonsense."

"Wouldn't you call Faulkner Aerospace a small empire? We don't have to guess who's the emperor, or who will succeed you." The journalist shot a quick smile at Raven, who did not return it. The journalist went back to his notes. "The Pentagon gives you a billion dollars a year, and then exerts political pressure in every corner of the globe to sell your product. A pretty sweet deal."

"The Pentagon doesn't work for me. We work for them, and we have to work hard or the Pentagon will give our contracts to General Dynamics or McDonnell or Boeing. Some 'empire.' "

"Maybe just a military-industrial complex—"

"Listen, in 1946, when Eisenhower was a general, he stated quite clearly that private industry was better qualified than the military to supply and build advanced technology. He suggested a partnership. In 1961, he was a politician and denigrated it as a *complex*."

"You don't like politicians much, do you?"

Buck laughed, stood up, and walked around his desk to shake hands with the journalist, saying, "I'm afraid I have some people waiting." When their hands were clasped, the journalist said, "One last question. If you're selling armaments, you sell to anyone who can pay, don't you—no matter what they'll do or whose side they're on?"

Buck held the hand and moved in close, looking down into the journalist's eyes.

"Are you going to caption my cover portrait with 'Merchant

of Death'?" He squeezed the journalist's hand a bit harder. "It won't be the truth, so say anything you want; I'm used to it." Buck picked up a model of the Raven from his desk. "This is who I am." He gestured out the window behind him as a C-1000 started down the runway of Faulkner Field. "And that's who I am. I don't have the luxury of making moral decisions about war and peace; go to Washington, or Harvard, for that."

He put the model back on his desk.

The journalist asked, "Will there be a war, Mr. Faulkner?"

"I pray not, but there's always been a next war, hasn't there? I look forward to reading your article." He smiled as Sam followed the journalist out and closed the door.

"Welcome to Faulkner Aerospace," Buck said as he walked across the office and sank down in an armchair next to Raven.

"You made it sound pretty good."

"I have to spend too much time these days doing that sort of thing. The problem is they take the truth and make news out of it."

Raven smiled. "Just as long as you know what the truth is."

"I do. And so will you." He returned Raven's smile. "I'm glad you're here. Was there anything I said that bothered you?"

Raven considered the question. "I didn't know you had such a clear picture of politicians."

Buck laughed. "Someday I'll tell you what I think of the military."

Raven saw his father had more to say and waited. "I got a report from our security people," he said, "about Melanie."

"Tell me everything."

"It seems Melanie pawned all of your things," Buck said.

The night that Melanie had left the Faulkner suite at the Carlyle Hotel, she had not gone shopping. Instead, she returned to Raven's apartment, where she packed her clothes and took Raven's stereo, television, tape recorder, and anything else that was valuable and portable. Then she disappeared.

"She stayed in a hotel for three days while she got a passport," Buck continued, "and then she flew to Athens, and from there to Tehran. She bought a one-way ticket. I presume she's visiting her father."

Raven nodded, "I wonder what he'll do when he hears about me."

"I doubt that he will," Buck replied. "I think the young lady enjoys her secrets."

"Did security find out what she meant about the twenty thousand?"

Buck shook his head.

"I guess that's that," Raven shrugged.

"Let's hope so."

They both smiled, then Buck stood up and walked to the window overlooking Faulkner Field. "Have you heard from Dan?" he asked.

"Not even a postcard."

"Neither have we," Buck said with considerable irritation.

"Isn't he still in Europe?" Raven asked.

"I presume so." Buck turned back and sat at his desk. "Now, what are your plans?" He obviously did not wish to discuss Dan any further.

"You tell me."

"I want you to go to classes at U.C.L.A. for two quarters, full time. Engineering, mainly, and some business. You can decide what other courses you need, and take them on your own time."

Raven scoffed. "My own time? When do I get some of that?"

Buck nodded, arching his brow.

The next day, Raven registered for classes at U.C.L.A. Two weeks after he moved into his apartment near Westwood Village, President Kennedy was shot in Dallas. For the next two days, Raven remained glued to his television set and, like half of America, was still watching when the assassin was shot in the arms of his own guards. The whole blood-splattered week filled Raven with a kind of hopelessness. His past convictions completely collapsed. He began to have nightmares of the watery-eyed man in the subway station. As the bone-handled knife punctured the man's chest, Raven would awaken, covered with sweat. Then he would get up and shower, or read, or go to the kitchen for milk. The rest of the night he slept with the lights on.

He was reading *Jane's All the World's Aircraft* one morning, when he heard a knock at his door. It was 4:15 A.M. When he opened the door, he was greeted by a uniformed chauffeur holding an envelope.

"Mr. Faulkner?" he asked, then he handed Raven the envelope.

The stationery was from the Connaught Hotel in London. The note read:

> Hey, big brother! Come with this guy.
> I need to see you. It's urgent.
>
> **D.**

"I'll get some clothes," Raven told the chauffeur. Raven hadn't seen his brother since the previous summer. Dan had gone to Europe on a whimsical search for culture, or so he told his parents. But when September came, Dan didn't come back, which caused Buck and Jennifer a good deal of anxiety, then anger. Dan wrote that he was having all of his credits transferred to Oxford, but Buck found out that his younger son was unknown to the university. Since then, there had been silence. Raven knew his parents had stopped any financial support in hopes that the need of money would force Dan home. The strategy hadn't worked.

The limousine which Dan had sent for Raven was enormous. As he sat back in the plush seat, Raven remembered how impressed Dan had always been by big cars.

Raven was driven across Los Angeles to the Hawthorne Airport, the largest airport for private aircraft in the world. It shared its runways with the Northrop Corporation. The limousine paused at the gates, then drove directly onto the apron and up to an old Martin P5M-2 Marlin seaplane.

As Raven got out of the car, Dan jumped down from the craft's loading hatch. Raven smiled at Dan's dress; he was wearing a tailored English suit. It fit him perfectly, but somehow Dan was not made to fit a suit.

"Hey, Big Brother, how you doing?" Dan said expansively.

Raven smiled and shook his brother's hand. "How elegant you look at five in the morning."

Dan shrugged. "Savile Row suits me," he laughed.

"And staying at the Connaught?" Raven added.

Dan laughed. "Listen, want to go down to Acapulco with me? We'll get there in time for lunch."

"Wish I could, but I have classes."

"Cut 'em."

"I can't."

Dan smiled unpleasantly and laid his arm on his brother's shoulder. "You mean D.O.D. would kick your ass. Dear Old Dad, he knows what he wants, doesn't he?"

Raven wanted to avoid an argument. He shrugged and changed the subject. "What are you doing with the Marlin?"

"Remember the seaplane Dad used for our first flying lesson?" he asked.

"Our first and only," Raven scoffed.

"We hit that submerged log, and he busted his nose, blood all over the goddam cockpit." They began walking over to Dan's plane.

"And Sam Priest swearing us to secrecy so the world would never know that Buck Faulkner cracked up his own plane." Raven shook his head.

"And Mother refusing to let us go again."

"After that, I didn't mind."

"Look, Raven, I've got to talk to you. Come on down there with me. We'll spend the night and have some fun. I promise you, I'll get you back by tomorrow."

"Can't we talk here?"

"Sometimes you can be dumber than shit, you know that, Raven? If you come, I'll cut you in on something big. You won't even need to go to school."

"I can't, but tell me about it."

Dan gave up, looked toward the plane disgustedly. "Okay, come on. I don't want anyone listening."

Raven didn't see how anyone would hear them. The chauffeur was back in the car; the plane's crew was waiting in the cockpit. Nevertheless, Dan strolled down the taxiway in the direction of the Northrop hangars.

"Do Mother and Dad know anything about what's happened to me yet?" Dan asked.

"Just that you're not a student at Oxford."

Dan laughed and nodded. "You bet your ass I'm not, and I'm not about to be. Well, listen—and I'd rather you tell them, than the State Department or some government asshole. I started a business." He paused to see Raven's reaction.

Raven nodded. "I'll tell them."

Realizing Raven was not going to ask for details even if he were curious, Dan said, "You fucking bastard, some day you'll beg to know what I'm doing."

Surprised at Dan's intensity, Raven looked at his brother. "What's that supposed to mean?"

"You figure it out. In the meantime, tell D.O.D. that my company, Onager Limited, put through the sale of thirty West German Sabre jets to some schoolmates of mine in the Middle East. My partner and I have options on ten more deals; we're filling contracts for just about any weapon you can name. Last week, I became a millionaire." He checked to see Raven's reaction.

"Congratulations," Raven said neutrally.

"Thanks," Dan replied, accepting more than was given.

"What's 'Onager' stand for?" Raven asked.

"Two things: it's the name of a medieval war machine for throwing stones, and it's a wild desert mule found in Asia. My partner's an Armenian." He laughed. "Listen, Big Brother, this guy's smart and ambitious. In fact, he's so damned ambitious I can't turn my back on him. I don't trust him, which makes it nice that I control the company. He does most of the work, but I come in and make the deal happen. Shit, I can't tell you how much the name Faulkner does in an arms deal."

"It always has," Raven observed.

"Yeah, but goddammit, it's more our name than his, right?"

Raven stared at his brother a moment. "You have any other messages for me to deliver?"

"No. Just one for you. I want you to come into Onager as my partner."

Raven was always on guard against Dan's many surprises, but he was totally unprepared for that one. He could only ask, "Why?"

"You piss me off; you always have. You're uptight and stubborn and screwed up with some pretty weird ideas. But I know I can trust you, and two Faulkners working this business could probably sew up the whole goddamm world. Big Brother, there's more market out there than Faulkner or the whole damn Pentagon can supply. You don't need to go to any more classes. You can be a millionaire next month! There's no end to this business. You get on that plane with me and I'll show you how simple it is, and I'm just delivering chicken shit."

Raven looked back at the Marlin. "Chicken shit?"

"Yeah. Ten thousand Mannlicher-Carcano rifles, the same kind that Oswald used to kill Kennedy. My partner set this up. He bought them for next to nothing from Adam Consolidated, the importer, who couldn't sell them after the assassination. We've already unloaded seventy thousand of them all over the world. These are going to a Filipino who's meeting us with a boat twenty miles off the coast of Mazatlan. We splash down there to unload and he pays us cash, forty dollars apiece. He'll sell them in Hong Kong for seventy-five to gun collectors—guys who like to show them off. You know, 'This is like the Luger that Goering used, this Thompson is like Al Capone's, and this Mannlicher-Carcano is like the one that blew Kennedy's brains all over Dallas.' The Filipino is going to make a fortune."

"Dan—"Raven started.

"So we make thirty dollars on each gun, minus expenses, the plane charter, crew. On the ten thousand rifles we'll net a quarter of a million. And that's hardly worth my time. I only came along to see you." Affecting a casual air, Dan looked off toward the Marlin.

"Dan, I appreciate your offer, but I can't do it."

"Sure you can," Dan said quickly. He waited, then his voice grew vicious. "What you mean is, you *won't*. And you want to know why? Because you're Buck Faulkner's *boy*. And everyone falls down on the ground when they hear 'Raven.' "

"Look, the name wasn't my idea, and you're Buck Faulkner's son, too."

"Bullshit. I've walked away. I don't report to anybody for anything." Again, he paused, waiting for an answer.

Finally, Raven shrugged and said, "You have your way, I have mine."

"Well, shit on you," Dan said. "On you and D.O.D. I don't need either one of you." He started walking back to the seaplane. "You just have to be a saint or something, don't you, Raven?"

"Yeah, just like you, Dan," Raven retorted, "making a few bucks on weapons and airplanes."

Dan's eyes narrowed. "Don't give me any of your moralistic bullshit. In case you haven't heard, Big Brother, there's no airplane business any more. It's armaments, pure and simple. You're working for the Department of Defense, and so is Buck Faulkner. He's got puppet strings all over him and he knows it. Hell, I'm just selling antiques and souvenirs. But nobody's telling me how. You're providing transport for napalm canisters, pretty heavy stuff for a *pacifist*." He spat out the word and continued, "But don't worry; it's legitimate and patriotic, so you can stay as self-righteous as ever." Without warning, he slapped Raven hard across the face.

Raven hesitated out of habit and surprise. Dan slapped him again harder. Raven grabbed his arm, yanked it, and sent Dan tumbling onto the concrete.

On his hands and knees, Dan shouted, "Son of a bitch, you tore my suit." He got up and lurched back toward Raven.

Raven backed off. "Dan, don't be stupid."

"Mother isn't here to save your ass this time." He swung with a closed fist and caught Raven's face. Raven nearly fell as he pivoted and swung up into Dan's stomach. Then he swung again at his descending chin, and kicked him in the ass which sent him sprawling again on the concrete. Again the suit tore.

"Shit," Dan said getting up. "Well, welcome to the real world, Big Brother." Dan threw another punch. Raven tried to block it, but Dan had power behind it and it found its mark. Raven staggered; Dan charged in, and punched twice into Raven's gut. Raven wrapped his arm around Dan's neck and held his head straight, punching it repeatedly until Dan's hold on him fell away.

Breathing hard, the two brothers stood facing each other. Blood dripped from Dan's nose and trickled from a gash on Raven's lip.

"We'll finish this another time," Dan said.

"Let's forget it," Raven replied.

"Why? I feel like I finally have a brother." Dan feigned a laugh.

"Don't depend on it. All I feel is that I'm as stupid as you are."

"I'll be seeing you," Dan said.

"Thanks for the offer," Raven offered.

"Anytime," Dan replied condescendingly.

210

The pilot was waiting, and Dan signaled him. Immediately, the starboard engine began to turn over.

"Say hello to Mom."

"I just thought of something. You have about five letters waiting at home from the Selective Service System. If you're not a registered student, you and your partner might already be drafted."

Dan laughed. "Tear them up for me. I'll tell you another secret you can pass on to Dad before he hears it from Washington. Just before the end of school last year, Mardigian and I were asked by one of our professors for Christ's sake, to work for the C.I.A. We've already taken our tests. You can bet your ass it'll be a hell of a lot better than the Infantry." He smiled to make a joke out of it. "Of course, it's not as good as having flat feet."

"Have fun in Acapulco," Raven said, wiping his lip.

Dan nodded and said, "You dumb bastard." Then he turned and climbed aboard the Marlin. Raven walked to the limousine and was driven back to his apartment.

For the first time in his life, Raven envied Dan. Dan knew what he was doing, and he didn't care.

20

The day that the Gulf of Tonkin resolution passed the Senate, Raven participated in a demonstration against the Vietnam War on the U.C.L.A. campus. He was drawn by nostalgia more than by conviction. With forty others, he burned his draft card, even though it read "4-F"; within minutes, he felt ridiculous and hypocritical. He was working part time, building military transports.

At Faulkner Field, Raven seldom saw his father. For the first two months, he was a floater on the assembly line for the C-1000 transport and worked on every part of the plane. He made some friends, despite the obsequious attention from his supervisors, and he learned the twenty-four-hour-a-day routine of building an airplane.

Raven observed the workers' devotion to the company and their innocent pride in its product. Although many of them had received pink slips over the years, they blamed their layoffs on "milksop politicians" or "the screwed-up economy." They never blamed Buck Faulkner; they knew he had fought for their jobs as hard as he had fought their union, and their respect for Mr. Faulkner included his son.

After several months, Raven was shifted from the plant floor to the design section. Working out of the chief engineer's office, he saw the development plans for "ten years down the tube," as the chief designer called the future.

Raven worked hard, and boned up on avionics, specifications, payloads, military armor, and ordnance. Late in 1965, he was assigned to the "Mole Hill" in Ajo, where the research-and-development team instructed him on missiles, electronic countermeasure pods, fire-control radar, pilots' head-up displays, and computer signal processors for the SwordDancer fighter that Faulkner Aerospace was building for the Navy.

Raven was working with two engineers on the problems of azimuth, the horizontal deviation of a missile's bearing. As they were theorizing how such a path could be projected by computer on a head-up display, an armed security officer approached and asked Raven to follow him outside. Raven found a waiting jeep, which drove him out to the end of the main runway. After several minutes, a Faulkner Execujet landed. The door of the plane opened and a steward welcomed Raven aboard, asked if he would like a drink, then escorted him inside the cabin to a seat in the rear.

Jennifer was seated in the forward armchair. She welcomed him with a kiss. Behind her, at a conference table strewn with graphs and charts, Buck was speaking with two Air Force generals. One was retired and worked at Faulkner Aerospace, the other was still on active duty at the Pentagon. With them were two vice-presidents of Faulkner, the controller, and the plant manager of the New Mexico facility. When he saw Raven, Buck nodded and continued the discussion. Raven sat down across the aisle from Sam Priest, who was wracked with a frenzy of coughing.

"Hello, Sam. Are you all right?"

"Yeah, sure," Sam finally replied as the plane took off. "Happens every time I get into a pressurized cabin."

The steward appeared with Raven's beer.

"You know where we're going, Sam?"

Sam nodded. "Over to the Albuquerque plant. Seems the boys from the wild blue yonder want some SwordDancer fighter planes. General Llewellyn sent out his messenger boy to close the deal." With a nod, Sam indicated the Air Force general sitting with Buck.

Raven looked at his mother. "A Faulkner family production?" he asked, knowing her discomfort with the role in spite of her playing it to perfection.

She nodded. "How are you? I've missed you."

"I'm fine. Learning a lot. Too much, I expect," he said, returning her smile.

"Meaning?"

"How close we are to blowing up the planet."

Jennifer watched him carefully. "There seems to be an echo in the plane, from some time ago."

Raven shrugged. "Don't worry. But it's funny. The big breakthroughs at the Mole Hill are usually about how to knock off several million people a little more efficiently. Does it ever strike you as kind of insane, what we're doing?"

She nodded as she said, "But this is the world we live in."

"So I've heard." He watched her.

Sadly, she smiled again.

"Raven," Buck called from the conference table. Raven unfastened his seat belt and walked over to his father. "General Dulaney, may I present my son, Raven Faulkner. I'd like him to sit in on this, if he may."

The general enthusiastically shook Raven's hand. "With a name like that you won't ever need a security clearance." Raven tried to smile politely. The surface of the conference table was cherry wood with an inlaid map of the world.

General Dulaney pointed to Guam, Japan, Korea and South Vietnam. ". . . Our SwordDancers will go to the Fifth Air Force, be based at Kadena, Okinawa, Yokuta, Japan, and Osan, South Korea. The B-52s will be coming over from Guam. The SwordDancers will sortie here and take them in, flying interference."

"The SwordDancer can do that and have time to burn some jungle too," said General Campbell. Raven knew that the retired general was known around the Faulkner offices as "Fry Cook" Campbell, because of his proclivity for napalm. It was said that he had given Dow Chemical stock to his children as wedding presents.

"You're going to have to haul ass on this one, Buck," Dulaney said, taking charge again. "There are four hundred thousand men going over to 'Nam now, and another hundred thou will go next year. We can't have any production delays or cost overruns on this one. And God help us if one crashes."

"Don't crack your whip over me, General," Buck said. "The procurement cost we gave you on four hundred and ninety units will hold unless you cut back on us. You'll be getting a system that will last you twenty years, and you're not even paying for the R & D. The Navy did that on the prototype five years ago." The general repressed a smile as Buck continued. "For one million seven a plane, you're getting a damn good deal. I promise you, we'll make our production schedule. I think you'll be impressed with the determination over here in Albuquerque. Right, Sam?"

"Absolutely," Sam said with an edge to his voice.

"But Jim," Buck said, just loud enough to be heard, "you boys have made a big mistake letting Lockheed build your heavy transport, and I don't appreciate it."

General Dulaney smiled warily. "Buck, they came in with the lowest bid."

Buck shot back. "They were buying in. Lockheed knows that contract is too low, and so do you. They underbid Boeing by four hundred million, us by two hundred, and Douglas by one hundred. They came in at twenty-eight million a unit just to get the contract and you know it."

Dulaney didn't move. "Buck, we get our money from the President and Congress. Twenty-eight million looks better to them than fifty or sixty million in one lump. We may have to go back for more, but it'll be easier for the Congress to give more down the road. In the meantime, we got a go on a vital system."

"Are you telling me to 'buy in' on future bids?"

"I'm not telling you anything, Buck."

The two men were silent. Then Buck nodded and said, "We want your help on something."

In that moment Dulaney's role changed from U.S. general to job candidate. "What's that, Buck?"

"The SwordDancer is a great plane. We're going to sell a lot of them to you boys and the Navy. But not enough to keep our plants at full operation. Now, McNamara is currently wild about General Dynamics' F-111. But I can promise you, that plane is going to fall on its rear end. It's at least five *tons* overweight; it'll punch a hole in any carrier it lands on. All I'm asking is that when the F-111 flops—and it *will*—you and Llewellyn get to McNamara fast, and sell some SwordDancers. Over the next twenty years, I want to sell at least five thousand, and I'd like you to have a lot to do with it, Jim."

At the mention of the figure, Sam Priest started coughing again and left for the lavatory with a Vicks inhaler.

"If the SwordDancer does what I think it's going to do for the Air Force," General Dulaney said staunchly, "I'll be glad to recommend it to anyone, Buck."

Dulaney had been trained in accounting and understood the price of his future. Faulkner Aerospace paid retired military executives a full salary with perks, plus a part of the commission on aircraft sold. The general had three more years to retirement. They had just talked around two billion dollars worth of airplanes. One percent of each five million was fifty thousand dollars commission per plane. Dulaney was smiling as the Execujet made a three-point landing and taxied toward the plant's main hangar. The Faulkner Industrial Park was set in the middle of four square miles of fenced-in, guarded desert on the outskirts of Albuquerque. Sam Priest had done his job well. Ten F-99 SwordDancers in full armament were lined up on the tarmac. They bore U.S. Navy insignia and designations.

Another SwordDancer had been parked at the hangar. This one had been freshly painted with Air Force colors, insignia and designation numbers. The Execujet stopped, and the hatchway stairs descended to a red carpet, leading to a platform with a bank of microphones. Between the microphones and a crowd of over a thousand Faulkner employees was a roped-off area for the press and television crews.

Raven got up to follow the others. His father, mother and General Dulaney went first. Waiting on the red carpet were the mayor of Albuquerque and the local Congressman, William Howe Bucknell, heir apparent on the House Armed Services Committee. The crowd cheered. Buck held his arms open to acknowledge the workers, who responded enthusiastically.

As Raven watched the ceremony, he remembered how, twelve years before, his father had chosen New Mexico for the plant site. Since then, fifty million dollars had been pumped into the state's economy. Employment had soared and there was an annual payroll of seven million. Congressman Bucknell had progressed as surely as rich cream through Washington's corroded arteries of influence.

When the ceremony was over, Buck signaled for Jennifer and Raven to follow him into the Execujet. The other executives, including Sam Priest, did not join them at the conference table, which had been folded so that only half the world showed. Raven happened to be looking at Southeast Asia when his father said, "I'm sorry not to have given you any warning about this, Raven, but I'm sending you to Saigon."

"That's funny."

"Why?" Jennifer questioned.

"After fighting the draft for three years, here I am going to Vietnam." Neither his mother nor father smiled. "When?" Raven asked.

"Tomorrow morning at nine," Buck said. "There's a troop charter from LAX. I'll have a car pick you up at six-thirty."

"*Tomorrow*? Wait a minute, my clothes are in Ajo."

"By now your clothes are in Los Angeles. I had them packed and shipped. We're flying straight home. Your mother and I hope you'll have dinner with us."

"What's going on?" he asked his mother, but she didn't answer.

"For one thing," Buck said, "you've just been made a vice-president of the company, the youngest in our history. Congratulations."

"Thanks. I knew someone with influence."

"I've heard you've picked up on things pretty quickly. You've impressed some good people."

"Who's going to tell Buck Faulkner his son's a jerk?" he shrugged.

Buck sat back and gazed at Raven. "Look, until there's combat, all we have is war games and theory. Vietnam is the biggest weapons showcase since Korea. You'll see the state of the art. I want you to check out every plane in the air. Then let the Mole Hill know what you find."

"I'm not sure I know enough."

"You know enough and you can get into the right places."

"You mean just drop my name."

"You'll be amazed at its effect."

"I'm sure."

"Something wrong?"

"No, sir. This is what I asked for."

"I'd send someone else, but no one else has the unique qualification of being my son."

When Buck smiled, Raven said, "Oh, I'm not the only one—"

"You're the only one who's available," Buck said with some annoyance.

"Too bad," Raven scoffed. "I think he assumes the right to throw the family name around better than I'll ever be able to."

"What do you mean?" Jennifer said sharply.

Raven was confused by her reaction. "I mean, you know Dan."

Buck took Jennifer's hand and said, "That deal in Germany never would have gone through without Faulkner written on every contract."

She did not look at him. "It's his name, and he can do what he wants with it," she said emphatically.

"Mother, are you all right?"

"Of course I am. I'm worried about your going to Vietnam. Mothers do that."

"Raven, when you get to Vietnam, you'll be making contacts that could mean sales. To them, regardless of rank or title, you represent a lot of money. Part of your job is the careful manipulation of giving money away."

"If we have the best plane, why all the baroque intrigue?" said Raven doubtfully.

Buck sighed. "Raven, the SwordDancer *is* the best plane. You and I know that, but how does an outsider judge?"

"So we try and buy them."

Buck looked pained. "Thank God you didn't choose diplomacy."

"Come on, Father, what else can you call it?"

"I'd call it, a sharing," Buck replied. Jennifer's face grew tense.

Raven laughed. "*You're* the diplomat."

Buck looked at him a moment. "Moral extremes are not realities, Raven. People have needs. I'll give you an example. Bob Gross ran Lockheed for thirty years; he was a fine man. He needed to sell his F-104 Starfighter in Europe, just as we had to sell our F-103, so he contacted Prince Bernhard of the Netherlands, also a fine man. The Netherlands bought the Lockheed plane, not necessarily because of Prince Bernhard, but his influence didn't hurt. All Bob Gross provided was some money—an equitable exchange."

"How much?" Raven asked.

"From what I've heard, around a million. A Prince's favor is not had for nickels and dimes. A Lockheed Jetstar was requested, but cash seemed more discreet."

"He *asked* for a Jetstar?"

"Of course not. Various friends made the suggestion."

Raven looked at his mother. "Did you know all this?"

She nodded, but said nothing.

"If these 'gifts' are all so legitimate, why can't everybody know about them?" Raven asked.

"Prince Bernhardt deserved the money for services rendered. If he had been a businessman, he'd be making millions."

Raven smiled wryly. "Money gets pretty abstract on those levels."

"Yes, it does," Buck conceded. "Just recently, when Fokker, a Dutch aviation company, needed capital, Tom Jones had Northrop buy in for twenty percent. He won't make any money off the deal, but he did get a seat on the board of directors. And do you know who else is on the board of directors? Prince Bernhardt."

Raven glanced around the cabin. "I'm surprised Prince Bernhardt isn't here somewhere."

Buck smiled. "I work the other side of the tracks, where the politicians and the military are."

"I guess all that matters is who pays."

"Well, in the case of Prince Bernhardt, Lockheed paid," said Buck.

Jennifer looked away as Raven leaned over the conference table and said, "No, I mean who really pays it?"

"It's a corporate expense, Raven."

"But it's an unusual corporate expense," said Raven, "because it's a secret. Look, I'm not trying to blame anybody. I just want to understand what's going on. There's no point in secrets between us, is there?"

Jennifer said tersely, "What is it that you want to know, Raven?"

"Just the truth, that's all. I don't believe you've ever told me anything else, Mother."

His words startled her and she looked back at him apprehensively.

219

"All right," she said.

"Jennifer, just a minute," Buck interrupted.

"He wants to know."

"And we'll tell him anything *he asks,*" Buck replied insistently.

Raven was startled by the degree to which his parents seemed upset. It wasn't the first time he had pressed them with hard questions. He decided to continue.

"I presume we pay out under-the-table money just the way Lockheed did," he said. "A corporation can't afford to just give away that kind of money. If the amounts are added to the price of the plane, the unaware customer pays it. That means the taxpayers of the country which is buying. If the 'gift' isn't added to the price of the plane, it means that the money is taken out of the company's profits, and the stockholder pays it. Since neither the stockholder nor the taxpayer knows what's going on, it means their money is in truth stolen." Raven let the word hang in the air.

Jennifer quickly looked down to her lap where her hand was slowly smoothing out the wrinkles in her skirt.

"We're not thieves, Raven," Buck said with conviction. "We simply practice our trade as best we can."

Raven was silent. He noticed that his mother was more relaxed even though his own tone had been harsher. He felt he had missed something in the conversation. He thought back a moment and realized that she had first become upset when he alluded to family secrets. He decided there was no reason to upset her further.

"Look, let's forget it," he said. "I just want to understand this business; I'm not second-guessing or judging you." He smiled at his parents, but his mother went on smoothing her skirt.

A long silence followed, which was relieved only by the steward serving drinks. Finally, Buck began to tell Raven about some of the people he could depend on in the Far East.

After they landed in Los Angeles, Raven left them at their limousine and caught a cab to Westwood so that he could pack for his trip. He promised to join them in Palos Verdes for dinner.

As soon as they were alone Jennifer said to Buck, "I thought he knew."

"So did I. But he doesn't. I'm sure of that."

"We have to tell him, Buck. I don't want him to learn from somebody else. We've got to tell him soon."

"We will."

"When?"

"When the time is right."

She looked angry. "I warn you, I *hate* this lie between us. And now he's going off to Vietnam thinking we're thieves. What if something happens to him?"

"Nothing will. I have too many of our people alerted to watch after him. Raven will be fine. I don't think tonight is the right time to take so much away from him."

"What do you mean, 'take so much away'?"

"I mean losing his parents. No matter how much he loves us, he'd feel abandoned."

Jennifer watched as Buck turned to open his attaché case.

Jennifer took a deep breath. "You never consider how much we'd be giving him, by getting rid of this tormenting lie."

Buck looked sadly at Jennifer. "We'd be telling him that his adoptive father destroyed his mother—and had an affair with his half sister. Let me keep those particular torments for myself, Jennifer, at least for now. There'll be a time, I know that. But when that time comes, I'm afraid I'll lose him."

21

Two Air Force escorts welcomed Raven to Saigon, loaded his bags and drove him into town to the Hotel Caravelle. In his room, he flopped down on the bed and slept without interruption until 6:00 A.M., local time, the next morning. It was not until he was eating breakfast that he learned the Viet Cong had had a busy night shelling targets just across the pier and burning an American tanker right at its dock.

As soon as he had eaten, two men from the American Embassy called for him. As they walked out to the car, one of them shook Raven's hand, saying, "I'm Al Mardigian. Your brother's a friend of mine. Dan and I were in school together."

"Yes, he told me. You did graduate work together at the C.I.A., didn't you?"

Raven realized his indiscretion as the other man shot a quick glance at Mardigian, who ignored him. Apparently Mardigian did not regard Raven's comment as much of a secret.

"Forgive the early hour," he said, "but your father spoke to the Ambassador, and we were hustled into action by His Excellency himself."

Raven felt a familiar twinge of irritation. "Good lord."

"You're an important guest. Certain employees of the Hotel Caravelle who work for us are on twenty-four-hour alert."

"That's enough, Mardigian!" the other diplomat interrupted angrily.

"Don't be so naïve, Georgy," Mardigian responded with a

cutting smile. "You don't need to worry; your career is on its way. I can already see you as a Consul General in Chad." He chuckled.

"I'm sure it'll be better than where *you're* headed," Georgy replied huffily.

Mardigian smiled as he turned back to Raven. "Anyway, I'd presume you have good connections at the Hotel Caravelle, because they got a message through Tan Son Nhut to your old man's little backyard bungalow, where I understand he can listen to Brezhnev snore, if he wishes." Mardigian chuckled. The car continued to crawl through a bevy of military shuttle buses, trishaws, motor bikes and cars.

At the Embassy, Mardigian walked to the entrance with Raven and said, "All the Embassy's military are quivering to meet you. I have several messages: His Excellency, the Ambassador, sends his greetings, and that if there's anything you need in Saigon, just ask for him. The Faulkner representative in Tokyo, Mr. Miki, will be arriving tomorrow at three. Oh, yes, and your father would like to receive some word of your well-being." Although he smiled, Mardigian's eyes indicated a sly contempt.

"I'll send him a carrier pigeon," Raven said.

"Needless to say, if there's anything I can do to make your stay more enjoyable, I'm at your service."

"Have you heard from Dan?"

"Yes. He's in Bahrain. Doing very well."

Raven left Mardigian, and he had little intention of seeing him again.

Over the next six weeks Raven attended numerous Embassy functions, at which the American military was represented by members of M.A.C.V. (Military Assistance Command, Vietnam). At one such occasion, he heard an officer comment, "What we have over here is an escalating military stalemate." Raven asked the officer how a stalemate could escalate, but the officer was more interested in discussing a Faulkner missile system.

Most of Raven's time was spent with Faulkner's consultant from Tokyo, Toshiharu Miki. Trained as a *kamikaze* pilot just before the end of the war, Mr. Miki was imprisoned for three years during the American occupation and then educated at

Stanford University. By the 1950s, Miki's friends in Japan were no longer regarded as war criminals, but as staunch anti-Communists; many of them had survived both the war and imprisonment with extraordinary fortunes intact. When Toshiharu Miki returned to Japan, Faulkner Aircraft was his first public-relations client.

With Mr. Miki's guidance, Raven traveled extensively. His father had been right; Raven's name was an open-sesame. He visited forward fire bases, airfields and radar bases near the D.M.Z.

As a civilian, Raven was not allowed near the fire-fights, but he did go in when they were over. On one such trip, Raven flew in on a rescue helicopter for "mop-up." The action had taken place about four kilometers south of Da Nang, near Marble Mountain, where a squad of Marines had been ambushed. As Raven helped load the wounded, a rifle lying near one of the dead Viet Cong caught his eye. Attached to it was an infrared night sight developed at the Mole Hill and manufactured at a special Faulkner subsidiary plant in Carlsbad, California. The night sight was an advanced development and as yet had not been issued to the American armed forces, except to certain elite units, none of which were in Vietnam. The Viet Cong, therefore, could not have stolen it.

Raven asked the X.O. at the scene about the rifle and scope.

"Have you ever seen a scope like this before?" Raven insisted.

"No. But that doesn't mean a thing. The gooks steal more hardware from us than they get from the Russkies. We sure as hell don't ask them where they get it."

"I'd like to take it with me."

Aware of who Raven was and what levels of authority had gotten him there, the infantry officer said, "With the compliments of what's left of the 3rd Battalion, First Marines. And tell your Daddy if he has any more of those scopes to send them to us before the Rangers."

Raven sent the night sight back to California, only to learn by return cable that it apparently was part of a consignment of the night sights sold six months previously to Iran. Rather than search for an answer in Vietnam, Raven let the matter drop;

Faulkner's security section would start work on it.

Raven was looking forward to going home. On December 22, two days before the Christmas cease-fire and several hours before his scheduled departure, Raven had lunch with Mr. Miki and several Japanese journalists, whom he briefed on the various advantages of the SwordDancer.

After their guests had left, Mr. Miki interrupted a discussion of future plans and suddenly began discussing California oranges. Raven looked up to see Al Mardigian coming toward the table.

"I understand you're leaving and I wanted to say goodbye," he said. "I hope we meet again."

Raven didn't respond to the statement.

"Mr. Miki, this is Mr. Mardigian."

Mr. Miki uncharacteristically did not rise. He was looking off in the direction from where Mardigian had come as he said, "Mr. Mardigian and I have met."

"Yes, once," Mardigian said. 'I'm sorry I didn't see more of you, Raven. Maybe when we meet again. Oh yes, the night sight you were so curious about." He chuckled. "A thousand of them were sold legally to Iran. They were then given as a gift, not quite illegally, to the Moslem state of Burma. There they were stolen criminally, by the private army of a dope-smuggler of the Golden Triangle. He planned to trade them for safe passage through Thailand, but his donkey train was intercepted by Communist insurgents. As a result, the night sights were quickly dispatched to Hanoi." Mardigian looked extremely pleased with himself.

Raven did not respond to the information. "When *will* we meet again, Al?"

"Here or there. Mr. Miki," Mardigian nodded and left the patio.

Mr. Miki watched him. "Mr. Mardigian is walking a very tight wire," he said.

"He's a friend of my brother's."

"I doubt it. Such people cannot afford friends. Mr. Mardigian is a *business associate* of your brother's."

"*Was.*"

"*Is.* The company that they set up, Onager Limited, to move the F-86 Sabre Jets out of Germany to their Arab schoolmates was never dissolved. Your brother and Mr. Mardigian have been dealing in all kinds of armaments ever since."

"How could they? They're in the C.I.A.—Oh."

Mr. Miki smiled at Raven's sudden understanding.

"Precisely. An organization such as Onager is an extremely useful cover for the Agency's own covert buying and selling. However, I understand that Langley does not look kindly on its junior associates' greed. And apparently Onager is making a great deal of money. I met Mr. Mardigian in Indonesia at the home of Sukarno's buyer, Mr. Dassaad. I had some used F-103s to sell President Sukarno. Mr. Mardigian either underpriced the Lockheed planes he was selling, or he offered "Old Das' more baksheesh than I did. Of course, we'll never know. What concerns me is why Mr. Mardigian was lunching with a man who is known around this District as a Viet Cong agent. I wonder if Mardigian would be such a fool as to sell his wares to the Viet Cong."

"I don't think my brother would let him do that. Still, I wonder why he wanted me to know the story on the night sights."

Mr. Miki looked at Raven evenly. "Who knows? Earlier this year, your brother managed to sell American tanks to both sides in the Pakistani-India war."

"Does my father know that?"

"If I do, he does."

Raven nodded but said nothing. Mr. Miki took note of Raven's silent agitation and said, "In our business, we sell much more than aircraft or missile systems. We sell symbols. Your father is the most perspicacious of dealers. Such discernment, let us hope for your brother's sake, is inherited." Mr. Miki smiled and inclined his head deferentially. "This is a dangerous bazaar."

They said goodbye, and Raven went to pack. A bellhop knocked to say Raven's car had arrived. Raven left his last piasters on the dresser for the maid and gave the bellhop dollars at the curb. As he climbed in the back of the embassy car, he was already imagining being at home in Palos Verdes.

They moved slowly up the broad boulevard. New office buildings stood on either side, protected by sandbags and guarded by M.P.s. There were two million people in Saigon;

more were coming in every day hoping to avoid the battle zone. Raven watched the crowds and thought about how hopeless the situation was.

The driver turned sharply to the left off Cong Ly Boulevard. The other Vietnamese in the front seat turned around and stuck an American Colt .45 automatic through the opening between the seats. In a thick accent, he commanded, "Face on floor! Quick. Quick."

Raven slid down and crouched behind the front seat. A roll of wide adhesive tape was thrown in front of him.

"Tape eyes. Shut. Shut. Quick. Quick!"

22

It was night by the time the American Embassy realized that Raven was missing. Any kind of search was impractical until morning, but the Ambassador knew that he could not wait to notify the boy's father.

Buck was used to having his sleep interrupted, but as he listened to the terse cable, he felt a jolt of dread. As if sensing his alarm, Jennifer looked at him and said, "It's Raven."

"He's missing."

"Oh God. I knew something would happen." She got out of bed and covered her eyes with her hand.

"All they know is that he was picked up at his hotel by two Vietnamese in a stolen embassy car. He's been missing for seven hours."

"Who else has been notified?" Jennifer asked, trying to stop crying.

"Red rocket to the Pentagon."

Jennifer shook her head. "The press will have it in twenty-four hours. Oh God. Buck—" She reached out for him and they held each other.

Again, the emergency phone rang. General Llewellyn was on the line.

"Buck, I've already sent a message requesting more details. I'll call you back in a half hour. I'm leaving now for my office; I can get information to you faster from there."

Buck was moved by the general's concern and action. "Thanks, Jack."

"And tell Jennifer to hold on. Raven's still alive. If they'd wanted to kill him, we'd have found him by now. They want him alive, probably to show off during the cease-fire. As long as he's alive, you've got the whole military machine of the United States looking for him. I'll have more in a half hour."

Buck hung up. "I agree with him: the Viet Cong want to keep Raven alive, probably for the duration of the cease-fire. That's from today to the Tet New Year, January 31."

"Buck, we have to think what *we* can do," Jennifer said. "Over there, we can't depend on anyone. Oh, they'll all try for the glory of finding him, but we can do better on our own."

"I've already been thinking that," said Buck. "I can't stand waiting for cables. I'd better go over there."

Jennifer stared across the bedroom. "Do you see what's happening? We kidnapped him, and never told him. Now they've kidnapped him from us—"

"Jennifer, there's no connection."

"How can you be so sure?" she spat out, then shook her head. "I'm sorry."

Buck walked over and reached for her hand. "Come on," he said, "let's go to the kitchen. I'll make some coffee."

As promised, Jack Llewellyn called back in a half hour with more information. The stolen embassy car had been found with Raven's bags in the trunk. A few hours later a Polaroid picture of Raven had been delivered to Reuters.

"That means it's public now," Buck stated. "Jack, we haven't made any specific plans, but if this lasts, we'll want to get over there. Jennifer and I would appreciate whatever cooperation your office can provide."

"Any way I can be of help, Buck, I will. I doubt if there's much you can do over there. I'd try to talk you out of it, but I know I wouldn't have a chance with Jennifer. Just keep me posted on what your plans are."

When Buck hung up, he paced the room for a time. Perhaps the V.C. wanted money, he thought. Perhaps negotiation through Switzerland was possible. He wasn't on the best of terms with the State Department, who often resented his business dealings abroad. Nevertheless, he would call them. As he continued to make plans, he happened to glance down at the notes Jennifer was scheduling on a pad. At the bottom, one name was outlined in a rectangle: Jim Owen.

"He may be the best chance we have," she said.

Buck nodded. Owen knew the right people, and he had proved in the past that he could work with astonishing speed.

"His fee may have nothing to do with money," Buck said.

"We can afford whatever it is," Jennifer said flatly.

"Well, if Jack's right about the cease-fire, we have a little more than five weeks," Buck said.

"It was always going to end this way, Buck," Jennifer said, pushing her fingers back through her hair. "We were fools to think we could—"

He interrupted. "We weren't fools, and it's not going to end."

Jennifer stared at him a moment, then looked away. "Something's going to end."

Raven had been transferred, bound and gagged, from the stolen embassy car into a large wicker container and wheeled through the streets on a trishaw. The wicker container was carried up some stairs and dumped onto the floor. His captors stripped him and gave him native clothes to wear. He was fed twice a day with *xoi,* which was glutinous rice, or *ché thung,* a mix of beans, lotus seeds, noodles and duck eggs. Hearing street noises outside, Raven assumed the hut was one of the thousands of ramshackle structures on pilings above the city's canals that drained into the Saigon River. A quarter of a million people lived in such disease-infested dwellings, because buildings over the water were not taxed.

Each day, several people entered the room. Speaking in Vietnamese, they untied Raven and tore the tape off his face. Before his eyes could adjust, a copy of *Stars and Stripes* was stuck in his hands and a flash bulb went off. Afterward, his eyes were taped shut again, and he was shoved back into a corner bound and gagged. The camera was the only thing that gave Raven hope.

On the third day, Raven was dragged across the room and made to kneel. As his captors tore off the tape around his eyes, Raven heard sirens approaching and then men giving orders in English and Vietnamese.

Four of his captors stood with Kalashnikov AK-47 automatic weapons pointing at the entrance to the hut. Beside them, in easy reach, was a pile of American M-67 fragmentation hand grenades. Raven could see an opening in the floor. Below, water was slowly moving past. A Viet Cong soldier came and squatted directly behind him holding a colt .45 just inches from Raven's head. The soldier was about sixteen. He put his finger to his lips and said, "No talk."

From the streets, Raven could still hear orders given in Vietnamese and English. He watched his captors waiting opposite the door. If whatever was happening on the streets found its way to that door, they were going to die, either in a fire fight, a siege, or with their grenades. Raven decided his only chance was to lurch forward and fall through to the water. He made the move but the guard behind him caught the rope which bound him and jerked him back sprawling. One of the Viet Cong watching the door came swiftly across the room and smashed the butt of his AK-47 across Raven's temple. Raven collapsed, unconscious.

In Palos Verdes, Buck and Jennifer decided they could wait no longer. It was time to call Jim Owen.

"Get me Jim Owen in Tehran," Buck told the technician. "Do *not* announce who it is that's calling." Then he hung up.

When the phone buzzed, the technician said that he had Miss Owen on the line, but that Mr. Owen was out.

"Put her on," Buck said, "and mix the line."

Buck and Jennifer watched each other as the clicks of rerouting matched their phones with the one being held by Melanie Owen.

"Hello?" they heard her say.

"Melanie, this is Buck Faulkner. It's urgent that I speak to your father."

After a pause, Melanie laughed nervously and asked, "I'd been expecting Santa Claus; this is too much. Where are you?"

"Melanie, we have to speak to your father," Jennifer said. "Where can we reach him? It's a matter of life or death."

"Really? Whose?"

"Raven's," Jennifer responded, controlling herself.

They both were prepared for some nasty crack and were

231

surprised when Melanie said, "Oh shit. I'm sorry it's him. Well, listen, I hope you and Dad can get Raven out of whatever trouble you got him into. Speaking as an expert, he's sure the best part of the Faulkner family." Melanie laughed, then said abruptly, "Daddy's at a party at the Air Force military attaché's house; I don't know his name, but you can figure that out." She hung up before Buck could thank her. Moments later he had Jim Owen on the line.

"I need your help," Buck said.

"You must be pretty desperate," Owen replied. His tone had not mellowed over the years.

"I am. My son, Raven, has been kidnapped by the Viet Cong."

There was a silence during which Buck and Jennifer could hear someone singing a Christmas carol in the background. "Your *son,* Buck? You know, I didn't think I could ever feel pity for you, but recently I've had the luxury of getting to know my own offspring. When did it happen?"

"Two days ago. He was picked up in a stolen embassy—"

Jim interrupted. "Any contact from the V.C.?"

"Polaroid pictures, three so far, showing he's healthy—"

"City or countryside?"

"Intelligence seems to think he's still in Saigon."

"Too bad," Jim Owen said. "It'll be like looking for a needle in a haystack. I'd rather be looking for a needle in a jungle. I'll need some credit. Send half a million to the Royal Westminster Bank's branch in Bahrain, care of Mr. Echols. Also, put another half million in an account for me in Zurich and send the number to my office in Paris. What are your plans?"

"Jennifer and I are flying to Saigon at midnight."

"Which hotel?"

"Caravelle."

"I'll meet you there. Don't tell anyone I'm coming; I have my own Saigon contacts. If there's any change, particularly regarding Raven's location, tell your people to let me know immediately. They can reach me through this number, *not* at home. Jake will know where I am; Melanie won't."

"Can you tell us what you're going to do?"

"I don't trust telephones, even with your fancy mix-masters. The Shah is getting good at listening, mainly because I'm helping him. I'll see you in Saigon." The line disconnected.

Jennifer stood up shaking and said, "I'm going up to pack. Those two are vile."

Hoping her anger would detract from her fears, Buck followed her out of the room.

Someone kicked his foot. Raven put a hand to his head. It felt as if a nail had been driven through it, but it was bandaged, which meant they still wanted to keep him alive. Someone lifted him into a sitting position. Immediately, he vomited.

The trap door was open. It was dark out. The streets were quiet. The same five men were in the room. Two of them dragged Raven over to the trap door. He could see a sampan floating below.

One of the Viet Cong looked at his watch and whispered something to the others, then he went down through the trap door into the boat. The others waited. They seemed to be listening.

Raven wondered whether it was still Christmas Eve.

In the distance, about a mile away, there was an explosion. The sound seemed to be what the Viet Cong had been waiting for. Another guard slipped down through the trap door, while two of them put a rope around Raven's chest and under his arms. The fifth soldier poured gasoline from a five-gallon tank over the floor and walls. As he was lowered through the trap door, Raven saw that the stack of grenades was being left behind.

He vomited again. Pain cut through his head as the Viet Cong lowered him into the sampan and laid him under the mat roofing. The boat, gliding between the pilings, eased away into the crowded canal.

The last thing that Raven remembered was the shack exploding into a burning torch that set fire to the whole street. All over the city, sirens were sounding.

Buck and Jennifer were met by a heavily armored car at Tan Son Nhut airport and escorted into Saigon by three Military Police jeeps. Mr. Miki was waiting inside their suite at the Caravelle.

"What's going on, Tashiharu?" Buck asked. "Nobody would tell us anything."

"The Viet Cong have indicated their compliance with the

cease-fire by blowing up an American officers' compound. Your arrival seemed an obvious opportunity for them."

"Any word about Raven?" Jennifer asked tersely.

"The photographs have stopped coming, but they're still certain that Raven is alive."

Jennifer turned away.

"The Viet Cong expended a great deal of effort on both his kidnapping and the propaganda it is creating," Mr. Miki continued. "If they were to kill him, they would make certain that he was found dramatically."

Buck and Jennifer exchanged a look, then Buck said, "Who are we working with here, Tashiharu?"

"Everyone from the Ambassador to CINCPAC to the intelligence units. They're all eager to be of help."

"Let's start with the C.I.A.," said Buck. "Who's working there?"

Mr. Miki hesitated. "There's a complication," he said slowly. "A C.I.A. agent has disappeared. Raven and I saw him lunching with a known Viet Cong agent the day of the kidnapping. In fact, he came over to our table for what I thought was a spurious reason. He, too, has not been seen since."

"So the C.I.A. man was a double agent," Buck suggested.

Mr. Miki nodded. "His name is Al Mardigian. I've learned that your younger son, Dan, has submitted his resignation to the Agency in Bahrain."

Buck looked at Jennifer. "Does anyone have any ideas about what that means?"

"No," Mr. Miki replied, "only incessant speculation about the nature of Onager Limited. It seems that—"

The phone rang. Buck picked it up, listened, and then said, "An embassy officer is on his way up. Tashiharu, you stay on top of whatever they learn about the Onager business. We can't be distracted by it while we're looking for Raven. How soon can we get our people in here to set up communications? And, incidentally, has the room been swept for bugs?"

As Mr. Miki nodded, there was a knock at the door. A young embassy officer came in, and without any introductory preamble, said, "We think we have a fix on your son's location."

23

It was very stuffy. There were flies on his face. He jerked his hand up to brush them away, but he couldn't move his arm. Raven yelled. He seemed to be lying in a matted coffin.

The top opened and two Viet Cong in black pajamas stood holding Kalashnikovs pointed down at him. One offered a U.S. Army canteen of water.

As he drank, Raven looked out at the jungle trying to ignore the sharp pain in his head. He could see delta about a hundred yards away. Groups of Viet Cong in black pajamas stood nearby. The mat container in which he lay had been strung with leather as a litter.

When Raven was finished drinking, two of the Viet Cong moved close to him and began removing bandages and cleaning his head wound. Raven noticed that they used gauze from a Johnson & Johnson package, and that the alcohol was from the United States.

One of his attendants abruptly began to comb Raven's hair, without any consideration for the wound. Before new bandages were applied, another copy of *Stars and Stripes* was thrust into Raven's hands, and he saw one of the Viet Cong with the Polaroid camera. Raven quickly started to read the date, December 28, and the headline—an American officers' billet bombed on Christmas Eve, two officers killed . . ."

Raven started yelling incoherently. He grabbed at the nearest Viet Cong, but was too weak to really fight. The soldier yanked him by the hair and forced him to hold the paper. The photographer moved to one side so that the wound, which Raven could feel bleeding again, did not show.

When the photograph had been taken, they dressed his wound again. Raven saw that the Polaroid picture was handed to two Viet Cong who left the camp instantly. From that and the date on the newspaper, Raven presumed he was still somewhere near Saigon.

Someone shoved a bowl of rice into his hands, and he ate it quickly. Looking around, he noticed that a number of the soldiers were watching him hungrily. Most of them were young and looked emaciated. Raven realized they were giving up a share of their own meager food supply to keep him alive.

He reached up to touch the bandaged wound. The pain in his head throbbed, but the cut seemed fairly shallow. He was surprised to feel that he hadn't any eyebrows left; the hair had been pulled out with the successive tearings of the adhesive tape.

Slowly, Raven tried to get up. The peasant clothes he wore stank of vomit and sweat. He felt faint, and the pain in his head intensified, but two Viet Cong grabbed his arms before he could collapse. When he was able to stand, the two soldiers let him go, backing away to size up his strength. Raven took a few steps, then staggered and the soldiers guided him back to the litter. In a few moments he was asleep.

At dawn the next day, Raven woke to the sound of helicopter engines coming in from the north. Before he could move, a guard thrust an AK-47 at his neck. Raven could see that the Viet Cong were already hiding in the undergrowth. Raven glimpsed the three Bell UH-1 Hueys through the trees.

As they cleared the edge of the jungle, the helicopters began to circle back. The Viet Cong troops quickly moved toward the delta as two soldiers grabbed Raven and pulled him to his feet. He heard an order, and immediately there was a burst of small-arms fire.

Prodded by his captors' guns, Raven was forced deeper into the jungle. As he broke into a trot, there was an explosion and Raven saw one of the helicopters crash. He knew the Huey's ordnance, two six-barreled miniguns, a 40mm. grenade launcher, and seven rocket pods.

The fire fight intensified as Raven moved deeper into the jungle. They reached a recently dug pit about ten feet deep. The two soldiers pushed Raven in and took cover to guard him. The run had left him weak, but seeing one of his guard's legs hanging down over the edge Raven thought he could pull the guard down into the pit with him.

As he was about to spring there was a second crash. Raven looked up to see the last helicopter rolling out of control in flames. Its rockets launched in all directions before it crashed not more than fifty yards away.

Raven's guards began to fire their AK-47s at the wreckage, then stopped to pull Raven out of the pit. One of them said, "Hands up!"

Raven could see the wreckage of the Huey. Several bodies were caught in the wreckage, and Raven began to shake violently.

A guard grabbed his wrists and tied them behind his back. Nobody bothered about the litter. Raven was forced to keep up with the soldiers. They stopped only once. Four Phantom Jets were speeding in over the tree tops. The Viet Cong fell to the ground as the planes surveyed the area three times. On the last pass, they dropped canisters of napalm, and two hundred yards away, a wall of fire consumed the jungle where they fell. The Viet Cong did not move until the sound of the jets had faded away. Raven tried not to think. He just concentrated on putting one foot in front of the other, fast enough to avoid being shot. At the same time, he couldn't imagine staying alive for very long.

Buck lay in their bed watching Jennifer pace the room. It was four-fifteen in the morning.

"Darling, come and try to get some sleep."

"I can't possibly." She kept pacing.

The failure of the rescue mission and the loss of the three Air Cavalry helicopters haunted them. Jennifer was still in control, but her voice was increasingly shrill. She stood at the window for a moment, then walked over and sat down on the bed beside Buck. When he put his hand on her back, he felt the rigidity of her spine.

"I've always believed I would have gone completely mad that

night," she said. Both of them knew what night she meant. "I held onto my baby all those hours as if I were holding on to my sanity. I was beginning to realize it wouldn't work when you arrived with Raven. Now I realize how much I've depended on him. If it weren't for him, where would I be? Where would we be?" She looked at Buck, her eyes wide in the dim light of the room. "If I lose him now, I'm afraid everything I've put together will collapse."

"Jennifer, nothing's the same as it was then. You couldn't go back to that point, even if you tried. Besides, we're not going to lose Raven."

"You don't know that," she replied angrily and jerked away from him.

"Jim Owen knows what he's doing."

"For a million dollars," she said curtly, "we deserve an occasional bulletin."

"Not from Owen—"

They both heard the door of the suite's living room open. In spite of knowing it was guarded by two Marines, Buck leaped out of bed. There was a light knock at the bedroom door and an unfamiliar voice said, "Mr. Faulkner?"

"Yes?"

"I'm from the Embassy. May we come in?" Without waiting for a reply, he opened the door. Buck was holding a chair, ready to swing it, but behind the man, he saw Jim Owen standing in the living room. Buck put the chair down at the foot of the bed and went to Jennifer.

"It's him," he told her. The man at the door said, "Please don't turn on any lights." Then as Owen entered the room, he closed the door behind him.

Jim walked to the chair at the foot of the bed, sat down and lit a cigarette. In the few seconds of wavering light, Buck saw that Jim had aged a great deal in the fifteen years since they had seen each other. His hair had become nearly white; his face deeply lined.

"Forgive the intrusion," he said to Jennifer. Then he turned to Buck. "I'll need another quarter of a million, delivered to Saigon. I'll open an account at the Chase Manhattan branch and send you the number. There's no great hurry, because we're all going to be here for a while."

In the dark, Jennifer searched for her husband's hand.

"The money's not a problem," said Buck. "Not knowing what it's paying for is."

Jim Owen nodded, "I'm sure knowing what the Air Cav was up to didn't give you much joy. I'll tell you as much as I can, but my people won't make radio contact until they find him."

Jim sucked deeply on his cigarette and Buck found himself following the movement of the burning ember.

"I hired twelve men; all of them have worked with me before. They're the best in the world, and the most expensive. I've arranged, through my own contacts and at considerable expense, for them to be dropped into the area where the Air Cav got shot down. These men are trackers; the V.C. have three days on them, and they know where they're going. It's going to take a while, so be prepared."

Jennifer said, "Who are these men? What uniforms are they wearing?"

"No uniform you'd recognize. They're here as private citizens, carrying no identification except their weapons. If anyone finds them, no one will be able to trace them to me, or to you."

"You're taking a double chance," Jennifer said furiously. "Your men could be shot by our Marines as well as the Viet Cong. Why do you use mercenaries? I thought you had contacts with—"

Owen interrupted her.

"Mrs. Faulkner, these men are very good. They could be in this room and you wouldn't know it. They're not going to run into Marines or anyone else until they find your boy."

Owen stood up and looked at his watch. "They're away. They'll drop into the delta in the first possible moment."

"Who else knows about this?" asked Jennifer.

"A few of my former colleagues here. They still have enough influence to do this without alerting Langley." He chuckled. "They're enjoying it."

As he walked to the door, Owen took a manila envelope out of the old World War II leather flight jacket he was wearing, and dropped it on the bed. "That's a Christmas card for you—cost me a lot. I hope you appreciate it."

"Let us know if you hear—" Buck began.

"I won't hear anything until Raven's ready for a Medevac,"

Owen said. At the door, he paused, "I have some good news for you though. Your younger son isn't a traitor. Dan and Mardigian are just businessmen. The reason Al was talking to a Viet Cong agent was to arrange for future purchases, not sales. The reason he and Dan resigned from the C.I.A. was simply because their arms business became too profitable to remain a sideline."

"How do you know all that?" asked Buck angrily.

Jim dropped his cigarette butt on the old parquet floor and ground it out with his foot. "Dan told me. Haven't you heard, Buck? I'm on a retainer from Onager as their Middle East consultant."

He left the room.

"That—sadist!" said Jennifer. "He's *enjoying* himself."

"It's part of his fee; we knew that."

Remembering the manila envelope, Buck went over to the bed and opened it. Inside was a photograph. He turned on a light. The picture was grainy and printed on an inferior kind of paper. Two figures were apparent. One was a man in a military uniform, unmistakably Russian. He was struggling with an old woman, white-haired, slack-jawed, with scabs on her forehead. Her eyes were angry, and her toothless mouth was drawn back as if forming a curse.

Jennifer came up behind Buck before he could conceal the picture. "Oh no. Oh God! No!" Buck turned and embraced her.

Buck might not have recognized Connie Mannheim, except for her eyes.

For the next two weeks, they seldom stopped moving. At times Raven was accompanied by as many as fifty Viet Cong, and at other times, as few as five. They traveled at night, across open delta, hiding in the jungle during the day. On two occasions, they entered native settlements in search of more rice, a pig or a dog. Raven was fed an equal share of whatever the Viet Cong managed to obtain. He regained some of his strength, and his head wound began to heal, but he frequently had to remind himself that he had reason to stay alive.

Except for a few days when the soldiers apparently were waiting for new film, they continued to take his photo every morning. Raven began to prepare for the pictures. He didn't know how they were being used, but he figured that his family might be seeing them and wanted to look as healthy as possible. It wasn't easy; his eyebrows were still stubble, and he began to lose weight because of dysentery. He tried not to think of his family. Controlling his mind, he recited odd bits of poetry, old political speeches, song lyrics, anything he could remember. The Viet Cong told him to stop it, but he did it anyway. It was the only way he could stay sane. One time when he wouldn't remain quiet, they beat him. Later he realized he couldn't stop talking to himself even if he tried. Finally, they lashed him to a tree and each time Raven would begin speaking, a V.C. would shoot at him, just missing his arm or head or crotch. At night, when they moved, he was gagged. Raven couldn't understand why they didn't kill him.

Finally they reached a camp that seemed to be their destination. There were a few concealed huts as well as a latrine; the latter was very important to Raven. As soon as they arrived in the camp, Raven was brought before an N.V.A. officer who spoke pidgin English.

The officer sat at a table, and Raven stood before him. "You nothing now . . . Cease-fire gone soon. You father, you government no find you . . . So. We kill you, or you tell SwordDance, you tell C-thousan, you tell *avionics*—" The last word he pronounced most clearly as if he had just learned it.

Raven kept thinking it was like the draft board. Without meaning to, he laughed.

The officer stood up, walked over to Raven, and looked at him closely. With no warning, he swung his elbow into the side of Raven's face.

Raven yelled and fell down on his knees. His mouth filled with blood, which he spat out on the dirt floor. His bowels were ready to explode as he said, "I can't tell you anything. I'm no engineer."

"*I* engineer. You tell. I know." The officer smiled, and pointed his finger at Raven like a teacher. "No hope now. Cease-fire gone soon. Here—" pointing to the ground—"no Vietnam. Here Cambodia. No Americans no here. You tell SwordDance or—" he kicked Raven on the side of the face where he had elbowed him before.

Raven sprawled on the floor, his mouth bleeding badly. His sphincter muscle finally gave way, which infuriated the officer.

He stepped back and kicked Raven in the ribs. Then two guards took his arms and dragged him out of the hut to the latrine. They shoved him inside and shut the door.

Raven peeled off the peasant pants he was wearing and squatted as best he could over the six-foot-wide hole in the ground. His ribs hurt and he kept spitting blood through his legs into the hole. The door opened, and the guards yelled at him, presumably to hurry.

"As if I could stop," thought Raven, laughing uncontrollably. His guards yanked him outside and pulled up his filthy pants.

Over the next few days, Raven was alternately questioned, beaten, and dragged to the latrine. He told the officer as little as possible and pleaded his genuine ignorance of details. On the fifth day, Raven went too far. He misdescribed the FLIR detection sensors. The officer, who seemed to know his radar, caught Raven in the obvious lie. For that, Raven's arms were bound in back of him around a pole which was then hoisted to the rafters of the hut.

That was the only time Raven gave up and wanted to die. He pleaded with the men standing below to shoot him, but they let him hang until both his arms were dislocated and he lost consciousness. Then they cut him down.

When he woke up, the dysentery had gotten worse and he begged to be taken to the latrine. The chafing sores between his buttocks and thighs made it difficult to walk. He was worried about being able to squat without falling in. As they got to the door of the hut, Raven turned to ask the guard if he could hold on to something.

Suddenly the soldier fell on top of him. Raven started to yell until he realized that the guard's throat had been slit. He looked up to see a man with a knife stooping down, his face blackened, his nostrils plugged, wearing a skull cap and black-knit combat clothes which were covered with shit. "OK, Buddy," the apparition whispered in a Southern accent, "we got sixty seconds to get down that." He pointed to a rope that stretched from the rafter down into the cesspool.

"I can't use my arms," Raven said.

"Figured as much. Can you stand up?"

Raven struggled up. Immediately, the man stood in front of him and wrapped several bands of wide elastic around them

242

both, binding Raven to his back. Then he pulled the pin on a signal grenade, which began pouring out pink and yellow smoke, grabbed the rope in gloved hands and started down the side of the cesspool.

They heard someone coming. Holding the rope with one hand, the man took a fragmentation grenade off his front belt, pulled the pin and rolled it out under the door. Then he did a fast free-fall until they hit the bottom.

"We'll sink," Raven whispered.

"Don't worry about it. I been down here already."

They heard a Vietnamese yell, and the grenade went off. Instantly, the earth above them exploded. Grenades, mortars, and machine-gun fire poured into the camp. Within seconds, Raven heard the whine of jets.

Earth from the sides of the pit fell down on them as the man said, "Only thing we gotta worry about is if some egg falls down in here by mistake." He took the rope from above and secured it on two pylons he had previously driven into the sides of the pit to prevent their sinking. Raven jammed his nose against the man's back, trying to breathe as little as possible.

After a few minutes, the sound of the jets faded, but the small-arms fire continued, heavier than before. Without warning, another rope fell down the hole and the man began to pull them up.

"The fish alive?" a voice bellowed in a French accent.

"Still flipping."

Raven heard the voice above say, *"Allons-y."*

At the top, five other men in similar black dress cut Raven loose and carried him to cover in a nearby bomb crater. The fire fight continued, but Raven saw there was nothing left of the camp. Bodies of Viet Cong lay everywhere.

Five Huey helicopter gun ships appeared over the edge of the jungle. They poured bullets at anything that moved. Two Chinook troop-carrier helicopters followed quickly and landed in the middle of what had been the camp. Raven saw several American soldiers examining the dead Viet Cong for booby traps.

The men who had rescued him remained in the bomb crater. One of them raised a walkie-talkie and said: "Ready for the tuna boat." Raven recognized the French accent again.

Less than a minute later, a Sikorsky Jolly Green Giant landed fifty feet away. Two corpsmen with a litter jumped out of the helicopter and ran to the bomb crater. They lifted Raven carefully and the men in black surrounded Raven as he was carried to the helicopter.

In the doorway, Raven saw a man in flannel slacks and a World War II bombardier's jacket. He never took his eyes off Raven as two medics began cutting off his clothes and cleaning him. As the Jolly Green Giant became airborne, they gave him an injection of morphine. As it began to take effect, Raven watched the men in black congratulating each other in the back of the aircraft. He noticed for the first time that none of them wore service insignia of any kind.

The man in the bombardier's jacket came over to the litter.

"How are you feeling?"

Raven was growing numb but was less interested in how he felt than what had happened.

"Who are you?"

The man hesitated, then said, "I'm Jim Owen."

Raven remembered the name.

"What the hell are you doing here?"

The man smiled bitterly. "I have a present for you."

Raven passed out.

24

For a week after Raven arrived at the Honolulu hospital, he found himself front-page news. Though Sam Priest felt that the publicity was not a bad thing, Raven turned down countless offers to appear on television.

Buck told him the details of his rescue. Jim Owen's twelve mercenaries had searched for two weeks before they found Raven and followed him into Cambodia. They then staked out the Viet Cong camp and contacted Saigon. Once the strategy for Raven's rescue was set, Jack Llewellyn gained diplomatic and military permission to cross into Cambodia. Prince Sihanouk agreed to ignore the raid under the condition that it be kept secret. So far, the press retained the impression that Raven had been rescued somewhere in the Mekong Delta.

On his last weekend in the hospital, Raven received an envelope marked only with his name. It was filled with large bills of American currency and a note that read: "$20,000 + 4.5% interest for 19 years." It was signed, "Jim Owen."

Raven remembered Owen's remark on the Medevac about having "a present," and Melanie's cryptic remark to Buck that night in the Carlyle, "Thanks for the twenty thousand." Raven decided to tell his parents about the money and watch for a reaction.

That weekend, when Buck flew in from the mainland, he had some news of his own. The moment he and Jennifer arrived at the hospital, he said, "Raven, we just put together some more information about the night sight that you found in Vietnam."

"More than what Mardigian told Mr. Miki and me?"

Buck nodded. "What Mardigian didn't tell you is that Onager Limited was involved in the transport of the night sights almost every step of the way."

Raven stared unbelieving at his father, then shook his head. "What's little brother done now?"

Buck scowled. "Because the night sights were a Faulkner product, Dan was approached by a representative of the Shah. Dan hid behind his cover, but Onager Limited took the commission. What Dan didn't know was that the Shah was buying for Burma, which has a leftist-leaning government that is in ill favor with the State Department.

"A corrupt Burmese official tipped off an opium trader, who managed to steal the night sights off the docks before they reached their official destination. Burma notified the Shah's government, who in turn notified Onager. Dan was determined to show the armaments community that no one could interfere with an Onager Limited deal. He had Mardigian inform the Viet Cong of the night sights' passage through Thailand."

"Jesus Christ," Raven said quietly. "I saw Marines who got killed by that night sight."

Buck walked to the window.

"Was Jim Owen the Shah's representative?" Raven asked.

Without turning around, Buck nodded. "And Dan has since hired Owen as a consultant to Onager."

Raven picked up Owen's envelope and handed it to his father. "Jim Owen's been busy."

Raven watched his parents, as Buck looked at the cash, read the note and passed the envelope on to Jennifer.

"Oh God, I *hate* this man!" cried Jennifer. "I don't know what this means, but he's trying to torture us."

"Isn't twenty thousand the amount Melanie Owen mentioned that night?" asked Buck.

"Yes," Raven said. "She thanked you for it."

"Which she indicated was a mistake," Buck said. "But it means she got that amount somewhere and didn't know from whom. So it's forty thousand now. Wait. Nineteen years—"

"Nineteen forty-six," Raven said. "I was five."

Buck was silent, his face the expressionless mask he used at business conferences. "I'm sure Jim has his reasons for this, and your mother's right. He's trying to hurt us again. We *can't let him* do that." He spoke the words emphatically, his eyes focused on Jennifer. Then he looked at Raven, to check his response.

They were hiding something; Raven was sure of it. "What's he got against us all of a sudden?" he asked. "Is he still hanging on to your affair with his wife?"

Buck didn't answer for a moment. "Not *us*. Just me. Look, I hate telling you this—"

Jennifer suddenly reached out and took his hand. "Not now," she implored.

Buck put his arm around her, saying, "I have to tell him this. When Jim Owen was in the O.S.S. he helped me get rid of someone who was trying to destroy the company. She had been blackmailing a lot of our executives, and one of my best men committed suicide. Jim's probably trying to use that incident to get back at me."

"When did he get rid of this person? In 1946?"

Buck nodded slowly. "The woman had been a Russian spy."

Raven looked quizzically at his father. His response seemed too pat, too quick.

"Is the money that Melanie and I got connected to the incident?" Raven abruptly had an idea. "Did any of those men actually pay the money?"

"One did," Buck said.

"How much? Do you know?" Raven stared as his mother's face seemed to tighten with fear.

"Fifty thousand dollars," Buck said.

"That's it, then," Raven said. "Jim Owen got hold of it, and for some reason gave it to me and Melanie."

Buck nodded. "It's possible. Whoever sees Jim Owen next will have to ask him why."

Raven was still watching Jennifer. "You all right, Mother?" he asked.

She nodded and smiled affectionately. "Raven, your father and I have been talking, and we think you should take a vacation."

"That'd be nice, but it's too late."

"Too late for what?" Buck asked.

247

"Stopping. Do you know how many people died because of me? There were the Americans blown up in the officer's billet, then the Air Cav people in the helicopters, and all the Viet Cong when I was rescued. That's a lot of bodies for my sake."

"It wasn't your fault," Buck said insistently.

"That's not the point," Raven replied angrily. "It happened because I was your son."

"Are you blaming me for—"

"No, but you're my father. I can't stop doing what I'm doing. There are too many people dead because of who I am."

"Stop it!" Jennifer cried. "I won't lose you just because—"

Raven looked at his mother, startled. "You're not losing me, Mother."

She turned to Buck. "Look what we've done."

He didn't answer. Her head sank down, and she covered her mouth with her hand.

"Your mother and I are going to the hotel now," Buck said quietly. "We'll come back to see you again in the morning."

"Okay," Raven said, getting out of bed and kissing his mother. "I'm sorry for how I've made you feel."

She stared at him, then kissed him and left the room.

"I'm serious about getting back to work," Raven said to his father.

Buck hesitated at the door and looked back at him. After a moment, he nodded and said, "Washington."

Driving to the hotel, Jennifer said, "I wanted to tell him today."

"It's getting harder not to. He figures things out so fast."

"I know," she said, staring straight ahead. "Everything is going too fast now."

Two weeks later, Raven was in Washington attending a poker game. It took place across the street from the House Office Building, in a suite of the Congressional Hotel. After greeting Raven effusively, the players settled down to the game. Raven himself was more interested in the players than the cards. On his left was Representative Bucknell of Albuquerque. Next to him sat Air Force Colonel George Lauter, a member of the Pentagon's Office of International Logistics, the sales force charged with selling American armaments abroad.

Following the deal around the table was a cigar-smoking Air Force lieutenant colonel named Jake Holcomb. He told Raven that he wrote "flimsies," the military policy proposals for the Pentagon hierarchy. Next sat Senator Broderick Sanderson (Republican, California), a member of the Senate Armed Services Committee and known in the press as "the soothing Senator from Aerospace." Raven had met him many times at his parents' home.

Last was their host, bald and bespectacled F. St. John (pronounced "Sin-Gin") Milton, with whom Raven was working.

Sin-Gin was a graduate of Yale Law School, had clerked for a California Supreme Court Justice, and then gone into corporation law. The firm for which he worked had been retained by Faulkner Aerospace. Sam Priest had spotted him early on and made him Vice-President for Governmental Affairs. In the eleven years he had held the job, he had become one of the most effective lobbyists in Congress.

"I'll raise you," Senator Sanderson was saying with the smug assurance that a bad poker player displays when holding three of a kind. Raven watched him. The Senator, he knew, was another of those charismatic "personalities" Californians elect as if they were casting a movie rather than a ballot. The Senator was not bright, but he worked hard for his state.

The cards moved around to Sin-Gin to deal. By then, Raven had learned that the dealer controlled the conversation. The shuffling could go on a long time, and the deck could even be laid aside, or cards could be dealt in a hurry.

"How was Beirut, George?" Sin-Gin idly asked Colonel Lauter, who had recently returned from the Middle East.

"Depressing," he snapped.

"Why?" Congressman Bucknell asked. "I hear that Beirut's the most swinging city that side of London."

Colonel Lauter shrugged. "I should have said 'frustrating.' We had countries from the Middle East lined up around the block wanting to buy airplanes. But our policies of embargo and balance of power have Israel buying from De Gaulle, and Nasser in love with Moscow. The other Arabs are screaming that they can't defend themselves, and they're right. Unfortunately the ones that can afford it get their arms from Russia, too. The poor ones can't pay, and they're the only game in town."

"Why's that a problem all of a sudden?" Congressman Bucknell took a handful of macadamia nuts and popped them one by one into his mouth. "Planes are exports; get the Export-Import Bank to lend the poor nations the money for the sale. Hell, that's all those fat cats over at Eximbank have to do."

Colonel Lauter smiled. "They're getting too much flak from the Senate Banking Committee. Half those countries can't afford what they buy; the other half just want to bomb their neighbors. We're ready to sell, but—"

"That's Proxmire, isn't it?" Senator Sanderson recognized the message and his familiar but unpleasant job of trying to neutralize a colleague.

"That son of a bitch is the most dangerous man on the Hill," said Lieutenant Colonel Holcomb. "Singlehandedly, he's holding up the best projects we have. And if we can't sell off our *old* planes to underdeveloped countries, let me tell you there won't be any market for *new* planes." He glanced at Raven, then checked his cards.

Sin-Gin shuffled the deck. "As far as I can tell, Eximbank is still willing to make funds available. They're mandated to unload eight billion dollars on financing exports."

"You bet," Colonel Lauter said, "they just don't like politics."

"Who can blame them?" Senator Sanderson laughed. "But I understand Eximbank's point of view. Lending a hundred million dollars to Yemen, for instance, where people are starving while the leaders spend a fortune to blow up the guys next door—well, it seems excessive."

Congressman Bucknell reached for more nuts. "Motives have nothing to do with the marketplace; free enterprise is supply and demand. Nothing else," he said, delicately sticking it to the Senator. "That's the trouble with Proxmire and his ilk; they're preaching Calvinism, while an entire American industry bogs down, and new markets go to the Russians. I mean who gives a real shit about Yemen?" He looked across the table at Raven.

"Seven card high-low," Sin-Gin announced, and started to deal. "What if the Eximbank didn't get involved with the country that wanted to buy the planes? Didn't even know which country it was? Ah, the Senator has an ace looking at us. Your bid, Broddy."

"Five without looking," the Senator said magnanimously.

Congressman Bucknell continued. "I'll *raise* you five, without looking. Doesn't the Eximbank have to know who they're giving money to?"

"Not the *final* destination of the loan, or its purpose," Sin-Gin replied, "as long as the loan is guaranteed by a reputable entity, such as the Pentagon."

The betting stopped. Raven noted the electricity flowing around the room.

Lieutenant Colonel Lauter was riveted. "How can the Pentagon guarantee a loan?"

"Over the years," said Sin-Gin, "the Pentagon has accumulated three hundred eighty three million dollars in its revolving arms sales credit fund. What if some of that were used to guarantee an Eximbank loan to, say, 'Country X'? And what if the Pentagon only had to pledge a third or a quarter of the face value of the loan? That would mean you'd have not three hundred million but a billion two hundred million to play with. It would finance a lot of airplane sales and the Eximbank could avoid involving itself in foreign policy."

"Making the Pentagon an international banker," Senator Sanderson said, "might seem improper, particularly in the Middle East. Please deal the cards."

Sin-Gin did as he was told, saying, "A possible flush for the colonel, nothing for the Congressman, and a pair of aces for the Senator. Still your bet, Broddy."

The Senator had lost interest in the game, even with a third ace in the hole. "What you're suggesting," he said, "is that Colonel Lauter's boss over at the Pentagon calls up the Eximbank and says, 'I want a loan of forty million dollars, which the Pentagon will guarantee with twenty-five percent of its face value, or ten million.'"

Sin-Gin smiled. "And then, of course," said the Senator, "the Pentagon would be in the position of negotiating the actual loan to Country X on its own terms—at even lower rates of interest to make the sale happen—any loss to be made up in the defense budgets of future years."

"Right!" Congressman Bucknell chimed in enthusiastically. "God Almighty, how soon can we get this going? This'll keep the SwordDancer in production until 1980!"

"I believe the Joint Chiefs meet tomorrow as usual," Sin-Gin said casually. "It might be interesting if the Air Force Chief of Staff were in a position to suggest something like this to his colleagues." He glanced meaningfully at Lieutenant Colonel Holcomb.

"I'll try it out on him tomorrow. I have a feeling it'll go up like an AGM-69!"

"A what?" Senator Sanderson asked impatiently.

"It's a SRAM, sir," Colonel Holcomb replied.

"A *what?*" the Senator repeated with irritation.

"A short range attack missile, sir," the Colonel explained patiently.

Sin-Gin continued methodically. "I wonder if the Office of International Logistics would be interested in the idea?"

Colonel Lauter nodded. "As soon as I win this pot, I'll call my boss at home."

"You're not going to win this pot," Senator Sanderson insisted. "It'll cost you fifteen big ones to stay in, and I've got three raises left."

The game continued for another hour. Sin-Gin was the big loser, Senator Sanderson the big winner. The two Air Force officers hurried off into the Washington drizzle anticipating the extravagant credit they would receive the next day for devising such a clever plan for the Air Force. Congressman Bucknell left soon after. Only Senator Sanderson tarried with his host and Raven.

"Very neat, Sin-Gin," he said as he finished a brandy and soda. "I'm sure Raven is impressed. I still see some trouble from the Banking Committee."

Sin-Gin nodded. "Nothing in this town lasts forever, Broddy, except you and me. I think this'll work for about a year. Then we'll find something else. When resistance begins in the Senate, I'll give you some legal reading that'll justify the Eximbank's involvement. And you can always champion the California aerospace worker, and the American economy. There are nearly five hundred thousand voters connected—"

"I know how many. You don't have to wipe my ass." The Senator got up none too steadily, and Raven and Sin-Gin walked him out to his car.

At the curb, he turned. "What happens if Country X doesn't pay back their loan?"

"That won't happen for two or three years. By then, the planes and systems are sold. Besides, the Eximbank has the U.S. Treasury behind it."

"Which has the U.S. taxpayer holding us all up," the Senator said, shaking hands with Raven. "Welcome to Washington, son. But be careful of this man you're with. He's dangerous."

Raven smiled. "I've been wondering why he's been spending so much time teaching me to shuffle."

After the Senator's car drove off, the Faulkner limousine cruised up.

"Can I give you a lift, Raven? Or should I say, can you give me a lift?"

"No. I feel like walking. I'm not used to the smoke-filled rooms yet. You play one hand of poker, ask one question about Beirut, and planes start flying in all directions."

Sin-Gin laughed. "Next you'll learn how to deal with only one hand." As the car turned the corner out of Raven's sight, Sin-Gin picked up the phone. A profitable game, he told Lieutenant General Jack Llewellyn. And no problems from Raven.

Several blocks away, Congressman Bucknell was in a phone booth. "Hello, Dan?" he said. "Yes, I know it's early in London. It's late here. Listen, I would urge Onager Limited to corner all the old planes you can and then let your customers in the Middle East and Africa know you can deliver them. Because they are about to get a line of credit as long as a rhinoceros dick. Who from? Why Dan, the Pentagon, of course."

25

In the spring of 1967, Raven was preparing for his first Faulkner sales mission in the Middle East. After many months of Sin-Gin Milton's Machiavellian tutelage, Raven thought he was ready to enter the international marketplace. Near the Sea of Galilee, the Israelis and Syrians were shooting at each other. In Egypt, Nasser's military commanders were making rhetorical speeches to their troops about a *jihad*, a holy Muslim war against Israel. There was speculation that Israel, with the help of France and the C.I.A., had developed a nuclear capability at Dimona. The time was perfect for major arms sales to the Arabs.

Raven waited in Buck's office, while an Execujet was fueled to take him to briefings at the Pentagon and the State Department, then on to the Middle East.

"Just remember," Buck said. "I'm a figurehead, not only for Faulkner Aerospace, but for the industry as well. The moment something goes wrong, if the plumbing backs up in Air Force One, or an airliner with a Senator on board has a flat tire, people start investigating me. So remember, any time you tell me anything, I may be forced to repeat it in a Congressional hearing room. I've been told I lie badly."

"You tell my jokes pretty well—"

"Thank you," Buck said. "Well, you seem all set to go. Any worries?"

"Only that there are no standards. Every deal I know about is different."

"That's right. Be ready for anything. And when a deal doesn't close, keep checking to see who still needs a commission."

"That's probably when I'll run into Dan—or Jim Owen," Raven said.

Buck seemed surprised. "You could very well run into them. They've been very active in the Middle East over the last year, but I'd prefer not to do business with Onager Limited."

"Agreed," Raven nodded. "I'll just ask Owen about the twenty thousand. That son of a bitch never answered any of my letters."

Buck stood up and walked over to the window overlooking the field. He saw that the Execujet had finished taking on fuel.

"Raven, may I ask a favor?"

"Sure, but I reserve the right not to grant it," Raven said, smiling. "That's part of my new negotiating style."

"If you do run into Jim Owen, don't mention the twenty thousand. It would only give him pleasure. Your mother and I have some thoughts about the money, nothing certain, but by the time you get back, I'll know more. If we're right, we'd rather tell you than have Jim Owen do it. Agreed?"

Raven hesitated. "I didn't know Mom was in on it."

"Your mother is in on everything I do."

Raven nodded. "Okay. Agreed."

It was time, Buck thought, as he watched his son cross the tarmac. When Raven returned from the trip, he had to know the story of his adoption. Watching the Execujet take off down the runway, Buck considered what it would be like to lose Raven. The idea seemed intolerable.

The Execujet carried Raven to many Middle Eastern capitals. The Faulkner sales team had coordinated its itinerary with that of the Pentagon Office of International Logistics' "green team," headed by recently promoted full Colonel Lauter. With such an assembly of military and civilian pitchmen, Raven thought it would be hard to fail. The strategy used with the Arab buyers was simple and time-tested: use Israel to provoke hate, and offer commissions to everyone in sight. In Saudi Arabia, Raven was careless in handling the latter and the oversight almost cost him his first deal.

Even after the Pentagon agreed to train Saudi pilots and

Faulkner threw in free maintenance, one Saudi air force general remained immune to the SwordDancer's charms. Raven put through a call to General James Dulaney, the ambitious Air Force general with whom he had flown to Albuquerque. When the connection was patched through, Raven implied that the sale of twenty SwordDancers to Saudi Arabia would influence General Dulaney's future with Faulkner Aerospace. Twenty-eight hours later, the general arrived in Riyadh for an elaborate dinner at the Equestrian Club, recently founded by King Faisal himself. The dinner party was attended by several members of the royal family, including Prince Sultan, the king's brother, who made all military decisions for the country. General Dulaney and his party appeared in full military regalia and extolled the Sword-Dancer with enthusiastic diplomacy. By the end of the evening, both the Saudi general and Prince Sultan seemed to be impressed.

For the next two days, however, Raven waited for a sign from the Air Ministry in Riyadh. None came. At the end of the second day, the "green team" left for Amman, where Jordan was apparently ready to request a Country X loan to purchase tanks. Raven checked with the American embassy, as well as his own sales team. No one had heard a word. Raven stayed in his suite and stared out the windows, absently watching the two most common conveyances, camels and Rolls-Royces, moving around the desert city. He remembered his father's warning. He was certain he had done as much as he could, but obviously he had missed something.

When the phone finally rang, it was the last person in the world Raven expected.

"Hello, Big Brother." Dan sounded as if he were in the next room. "I heard you had a terrific party at the Equestrian Club. I'm really hurt you didn't invite me."

Raven knew from long experience not to react to Dan's access to inside information.

"Where are you?" was all Raven said.

"Just over in Bahrain. I heard you asked that asshole Dulaney to come, as if he could do you any good."

"Gee, Dan," Raven said with exaggerated incredulity, "what else do you know?"

"Enough to be sure you'll sit in that hotel till Christmas and not sell any SwordDancers." Raven recognized the switch in his brother's tone.

"Who tells you all these wild stories, Dan, your former C.I.A. buddies?"

"They don't tell me a thing. We tell them." He laughed contemptuously. "If you'll come over here for dinner, we'll tell you how to move a few planes."

"Who's we?"

"Onager Limited. I figure you can get here by seven. There'll be a car at the airport. I have a surprise for you."

Raven didn't like playing Dan's games, particularly when Dan was making the rules. "I'm leaving tomorrow. Tell me over the phone."

Dan's tone changed again. "Big Brother, if you want the Saudi's business, you have to talk to me, and I don't talk this kind of business on the phone."

"You know me, Dan; I love surprises." Raven hung up, then called the Execujet's crew.

The flight took less than an hour. They landed at Muharraq Island Airport off the north tip of Bahrain. At the private terminal, a large Mercedes limousine was waiting. Inside was a mahogany bar with a bottle of Champagne in a crystal ice bucket. An engraved card propped beside it read, "Onager Limited welcomes you." Dan was really showing off.

The limousine sped over the causeway into Manama. At the Gulf Hotel, the driver escorted Raven to the elevator and pushed the top button. When the elevator doors opened, Raven stepped directly into a penthouse with a view overlooking the city to the Persian Gulf. Dan watched his brother's reaction, then got up to greet him. Across the coffee table, sitting in a straight-backed wooden chair, smoking a cigarette, was Jim Owen.

"Big Brother, come in. You've lost some weight since I saw you. When was that? Back on the Hawthorne runway. We've all come a ways from there, haven't we? You remember Jim Owen, don't you?"

Owen didn't move, and Raven just nodded.

"Have a drink, Raven." Dan pushed a button by the couch, and an Arab houseboy came out of the kitchen with skewers of hot mint-flavored lamb bits.

Dan was wearing a cashmere sweater with its sleeves pushed up his forearms. "It seems Allah has been good to you," Raven said, looking around.

Dan laughed softly. He dropped his forearm on his brother's shoulder and sat down with him on the oversized sofa. "Have some Champagne while you can get it. Those Saudis will cut your tongue out if it touches the stuff." He laughed again, then impatiently stood up and left the room saying, "I'll be right back."

When they were alone, Raven said to Owen, "Did you get my letters?"

"I did, but I didn't read them." He lit another cigarette.

"Why not? I wrote to thank you."

Jim Owen didn't seem to be particularly interested. "My pleasure." Since Raven had seen him in Vietnam, Owen had become alarmingly gaunt. His hair was thin and white, his hands skeletal.

"You know, your daughter and I were friends once," Raven said, hoping the revelation would cause a reaction. He wouldn't mention the twenty thousand since he had promised his father, but Raven wanted any other information he might get out of Owen.

Owen was too used to surprises to reveal anything. "Were you really?"

"Yes. We lived together for about five months when we were at N.Y.U."

"She never told me that," Owen said without the slightest sign that the information meant anything to him.

"No?" Raven responded, smiling easily. "One thing Melanie could do was play on a secret. It took her four months to tell me that my father had had an affair with your wife. Maybe we should talk about that sometime."

The older man's face didn't change. After a moment, he asked Raven, "Do you play poker?"

"Once in a while."

"I'll give you some free advice: hold your best card for last. It has a more dramatic effect."

He crushed out his cigarette as Dan returned and said, "Surprise!"

Standing next to him was Melanie in a translucent turquoise

258

caftan. She wore heavy gold jewelry, and her hair was braided stylishly with a gold cord. Without concealing his astonishment, Raven stood up.

"Melanie, this is my brother," Dan said smoothly.

"I told you, Dan," she interrupted, "we met at college." She came over to Raven and shook his hand. "Hello, Raven." There was no familiarity in her look, but she seemed prepared for whatever Raven might choose to reveal.

"That's right," Dan said, "but Big Brother, did you know you went to college with Jim Owen's daughter?"

Glancing at his brother's smiling face, Raven realized that Melanie had kept her secret very well indeed. He turned to Jim Owen, who stared back at him placidly.

"What a surprise," Raven said; both Melanie and Dan laughed.

"And I have another one for you, if you can keep a secret," Dan said.

"I'll try."

Dan held up Melanie's left hand. On the ring finger was an enormous emerald.

"She and I plan to get married. Jim's given his permission, but for God's sake, don't tell Mother and Father yet. There's a lot of bad blood at the moment."

Raven could think of nothing to say other than, "Congratulations."

"Thanks, Raven," Dan replied. "I've never been happier. Come on, let's eat. I'm starved."

Throughout dinner, they talked airplane gossip: McDonnell's takeover of Douglas, the rumored takeover by a Pittsburgh conglomerate, Rockwell, of North American Aviation. Raven remembered meals from their childhood when they had both rattled off such current facts to impress their father.

Melanie joined in from time to time, curious about Dan's interests, and looking, as Raven had to admit, ravishing. Her father said little. Eventually his silence became oppressive, so Raven decided to break it by asking, "When's the war with Israel going to start, Jim?"

Owen barely looked up from his baked *kibbee*. "It started in 1948. They'll start *fighting* again when one side or the other gets ready. The Jews are ready now, but they can't let the world think they're aggressors. So they'll wait for Nasser to give them an excuse."

"You don't seem to be an Israeli sympathizer."

Dan laughed quietly. "That's the understatement of the year. That's why Jim got canned from the Agency."

Jim Owen glared at Dan. "That's not true."

"Sorry, Jim," Dan said and turned to Raven. "He resigned."

"For a number of years," Owen explained, "I had disagreed with one of my superiors. I thought my talents, such as they were, might be more useful elsewhere."

"They are, Jim, they are," Dan said. "As you're about to find out, Big Brother. Melanie, would you see about coffee?"

Melanie took her cue and left the room. Dan continued.

"Jim thinks you might have missed something over there in Araby."

"We were *told* you missed something," said Jim.

"The point is," Dan hastened to elucidate, "that Jim's the one they told."

"You have my undivided attention," Raven said.

Pressing out his cigarette, Owen lit another as he began to talk.

"You didn't get to the right man," he said simply.

"We got to everyone," Raven said. "The ministers, the Air Force, the royal family . . ."

Jim Owen shook his head. "It doesn't make any difference. They don't know you. There's no reason for them to trust you, because what you're selling to them, you'll sell as quickly to their enemies. Besides, they can buy planes from many places. Your concern is money; theirs isn't. Therefore, they regard you as little more than the dogs that beg to eat their garbage."

"Who did I miss?"

"You missed the classic 'inside-outside man' in a feudal court. He's *inside,* because he's one of them, connected in some inconspicuous way to the power. He's also *outside,* because he's not part of the royal family or the military, and because he knows the outside well enough to reassure those on the inside. No Arab trusts the West. The royal family is forbidden by Faisal to deal in business. Therefore, they insist on their inside-outside man. As far as the SwordDancer is concerned, they want the plane, but they're insisting that business be done their way."

260

"Your advice is that we should hire a local agent?" Raven noticed that Dan was watching the conversation as he would a tennis match.

"No," Owen said. "You don't hire anyone. You don't mention commissions. You make an arrangement with whomever they've chosen."

"And does this anointed one work for nothing?"

Jim Owen sat back in his chair and smiled. "You'll pay him more than Faulkner Aerospace has ever paid anyone before, and Buck won't care, because his planes will sell like nothing he's ever seen."

"Can I reach the miracle man later tonight?"

With a bursting look of pride, Dan answered, "No. You can't. We can."

"What's the deal, Dan?" Raven said.

"Two nights ago, I was in London; Jim was in Tehran. A friend of Onager Limited called each of us from Paris, where he has an office. He told us in very specific terms what you were up to over in Riyadh. That means that the Saudis called him after your little party at the Equestrian Club. Our friend suggested that you might need him and asked us to act as contact. We flew here yesterday, and we have his terms. Ours aren't as pricey as his, but we'll give you those, too, if you're interested in selling *any* SwordDancers."

Raven looked over at Owen, who seemed disinterested.

"What *is* the price, Dan?" Raven asked.

"He wants two percent commission; we want one percent."

Raven thought a moment and said, "Three percent adds about forty-five thousand dollars to the cost of a plane."

"It's nothing," Dan shrugged.

"Twenty planes would make it about a million for you and your magic man."

Dan leaned over toward Raven, and said confidentially, "And those Saudi sons of bitches will pay it. They know what's going on, Raven. They just want to humble you a little by making you go their route. So just jack up the price. You'll be selling thirty million dollars worth of airplanes." Dan smiled as if money were the solution to any problem. "If this deal goes through, we want Faulkner to use us as their agents in the Middle East and North Africa. To prove Onager's ability, we'll line up an Iranian deal

261

for SwordDancers within a month."

Raven remembered his father's warning.

"Well, Dan, you have it all worked out. But how do I know that this 'inside-outside man' can perform?"

Dan turned in his chair and opened a drawer in the sideboard behind him. He took out an alligator-skin folder and flipped it down at Raven's place. "You sign these agreements and get back to Riyadh. If the deal doesn't go through, you don't pay anyone anything. But I'd tell your flight crew to be ready to leave by noon tomorrow."

Raven believed him. There was little risk, yet the price had gone up alarmingly. Raven didn't open the folder.

"We don't make deals with people we don't know."

His brother leaned across the table. "You'll meet him. He's a friend of Jim's." Raven met Owen's eyes as Dan went on insistently. "But there's no time for that now, or you'll blow the deal—" He stopped, trying to restrain himself from pushing his brother.

"In the case of Onager Limited, we don't make deals with people we know," Raven said suddenly, changing the tone of the meeting.

Dan stood menacingly. "If you think the old man will pat you on the head for losing a twenty-plane deal, you have your head farther up your ass than I thought, Big Brother."

"Your father won't be happy that I'm involved," Owen said. "But if he wants to do business in the Arab countries, he'll have to come to us. I know your father well enough to know that he'll put his company before any personal feelings." He stubbed out his cigarette.

"No, he won't," Raven said. "No deal."

For a moment there was silence until Dan said, "You crazy bastard!" Owen stood up and went to a telephone in the next room as Dan continued. "What's the matter with you? You're going to blow Faulkner Aerospace right out of the Middle East."

"How much did you make on the night sights, Dan? And Jim," Raven called into the next room, "how did you get hold of the forty thousand you gave to me and Melanie? It didn't belong to the person who gave it to you."

Jim put his hand over the phone and said flatly, "That's a private matter. Maybe we'll talk about it some other time."

262

"And the night sights," Dan spat out, "are none of your fucking business."

"Faulkner won't use anyone who supplies our products to the Viet Cong. A lot of Marines have died because of you. What you did comes close to treason."

"Don't you judge me, you son of a bitch. A lot of people died because of you, too. And besides that, we're both in the same business. The difference is, you're working for a government and I'm not. I don't declare any wars; I just profit from them like everyone else, including you and Buck Faulkner."

Raven stood to grab his brother, but Jim called out from the next room. "Raven! I have your father on the phone."

Raven hesitated, then went into the living room, as Jim Owen said, "Tell him the deal. There's no point in us arguing about what he wants. He can tell you himself."

Raven took the phone and sat with his back toward the dining area.

"So you ran into Jim Owen." Raven could hear Buck as clearly as if it were a local call.

"And Dan as well." He decided not to overwhelm Buck with news of Melanie.

"What's the problem?"

Quickly, Raven explained the Saudi situation and Onager Limited's proposed solution.

"Who's the inside-outside man?" Buck asked.

"I didn't bother to ask," Raven replied. "I turned them down." When there was no response, he said, "You told me to use my own judgment, and that Onager wasn't—"

"Raven, if the third party is a company called Triad Corporation, sign the agreements."

For a moment, Raven didn't speak. "I told them you'd never—What's Triad?"

"It's one man named Adnan Kashoggi, who controls most of the Arab market. He already works for Lockheed and Northrop. We can use him."

"There are a lot of other markets."

"None as big as that one."

"You'll have to work through Onager."

"Yes, we will. Adaptation is something you have to learn in this business."

"Father, why don't I just *not* sign and not tell you about it? You wouldn't even need to know about me being here."

Buck paused. "Raven, I hear about everything. Sign." He hung up.

Raven didn't put the phone down for a moment. Then he went back to the dining room and picked up the alligator-skin folder. The two agreements were very short. One was with Onager Limited; the other was with the Triad Corporation. "I'll sign," he said.

Dan smiled and said, "Big Brother, we're going to do some business together. Give us a month and we'll have something for Faulkner Aerospace in Tehran. Now where's our coffee? Jim, that daughter of yours is slower than—Melanie?" Raven had the feeling that Jim had told Dan not to continue the argument and not to crow over their triumph.

Melanie appeared instantly as if she had been listening on the other side of the door. An Arab servant followed her with a tray. As they had their coffee, she barely spoke, seemingly content to listen as Dan described his version of their meeting in Tehran. Melanie had been entrenched in the royal court and had even attracted the eye of his Imperial Majesty. Impressed with her status, Dan had courted her lavishly, sending flowers every day and commuting from London on weekends.

Raven listened patiently, but he was distracted. As soon as he could, he took his leave.

"Nice to see you again," he said to Melanie.

"Thank you, Raven. We'll look forward to seeing you in London sometime." She watched the Arab servant collect coffee cups and followed him into the kitchen.

When Dan went to phone down to the car, Raven said quietly to Owen, "I see what you mean about holding on to your cards."

Owen nodded.

"You seem to be holding quite a few," Raven added.

"People keep slipping them to me under the table. The money was yours. Connie Mannheim wanted you and Cass to have it. She told me about it in Berlin, just before—"

Seeing Raven's shocked surprise, Jim realized that the boy knew even less than he had supposed.

"Car's waiting, Raven," Dan called, and he headed for the elevator.

"We'll have to talk some time," Raven said to Jim.

"You can talk to Buck."

Raven turned and walked with his brother to the elevator. As they waited, Dan stuck out his hand and said, "Maybe we'll be better partners than brothers."

Raven stepped into the elevator without shaking Dan's hand. "I'm not your partner. Father is." The doors closed on Dan's infuriated look.

Raven returned to Riyadh. He knew that "Cass" was Melanie's mother. But the name "Connie Mannheim" meant nothing. That night he slept little. At nine the next morning, however, he was summoned to the Saudi Air Ministry, where a contract for twenty SwordDancers at a unit price of one and a half million dollars was signed by Prince Sultan himself. As predicted, the Faulkner Execujet took off at noon for Beirut. The sales team was ecstatic, but Raven remained noticeably reticent.

When they landed, the head of the Beirut office met the plane to say Nasser had blockaded the Gulf of Aqaba proclaiming that the *jihad* against Israel was about to begin.

Massive Arab orders for aircraft were anticipated; the sales team was to remain in Beirut to take advantage of them. Raven was expected in Paris the next day. Just before he reboarded the Execujet, Raven sent a cable to his parents at Palos Verdes. The message was short: "Connie Mannheim. Love, Raven."

26

When Raven cleared customs at Orly airport, he was surprised to find his mother and father waiting for him. Jennifer hugged him silently, but Buck said, "We got your cable."

"We were already on our way to meet you," Jennifer said. "They forwarded it here."

Raven felt a considerable dread and didn't know why. They walked in silence to the car. As the driver pulled on to the highway, Buck said, "We heard the Saudi deal went through. Congratulations."

Raven looked at his parents. "Don't congratulate me. I'd have blown it." He turned back to stare out his window. "As a matter of fact, I'm resigning because of it."

Buck and Jennifer glanced quickly at each other. No one spoke again until the car stopped a block west of the Champs-Elysées in front of a luxurious building, where Faulkner Aerospace kept an apartment. When they were alone in a drawing room, Buck closed the doors and opened his briefcase. He took out the photograph which Owen had given to them in Saigon. He gave it to Raven.

Raven studied the picture, then looked up with anticipation.

"That's Connie Mannheim," Buck said, watching for Raven's reaction.

Raven looked at the picture again, then looked directly at Buck. "Why did she give me and Jim Owen's wife forty thousand dollars?"

Buck hesitated, then said, "I'm going to tell the story from the beginning. If I repeat anything that Jim told you already, you can stop me."

During the next hour, the only movement in the room was Jennifer's hands, which continuously fingered the folds of her skirt. Buck began with the first time he met Connie Mannheim, when she slapped his face, through all her various attempts to wring money from him.

"In the end," Buck said, "she agreed to all my conditions, including having her child. That child was you."

Raven looked at Buck with disbelief. Then he fixed his eyes on Jennifer, who lowered her head and said, "I'm sorry we waited so long to tell you."

When Raven didn't speak, Buck cleared his throat and went on, describing Connie's desperation, Jennifer's pregnancy, and the birth of their first child.

Raven sat forward in his chair. The Paris humidity was stifling; he could feel his shirt sticking to his back. Buck's voice thickened as he revealed the infant's death and finally, his trip to Saugus.

"What happened to my mother?" Raven said, interrupting for the first time.

At the reference, Jennifer winced.

"We'll tell you everything, Raven, I promise," Buck said. Raven didn't speak again until Buck came to his affair with Cass Owen. Then Raven blurted out, "Jesus Christ, you knew she was my half sister. That's insane."

"It had nothing to do with her relationship to you," Buck said.

"You don't think so? A psychiatrist would have a field day." Raven looked at Jennifer. "Don't you agree?"

"Don't blame your father," Jennifer said, letting her anger show. "You don't know what it was like for him. I stopped being his wife."

"Can I blame him for getting rid of my mother?" Raven asked, holding up the picture of Connie Mannheim.

"No!" Jennifer shouted. "No one, not you, or the law, or God Himself can blame us more than we have blamed ourselves. We've paid, Raven, and if Jim Owen has his way, we'll pay some more."

"I still don't understand how Jim knew about the money."

Buck cut off Jennifer's tears, trying to finish the puzzle.

"Owen mentioned being in Berlin with Connie Mannheim, 'just before—' " Raven said. "Maybe he was there when she was traded to the Russians."

"It's possible," said Buck. "Connie had a way of using everything—"

Without warning, Raven stood up. "So what am I supposed to do now?" He looked from one to the other. "I can't blame you or hate you. I *can't*."

"We don't want to lose you," Buck said.

Jennifer kissed him, her cheeks still wet with tears.

"You can't lose me," Raven said. "Who else is there for me to be, except Raven Faulkner?"

"Raven Faulkner is our son," Buck said. "That's the most important—"

"But why did I have to hear about it from Jim Owen?"

"We regret that more than you know."

"Really? You've had twenty-seven years to tell me. I'm kind of grateful to him."

"You're wrong, Raven," Buck said angrily. "When should we have told you? I was nine when I learned that my biological parents hadn't cared enough to keep me. The information didn't help me much. Should we have told you when you were nine, or sixteen or twenty-one? Are you ready now?"

"I don't know," said Raven. "Would you ever have told me if you weren't afraid that Owen would?"

Buck considered a moment, then said, "I think so. Your mother has always wanted you to know. I was the one who insisted on secrecy."

Raven walked over to his father's chair and stood looking down at him. "It was different for you. All those years when you knew you were adopted, you had a kind of freedom. If you wanted to fly the Atlantic, you went ahead and tried it. If you wanted to build a plane, you built it. If you wanted to take someone's baby or wife, you took them. But it's not so easy any more, is it? Maybe if you'd told me all this sooner, I'd have had the chance to find out what I really am. Now it's too late. I'm in too deep."

"You can do anything you want," Buck said. "We'll see to it—"

268

"That's not possible," Raven said sharply. "We're trapped in these roles. You've had a lot more practice; I only hope that I can measure up." He walked toward the door.

"You're making one mistake," Jennifer said suddenly. Raven hesitated. "You spoke of Connie Mannheim as your *real* mother. Don't fool yourself." She finally looked up. "*I* am your *real* mother, and Buck is your *real* father. You may want to hate us for what we've done, but we are, and we'll always be, your *real* parents."

"I know that," Raven said quickly.

"Raven, give yourself some time," Buck said walking over to Jennifer. "We're going to fly back as soon as we get some sleep. You can stay here as long as you wish. Or if you want, you can come home and stay with us. We—"

"Stop being so goddam accommodating." Raven tried not to shout. "I told you, I don't know what to do." He held up the picture of Connie Mannheim. "What am I supposed to do with this?"

Dropping the photograph on a side table, Raven hurried out of the apartment. All day, he didn't stop walking. As the sun set, he finally sat down to drink a *café au lait* and eat a stale croissant at a market café. He picked up a discarded newspaper, and read how the Israeli Air Force had attacked Egypt and destroyed its Russian planes before they left the ground. Then he began to walk again. It was dawn before he returned to the apartment. His parents had left, but next to his bed was a short note from Jennifer. "We love you," was all it said. Without undressing, Raven lay down on the bed and fell asleep.

For several days, Raven did little else in Paris but walk and sleep. If the phone rang while he was in the apartment, he didn't answer it. If someone knocked at the door, he didn't respond. He knew no one in Paris, and he wanted to be left entirely alone.

Then one morning when he was sitting at a sidewalk café around the corner from his apartment, a man walked over to Raven's table.

"Good morning. I can't join you." It was Jim Owen.

Raven shrugged.

"We've been invited out to dinner tonight," Owen said. "You won't want to miss it."

Raven's fists clenched.

"I'll pick you up, if you'd like," Jim said. "Eight-thirty, in front of your building."

Unable to stop himself, Raven jumped up and grabbed Owen by the shoulders. "Where's my mother?"

In an instant, Jim's initial surprise changed to comprehension. He punched Raven once, knocking over the table. Then he helped him up and began handing bills to the waiters, explaining in perfect French that his friend had stumbled. When they were alone again at the righted table, Jim spoke quickly. "Last time I heard, she was in the Gulag. You saw her picture?"

Raven nodded.

"Well, don't take it out on me. I didn't put her there." When Raven didn't answer, Owen added, "I'll be outside at eight-thirty."

In the end Raven decided to go. He was driven to a Russian restaurant that specialized in caviar and stylish excess. The party was large; the women were lavish and beautiful, the men tailored and rapacious. Their host was Adnan Kashoggi; the center of attention was Richard Nixon. At one point, the short, round-bellied Arab came around to their table and greeted Owen effusively. When Raven was introduced, Kashoggi chatted enthusiastically about the SwordDancer. Then he returned to his guest of honor.

"Now you've met Triad," Jim Owen said. "For Onager's sake, I hope you'll impress on Buck his importance, and ours."

"My father's already impressed." Raven looked across the room. "What the hell's Kashoggi doing with Nixon?"

Owen smiled. "Nixon wasn't received in Morocco last week in the manner in which a presidential candidate likes to be received. King Hassan wouldn't even see him. Kashoggi will help him get some statesmanlike attention in other Arab countries."

"Why?" Raven asked. "Nixon couldn't even win the governorship of California."

Jim Owen shrugged. "Then Kashoggi hasn't lost a thing, has he? But what other presidential candidate does he know that's open to his kind of favors?" He gestured to the room, filled with excitement and ambition. "And what if he wins? I'm sure Buck knows Nixon."

"Everyone knows Nixon," Raven replied. "Tell me about Triad."

"Triad is incorporated in Liechtenstein, headquartered in Geneva, and is run from wherever Kashoggi happens to be. He's a Saudi, the son of the late King Ibn Saud's doctor. He attended Victoria College in Cairo with King Hussein of Jordan, then he went to Stanford University for a time. After that, he went back to Saudi Arabia, mined gypsum, and became an agent for Rolls-Royce and Marconi. He has since expanded. His royal connections are very strong, not only in Saudi Arabia, but elsewhere around the Mediterranean and Persian Gulf. He's obviously the man to know in the Middle East. Buck will be pleased with the affiliation. Because of it, Faulkner Aerospace will receive a commitment next week from Iran for fifty SwordDancers."

"Even though Kashoggi's a Lockheed agent?" Raven said.

Owen lit another cigarette. "Buck takes a certain delight in making use of Lockheed's facilities. As long as Kashoggi assures Faulkner sales, his other obligations don't matter."

"Let me ask you something else," Raven said. "Isn't it kind of pathetic to hang on to an affair that took place twenty years ago? It's a pretty weak reason for revenge these days."

Jim Owen sat silently for a moment, his head bent down over his chest. Then he straightened and looked at Raven. "Sometimes when you lose, there's nothing much left. I didn't start out my life to play this role. Buck Faulkner ruined my marriage."

"What about Melanie?"

Owen sighed. "Melanie doesn't give. She takes, and I owe her a lot. So, she takes what she wants, and it gives me some happiness."

"There's only one thing I don't know," Raven said. "Did Connie Mannheim tell you about the forty thousand herself?"

"In 1946, Buck fingered her as a Communist agent. I arranged for her to be part of a trade with the K.G.B. for some American operatives. What Buck never knew was that I was actually present at the trade. In her last moments in the West, she told me where she had buried forty thousand dollars." Owen shook his head. "She never knew I had married her daughter. Just before they took her away, she asked me to deliver the money to her two children, one being my wife, the other being you." He

271

looked over at Raven, who had not moved. "That's when I learned that there's no such thing as coincidence."

"You believed her?" Raven said, hoping to shake Jim's certainty. "She was a Communist agent. She knew who you were, and she played you along."

"That occurred to me," Owen replied, "even after I dug up the money. But over the years, I did my homework. I assure you, the money belonged to you and Cass."

"What makes you so certain?"

"If you're interested enough to get it, there's a file in the safe at my Tehran office. It contains the F.B.I. reports, Faulkner Aircraft employee records and pictures."

"Terrific. I'll just ask Dan to send it."

Owen shook his head. "He knows I don't like your father, but he doesn't know why. I don't mind causing Buck any amount of grief. But I've nothing against his sons."

"How noble," Raven said.

"One other thing. I heard Connie Mannheim died in prison two years ago."

Raven stood up and, without saying goodbye, left the restaurant. Outside, he couldn't decide where to go. He didn't want to think about what Jim Owen had just told him. As he started toward the Champs Élysées, one of the women whom he had seen at the party came out and asked if she might walk with him. She was English, a "model," who spoke of Deauville and "Monte," and all the parties she had attended. Raven knew none of the names she dropped; they had nothing in common, and he didn't care. At one of the sprawling sidewalk cafés, they drank a lot of cognac. She kept talking, while Raven tried to get drunk. Finally, without any discussion they went back to the apartment.

It was the least enjoyable sex Raven had ever known. When it was over he silently got out of bed and packed. Not knowing the woman's name, he left two thousand francs on the mantel. Then he let himself out of the apartment and took a taxi out to Orly. In the lounge of the executive terminal, he called the Execujet's crew and drank coffee until they arrived. Then he boarded the plane and began the long flight back to Faulkner Field.

27

Raven knew he could not go back to his parents' house. For the first few days after his return, he went to the nearest Holiday Inn and slept off his exhaustion. Then he bought a furnished house in Pacific Palisades, lived in it for ten days and put it back on the market. He lasted only two days longer at the Beverly Hills Hotel, then he moved on to the Bel-Air. After that, he took an apartment in the Faulkner Building in downtown Los Angeles and commuted to Faulkner Field by company helicopter. Finally, he bought a fifty-five foot sloop which was berthed at Marina del Rey. His restlessness never let up. Every day he got up as soon as it was light and drove to work, where he would stay until long after dark. Occasionally, he went to Palos Verdes for a meal, but his relationship with Buck and Jennifer remained cordially distant.

They were all pleased to be distracted from their personal problems by the myriad details involved in the Iranian sale. The letter of intent had been signed, but in order to close the deal, Buck told Raven he'd have to visit Tehran. The necessity of a deal with the Shah increased as public pressure for peace in Vietnam escalated, and military contracts were canceled. Faulkner had plenty of competition for his Majesty's favor, even from the Russians. Fortunately, the company was linked to Jim Owen, and Owen not only had helped to save the Shah's throne in 1953, but had remained a close adviser to the Shah, first in, then out of the C.I.A. His Imperial Majesty was therefore willing to grace Onager Limited and Faulkner Aerospace with his saving beneficence.

A few days before his trip, Dan called Raven at his office.

"Hey, Big Brother," Dan said. "Ask me for the good news."

"What's the good news, Dan?" In spite of Dan's cheery mood, Raven knew that Dan hadn't forgotten their enmity.

"Well, I just talked to Melanie and I asked her to marry me again. She said yes. So, Big Brother, I want you to be my best man."

Raven hesitated. "Well, Dan, congratulations."

"We're thinking about having it in London, a really big bash, maybe the service in Westminster Abbey and the party at the Savoy. I'll let you know."

"Should I say anything to Mother and Father?"

"I'll tell them myself." His tone shaded to the defensive.

"Is Jim pleased?"

"As punch. He's in Tehran and says he'll try to get the SwordDancer order up to a hundred as a wedding present. When are you heading for Tehran?"

"The end of the week."

"Hot damn, you're getting rich, aren't you?" Dan laughed as he hung up.

Oh yes, Raven thought, getting rich all right, with a numbered Swiss account into which his untaxed commissions flowed, and nearly a half million dollars transferred from it to another blind account in Liechtenstein. The Iranian commissions would be added to it, and when he had time, he would set up a tax-free blind holding company in Liechtenstein to invest his assets. Oh yes, he was getting to be very rich.

Five minutes after Dan's call, Raven's phone rang again. When he answered it, the voice said, "This is Cass Owen. I'm sorry to bother you. Believe me, I am. But could you meet me for an hour tomorrow morning at the Los Angeles Airport? I won't need more than that." Her voice was anxious.

"Yes, of course, Mrs. Owen," Raven could barely keep his voice steady. "What time?"

"I can be there by nine. I'll meet you at the Admiral's Club."

Raven arrived at the Admiral's Club almost an hour early. When Cass came into the Club, Raven saw that although her eyes were dark from a sleepless night, her face was still lovely.

She clutched a small green purse which matched nothing she wore.

"Can I get you some coffee, Mrs. Owen?"

"No, thank you. You look different from your pictures," she said, sitting down.

"I guess so."

"I didn't want to call. I wouldn't have except for this engagement. If you talk with my husband or your father, please tell them I would never have contacted you except—" She stopped, then went on. "I called you with the idea of asking you to help stop this relationship between your brother and my daughter, but as I flew down this morning, I couldn't think of any way you could help. I'm a little embarrassed now, because all I can say to you is how horrible this is for me."

Raven nodded. "I can understand why."

"Can you?" She smiled sadly and said, "I doubt it. I don't know how much you know about me." She hesitated. "Do you know about my relationship with your father?"

Raven nodded.

"I presume my husband told you."

"No, Melanie did. My father filled in some details when I asked him about it." He did not want her to know of his early relationship with Melanie, and let her assume Melanie had only told him recently.

Cass looked surprised, then smiled bitterly. "I see. I suspected she knew. You know I loved my husband very much, even after I met Buck Faulkner. But with Buck I lost control. I still don't completely understand what happened."

Raven nodded.

"But the results of that affair I've had to understand all too well."

She hesitated and Raven said, "I know. Owen told me a little about that."

She eyed him appraisingly and said, "I think it's important that you know how hard we tried to save our marriage." As she talked she undid a button on the cuff of her blouse. "I'm not showing off." Across her wrist ran a jagged slick-skinned scar. "When I did this, I was much more interested in destroying the part of me that was still devoted to Buck Faulkner than ending my life." She rebuttoned the sleeve of her blouse.

Raven wanted to say something sympathetic, but he couldn't speak.

"Since that time, I've worked hard to forget your father. Jim and I tried to live together; we even had Melanie. But it didn't work. Our love didn't grow. It festered. In spite of that, I'd have stayed with Jim, but his hate for your father grew, until I realized that I'd never be able to forget Buck Faulkner if I stayed with Jim."

Her eyes widened noticeably. "I finally left. But Jim's hatred has never slackened, and I warn you, it's very dangerous. It's more dangerous to you and your brother than it is to your father. Jim needs Buck. You boys are just tools. He'll try to use you as weapons." She looked at him quizzically. "Does your brother understand any of this?"

"Only what he feels for your daughter."

"I hope what he feels is more complex than Melanie's impulse. When she was seven, she announced to me that she was going to be beautiful. She was right. She also said she was going to be rich. I suppose she was right again. Do you know how she found out about Buck and me?"

"You had some letters. She found them."

Her shoulders sagged. "What can I do?" she asked. "You know Jim is dying. He has emphysema and he won't stop smoking."

"Why?" asked Raven.

Her sad eyes slowly met his. "Because Jim wants to die. He has for a long time. Smoking is just a more socially acceptable form of suicide."

"Well, he'll get his wish if he—"

"Maybe. On the other hand, hate has kept him alive against worse odds than emphysema. And I don't think he'd let himself die without causing Buck some kind of pain. This is why you and your brother should be careful."

"What do you want me to do, Mrs. Owen?"

Cass Owen sank back into the couch and sat quietly for a moment, looking up toward the ceiling. "I want you to stop the marriage."

Raven looked at her dubiously. Cass nodded.

"Yes, I know, I doubt if you can. Other than that, be very careful with Jim. And warn your brother."

As she started to rise, Raven asked her, "Mrs. Owen, Jim gave you twenty thousand dollars once. Where did he say he got it?"

She looked at him curiously. "Why would he tell you about that? He said it was a bonus, I presumed from the Shah of Iran. It was for Melanie's education."

Raven saw that the woman had enough to live with, and obviously she did not want to know any more. She was standing by the table. "One last request. Please don't try and contact me. If Melanie does marry your brother, I'll live with it, but I won't want to talk." She leaned forward and shook his hand, then hurried out.

Three days later, Raven arrived at Mehrabad Air Base outside Tehran. He was accompanied by two Air Force F-99C Sword-Dancers, which he intended to display to as many members of the Imperial household as he could get to watch. He had also brought each male in the royal family a tailored powder-blue flight suit with the Pahlevi crest over the heart.

As soon as Raven dropped his bags in his hotel, he went to Jim Owen's office. Jim looked even thinner. His office had a view of the Elburz Mountains to the north. On the opposite wall Raven saw photographs of every Arab head of state in the last twenty years, each taken with Jim Owen. There was a large formal picture of the Shah, his wife and four children all smiling happily. As Jim lit up a cigarette, Raven said, "I heard you want to die."

Owen squinted his surprise, then smiled. "You've been talking to Cass. Notice any resemblance between you and her?"

Raven shook his head. "All I got was some warnings about you."

"How was she?"

"Bitter."

"Did you tell her who you were?"

"No."

Owen smiled flatly again. "Don't believe everything you hear." He coughed deeply, gasping for air.

Raven let him finish before he replied, "If you're crazy enough to keep smoking with emphysema, you're crazy enough to be really dangerous. I don't know what you have in mind, Jim, but I don't want my life messed up any more than it is already. I intend to take very good care of myself when I'm around you."

Jim paused to inhale, then said, "I'll show you what I have in mind."

He reached into a desk drawer, drew out a Colt .45, and put the gun to his temple.

Quietly, Raven said, "Don't."

"Why not?" Jim cocked the gun.

"Because nobody's going to regret it except you."

Just then the door of the office opened and Al Mardigian walked in, all smiles, until he saw the gun. "What the hell's going on?"

Jim Owen thumbed the hammer of the revolver and tossed it on his desk. Mardigian looked at Raven, who offered no explanation. There was an awkward silence until Owen said, "You can stay around here long enough to get your SwordDancer commission. After that, stay away from me. As far as *I'm* concerned, you're still Buck's boy."

Two days later, His Imperial Majesty and his seven-year-old son, both wearing Faulkner flight suits, arrived with their party at the Mehrabad Air Base. They proceeded to a royal enclosure, which was a luxurious version of a Shahsavan tribe's tent. From there the group watched the two SwordDancers perform.

Three days later, the sale was finalized. The price had gone up to two and a half million per plane. Raven left without seeing Jim again.

28

In early December, Faulkner's stockholder's report included a page on the state of the aerospace business.

"Nineteen sixty-eight is a record year in the aerospace industry, which currently employs one and a half million Americans. Six hundred thousand of those jobs are here in California. . . ."

Sam quickly scanned the rest of his report and threw it in his out box. On a yellow pad, he listed thirty-seven foreign countries, and followed each with initials indicating title or rank. Then he took a plain file out of his desk and opened the large sheet of graph paper folded inside. Frowning, he transposed the cryptographical columns to the appropriate lines on the yellow pad.

Sam didn't believe in office safes. He kept what he needed to know in his head, or on graph papers that no one else could decipher. When he finished transposing the figures to the list of abbreviations, he added up the total: $2,780,500. Below it, he added, "N.B.! *Not* including U.S." He tore off the sheet, put it in his pocket, and left his office by its private door.

The initials on the yellow sheet indicated clandestine Faulkner contacts of considerable influence in each of the countries listed. Not only did they pull strings on Faulkner Aerospace's behalf, but each acted as local oracle of political, military and economic matters. The funds they received could not be justified on a corporate balance sheet, and the contacts, many of whom were well known, never tolerated the usual scrutiny. Over the years, each had been contacted discreetly by Sam and regularly paid with cash.

As he walked back to Buck's office, Sam greeted several members of the Board's executive committee. As they took their places around the conference table, Sam handed the folded yellow sheet to Buck. Buck opened it, glanced at the total, and looked incredulously at Sam. Buck shook his head indicating that he would not discuss the situation.

Buck was uneasy. He knew that if such a large figure went unreported he could be in serious legal trouble if it were later discovered. Buck knew that neither the S.E.C., the Board nor the stockholders would accept such surreptitious practice, even though the payments had become an expected courtesy abroad.

Buck remembered the fifties, when the British stopped giving discreet boodle to their foreign markets. As a result, the British aircraft business lost most of their customers to France and the United States. The price of influence, however, was going up faster than sales or inflation. To Buck, cost of production was not the problem; to cover it, the product's price was simply increased. The problem was that there was no ceiling to such payoffs in sight. What's more, 1968 was an election year, so off-the-record political contributions in the United States would fill yet another yellow sheet, and the slide from "commission" to "bribe" and then to "extortion" would become dangerous.

Sam sat down next to Raven at the end of the table. Both attended executive committee meetings when able, but they did not speak unless called upon.

Buck began. "Now that Mr. McNamara has been kicked upstairs to the World Bank—and may I say respectfully, God help the world—" Several executives laughed obediently. "His successor, Mr. Clifford, seems to be in favor of offensive weapons, namely the B-1 bomber, to finally replace S.A.C.'s old reliables, the B-52. The two questions which face us are, do we want the contract and can we get it?"

"How much have we invested?" someone asked.

"Ball park, twelve million."

Several committee members seemed concerned.

"It's worth it," Buck insisted. "The contract just for prototypes will be a couple of billion. The other companies in on this are outspending us by far."

"The Pentagon is talking about seven prototypes," said the vice-president for finance. "Committing that kind of capital will extend us beyond our limits. The only other way is to do what North American did with Rockwell: merge to increase operating capital."

The discussion continued. Each member of the executive committee expressed his reservations, but each knew that Buck wanted the B-1 contract.

"What if we don't get the contract?" Raven asked.

Buck scowled dangerously. "Does that prospect appeal to you?"

"It might. How do you sell a hundred-million-dollar bomber that's vulnerable to a hundred-thousand-dollar missile? In ten years, when the B-1 becomes operational, missile technology applied to our own Brick-Bat missile may make such a bomber an instant antique."

"Your point seems irrelevant," Buck said.

"Is spending ten years and billions of dollars on a potentially defunct airplane irrelevant?"

"Yes, because the B-1 could keep our plant going for ten years at *full capacity*. If the Pentagon wants to build that plane, 'ours is not to reason why.'" Buck moved quickly to a vote, carefully avoiding his son's eye.

"All those in favor?" The response was expected. "All those opposed?" Raven remained quiet.

During the 1968 election, Faulkner Aerospace contributed two hundred and thirty thousand dollars to various campaigns. When Richard Nixon was elected in November, the badly depressed aerospace industry knew that they would have a patron in the White House. By the time Nixon was sworn in, there were so many aerospace executives in town that Washington, D.C., resembled the Paris Air Show.

Buck sent Raven to help fight for the B-1 contract. Raven worked hard on the project, discovering what politicians wanted and getting it for them. His personal concerns became as abstract as the B-1 bomber itself, which despite his unremitting attention, no longer seemed a plane, or a weapons system, but merely a contract. Ethics no longer interested him. They were part of a world he had left behind.

In contrast, Washington seemed to galvanize with power and

tension. Its insecurity, paranoia and incurable lust for recognition bemused Raven. The town seemed an endless spectacle of human egos, full of monuments to folly. The parties were as complex as government itself, microcosms of the power structure. In no other milieu than a Washington party would he have met Mrs. Wheatley.

First Raven noticed her hair, which was flaming red. Her skin had the translucent sheen of polished marble, with which lucky redheads are blessed. She had widely set blue eyes and a slightly upturned nose. Her mouth was misleading; in repose it was small, yet her smile was the widest of welcomes. Raven noticed, however, that the smile never quite covered a wary watchfulness.

General and Mrs. Dulaney had arranged the dinner at the Army-Navy Club. The occasion was referred to as a Faulkner "in-house do." Raven was one of the few civilians present. He noticed that Mrs. Wheatley resolutely stood in one place, allowing the party to come to her. She seemed to know everyone, and just about everyone came across the room to greet her. Since Raven didn't know who she was, he awaited his turn.

"Hello. I'm Raven Faulkner."

"Oh yes," she said. "You were named for an airplane."

"I'm afraid I don't know your name," he said, ignoring her mockery.

Her eyes lifted in surprise. "You don't?" she said, then added, "How nice."

"Why?" Raven asked.

She stared at him for a moment. "I'm Babs Wheatley." Raven saw that she expected recognition.

"Representative Wheatley's daughter?" He remembered that several years before, the old Oklahoma Congressman had been defeated for reelection, which gave Bucknell of Albuquerque the chairmanship of the House Armed Services Committee.

"No. His former wife." Putting her glass down on the piano, she walked away.

Raven watched her cross the room as she was greeted by a group of Air Force officers. He remembered that Sam Priest had mentioned some scandal connected with the old Congressman. When they lined up for the buffet, Raven found a spot behind her.

"I'm new in town," he said. "May I try again?"

"Try what?" she said coolly.

"Charming you—without the usual game of rank and vile."

She smiled. "Did you say '*vile*'?"

He nodded.

"You're not so new in town!"

He said, "Tell me who you are."

"Tell *me* about airplanes."

"It's boring."

"So am I. Nice try." She walked away again.

Raven followed. "What am I supposed to know about you?"

"Everything. Nothing."

He shrugged. "I'd prefer everything."

"I'm sure you can hear it all at this party."

"I'd rather hear it from you."

She suppressed her smile. "You are charming."

"I'm trying my best."

"Since you're new in town," she said, "I'll explain something that took me a long time to learn. If you stay around Washington, you get a character created for you. A cartoon with a little dirt." She looked away.

"So why not leave," Raven said. "Go back home?"

"In my case," she said with a sigh, "home is a town of two hundred rednecks in eastern Oklahoma. Besides, I couldn't afford the moving van."

Raven glanced at the ring and bracelet on her right hand. "They say the price of diamonds is up."

"I'd never sell these," she said touching the necklace. "They're my scarlet letter."

"Part of the cartoon."

She nodded. "You learn fast."

"Maybe you're stuck with me."

"It seems that way." She looked at him for a moment. "Why don't you take me in to dinner?"

He took the glass out of her hand and put it down on a windowsill. Taking her hand, he said, "Let's get out of here."

"That'd be rude."

"No. Raven Faulkner's the host."

"I'm never going to call you Raven," she said, watching him. "Why not?"

"Because that's an airplane."

He nodded slowly. "How about Ray?"

"Better," she said, and they walked to the door.

Most of the guests had gone into the dining room. Only Sam Priest saw them heading for the elevator hand in hand. Raven smiled at him with mock innocence; Sam rolled his eyes fatefully toward heaven.

Outside, Raven helped Babs into his limousine, gave the driver the name of a restaurant in Alexandria, and closed the divider.

Babs pointed to the small bar and said, "Do you have any wine in there?"

Raven had never used the bar and leaned forward to fold it open. In the small refrigerator were beer, wine, and four splits of Champagne.

Babs said, "Perfect."

Over Champagne, they began comparing childhoods. "Yours was rich, mine was different," Babs said laughing. The car stopped in front of the awning to the restaurant. Raven opened the door and said, "For the next episode, I need oysters."

"I wouldn't miss it."

Talking about everything from "Oklahoma prude" to pacifism, they ate oysters and half a loaf of French bread. When the rack of lamb arrived, Raven said, "Enough about us. Tell me about you."

"I can't talk," she said quickly lifting up her fork and taking a bite, "when my mouth is full."

Another hour passed. They discussed Washington. She was funny one minute, blisteringly insightful the next.

As the pastry cart wheeled past, Raven said, "Can you resist that?"

"Oh yes. I only eat one thing for dessert," she said.

"What's that?"

"Blackberry swirl double butterfat ice cream."

"Where can we get that?"

"At my house," she replied without the slightest implication.

When the limousine turned into the driveway off Foxhall Road, Raven recognized the house. The classic French château was often taken for an embassy. As they walked up the stone steps to the front door, Raven heard a dog growling.

"It's all right, Kitty," Babs said as she unlocked the front door. Kitty, an Irish wolfhound, greeted Raven affectionately.

"Nice horse you have," he said.

"Kitty's an old bitch," Babs said, "but she's a good burglar alarm. Come on in. She won't bother you."

Even in the dim light, Raven could see the deterioration of the carpets. Babs took his hand and led him through the rooms of the ground floor. The huge dog accompanied them, panting with pleasure. The rooms were empty; only the windows, which faced Foxhall Road, still had drapes.

Finally, she stopped. "This was the dining room. We sat down in here with thirty people every other Friday night."

"Were those the days?"

He was close enough to see her nod slowly. "For a while." She took a few steps away from him. "I loved my husband—" she said turning away. Raven thought that she didn't want to take a chance on his reaction. When he offered none, she added, "—as long as I could. I loved this place, too. It's the first place I've ever lived where the roof doesn't leak. Well, at least I haven't cut up the drapes for dresses."

"Tara got Scarlett through the war," Raven said with a thick Southern accent.

She laughed. "If Scarlett O'Hara had owned this place, she'd have gone crazy. I owe my soul to a Georgetown plumber. Come on."

She led him through a swinging door into a huge kitchen. Capped pipes stuck out of the wall where multiple appliances had once stood. One refrigerator remained, along with a two-burner hot plate. The room was lit by a single fluorescent tube, which Babs snapped off. She struck a match and lit the four-branch silver candelabrum on the kitchen table. Kitty curled her massive form onto a piece of rug in a corner.

Holding out her hand, Babs said, "We have to go downstairs for the ice cream. Will you carry the light?"

Raven picked up the candelabrum and followed her through a door. They descended a flight of steps to the basement, where she stopped for a moment and held his hand tightly.

"You all right?" he asked.

"You bet," she said. Then she opened the top of a freezer crammed with frozen food. "I guess it's finally time to sell the place. You know, nobody's been here since the divorce." She glanced at him, and he smiled. "Keeping it has been crazy. I moved in here when I was nineteen. Back home there were ten of us kids, and I swear one reason I married the Congressman was to get a room of my own."

She lifted the pint of ice cream up.

"Go on," he said, following her back up the stairs.

"My daddy thought Congressman Wheatley was God for making sure the Oklahoma tobacco growers got the same benefits they got in Tennessee and North Carolina. It was a real kindness; there just aren't too many voters in Oklahoma that care about tobacco. It's all oil, and the Congressman had more of that than mustard. He came up here to look after it. Anyway, when I was growing up, there was a signed picture of Congressman Wheatley in our dining room. When Daddy died, I was sixteen. The Congressman came to the funeral; he was that kind of old-fashioned politician. That was a problem too: he was old, and he didn't want to be."

Raven watched her carefully as she took two bowls out of a kitchen cabinet and tried to scoop the ice cream into them.

"Damn," she said. "This stuff is frozen solid."

Raven took the scoop out of her hand and saw that there were tears in her eyes.

"Tell me," he said, touching her cheek.

She nodded. "He was so sweet to me." She shrugged. "For the next three years, he came around the house when he visited the district. During that time, he had a face lift, transplanted some hair, and when I was nineteen, he proposed. He was sixty-three. By then, I loved him as much as I thought I could love anyone."

Raven handed her the ice cream, and she opened a drawer and took out two spoons.

"I just adored him. For ten years I campaigned for him, ran his house, entertained, and never asked for anything more. But it came anyway. That's when someone drew my Washington cartoon. Let's eat."

They sat at the kitchen table and ate in the light of the candelabrum. She watched him doubtfully, then said, "It'll be interesting to see how long you'll believe me when you start hearing what everybody else says."

"Try me." He began to eat the ice cream.

"Well, 'the affair' was with a married man, very high up around town, who had very grand ambitions. I loved him, so I kept him a secret—but, of course, everyone eventually found out about me. They always do, especially in Washington. Then the rumors put me in bed with almost everyone in town." She slowly moved the spoon through the dish. "Then, Mr. Wheatley got mad—very mad—and decided to divorce me. Big scandal. Washington loved guessing at who the other man was. Don't ever ask."

"I didn't deny much in court. I was hurting too much to care. The judge gave me the house *without* most of the Wheatley furniture, and my 'personal effects,' which included some of the Wheatley diamonds. My lawyer made me wear them to court every day to establish ownership." She laughed sadly.

They ate silently. Raven was already thinking that if Sam liked Mrs. Wheatley, she would make a terrific consultant. He wanted to tell her, but decided to wait.

"Anyway, Faulkner Aerospace is in my debt," she said.

"What for?" he said with surprise.

"I'd say I had a lot to do with my husband's retirement from politics, which allowed your friend Bucknell to become chairman of the House Armed Services Committee."

He nodded. "Sounds like you're pointing the guilty finger at yourself."

"I'm the one who did it to him. Wheat never would have been defeated otherwise."

"A sixty-year-old man going after a sixteen-year-old girl takes his chances. The dice came up his way for a long time, then he lost. He came off pretty well—a hell of a lot better than you did. He won ten years; you paid them. You didn't exactly steal those diamonds."

She sat without responding, then slowly reached across the table for his hand. "Tell me that, over and over again. I don't know if I should have told you so much."

"You took a chance, so now I'll take one." He leaned over and kissed her neck. When he finally sat back, she smiled at him and said, "Nice try. You win."

She picked up the candelabrum, and the two of them went out through the swinging door, followed by the Irish wolfhound.

They walked back through the rooms to the front hall. At the foot of the stairs leading to the second floor, she turned and handed him the candelabrum. "There's no point in your chauffeur staying out there all night. I'll meet you upstairs."

"Where?"

"The only room with furniture."

Raven dismissed his driver and then followed Babs upstairs. Light came from a doorway. When he walked into the bedroom, he saw Babs sitting on a heavily draped four-poster bed. The room was crowded with storage boxes stacked around lounges, a marble table, some odd chairs, two couches and many lamps. Several pictures and mirrors in ornate frames were leaning against the wall.

"This isn't as crazy as it looks," she said, "but it *is* crazy."

"What is all this?" Raven put the candelabrum down on a table.

"Personal effects! My lawyer said the court might let me only keep the furniture in my room, so every night I dragged stuff in here. I never bothered to drag it out again. If you think this is bad, you should see what I have stacked in the bathroom." She looked back at him. "You're the first visitor."

"And the last," Raven said. "You can move into a larger room tomorrow."

"What?"

"As you said, we're in your debt, and we hate debts. What if Faulkner Aerospace leases the house for five years at top dollar for corporate entertaining, with the understanding that you'll live here, redecorate and throw the parties?"

"Wait!" she said, "Ray, come over here and make love to me. I've been anticipating that for a couple of hours now, and I don't like being overwhelmed with more than one thing at a time."

29

The Sunday morning after the Senate allocated one hundred million dollars for the development of the B-1, Raven sat drinking his morning coffee in Babs's newly decorated bedroom. As he finished reading the paper, Babs came out of the bathroom, swathed in cashmere, with her hair wrapped in a towel.

"Would you pour my coffee, Ray? Leave it black, or I'll probably fall asleep. I'm flying six Air Force wives down to Williamsburg for lunch. Why, I'll never know. They wouldn't know a B-1 from a B.M."

"Don't tell them," Raven smiled up at her.

"I wouldn't waste my time. I pre*sume* you and your Daddy'll name the prototype for me after all I'm doing for Faulkner Aerospace." Sitting on his lap, she put his paper aside and kissed him. "I think your daddy likes me."

"I think so, too. He ought to. That was a pretty impressive gathering you put together on Friday. I hear he wants to be invited to all your parties."

"He told me that. I said as long as he kept paying for them, he could come."

Raven smiled and kissed her. She laid her head on his shoulder and said, "Funny, though. He's wary about something, kind of circles around me."

Raven didn't respond.

"What are you doing today?" she asked.

"This morning Sam and I helicopter down the Chesapeake.

There's a duck-hunting lodge we're thinking of buying as an R-and-R resort for the brass. This afternoon, I have a box at the Redskins' game for three Admirals and a Senator."

Babs said, "You don't sound happy in your work."

He didn't answer. Sitting back on the ottoman, she put a hand on his knee.

"You know, Ray, it doesn't make any difference to me if you don't care about this damn airplane contract, but I'll tell you, it'd be a whole lot easier on you if you did."

Raven shrugged. "You're right, but I don't."

"Seems to me you're the one who should care the most. I mean, Buck Faulkner's one of the few men left on this earth who can say, 'Son, one day all this will be yours.' " Her mimicry was exact. She took his hand. "But you're just walking through it."

"I guess so."

"Killing time," she said, looking at him closely.

He nodded.

"Take it from one who knows," she sighed, "you start killing too much time, it'll stay dead."

"I suppose."

"So listen," she said, getting up and going into her dressing room, "what I want from you is a little enthusiasm. After all," she drawled, "we have to get us a contract."

"What if we don't?"

"Well, I'll just go back to living on hominy grits and hors d'oeuvres. But have you ever thought what it'd be like for you without Faulkner Aerospace?"

Raven didn't answer. Her question, however, stayed in his mind for days.

A month later, the Pentagon officially "requested" bids for five prototypes. Four companies received the invitation: North American Rockwell, Faulkner, General Dynamics and Boeing. Like the other companies, Faulkner Aerospace already had been working on the project. For six years, a thousand engineers and millions of dollars had been spent on the B-1 proposal. The preliminary specifications already ran eight thousand pages, bound into sixty-five volumes. It was the most expensive commitment Faulkner had ever made to win a contract, and while they were still planning, the project was coming under intense Congressional criticism.

Concerned, Jennifer and Buck took a furnished apartment at the Watergate. Babs and Jennifer met soon afterward, but the nature of the evening was business. Babs called Jennifer the next day and invited her to lunch. Jennifer was delighted and insisted on being the hostess.

"I'm so glad you phoned me," Jennifer said, as they sat down at a table at the Sulgrave Club.

"So am I," Babs said with a wry smile. "I imagine you've heard a good deal more about me than either your son or Mr. Faulkner told you."

"Yes, I have."

Babs's eyes flickered as she picked up her menu. "I was afraid of that."

Jennifer looked at her, "I don't believe everything I hear."

Babs laughed. "Well, it's a long story. Do I have to talk fast?"

"As far as I'm concerned, you don't have to explain anything. You're doing a splendid job for the company and I'm sure we'll be seeing a lot of each other in the next months."

"I'd like that. I like my job. And I like your son."

Jennifer nodded. "I suppose it's natural for a mother to hope that her son won't be hurt."

Babs leaned on the table. "Mrs. Faulkner, I wouldn't hurt him. I adore him. Furthermore, he and I are friends, the best kind. He's tired of being alone, and so am I. I'm not sure that we're in love with each other. For the moment, maybe we can't be, but he makes me happy, and I make him laugh, a couple of honest accomplishments."

"You said, 'being alone'?" Jennifer said.

Babs sat back in her chair. "I've seen him in a room with a hundred people, shaking hands, asking about their families, listening to their problems. And it's always as if he were alone inside a glass bottle looking out. I don't know what it is, except I've seen the same kind of look on your husband's face. Like father, like son maybe? You'd know that better than I would."

Jennifer found herself somehow disappointed that Babs didn't know more. On the other hand, she had heard that Mrs. Wheatley had a reputation for never keeping a secret. Jennifer said nothing more and they turned their conversation to business.

As they were leaving, Jennifer said, "Babs, whether we get this contract or not, I look forward to knowing you better. I must

291

admit that I'm a protective mother, but I'm also a good friend, or so I'm told."

Babs smiled. "I need as many of those as I can get."

A month later the B-1 project looked as if it were headed for real trouble. The doves in the Senate seemed determined to shoot it out of the sky.

"I think Proxmire, Kennedy and McGovern should be our next team of astronauts," Babs suggested at one meeting in the Faulkner offices.

Sam Priest smiled. "Send 'em right on up to heaven, so they can replace the Trinity."

Jennifer said, "They won't be joked away, Sam."

Buck had flown in from Faulkner Field the previous night. "There's no point wasting our time on three doves cooing at each other," he scowled. Turning to a chagrined General Dulaney, Buck added, "The Pentagon has a small army of public-relations people. Tell them it's time to send out their generals to scare hell out of the American public." He turned to Raven. "Get a picture of a B-52 that's falling apart and put it next to something sleek and Russian. Sin-Gin, you pass it around on the Hill. The Russians are already flying a Mach-2 airplane with a range of five thousand miles."

Raven listened with an increasing sense of disbelief. "Is Congress that stupid? Because if it's not, this could boomerang."

"What do you mean?" Jennifer asked carefully.

Raven slumped in his chair. "Forget it," he said.

"No, let's hear what you have to say," Buck commanded.

Raven took a deep breath and glanced at Babs. Unseen by the others, she shrugged and looked to heaven. "You want me to put a picture of the B-52 up against a 'sleek' Russian bomber," Raven began. "The only intercontinental bomber they have is the TU-20 Bear, which has turboprops, *propellers!* It's as *old* as the B-52 and it's *slower.* The Russians are phasing them out, using them for reconnaissance. We have twice as many B-52s, armed and programmed for attack. I don't think it's such a great idea to compare them." Raven was surprised at his growing anger. "Maybe I can dig up a rendering of the Russians' new Backfire Bomber and make it scarey as hell. But the intelligence people, ours as well as everyone else's, know the Russians are having design problems. And even if it were in the air today the Russians wouldn't use it to attack us. If they wanted to bomb the U.S., they would use an unmanned I.C.B.M."

Disgusted, Raven shook his head. "We've *always* overestimated Russian technology. The Soviet Union has more planes than the U.S., but their planes aren't as good. Of course, they aren't as expensive, either, and that's really what we're talking about: money and Faulkner Aerospace. All this is just a rationalization for getting the money to keep the company going. The end product is irrelevant; building it is everything. We're talking about fifty to seventy-five *billion* dollars to fly, refuel and arm a fleet of two hundred and fifty fancy, but immediately obsolete, B-1 bombers. What if the American public wakes up and becomes scared about going broke? This contract would force Faulkner Aerospace to be completely dependent on the Pentagon. Cancellation of this contract would do more damage than losing it in the first place."

"He sounds like the old closet Quaker to me," Sam said with a grin, trying to release the tension. No one laughed except Raven, who said unexpectedly, "Sam, that's probably who I am."

In the awkward silence that followed, Raven noted a shadow of fear cross his mother's face.

General Dulaney started to speak, but then thought better of it. He didn't want to interrupt a family argument.

Buck tried to control his anger. "In our business, you supply the market or close up shop."

"Then shouldn't we admit, at least to ourselves, that what we're doing is dumb—or dangerous?"

General Dulaney suddenly stood up. "I see no reason to discuss this further."

Buck nodded. "We'll talk again tomorrow. Raven, you wait here."

As soon as everyone except Babs and Jennifer had left, Buck turned to Raven. "You're off the B-1 project."

"Fine," Raven answered. He stood up to leave.

"Wait," said Jennifer.

Angrily, Buck continued. "Dulaney will report Raven's military interpretations right to Jack Llewellyn, and from there, throughout the Air Force. I want news of Raven's removal from the project to reach them just as quickly. I hope you'll get right to work on that, Babs."

Babs nodded, not at Buck, but at Jennifer. She stood, and with only a quick look at Raven, left the room.

"Raven, please sit down for a moment," Jennifer said.

He took his place at the table.

Jennifer continued. "Buck, it'll be a mistake to take Raven off the project. It will appear to everyone that our house isn't in order."

"And if he remains, the Pentagon won't touch us with a ten-foot pole."

There was a long silence. Then Jennifer spoke quietly but firmly. "I agree with everything Raven said. I've thought that way for years."

"You're arguing to keep him our son, and doing better than I could do. He may be trying very hard not to be."

Raven stood up. "I didn't say all that because I'm adopted."

"Are you sure?" Buck stood up and went out the door.

When Jennifer looked at Raven, he shook his head, but said nothing.

"He's afraid that what happened to him will happen to you," Jennifer began. "When he finally found his biological parents, they died inside him."

"Connie Mannheim's already dead," Raven said, as he sat down across from his mother.

Jennifer gasped. "How do you know?"

"Jim Owen told me."

"When?"

"Just after I saw you in Paris."

Jennifer nodded. "I see. All this time you've known."

Raven looked at her. "Do you really agree with me about all that stuff?"

"Most of it."

"Not just because you're a clever lawyer and a faithful mother?"

She looked at him and smiled sadly. "You know that you haven't called me that since Paris?"

"I'm sorry."

Jennifer shook her head. "I'd promised myself not to mention that to you. I suppose I've missed it too much. Raven, stay Buck Faulkner's son for a while longer. He needs you very much. You were right in Paris when you said it's so different for him now. It's crippling to be controlled by these military people. Help him with the B-1 contract. Even if we don't get it, he'll remember that you were with him."

Jennifer waited for an answer. Finally, Raven got up to leave. "I don't know how much longer I can forget everything I believe, just because I want a father and Buck Faulkner wants a son."

30

In early January of 1970, the four bids for the B-1 bomber were submitted. Faulkner's proposal reached seventy-two volumes, standing five feet tall. Its estimate came in at $1.45 billion for five prototypes. The proposals were scored by six hundred Air Force technical experts. During the process, intense unofficial manipulation continued. Buck was not surprised when Jack Llewellyn called to set up a meeting with the Under Secretary of the Air Force. What intrigued Buck was Jack's insistence that Raven attend.

Strangely, Raven's impulsive statements had not seemed to create any ramifications in the Pentagon although General Dulaney had not returned to the Faulkner offices. Buck presumed that once again, he was indebted to Jack Llewellyn.

Buck called Raven into his office to make sure that his son would not repeat his ideas to the Under Secretary of the Air Force.

"I've heard you've done well on the Hill," Buck began.

"Who can tell? It's insane up there."

"Why?"

"You know how they really think the contract should be awarded? Not to the best plane. To the company that needs it the most." He laughed and shook his head.

Buck smiled. "And how do you convince them that we need it the most?"

"I tell everyone there are a hundred thousand unemployed aerospace workers in California. That's more than Seattle or

Texas. Then, I have to convince them that Faulkner needs it more than our neighbor Rockwell does. So I've been reminding the California delegation of Faulkner's thirty years of California history, along with Rockwell's headquarters in *Pittsburgh*. But who knows?"

"I think we're all right," said Buck. "If you still want to get out of this, you can."

"No. I'm in this—if you are."

Buck hesitated. Raven was making a statement of affection, rather than commitment.

"Well," Buck said, "we've been invited to the Pentagon for a meeting with the Under Secretary of the Air Force."

"I've been waiting to see what Uncle Jack is going to do for us," Raven said, laughing, and they went down to their car. Fifteen minutes later they arrived at the river entrance of the Pentagon. An Air Force colonel met them and escorted them to the Under Secretary's office.

"Mr. Faulkner, all my life I've wanted to meet you." The Under Secretary came around his desk to shake Buck's hand. "I've been flying since I was ten, and I've admired your planes ever since I found an old Raven at a National Guard camp."

"And this is Raven Faulkner," Jack said proudly.

The Under Secretary's expression changed slightly from lavish charm to quick appraisal. They were about the same age. "Hi, how are you, Raven?" Then he returned to his chair behind his desk. For the first time, Buck began to suspect that the meeting was not exclusively about the B-1 bomber.

"First of all," said the Under Secretary, "what's said in this room will remain between us. As General Llewellyn can tell you, I've wanted Faulkner Aerospace to build the B-1 bomber from the beginning."

"That's absolutely true," Llewellyn said.

Buck noted the rehearsed tone of their statements.

"General Llewellyn and I want to try to help," the Under Secretary continued. "We want you to know some of the reasons why you might not get the B-1 contract. Then maybe we can solve the problem among ourselves."

"I don't know of any problem," Buck said.

"Buck," the Under Secretary said, "you and I know there's no reason, but other people have ideas of their own."

"What, for example?" Buck asked.

"The main thing we hear is that Faulkner is too small."

"And when they say something so ill-informed, what do you tell them?" Buck asked.

"What *should* we tell them, Buck?" Jack asked.

"Boeing is bigger, but General Dynamics and North American Rockwell are only bigger corporately. Faulkner Aerospace is in the same league with both of those companies' aircraft divisions. Therefore, the advantage we have is that our entire business is airplanes. With some conglomerates, you'll end up with an airplane made of feathers just because they own a chicken farm."

The Under Secretary laughed nervously at Buck's joke.

"May I interrupt?" Raven asked.

Apprehensively, Buck turned to his son.

"We're at a disadvantage," Raven began. "You know we want the B-1 contract, but we don't know what you want. Wouldn't it save us all a lot of time if you just told us?"

The Under Secretary's face tightened. "Sure, Raven, we don't want to waste *your* time, so let me give you a picture of Faulkner Aerospace as we see it here at the Pentagon."

The general smiled as the Under Secretary began his interpretation. As he talked, he casually flipped a ball-point pen end over end. "Faulkner basically makes two good planes, the C-1000 transport and the SwordDancer. Both are reaching the end of their production runs. Your subsidiary missile and communications divisions aren't large enough to carry you. Your plans for a new wide-bodied jet liner are putting pressure on your financing. Wall Street already suspects your vulnerability. Your stock is down, your credit's extended to its limits, your cash reserve is negligible. Our view is that, if you lose the B-1, you could be forced to sell out. Even if you didn't, you'd be just about the best candidate for a takeover on the Big Board. Aside from that, you make some of the best planes America has, and we'd like to make sure it stays that way. The Air Force needs you, and so does this country."

"Thank you," Buck said. "How do you plan to do that?"

The Under Secretary stopped flipping his pen. "The B-1 is going to take a lot of capital cash flow. You don't have it, and probably can't get it from your banks. If a takeover is inevitable, why not get together your own conglomerate, one that will allow you to gain immediate cash for the B-1—"

"In this conglomerate," asked Buck, "do you have any idea who Faulkner Aerospace might take in?"

"Oakland Terminal and Dry Dock, Dominion Steel, and Trans-National Electronics."

"Have you discussed this idea with any of them?" Buck asked, indicating no surprise.

"All of them. Their reactions were positive." The Under Secretary stood up. "Buck, Ben Hoffman of Dominion would accept vice-chairmanship *under* you."

Buck nodded. He knew Ben Hoffman and liked him, but he also knew that because of Japanese steel imports, Dominion was in serious trouble. They desperately needed an Army contract to cast the turrets for the new battle tank. Oakland Dry Dock built ships for the Navy, and Trans-National was a rival with Faulkner for in-board computer technology. On the surface, the merger appeared a perfect one.

"Have you come up with a name for this conglomerate?" he asked.

"No, sir," the Under Secretary replied, smiling. "We thought that that should be your honor; after all, it would be your company."

"Would it?" Buck mused. He turned to Raven, who said abruptly to the Under Secretary, "Where do you fit in?"

"I'd like to answer that, Raven," Llewellyn said. "As we said, Buck would be chairman; Hoffman would be vice-chairman, and, because he conceived the idea, the Under Secretary would be its president—"

"But only for the first four years," said the Under Secretary. "When I resign, Raven would take my place."

For a moment, no one spoke. Then Buck laughed. "I just saw 'the picture.' The conglomerate isn't just good for business, but for politics, too." Buck laughed again. "Faulkner Aerospace and Oakland Dry Dock are in California, Trans-National is in Texas, and Dominion is in Pennsylvania. Four years of running a company in those three power bases would make a nice springboard for a Senate seat. After all, well, you'd still be in your forties with a chance for the White House. As for you, Jack, I doubt if you're after a job with just another aerospace conglomerate. So what is it? Secretary of State or Secretary of Defense?"

Llewellyn did not enjoy the astuteness of the perception. "Buck, there are a lot of responsibilities facing us in this world, and one of them is finding our future leaders. I haven't met a better possibility than the Under Secretary. He would represent the best interests of this country—"

"Not to mention the military," said Raven. "I can see the Defense budgets now."

"Good, Raven," the Under Secretary spoke quickly, "and I hope you can see the share of them Faulkner would get. Our future would be guaranteed."

"By the government, just like the Tupolev works." Raven turned to the general. "Uncle Jack, you already have a little Kremlin over here. Do you really need your own czar in the White House?"

"You're out of line, Raven," Llewellyn snapped.

"We've heard a lot about your politics, Raven," said the Under Secretary. "Frankly, they don't matter. What we're talking about here is business, pure and simple. You might be interested to know that your last harangue only succeeded in converting General Dulaney to Rockwell's cause."

In the pause that followed, the Under Secretary sat back in his chair and flipped his pen. His jaw clenched spasmodically.

"The company you've outlined," Buck said, "would be a captive of the military. Besides, I can't conceive of Faulkner as a division of a conglomerate. So I have only one question. If we decide *not* to join, will you still support the Faulkner Aerospace bid for the B-1?"

The Under Secretary's pen flipped too high and fell behind him on the floor. "You don't get it, do you, Buck? I just explained to you why you can't build the B-1 on your own. Do you want me to tell you what's going to happen to Faulkner Aerospace *without* the B-1 contract? *Slow death,* while your stock goes through the floor, and finally someone buys you out to build high-rises on Faulkner Field. And I'll tell you something else: the Pentagon has the longest memory in town, so don't think for a second the B-1 is all you'll lose. Even when I leave, General Llewellyn will remember your decision."

"Is that right, Jack?"

The general met his look. "I want the merger to go through, Buck. I think you owe it to me."

"I owe you a lot, Jack, but not everything, particularly when you want to waste it on making a President out of this—Under Secretary."

"Okay, Buck. Thanks for coming over," said the Under Secretary, smiling maliciously. He swiveled around in his chair so that its back faced his visitors.

Jack Llewellyn didn't move. "Buck, I've helped you save your company time and time again. I delivered sales teams, projects, and off-the-record information. I kept your affair secret and rescued your lover's husband." He watched both Faulkners, but neither reacted, so he went on. "I monitored Raven's captivity and went to the White House myself to clear his rescue. I didn't do all of that for nothing, Buck. If you walk out of here without accepting this plan, I promise you things will be different."

Buck remained silent, but Raven said softly, "Uncle Jack, if you think you're the foundation of Faulkner Aerospace, you're crazy."

Jack Llewellyn remained sitting in his chair. "Raven, you may not like to hear it, but without me, Buck Faulkner would not be where he is today. And you, Raven, might not be alive."

Buck interrupted. "You haven't done a damn thing but gamble on me. Years ago at Old Orchard, you lost. Every other time you won, and don't pretend I haven't contributed to those stars on your shoulder."

Sitting ramrod straight in his chair, Jack said calmly, "I'll destroy you, Buck. I can do it from here, you know."

"So you said. Come on, Raven."

Outside, they hurried down the steps to their car. "They live on different gases in there," Raven said.

The driver hurried to open the door. As Buck got in, Raven said, "You were terrific."

"I'm glad you were there." Buck motioned the driver to start.

"I want to tell you something," Raven said. "No matter what they said, they were playing on heritage. I don't want you to ever make a decision because of me. I don't expect anything. In fact, if you give it to me, I might not take it. Dan's a better bet."

"I appreciate your telling me, but I make my own bets."

"All right, what do we do about the B-1?"

"We have to keep after it."

"But we won't get it."

Buck shook his head. "Jack was playing from considerable strength in there."

"Any contingencies?"

"I'll think up one or two, as usual. You and Jack Llewellyn can't change that habit, even though you both may be pleased in your own way that we don't receive the contract."

"That plane's a loser. Some day you'll be glad."

"That's something I wouldn't bet on."

"What do we do about Uncle Jack?"

"We stop calling him 'uncle.'"

The day that the contract was awarded, Buck made sure that Congressman Bucknell was at the Faulkner offices. Senator Sanderson called to express his regrets. Buck hung up and turned to Sam, Raven and Babs, who were waiting with Congressman Bucknell. "Rockwell got it," he said.

Bucknell shot up out of his chair. "I don't believe it! Those sons of bitches, we'll kill—"

Buck interrupted him. "Sam, get the Execujet ready. We're leaving for Faulkner Field tonight. Call the members of the executive committee and have them in my office tomorrow morning at eight." He then turned to the Congressman. "Sit down, Bucknell. We just lost thirty million dollars making this proposal. I want it back and you're going to get it for me."

"How the hell—"

"I told you to listen! We're going to retool the SwordDancer, and the government's going to pay for it. I want you to kick every member on your House Armed Services Committee wherever it hurts, so they support us. We'll upgrade the design, make it more versatile and cheaper than any other fighter coming down the pipeline. And then we'll sell it—" he looked hard at Raven—"overseas, and we'll never be dependent on the Pentagon again."

Raven met his glance, but Buck didn't wait for a reply.

"Until now," Buck said as he stood up to leave, "I've been able to hold the Faulkner family together pretty well. But tomorrow we'll have to send out fourteen thousand pink slips. Before we're done, by God, I'll hire every one of them back."

302

31

After some arm twisting, the government financed the Sword-Dancer's retooling. The fighter would be equipped with state-of-the-art avionics and missile systems equal to those of Grumman's F-14 Tomcat, McDonnell Douglas's F-15 Eagle, and Northrop's F-5E Tiger II. Four such advanced aircraft, however, glutted the market, and every SwordDancer sale became crucial.

Faulkner Aerospace wasn't the only company affected by the loss of the B-1 contract. The entire industry went into a tailspin. Two hundred thousand highly trained technicians were out of work, and Congress found it necessary to approve a quarter-billion-dollar loan guarantee to save Lockheed from bankruptcy.

As expected, the commercial airline companies stopped ordering the Faulkner CF-102. Buck ramrodded bank loans for the development of a new wide-bodied commercial passenger liner, what he called the Gamma. In order to secure the loans and build the prototype, however, he had to put up the valuable real estate of Faulkner Field as security. The company had never faced such financial jeopardy, and Buck knew that the Pentagon could not be relied on to bail him out.

In the following weeks, Raven traveled through Europe briefing the commercial airlines on the new Gamma jetliner and exerting steady pressure on NATO countries to purchase the upgraded SwordDancer. As the cities blurred together, he tried to blame his general depression on the vile weather.

Raven hoped Babs's arrival in Paris would lift his spirits. As he waited for her at Orly, he realized that he was probably counting on her too much.

"Hello, stranger," she said, hurrying out of customs. Raven hugged her, but Babs could read an embrace better than most.

"You've been away too long, Ray. Remember me? Try again."

Raven laughed and hugged her again.

"That's much better," she said as she handed the driver her baggage tags. She took Raven's arm. "When a girl comes all the way to Paris to see you, you have to let her know that your intentions are dishonorable. How are you, Ray? You look rotten."

"I am rotten, but I'm glad to see you."

"What's going on with you?"

Raven shrugged. "Nothing that spending a week with you won't cure. What's going on on the Potomac?"

Babs gave him a knowing look. "Oh, I see: Dr. Wheatley and her magic distractions. Well, anything I have is yours, but I don't know if there's a cure for whatever you've got."

As they drove to the Hotel Crillon, Raven began to enjoy himself.

"Why aren't we staying at the apartment?" Babs asked.

"I don't want to answer a Faulkner phone all week."

When they reached their suite, Babs took a deep breath and said, "Well, if we're going to have a week without Faulkner, I better get rid of the family news. Your brother got married."

"When?"

"Last week, at the Chelsea Registry Office in London. He called to tell your mother and father."

"How did they take it?"

"Not too well, as far as I could tell. When they talked to me, they didn't seem too happy about the bride. Do you know her?"

Raven nodded.

Babs noted his reaction carefully. "You'll have to tell me about her some time. The way you and your family act, she must have quite a story. From your mother's comments, I gather that the bride's parents didn't attend the wedding either. Her mother refused; her father was in a Swiss sanitarium. Buck wanted you to be sure to know that."

304

"Why?"

"I don't know. Maybe it has something to do with this." She opened her attaché case and took out a large formal envelope embossed with what Raven recognized as the Pahlevi crest. "When Dan spoke to your parents on the phone, he said that, in honor of the marriage, he had arranged for Iran Air to buy ten Gammas, at thirty-two million each."

Raven was amazed. "That's our first big order."

Babs nodded. "Yes. The Shah wants to close the deal next week at the party to celebrate the twenty-five-hundredth year of the Persian Empire. Dan wanted your father to be there, but Buck's going to be in Tokyo. You're supposed to go instead."

"What was Dan's reaction to that?"

"I don't know."

Raven gave the envelope back to her, without opening it. "I don't want to think about it while you're here. Anything else?"

"No. Just Paris." She kissed him.

"I'm going to take a shower," Babs said. "When I get out, I'd like to find you in that lovely bed in there. Then you can show me how much you missed me." She started into the bedroom, but Raven took her hand.

"I missed you," he said.

His sincerity surprised her. She kissed him gently and put her hand on the side of his face. "You look worried," she said.

He shook his head and kissed her. After a moment, she hurried into the bedroom.

Raven wandered over to the French doors and stood looking at his reflection, listening to the sound of the shower. He suddenly began to smile. He took off his clothes, picked up a Champagne bottle and two glasses, and went into the steaming bathroom. As he slid open the glass shower door around the tub, Babs turned quickly and gasped, "Ray, I have soap in my eyes."

"Keep them shut, then."

Reaching her arms out, she let the shower rinse her face. "Where are you?" she asked.

"Here," he said, directing her hands downward, as his hands slowly moved over her soapy breasts and around to her buttocks. Standing on tiptoe, she gently parted her legs and pulled him toward her. The water from the shower slicked her red hair down her back. As he entered her she clung to his neck. He let his back slide down the tile wall, and they sank into the tub.

Afterward, Raven reached over the edge for the Champagne. He handed Babs her glass and poured.

"Here I am in Paris," she laughed, "skinny dipping for the first time."

Raven stretched out his legs. "I'd have thought most of the male population in eastern Oklahoma would have hung around swimming holes in hopes you'd turn up."

"Not me, honey, I was too shy." Slowly, she slid under the water, while keeping one arm elevated with the champagne glass.

When she surfaced again and wiped her eyes, Babs saw that Raven's smile was gone. She looked at him and cocked her head to the side, questioning him.

"Listen," he said, "I want to tell you something."

"You're married?" she guessed.

"That's about the only thing I don't have to tell."

"Really?"

He nodded and set down his glass. "First of all, I'm not Buck and Jennifer Faulkner's son. They adopted me when their first son died."

Babs nodded. Seeing that he was having such a hard time, she didn't dare to interrupt.

"I killed a man. In a New York subway. He pulled a knife on me, and I stabbed him with it. It was a long time ago. No one else knows."

Babs kept her eyes steady and waited.

"Around the same time," Raven's face tensed with annoyance, "I had a rather peculiar affair with Melanie Owen."

Babs's eyebrows lifted.

"Melanie Owen," he continued, "is the daughter of my half-sister. She and my father had an affair. Our mother was a Communist spy. Can you believe all that?"

With her eyes rolled up to the ceiling, Babs said, "I can't even follow it. Could we go back to the baby who died?"

Raven slowly told the story. They drank Champagne as he filled in details up to meeting Melanie again with Dan in Bahrain. As they moved back to the bedroom, Babs said, "It worries the hell out of me already."

"Why?"

"I don't know. I was already worried about you, trying so hard to do something I knew you didn't want to do. Now I'm worried the dangers may be more than emotional. I've heard about Jim Owen from some friends of mine in Intelligence. He's not exactly a sweet man, and Buck Faulkner's given him a lot of ammunition."

"He's been using it on us for years. The guy's a sadist. He wants it to last a long time."

"It sounds like he doesn't have a long time."

Raven nodded.

"Ray, is this why we're staying here instead of the apartment? Are we hiding from anyone?"

Raven saw her concern and slipped his hand into her tangled wet hair. "We're in love. We came here to have an affair." He took her in his arms. "Don't worry."

"I wish I didn't." She kissed him longingly, then said, "I've got to sleep. It's four in the morning in Washington." She slipped on her robe and without turning to Raven said, "Do me one favor, Ray. Don't say anything more about love. I'm not ready for it."

"You've never been more ready. Neither have I."

She turned quickly to him. "It scares the hell out of me."

"Sure it does," he said. "You've loved a couple of men and both of them kicked you in the face. Why should you trust me, particularly after what I've just unloaded on you?"

"It's not you that's the problem," Babs said.

"It's just me saying I love you."

She shook her head hopelessly as they settled down to sleep.

For the next week, Paris was good to them. The weather brightened, and they walked the streets and sat in cafés. By catching up with Raven's past, they avoided discussing the future. Babs's amazement gave way to even more apprehension, not only about his safety, but about what she felt for him.

Their last lunch together, they sat side by side on the old-fashioned red velvet banquettes at the Lucas-Carton. Babs was scheduled to fly back to Washington that afternoon. She carefully opened her purse and handed Raven the Shah's invitation that he had refused the morning she arrived.

"You want to go to Persepolis with me?" Raven asked. "It says I can bring a guest."

"The first thing I ever learned was not to make love on the beach or in the desert. Besides, I've got to get back to work."

"When will I see you again?"

"I don't know."

"I can hear you making all kinds of resolutions to yourself," Raven said.

"Damn right."

"They won't do any good."

"We'll see."

"I'm in love with you."

"Affairs are fun; love isn't."

"Affairs always end. Look, Babs, we don't really have a choice any more."

"The hell we don't. I can get on the plane this afternoon and say goodbye and mean it."

"I'll fight you."

"How come you're so damn sure? You might get away from Paris and think about it a little. You might see that you got stuck with the wrong girl."

"I'll let you know," he said.

"About what?"

"If Paris has fooled me."

Babs nodded and squeezed his hand. "You go to Persepolis, and I'll go on back to Washington. I need some time to think. And don't tell me you love me at the airport or I'll scream rape."

He didn't. Instead, he presented her with a box of Hotel Crillon bubble bath, for which he received a long kiss.

"Be careful, Ray. They may cure Owen's lungs in Switzerland, but I doubt if they'll untwist his head."

"You're worried about me. A good sign."

She hit him softly on the arm and turned to go aboard her flight.

The next day, thirty tons of pink Dom Perignon Champagne and eighteen tons of food to be catered by Maxim's arrived at Shiraz. So did Raven. The Shah's celebration of the founding of the Persian Empire by Cyrus the Great was to take place sixty miles away, near the ruins of Persepolis. The guest list numbered five hundred, although it included only a few of the world's truly powerful statesmen. As one wag was heard to say, "If you weren't invited, you weren't very important, but if you showed up, you were even *less* important."

The Shah was spending a hundred million dollars on his *jash'n,* or celebration, to "show the rest of the world that Iran is again a nation equal to all others, and much finer than many."

Raven had a room at the Kourosh Hotel in Shiraz and commuted by limousine to the elaborate tent city at Persepolis. The more important guests were given individual tents at the site, each of which provided bedrooms, salons, kitchenettes, his and her bathrooms, blue matchbooks stamped with "Persepolis," and a supply of Alka Seltzer. Even at such a lofty diplomatic level, there was a continual and distasteful bickering over accommodations. Cardinal de Furstenberg, representing the Vatican, refused to accept anything less than a royal tent. Spiro Agnew, representing the United States, refused to drive from the Shiraz airport to Persepolis and insisted on a helicopter. In the end, royal rank seemed to take precedence over political. The President of the West German Bundestag lost his tent to an Afghanistan princess.

Dan and Melanie were also in Raven's hotel. When he went up to their suite, they did not bother to stop a vicious argument over what she should wear that evening.

"I don't give a shit what you wear," Dan shouted, "just so long as you get your ass wrapped in time."

Glaring at Raven, Melanie stormed into the bathroom.

Dan looked angrily at the closed door. Then he turned to Raven. "Every time we hit open water, she threw up all over everything. Great honeymoon, Big Brother. You ever spent a month on a yacht? I don't care how big it is, it's like a prison."

"Congratulations on your marriage," Raven said with little enthusiasm.

"Go fuck yourself. To tell the truth, it was a big mistake. Take my advice and don't change Mrs. Wheatley's name. Better to have a week at the Crillon than a divorce in Vegas."

"Gee, Dan, how did you know about the Crillon?"

"It's my business to know, Big Brother. I had to make sure *one* of my goddam relatives showed up to sign this contract. D.O.D. sure as hell made it clear he wasn't going to come, even though I'm busting my ass saving his company. Another thing it's my business to know is that Uncle Jack's put the word out on Faulkner. You guys are in trouble."

"We'll be all right. The Pentagon isn't the only buyer."

Dan smiled maliciously. "You think Japan will buy enough Gammas to get you off the hook? There isn't an aerospace company in the U.S. that could survive without its government fix. You should have come in with me, Big Brother. The future looks bright."

"It always will for you, Dan. When do we sign the papers?"

Dan stared at Raven a moment. "Melanie's old man is dying. You could take his place at Onager."

"Why?"

"Because you're my brother—because I trust you."

"That's bullshit, Dan. You want me working for you instead of working for your father. A little triumph over Buck Faulkner. You've wanted to get back at him for a long time. His company going under and me working for you would really give you joy, wouldn't it?"

"What the fuck are you talking about? Is that why I'm selling ten of his planes without his even asking?"

"I didn't say you were consistent. You either want him to love you best, or crawl on his knees."

"Why would I want that?"

"Because of you and me, Dan." Raven suddenly wanted to tell his brother the whole story, but the phone rang. General Khatama, the head of the Iranian Air Force, commanded their immediate presence.

The moment was lost. The contracts were signed the following day, and Raven left Iran without finding another chance to speak to his brother alone.

32

A week before the Japanese Minister of Trade and Industry, Kakuei Tanaka, was to meet with President Nixon at San Clemente, Babs Wheatley set up a lunch for Buck with one of Nixon's advisers. Over lunch at the White House mess, Buck asked, "Do you think the President might say a kind word to Mr. Tanaka about the sale of the Faulkner Gamma to Japan?"

"I'm sure that could be arranged, Buck," the adviser said. "In fact, I have a good many connections of my own in Japan."

"I'd be grateful for anything you could do."

"Good," the adviser smiled. "Relationships can last a long time, can't they? Even after we get out of government."

Buck had heard such proffers before, though usually made with more subtlety. He said, "Our relationship in the past has always been enjoyable." The adviser had received consulting fees concerning several foreign sales to Faulkner.

"The Japanese aren't too happy with us at the moment," the adviser continued, negotiating his price. "It's going to be hard for the President to ask them for any favors."

"I sympathize," Buck said, "but if he can, there are thirty thousand Faulkner voters who will be grateful."

"Thank you, Buck. I'll be sure to inform the President." They had finished eating, and Buck followed the adviser outside. He knew the real negotiation would have to take place away from neighboring diners or possible hidden microphones.

"Buck, you know what I'd *really* like to tell the President? I'd like to tell him you're going to help us get him reelected."

"We've supported Dick Nixon from the beginning," Buck said.

"You've supported a lot of others, too. What I'm hoping is that you might use your Agency for Institutional Unity down in Panama to contribute some cash." He laughed, noting Buck's surprise at his mention of the Panamanian Foundation. "Well, Buck, don't be naïve. We all read the C.I.A. reports."

"What kind of cash are you talking about?"

"Dollars would be fine. About a million of them." The adviser continued toward the Executive Office Building. Buck wondered what would happen if he turned the adviser down. Then he said, "We'll give a quarter of a million now; then we can see how it goes."

The adviser turned back quickly. "You don't haggle with the President, Buck."

"I'm not," said Buck. "I'm haggling with you. I want to see how effectively you can deliver messages." Buck turned and walked away, saying, "Thanks for lunch."

When he called California, Buck was surprised by the degree of Jennifer's opposition.

"We can't afford this, Buck. I don't mean the money, I mean the consequences if these amounts become public."

"If we don't go along, what's our choice?"

There was silence on the other end of the phone.

"I made a reservation at the Hotel Okura for two," Buck said.

"For what day?"

"Thursday. I'll be home tonight."

"I'll pack," she said. "Have Raven join us. I don't trust myself on this."

After he hung up, Buck asked Babs Wheatley to come in.

"I need to get a message to Raven. Can you reach him?"

"I think so."

"Please tell him I want him in Tokyo next Thursday, and book him a room at the Okura."

Babs knew that she hadn't been called in just to convey a travel plan, but she wasn't sure she wanted to know more. "I'll get right on it," she said, standing up to leave.

"I'm afraid he won't be getting to Washington quite as often as he has been. We'll be over there for some time."

She knew most of the plans of the Japanese sales campaign. "It's a pretty long commute from Tokyo."

"They used to say that absence makes the heart grow fonder."

"They also say out of sight, out of mind."

"I hope it works out. I wanted you to know that."

"I'm glad," she said, surprised. "I've often wondered what you and Mrs. Faulkner thought. I hope she knows I'm not trying to steal her baby right out of the cradle." With a shock, she remembered the first baby. Her stunned reaction was only a split second in length, but Buck caught it. Babs was not used to revealing her thoughts unintentionally and didn't handle it well. "That, that, was really a stupid thing to say."

"Why?" Buck said, knowing the answer.

She stared at him. "I suppose this was bound to happen."

"How much do you know?"

"The whole mess, I'm afraid."

"He must trust you."

"So he says."

"Have you told anyone else?"

She smiled with exasperation. "Not a soul until right now. Let me tell you, the two things I've been trying to avoid are love and secrets."

"Welcome to the family, Babs."

She smiled and said, "Thanks a whole hell of a lot." Buck watched her leave and liked her even more. Then he pulled out the yellow sheet that Sam had prepared for the Japanese campaign. There were three groups of names: Japanese who were working for Boeing, for McDonnell Douglas, and for Lockheed. Each man's connection with Japan Air Lines, the international carrier, or All-Nippon Air, the domestic carrier, was noted. After memorizing the list, Buck tossed the paper in the shredder.

Later that afternoon, after Buck had left the office, Babs's phone rang.

"Hello?"

"I'm sick of making love over a telephone." Raven's voice caught her by surprise.

"Ray . . ."

"I mean it."

"Ray!" she repeated more forcefully. "The switchboard puts

313

your calls on the speakerphones."

"Really? Let's drive them crazy. Will you have dinner with me on Saturday?"

"You won't be here, I'm afraid."

His tone changed abruptly. "What's up?"

"Where are you? I'll call you back."

Raven rattled off a phone number in Brussels. When they were reconnected, Raven's voice had lost all its enthusiasm. "Where am I going to be, for Christ's sake?"

"In Tokyo at the Hotel Okura."

"Get me a king-size bed. You've always wanted to see Tokyo, haven't you?"

"Your parents will meet you there."

He paused. "Oh. The big push. Did you put that stuff together for me?"

"As much as I could. Information wasn't easy."

"Are we in trouble?"

"This man named Nogato sounds like more than trouble to me."

"My father seems to think he's our main chance."

"It depends. Hiroshi Nogato is *not* a nice person, but in Japan he does seem able to make things happen."

"Give me what you've got."

Babs read from her notes. "During the Second World War, he hoarded gold. Afterwards the American occupation sent him to prison as a Class-A War Criminal. Since he was released, Nogato has financed the election campaigns of three prime ministers. He doubled his fortune selling goods to the American forces during the Korean War. He did it again in Vietnam. He underwrites one of those small private armies some people have in Japan, recruiting most of his soldiers from prisons. Then he trains them for his own purposes. The liberals call him 'The Nazi.' "

"How long has he been retained by Faulkner?"

"I'm not sure. I didn't want to ask around here, but at least eight years, maybe longer."

"Eight years?! God."

"Nogato's also funded by the C.I.A."

"Are you sure?"

"Yes. The Agency knows about Faulkner's payments, which

could be considered implicit consent if anybody ever finds out about it."

Raven was silent for so long that Babs thought they'd been cut off.

"Ray?"

"I'm here."

"What are you thinking?"

"That I shouldn't go. All I'll do is fight them. But I'll go anyway."

"Why?"

"Because Buck Faulkner wants me there," he said disgustedly.

"If you go, you have to help."

"I know. I know."

"Ray, help them. I don't mean go along with everything. Try to keep Faulkner's feet out of the mud as much as you can, but get your parents through it. Afterwards you can quit, but right now they need you, and I don't mean because of the company. By the way, Buck knows you told me about Connie Mannheim."

"How did that happen?"

"I made a slip. He caught it."

"That's a relief."

"Why?"

"It means he didn't bug the bathroom at the Crillon, and it might mean you wanted him to know you knew."

"Why would I want that?"

"Makes you a member of the family, doesn't it?"

"That's what he said."

Raven laughed. "Well, any time you want to fly to Tokyo, just get on a plane. We'll all meet you," he said and hung up.

Five days later, Raven joined his parents for breakfast in their suite at the Okura Hotel. They were all unusually edgy.

"Have you seen Dan recently?" Jennifer asked.

"Not since Persepolis."

"Have you heard anything?" she continued.

"No more than what we get on the weekly briefing sheets. Seems that he and Melanie are making the scene in swinging London."

"Onager Limited is no longer pushing our planes," Buck said.

"I'm not surprised. I don't think he heard you say thank you."

"I didn't say it."

Raven shrugged and buttered some toast.

Jennifer asked, "Do you think they're happy?"

"Knowing Dan and Melanie, I doubt if 'happy' is the word."

"We were hurt he didn't invite us to the wedding," she said.

Raven looked up from his plate. "Would you have gone if he had asked you?"

Jennifer looked at him steadily. "He could have given us that choice."

"And taken a good chance that you'd have hurt him."

"I doubt," Buck said, "if Dan can be hurt by us."

"You're wrong," Raven said intensely, then went back to his breakfast.

"I spoke to Babs yesterday," said Jennifer changing the subject. "I told her we wanted to hear from her every day at noon." She smiled. "Does she love you?"

"Yes, but she hasn't admitted it yet. I don't think she will until I've figured out what I'm doing bribing everyone in sight to buy Faulkner planes."

Buck put down his silver. "You don't bribe anyone."

"Let's not play games with ourselves." Raven knew his timing was bad. He tried to finish eating, but he couldn't. "You might as well tell me your plans with Nogato."

"And you can explain why you flew all the way to Tokyo to accuse me of corruption."

Raven shook his head and said quickly, "There's only one reason I'm in Tokyo, and you're it."

Buck hesitated. "All right. I'll tell you what we're in for, and then you decide to stay or go."

"I've already decided. I'm staying until this is over."

"Well, to begin with," said Buck, "I've contributed a quarter of a million to Nixon's campaign in cash. I don't know what Nogato is going to need, but Toshiharu Miki has guessed in the neighborhood of four or five million."

Raven watched a moment, then said, "Any accountant will fall all over four or five million."

"When?" Buck said quietly.

"It doesn't matter when," said Raven.

"Of course it does," said Buck. "By the time anyone notices

anything, we'll have our contract. After that, I'll take the consequences. That's part of my job. Do you understand?"

"I understand you're crazy enough to destroy yourself to save your company."

"Certainly I am! I've been willing to destroy myself for a lot less." His eyes blazed with anger. "You'll never understand what this company is to me. I suppose your mother and I should be gratified. You'll never *need* to understand, because you have parents."

There was a knock at the door.

"That's Toshiharu. He's taking me to Nogato," Buck said, regaining his composure. "Are you coming with me?"

Without hesitating, Raven nodded.

33

As their car moved slowly through Tokyo's glutted streets, Mr. Miki opened *The New York Times*. A small article on the front page had been circled. The headline read, "Tanaka-Nixon Meet at San Clemente."

"We'll start with the politicians," Mr. Miki said.

"I've already started," Buck said. "I hope that Nixon helped us with Tanaka."

Mr. Miki nodded. "Of course, the other American companies have the same hope."

"I know," Buck said.

"My greatest concern," Mr. Miki continued, "is Lockheed. Their TriStar is being built with a U.S. Treasury guarantee against bankruptcy. Rolls-Royce, a company similarly propped by Her Majesty's Exchequer, is providing the engines. A Lockheed contract would solve two countries' balance-of-payments problems with Japan."

Nogato's office was off an alleyway behind the Ginza. The building was guarded by seven young men dressed in black leather jackets and paratrooper boots. The interior was sparsely furnished, and Mr. Nogato waited behind a simple teakwood table. He wore a three-piece Western suit, a silk tie, and highly polished paratrooper boots. He spoke in a careful monotone.

With Mr. Miki translating, Nogato said that President Nixon had discussed the sale of the airplanes with Mr. Tanaka, who was expected to become prime minister within the month. To gain influence for such a large undertaking as the All-Nippon contract, Mr. Nogato suggested a gift to Mr. Tanaka of five hundred million yen. The head of All-Nippon Airways, as well as numerous bureaucrats in the Transport Ministry and the Ministry of Trade would have to receive smaller gifts. While Mr. Nogato continued listing additional names, Raven was figuring a total on a pocket calculator. Then he heard Mr. Nogato say one word of English:

"Cash."

Buck took a long time to react. Finally, he nodded.

Mr. Nogato rose and said, *"Yosha,"* meaning, all right. Then he bowed rigidly.

The meeting was over. Mr. Miki led Buck and Raven out to their car.

Buck began to consider the financial groundwork. "I don't want anyone's signature on any paper. I don't want any thefts or losses that insurance can't cover quickly. Once the cash is here in Tokyo, one of the three of us will deliver it. *No one else* is to be involved. Is that clear?"

Miki nodded as Raven asked, "Does insurance cover bribes?"

"Commissions and operating expenses are covered," said Buck, "but I don't relish explaining to an insurance company or anyone else what we were doing with that amount of cash."

"Will five hundred million yen fit in a suitcase?" Raven asked.

"Yes," said Mr. Miki adding circumspectly, "but I suspect your couriers will need more than one. When the moment comes, enough cash must be on hand to satisfy everyone."

"We'll get it," Buck said. "But where do we keep it? We can't take it to a Tokyo bank, and I don't want to leave it in a hotel room."

"You could stockpile it in Hong Kong and fly it here as it's needed," Mr. Miki suggested.

"Good," Buck said, and then turned pointedly to Raven. "Set that up."

Raven didn't blink. "How much?"

Buck didn't answer for a moment, then said evenly, "Five million dollars, whatever that is in yen."

Raven sat back in his seat. "I'll buy a steamer trunk."

In their luxurious Georgian home on Belgrave Square, Melanie realized that she was bored. Dan was sitting on the edge of their circular bed carefully cutting his toenails. Melanie stared up into a large mirror on the ceiling above the bed. She admired her body and languidly touched her breasts, then ran her hand down over her stomach and between her legs. Rolling over slightly to check the tan on her buttocks, she sighed with irritation.

"What's wrong?" Dan asked idly as he added his latest cutting to a small pile on the bedside table.

She didn't answer, but continued posing for herself. Melanie's problem was that swinging London had gone limp. Dancing and gambling at Annabelle's filled only so many nights. Melanie spent her afternoons preparing for her entrances.

Dan took her wrist from between her thighs.

"What're you doing?" he asked.

"What do you mean?"

"You know what I mean. What're you doing?"

"Nothing."

"No playing with yourself when I'm in the same goddam room!" he said as he went back to finish his pedicure.

"Jealous?" she suggested.

"No, I'm not jealous. If you want to get it off, you get it off with me."

"Okay, I want to get it off."

"I'm not in the mood," he said, putting the clippers in their place beside the bed. "I'm going to take a sauna. You know what I'm really in the mood for? A good old-fashioned peanut-butter-and-jelly sandwich and a glass of milk. Make me one, will you?" He got up and went into the next room.

When she heard the door of the sauna slam shut, Melanie was angry. On the bedside was the silver-framed picture of herself and Dan at their wedding. Next to it was Dan's pile of clippings.

By the time she returned with the sandwich, Dan was in the bathtub, rotating his spine in front of one of the Jacuzzi nozzles.

"Here's your sandwich," Melanie said.

"That's what I like—a little service around here. You want to get in here with me?"

"Maybe. Eat your sandwich first. It isn't waterproof."

He took a large bite. "Very good." His teeth bit on something which he extracted and examined. It was the crescent of a toenail.

"You bitch!" he said as he sprang out of the tub. Melanie was laughing. He slapped her hard across the face.

"Don't you dare hit me," she screamed.

He slapped her again, harder. "I'll hit you any goddam time you deserve it."

As she stared at him, blood began to trickle from her lip and drop on her breast. "You stupid son of a bitch. You think you're so fucking smart. You just don't know how stupid you are, but everybody else does."

Dan started moving toward her, and she cringed back against the marble wall. "You hit me again, I swear you'll be sorry."

"What are you going to do, scratch my eyes out?" He raised his arm. Melanie fell on her hands and knees and crawled clumsily out of the bathroom. Dan laughed and followed her into the bedroom, where he saw her reaching in the closet. "Come on out and fight like the spoiled bitch you are."

She turned holding up a folder of papers like a weapon.

"What's that for?" asked Dan.

"My father has a safe in Tehran. He told me how to open it in case anything happened to him, but I decided to open it before that." She threw the papers at him. "I made copies of what I found. Read them. You'll learn a lot of things you were too dumb to figure out. And, by the way, Raven and I were lovers for a couple of months, and it was the best couple of months of my life."

Dan moved so quickly she had no time to duck. He hit her in the jaw with his closed fist, throwing her head onto the corner of her dressing table and knocking her unconscious. When she didn't move, Dan went over to her. He couldn't see too much because of the blood, but it looked like part of her face was caved in. He called an ambulance. While he waited for it to arrive, he picked up the papers on the floor and read them.

Within twenty-four hours, Melanie's jaw, which had been broken in four places, was wired shut and she was being fed through a tube. The press had discovered her presence in the hospital and a number of lurid items had appeared in the gossip columns. In order to avoid photographs, Dan had posted private guards at Melanie's door around the clock. A picture would not have been pretty; both her eyes were blackened, and there were bruises over her cheeks and down her neck. Dan had explained to the doctors that she had tripped and fallen. Melanie was in enough pain for the moment not to contradict him.

She was awakened, several nights later, by a man coughing. Through her drug-induced haze, she saw someone standing by the window. She was terrified.

"Get out," she said between her teeth. "What are you—"

"Melanie, it's me."

She reached for her father's hand and began to cry.

"Daddy, you look horrible."

His face looked ravaged; his clothes seemed several sizes too large.

"Never mind me," he said. "What happened?"

"Dan beat me up." Thinking fast, she continued. "It's been going on for a long time."

"Why didn't you tell me?"

"I didn't want you to know. You've been so unhappy all your life."

"Not all of it." He turned away and took out a pack of cigarettes.

"Daddy, please don't. You're not supposed to."

He ignored her and lit his cigarette. "It doesn't matter any more."

"Oh, Daddy, no." She wanted to cry, but couldn't.

"Don't tell anyone, particularly your mother."

"What are you going to do?"

"Anything you'd like me to do?" Melanie didn't answer; his voice was so vicious that it scared her. "I owe you so much that I couldn't give you," he said, "and I end up giving you this. I'm sorry, Melanie. I knew when you married Dan it would infuriate his father, but I didn't know this would happen."

"Is that why you wanted me to marry Dan?"

"In part."

"Well, I'm glad I could be of some use to you."

"Melanie—"

"You sure weren't much use to me. How could you leave Mommie and me all that time? If you hated Buck Faulkner so much, why the hell didn't you do something about it, instead of letting Mother dry up into a bitter old woman and letting me get my face torn apart?" A wire shifted in her mouth and she screamed through her teeth and pressed the call button.

Jim Owen came to her side and said, "This time you can depend on me. I promise you."

The nurse arrived quickly; Melanie demanded a shot for pain. She held her face in her hands and groaned until the nurse administered the needle. Its effect was almost instantaneous; as Melanie began to float into unconsciousness, she looked around for her father, but he was gone.

A week later, five men were arrested breaking into Democratic Party headquarters at the Watergate. The caper became the joke of Washington, and Babs laughed as loudly as anyone until she heard from one of her sources that some of Buck's cash had been used to finance the operation. Luckily, the presidential campaign had begun in earnest, and the Watergate break-in was quickly forgotten. Babs, however, kept alert. She made certain that she was always in the office to receive Jennifer's call. Tanaka, as Nogato had predicted, became prime minister. Support from the Nixon Administration became vital, and Babs was in charge of finding out its price.

Babs spoke to Raven almost as often as to Jennifer. Their conversations were longer, and of a different kind. At the end of each call, Raven asked Babs to join him. She continued to refuse, saying either she couldn't leave her work, or that she wasn't ready to take on so many Faulkners at once. But as the days dragged on she grew increasingly lonely and began filling her empty evenings with the parties she had spent the last few months refusing.

On her way to one long weekend in New York she noticed General Jack Llewellyn sitting two seats ahead of her on the shuttle. When he turned to check for any familiar faces, Babs ducked behind a copy of *Vogue*.

They had known each other for years. As a young general at the Pentagon, Jack Llewellyn had courted Babs's former husband, and they had met more recently when Babs started working for Faulkner. Babs was aware of the general's role in the loss of the B-1 bomber contract and no longer regarded Jack as a friend.

When their plane landed, Babs lingered out of sight behind the general, hoping to avoid an awkward meeting. As she waited for a phone to call her host, she noticed him disappear into the men's room. The phone was busy, and she was still waiting a few minutes later, when Jack Llewellyn emerged in civilian clothes, wearing a large pair of dark glasses and a Homburg. Babs hung up the phone and, staying carefully out of sight, followed the general to a locker, where he left his bag, and then to the taxi line. As his cab sped off, she tipped the dispatcher ten dollars and learned that Llewellyn was headed for Kennedy Airport. Her weekend plans were forgotten. Carrying her bag, she jumped into a cab to follow him.

Llewellyn got out of his cab at the International Arrivals Building, and Babs watched as he went to the B.O.A.C. service booth. When he took the escalator to the observation area, Babs went over to the attendant, to see what she could find out. Inventing quickly, she said Llewellyn was her uncle and that she was planning to surprise him. She just wanted to check which plane he was meeting. After looking over Babs's elegant clothes, the attendant smiled and said that Llewellyn had been checking on the six-o'clock flight from London.

For half an hour, Babs had little to do except make sure that Jack Llewellyn didn't see her. Fifteen minutes before the plane landed, she decided to hurry to the souvenir shop to buy a camera. When she returned to the observation area, she was panicked to see that Llewellyn had left. She looked at the information board; the B.O.A.C. flight had landed early.

She ran down to the arrival area just in time to see Llewellyn stop a man who had come through the customs area. As they exchanged greetings, Babs was able to take a couple of pictures. Then she followed the two men outside. Instead of hailing a cab, she was surprised to see them walk over to Japan Air Lines.

For the first time, Babs decided that Llewellyn might be planning something that could be directed against Buck. Peering in through the glass she saw the general hand his companion a thick envelope. Then Llewellyn strode toward the entranceway, and Babs quickly continued down the sidewalk.

She had a choice—to continue following the general, or to find out more about the man he had met. She chose the latter, and after Jack had found a cab, she returned to the J.A.L. departure area. The stranger was in the lounge, apparently waiting for the 9 P.M. flight to Tokyo. She sat down nearby and watched him smoke. Certain now that the man was involved in Faulkner's efforts in Japan, she wondered what more she could do. In less

324

than five seconds she decided that Raven would get his wish. She always carried her passport and her air travel card; she had her toothbrush and a party dress in the overnight bag she had been lugging between airports. Thinking of Raven, she smiled and, at the same moment, realized that the man was looking at her. She adroitly turned the full force of her charm on him and said enthusiastically, "Is this your first trip to Tokyo?" Shaking his head he turned away, indicating a sour certainty that he was not inclined toward conversation. Babs got up to buy her ticket.

During the flight she slept as much as she could, but each time she got up she noticed that the man was wide awake, smoking. On the final leg of the trip, from Manila to Tokyo, Babs woke up to find the man's seat was empty. When he didn't return for a half hour, she decided to investigate. None of the lavatories was occupied, and after walking the aisles in both seating sections, she decided to ask a stewardess. She went up to the galley and saw the man himself sitting on one of the stewardess's jump seats, with an oxygen mask over his face.

He glared angrily at Babs, who smiled and said, "Oh, I'm so sorry to interrupt, but I'm kind of desperate myself." She glanced meaningfully at the stewardess and whispered. The stewardess obliged, but as Babs left the galley, clutching a tampon, she suddenly realized that she was flying to Tokyo with Jim Owen.

34

It was nearly midnight in Japan when Dan reached his parents by phone. He was so upset that it took several minutes before they understood that his house on Belgrave Square had been bombed.

"Oh, God," Jennifer said. "Where are you?"

"I left for Paris. I didn't want to answer questions," said Dan.

"Is Melanie all right?" Buck asked on the extension.

"Oh hell, yes. Luckily, she's been in the hospital. She had an accident, fell and broke her jaw in a couple of places. She's fine now. People knew she wasn't home, but I was supposed to be. *That's* the point."

"Where were you?" Buck asked.

"I stayed with a friend. I thought there might be some trouble because a couple of days before, Jim Owen showed up out of nowhere to see his darling daughter. That crazy bastard thinks I was responsible for Melanie's accident. Her jaw is all wired up, but goddammit, she'll be all right. I have the best plastic surgeons in Europe—"

"Why did you leave the country?" Jennifer interrupted.

"Jesus Christ, Mother, I'm not going to stay around and give that crazy son of a bitch another chance at me. Besides, Scotland Yard thinks terrorists were responsible, and they want all my records. I burnt everything in my office and got out of London on a train."

Jennifer and Buck looked at each other, then Buck asked,

"Do you want some of our security people to—"

"Hell, no, I can take care of myself. I always have, haven't I? I'm just calling to let you know that if Jim Owen can't get to me, he may come after you. I'm at Orly now. I'm getting out of France. Take care of yourselves. All of a sudden, we have a lot to talk about." He hung up.

Apprehensively, Jennifer turned to her husband.

"Let's tell Raven," said Buck. "He may have an idea."

But Raven was as mystified as his parents. He thought that Melanie might have told about their affair, but doubted whether she knew more.

A few hours later, Raven's phone rang again.

"Hello, stranger. Guess who's here?" Babs announced.

"Good God almighty. Are you in Japan?"

"Yes."

"You're sure?"

"Yes. I got hungry for some sushi. Is your phone clear?"

"They're checked every day. So you finally couldn't stay away."

"It wasn't you. I saw General Llewellyn making some very surprising moves. He met someone getting off a flight from London and boarding a plane to Tokyo. I'd swear he was making a payoff, *and* I think I have pictures. So tell your mother not to call me in the office. I'm up in Room—well, what the hell is it?— twenty-fourteen, and I expect a big bonus."

"What did the man look like?" Raven asked tensely.

"Why haven't you hung up and started running on up here?"

"I'm on my way. Did the man have white hair and leathery skin—?"

"He smoked a lot," Babs added, "and he needed oxygen. You think it was Jim Owen?"

"Lock your door, don't go out, and don't let anyone in until I get there."

"So this is the serene Orient."

"I'll be there as soon as I can."

Raven hurried to Buck and Jennifer's suite and told them Babs's story.

"Call Faulkner Field and have two dozen security people sent over here instantly," Jennifer said.

"We can't," Buck countered. "We'd have the press swarming

all over us, asking why. When we didn't tell them, they'd make up their own stories. At this point, we can't even ask the Japanese for help."

They were silent, until Raven said, "Have the best four people in our security section flown over here. They can be here in sixteen hours. That won't attract attention. Anybody who's anybody has a bodyguard. I doubt if Uncle Jack has paid to have us murdered. He probably just hired Owen to screw up our campaign."

"Yes, but Jim has his own ideas," Jennifer said, deeply alarmed.

"Babs and I will stay in room twenty-fourteen until someone comes to get us," Raven said, adding as he went out the door, "and send someone to have Babs's film developed."

When he knocked at twenty-fourteen, Babs said, "Room service?"

"I'll do my best," he answered as she opened the door and kissed him.

"Raven, I've missed you so. There just isn't enough time to waste any more of it commuting."

"I've been saying that for weeks."

"Isn't it nice to be right? I hope your daddy's going to let me stay for a while."

"He's leaving that to me."

"Good. Come on over here—"

"Someone's coming up here for the film."

"Now?"

"Yeah. Where is it?"

Grumbling, she went to the bureau. "Business before pleasure, but *never* before necessity." She handed Raven the camera.

As he carefully took the film out of the camera, he asked, "How many did you get?"

"Three, I think."

"Both of them?"

"I don't know. I think both."

There was a knock at the door. Raven answered it and gave the film to the bellboy.

"We'll know in an hour."

"I'm not letting you out of this room," Babs said.

He smiled. "I'm not going anywhere. Neither are you. Not until tomorrow, when the Faulkner security people arrive."

"That's pretty exciting," said Babs, trying to hide her fear. "What'll we do to pass the time?"

Early the next morning, Buck called to say, "Nogato wants six hundred million yen in twenty-four hours. He's about to make his decision."

"All right," Raven said.

Jennifer took the phone from her husband. "We don't want you to leave the hotel. Can you do it by phone?"

"And have every call recorded on the hotel's records? No. It's all ready. I'll take care of it. Owen hasn't been here long enough to get set up."

After a moment, Jennifer said, "Be careful. Please be very careful."

"I will," Raven said.

"The security people will be here late tonight," Buck added.

"I'll look forward to that," Raven answered, and he hung up.

Before Babs had a chance to object, Raven kissed her and said, "I'll be back in an hour. Don't leave the room. I don't want Owen to have an opportunity to identify you."

Babs didn't argue, but said, "If you're not back in an hour, I'm calling the Marines."

"I'm sure they'd be delighted," Raven said, and he went out the door.

He took a taxi to the Ginza subway station. Down on the platform, he waited for the first train. Just as the door closed, he jumped on, rode for two stations, then doubled back for one. When he was sure no one was following him, he walked to the K.D.D. Building, Tokyo's international telephone-and-telegraph center.

The five million dollars had been stockpiled in Hong Kong. Sam Priest had withdrawn the money in numerous small sums from Faulkner's banks all over the world and delivered it to an international currency dealer. In the United States, currency dealers did not come under the scrutiny of the Treasury's Comptroller of Currency, so the money could be transferred out of the country without detection.

Because someone would have to sign for the yen when they

were withdrawn in Hong Kong, Raven paid a Philippine junk dealer a fee of fifty thousand dollars to handle the transaction. The man had once worked for the C.I.A. and Raven felt he could be trusted. A former missionary whose faith had lapsed would bring the cash to Tokyo as needed for five thousand dollars a trip.

Raven activated the plan on one of the K.D.D.'s sophisticated scrambler telephones and returned without incident to Babs's room.

Within ten hours, the six hundred million yen arrived in Tokyo. Mr. Miki met the courier and took the money to the Ginza subway station, where he delivered it to three of Mr. Nogato's lieutenants. From there, the yen were Nogato's responsibility.

Late that night, the Faulkner security team arrived—three men and one woman. Babs and Raven joined his parents in their suite. One of the security officers explained their routine. Besides walkie-talkies, they gave Babs and Raven a tracing monitor to be hidden on their bodies.

Then another member of the security team spread out copies of Babs's pictures. Without a doubt, the man was Jim Owen. In one of the photographs he was shown facing Jack Llewellyn's unmistakable profile.

Buck put his arm around Babs and said, "What you did was very impressive. You've given us Jack Llewellyn on a platter."

"Unfortunately," said Babs, "I also brought you Jim Owen."

Buck nodded. "That's going to make the rest of our stay in Tokyo an uncomfortable one. The security people insist we stay in our rooms. We'll fly out the minute the contract's settled."

"How long do you think it's going to take?" Raven asked.

"I don't know. The pump is primed with two million dollars. At that price, I'd like to think we'll get a speedy decision, but somehow I doubt it."

Buck was right. For five days they heard nothing, neither from the Japanese airlines, nor from Nogato. The two couples tried entertaining each other with room-service meals, but they never relaxed.

The news from London only added to the tension. As Dan had stated, Melanie Owen's father had visited her the day before the bombing, but Scotland Yard insisted that one person working

330

alone could not have planted the explosives so professionally. They continued to speculate that Onager had offended a group of terrorists.

In the meantime, nothing more was heard from Dan. Buck received one piece of information that he did not share with anyone else: the reason that Dan had not been at home on the night of the explosion was that he had gone home with a girl he met at Annabelle's.

On the fifth day, Buck decided that he could wait no longer. He asked Babs and Raven to his suite to meet with Mr. Miki.

"I've decided," Buck began, "that the Japanese are waiting for some last gesture. At first, I thought it might be more money, but I think now it's more a matter of style. I've arranged for Toshiharu to fly to Faulkner Field, pick up a cash contribution from Sam and deliver it to Nixon's campaign people. I'm writing a personal note asking the President to contact Tanaka for us."

"Nixon doesn't need any more money," Raven said, "he's going to win by a landslide."

"It doesn't matter," Babs said. "The Committee to Reelect the President is taking in as much money as they can, and they prefer cash."

Buck continued. "Toshiharu will also deliver Babs's photos to Jack Llewellyn. That should prepare him for my call asking him to defuse Owen and to pressure the Secretary of Defense to recommend the Gamma to Tanaka. That should be 'stylish' enough."

"Are we sure this is necessary," Raven asked, "or are we doing it just to be doing something?"

"We can be sure Lockheed's doing something," Buck retorted.

"Yes, but to what effect?" Jennifer asked. "Raven's question is valid. We sit around wondering who else we should give money to. Pretty soon we'll be begging people to take our money."

"We're just tired of sitting in a hotel room," said Raven. "I figure we're in for another payment. They'd rather have money than gestures."

"I've considered that," said Buck. "If they want more money, we'll give it to them. But even if the Japanese don't want the gesture, it can't help but impress them. And besides, there might not be another chance to use everything we've got." The implication was clear. Without the All-Nippon contract, later manipulation of a Llewellyn or a Nixon might be superfluous.

Mr. Miki left, and the two couples were alone again, tense and silent.

"Let's get the hell out of here," Raven said finally.

No one responded until Jennifer said quietly, "Where can we go?"

"Out!" Raven replied. "Nobody's expecting us to leave. Let's just go."

He looked at Buck, who said, "The security people won't want it."

"They work for us. Hell, they need fresh air as much as we do."

"If my skin doesn't get some direct sunlight, it'll start to mold," Babs added.

They all looked at Buck. After a moment, he said, "Get your coats. Babs, you'd better disguise yourself a bit. Owen may have spotted you."

"I don't care if Jim Owen is set up for a turkey shoot," Raven said. "We have to get out of here."

Ten minutes later, the elevator doors opened in the lobby and two Faulkner security men hurried out, one of them talking low and fast into his walkie-talkie. They waited at the front entrance until the two couples they were watching got out of the next elevator followed by the other two guards.

Babs wore dark glasses, a coat with a high collar and a scarf that concealed her hair. They proceeded down the street, the security team surrounding them.

A light rain began to fall; the sidewalks were clogged with umbrellas. They passed the American Embassy and turned on to a side street.

Jennifer said sadly, "I've never wanted to be a tourist so much in my life."

"You sound like you just got out of San Quentin," said Raven, laughing.

"If they ever catch us," Buck said, "that's probably where we'll be going."

Babs laughed. The security woman urged them to spread out as much as possible. As they separated, Raven had an unpleasant vision of being followed by a telescopic gun sight.

At the next corner, he saw a small "country house" restaurant. "I'll buy you dinner," he said to his parents.

Buck shook his head. "We can't."

Raven stared at Buck. "If we can't even go out for dinner, for Christ's sake, there's not much point to any of this."

Buck paused, then he motioned to a guard and told him to check out the restaurant. Relieved to be getting the family off the streets, the man went in the front door. A moment later, he signaled for them to enter.

In a room overlooking the street on the second floor of the Okura Hotel, Dan put his binoculars down. His electronic receiver could no longer pick up the security team's walkie-talkies. "They've got to be nuts, walking around like that," he said to himself. But he knew that Jim Owen was not in the neighborhood. After closing the drapes, Dan turned on the television and flopped down on the bed to wait for Al Mardigian's return.

35

After speaking to his parents from Paris, Dan had flown to Manama, Bahrain. From there he contacted Savak, who informed him that they had not located Jim Owen, but they assured Dan that his father-in-law was not in Iran.

Dan then flew to Tehran. When he reached the Onager offices, he immediately arranged to have Jim Owen's safe opened. Besides stacks of currencies from four countries, an old Browning automatic, and a small chamois bag of loose diamonds, Dan found several files, including the one titled "Mannheim, Inc." The original material that Melanie had copied revealed no new information, except the picture of Connie Mannheim in a Russian prison. Dan put the file in his attaché case and carried it to his own office. Stacking the original with Melanie's copies, he fed them all into a shredder. His father would be pleased.

Then he went to see Savak, who provided Dan with a false passport and drove him to the airport, where he caught the night flight to Tokyo. The moment he cleared customs a man came up identifying himself as one of Savak's agents. Savak had traced Jim Owen to Tokyo. Dan was about to ask for more information, but the agent refused any further discussion. Dan concluded that Savak was going to wait on the sidelines, to see which of their friends at Onager, Limited, would survive.

Dan's original intention was to join his family. As he drove into the city, however, he realized that he had a chance to hunt the hunter and could be more effective if no one knew he was there. After checking into his room, he went out and observed the Faulkners' elaborate security. Deciding that his father must have good reason to be so cautious, Dan stayed where he was and phoned Al Mardigian, who was in Macao.

Dan knew the equipment that Buck's security team used and what would be needed to listen in on it. He also knew what guns he wanted. Mardigian said he would need two weeks to get the gear into Tokyo, but Dan gave him forty-eight hours and hung up.

The communications equipment was a simple matter; it arrived the next day by air charter. The guns were more of a problem, since Japan had the strictest gun control laws in the world. Mardigian decided on a technique used by the Japanese underworld. He located a corpse in Hong Kong that was to be shipped to Tokyo for burial. For a substantial bribe, he had two Atchisson 9-mm. submachine guns sealed in plastic wrap and surgically implanted in the cadaver's stomach. The weapons' two 32-round magazines were sewn into each thigh. The Japanese undertaker who received the remains in Tokyo removed the weapons for another substantial fee, and forty-seven hours after Dan's call, Al and the two submachine guns arrived at Dan's room.

While Dan stayed in the hotel room, Mardigian watched for Jim Owen and reported upstairs by walkie-talkie from a car parked near the hotel's entrance. Dan was able to monitor the Faulkner security team's transmissions, including their conversation about a possible exchange of money in the Ginza subway station.

The boredom of waiting, however, was numbing. When Mr. Miki came out of the front entrance of the hotel, Mardigian almost missed the man following him. His hair was dyed black, he wore thick horn-rimmed glasses, and his cheeks had been padded. Still, Mardigian recognized Jim Owen. Yelling the information over his walkie-talkie to Dan, Mardigian drove off behind Owen to the Tokyo Airport.

Soon after, Dan heard his family leave the hotel and watched them until they turned a corner. As the walkie-talkie moved out of range, he thought of his last conversation with Raven. Lying in the dark room, watching the Hotel Okura's English-language news service, he wondered whether his brother had been about to tell him the truth, and tried to decide how long Raven had known about his birth. If he hadn't found out himself, Dan wondered whether his family would ever have let him in on the secret. It made no difference. Dan was sure that he would soon earn Buck and Jennifer's gratitude once and for all.

On the road to the airport, Owen was congratulating himself on deciding to follow Mr. Miki rather than Buck. By doing so he had monitored the first transfer of cash to Nogato's men in the Ginza subway. Now he suspected Mr. Miki was about to make the final payment.

Sitting in the cab, alternately smoking and trying to control his cough, he watched Miki's limousine out the front window. Reaching inside his coat, he touched the butt of the .357 Magnum, for which he had paid three thousand dollars to a black-market dealer. Uncharacteristically, he didn't look out the back window of his cab to check whether he was being followed.

As he watched Mr. Miki board a plane bound for Los Angeles, however, Owen's expectations dissolved. He walked away from the departure area and tried to figure out what had happened. Sensing an old instinct, he abruptly changed direction and glimpsed Mardigian attempting to disappear into a crowd. Jim Owen lit another cigarette and quickly figured out a contingency plan that included Dan in its resolution. He knew that Mardigian would never be in Tokyo following him, if Dan weren't there as well. Then he deliberately let Mardigian pick him up again.

Before seeing Mardigian, Owen had believed he had two advantages. One was that the Faulkners did not anticipate violence. The other was that Owen didn't care about his own survival, once the Faulkners were destroyed. But with Dan in Tokyo, Owen presumed they were concerned with more than negotiation and decided the .357 Magnum might not be enough.

Owen returned downtown and quickly lost Mardigian, then expertly followed his former business colleague back to the Okura Hotel. After tipping lavishly to learn Mardigian's room number, Jim realized that he had all the Faulkners under one roof.

As he started out of the lobby, he nearly ran into the rest of the family, who were just returning from their dinner. Fortunately, his disguise seemed effective. Owen quickly left the hotel.

That night, just as Raven and Babs were falling asleep, Buck knocked at the door. When Raven let him in, Buck said, "I just heard from Nogato. He needs more money, by five tomorrow morning. They're going to announce our contract at nine, but certain tokens must be paid before that." He hesitated, then said, "You were right; they aren't interested in gestures. They want money. A lot of it. Can you get the money from Hong Kong?"

"Not in four hours. How much do they want?"

"Another two million dollars in yen. I'll have to make a lot of phone calls."

Raven said, "The K.D.D. is open all night. You can call from there. It's not far, on Kasumi-gaseke Dori. I'll go with you."

Buck nodded. "Knock on my door when you're dressed."

Raven started for the closet, but Babs was standing in his way.

"Don't ask," Raven said.

She nodded. "I won't. I'll just tell you I love you, so I damn well expect you to get back here in one piece." He kissed her.

On the second floor, Dan heard the security team begin organizing themselves. He crossed the room and shoved Mardigian with his foot.

"Come on, Al, get your ass in gear. This is probably the shooting match."

Mardigian was immediately alert. He hung one of the submachine guns on the strap around his shoulder. As he put a raincoat on, he said to Dan, "Don't kick me. I don't like it."

"Sh!" Dan responded, listening to the receiver. "Father and Raven are going in the limo. It's a goddam big Cadillac; you should be able to see it well enough."

Mardigian smiled. "I won't lose it."

Dan picked up his gun. "I'll be at the phone booth near the Ginza subway in fifteen minutes. You have the number in case anything goes wrong?"

Mardigian nodded.

"All right. Be careful going out. Raven could see you."

"Thank you, Dan," Mardigian said sarcastically, "I will."

On the first floor, Mardigian checked and hurried across the lobby. Dan left the hotel by a service entrance and hailed a taxi.

Outside, Mardigian waited as the limousine drove past. He turned the ignition key in his car, but nothing happened. He tried the ignition again and again as the limousine disappeared into the night. He jumped out of the car and opened the hood. Every cable had been cut.

Smiling, he went back into the car, unclipped the submachine gun, took a small automatic revolver from under the front seat, and stuck it in his belt. Then he walked the block to the American Embassy and, pretending to search for a coin, let the Japanese police see his weapon. He was instantly arrested. If Dan survived whatever Owen had planned for him, which Mardigian doubted, Mardigian would have a perfect excuse for not having been able to call with a warning.

Raven and Buck arrived at the K.D.D. building without incident. It was early morning in California, which made it easier to reach people. Buck's first call was to tell Sam Priest to stop Mr. Miki's mission. Then he spoke with various financial officers of the company, and to the banks. Raven sat in the private cubicle and watched Buck work. When he was finished, Buck handed Raven four names and addresses. Beside each name was a figure which collectively added up to two million.

"This should do it," Buck said. "These people will be expecting you. Nogato's people will be at the usual place at five A.M. The password is for one of them to say, *Mokari makka,* which means, 'How's business?' We'll say, *Chigai-masu,* 'It's different.' Nogato seems to enjoy his little ironies."

Raven looked at the list, then at his father.

"Even if Owen doesn't get to us," Raven said slowly, "we're going to get burned for this."

"Almost certainly," Buck replied.

Raven folded the list and put it in his pocket.

"You take two security men and drop me at the hotel," Buck said. "We'll meet you at the Ginza subway entrance just before five."

"What for? You stay in the hotel. When somebody starts asking questions they'll start with you. I can deliver the money."

"I know. But as you said once, 'If you're in this, so am I.'"

"That's sentimental. Let me do it."

"I'll meet you at the Ginza," Buck said as he headed for the street.

Raven crisscrossed Tokyo, meeting sleepy Japanese businessmen who kept large amounts of cash in their homes for various emergencies. By 4 A.M, they reached the last house. Raven and one security man hurried inside.

The chauffeur was the first to notice smoke coming from the limousine's trunk. Fortunately, he had a small fire extinguisher under the front seat, which he handed to the guard while he quickly opened the trunk. For a moment, all he could see was smoke. Then he saw a man wearing a plastic nose cone, who aimed a pistol with a silencer at the security guard and shot him in the forehead. The chauffeur did not utter a sound. Owen climbed stiffly out of the trunk, tearing off the nose cone, which was attached to a portable tank of oxygen.

"Do you speak English?" Owen whispered.

The chauffeur nodded. Owen frisked him and said, "If you make any noise, I'll kill you. Go sit behind the wheel."

The chauffeur did as he was told, as Owen closed the trunk and took a position where he could watch both the car and the house.

Raven and the guard crossed the lawn. Before they noticed anything amiss, Owen stepped out from behind a pine tree and shot the guard in the back of the head.

"If you want to live," Owen said, training his gun on Raven, "open the back door and get in the far jump seat."

Raven did what he was told, and Owen sat on the seat behind him.

"Driver," Owen said, pitching the chauffeur the keys. "Take us to the Iriya subway station on Kototoi-dori. I don't want to talk until we get there, Raven. Just face straight ahead, and believe me, I can shoot faster than you can jump."

They rode silently except for Owen's frequent cough. By the time they reached the subway station, Raven had sweated through his suit.

Owen told the chauffeur to turn a corner and double park. Then he said, "Take the subway to the Ginza. If Mr. Faulkner is there, tell him to call his hotel. If he isn't, go find him at the Okura. Tell him what's happened, and that my name is Jim Owen. If you call for the police on your way, as soon as they find us I'll shoot Raven. Do you understand all that?"

The chauffeur nodded.

"All right. Leave the keys and get out."

They watched the chauffeur hurry across the street and enter the subway. As soon as he had disappeared from sight, Owen said, "We're moving. Let me warn you: Don't do anything to attract attention. Open the door."

Raven did so, and stepped out. Owen followed, the revolver under his coat. "Get the keys and open the trunk. Bring the tank and face mask you find with you. Then close the trunk and leave the keys in the lock."

The street was empty. When Raven had the oxygen tank and mask, Owen said, "There's a blue Toyota parked across the street. Unlock it with these keys. Put the tank and the mask on the back seat, then get in front. We can chat while I get that smoke bomb out of my lungs."

Again, Raven did as he was told, realizing that Owen must have been in the limousine's trunk the entire time they had driven around Tokyo.

When they were both seated in the Toyota, Raven listened to the low hiss as Jim turned on the oxygen and breathed through the nose cone.

"Just look straight ahead," Owen said.

"Sure, Jim. What happens now?"

"In about twenty minutes, Faulkner Aerospace starts to crumble."

"Probably the two people who care the least about that are sitting in this car."

"I care," Owen said, before he coughed and breathed again into the mask.

"Sure you do, you and Uncle Jack. He'll be proud of you, or at least impressed with you."

Owen didn't respond immediately. "Who?"

"Jack Llewellyn. We have pictures of you and him at Kennedy Airport. He looks pretty silly in a Homburg, don't you think?"

Again Jim Owen paused, then said, "You still haven't learned to hold onto your strong cards, have you?"

Raven felt a jab of pain in his neck. In two seconds, he was unconscious.

After propping Raven up, Owen let the hypodermic needle fall and started the car. He stopped two blocks away, beside a blue intercity phone booth. Depositing a ten-yen coin, he dialed the

340

Hotel Okura and asked for Buck Faulkner. Halfway through the first ring, Jennifer answered.

"Mrs. Faulkner, this is Jim Owen. If Buck's there, tell him to pick up the extension."

"He's not here."

Another click sounded and Owen knew that someone was listening.

"Then you'll be hearing from him shortly. Listen carefully. I have Raven." He heard a sudden gasp as he continued. "I want Dan, and I want him at eight this morning."

"Dan's not in Tokyo. We can't possibly . . ." she started to plead.

"Mrs. Faulkner, don't lie to me. Dan and Al Mardigian are in Room 210, and I know it." He coughed. "If you want to see Raven again, Dan will have to go to Ueno Park. At the south end there's a statue of Takamori Saigo. There's a bench directly behind it. Under the left end of the bench, he'll find a pair of handcuffs. He should put them on and carry his coat over them so they won't be noticed. If he has a weapon, you lose Raven. If he's not there by eight, you lose Raven. If he wears any body transmitters, or if anyone comes with him, you lose Raven." He chuckled, which made him start coughing. "It should be an interesting choice for Buck."

"How do we know you'll let Raven go?"

Owen was impressed; she wasn't giving in to anger or hysteria. "You don't, but it's the only hope you have."

"And then what are we to expect from you and whoever else you've hired?"

"I'm alone, Mrs. Faulkner. Tell Buck that. I want him to know."

"What will happen to Dan?"

"We have some business to finish. You have three hours."

The warning chime began on the phone, signaling the end of three minutes.

"Wait!"

"Sorry," Owen said. "Eight o'clock. Ueno Park." He hung up and lit a cigarette. Then he hurried back to the blue Toyota. He grabbed for the mask in the back seat and turned on the tank. The slight amount of oxygen that escaped from the mask made his cigarette burn down twice as fast as usual. When he finished

341

smoking, he got in the front seat and took a bottle of plum wine out of the glove compartment. He poured the bottle into Raven's mouth. Still unconscious, Raven gagged, then Jim Owen took a swallow, rinsed his mouth, and spat the wine on Raven. Throwing the open bottle on the back seat, Owen drove away.

By that time, Dan had been waiting at the Ginza subway station entrance for nearly three hours. He was cold and jumpy. He paced around a blue phone booth, on which he had placed a Japanese "out of order" sign. Dan believed that if he didn't hear from Mardigian, sooner or later the transfer would happen. He felt the outline of the Atchisson under his arm. He squeezed his fingers into fists, trying to keep the circulation going in his hands.

Even at 5 A.M., the Ginza was far from deserted. The air had been washed down by the night's rain, so the usual smog had not yet blanketed the city. Dan tried to remain inconspicuous, but it was difficult because of his size.

A *haiyo* car pulled up to the curb, and Dan saw his father sitting in the back seat with a woman. The man sitting beside the driver got out of the car and examined the pedestrians as they walked by. Dan presumed that they were two of the security people whom he had heard talking over the past few days. He walked to a nearby newsstand. It was five o'clock. He unbuttoned his overcoat.

Nothing happened. At three minutes after the hour, Buck jumped out of the car and stared desperately up and down the broad avenue. Raven was obviously late; Dan smiled. Suddenly, a Japanese man in a chauffeur's uniform came running out of the subway entrance. When he saw Buck, he started yelling. Dan thought that was it. As the chauffeur ran toward Buck, he was intercepted by the security guard. Dan presumed that they were being set up as targets. He wondered where the hell Raven was—and Mardigian, for that matter. The chauffeur had fallen to his knees and was babbling hysterically. Dan gripped his gun and began walking toward them. He expected to see Jim Owen and wanted to be in place. Instead a sharp object jammed into his back and a woman quietly said, "Hold it there and don't move."

Dan's first reaction was to turn and shoot her. As he started to pivot, he felt a leg go between his, a quick shove, and he was on his back with the submachine gun clattering down beside him.

342

The woman from the car stood over him and lifted her heel toward his eye as Buck called out, "Wait!"

The woman stopped, but grabbed Dan's neck and squeezed enough nerves to paralyze him. She unclipped the submachine gun and concealed it under her coat.

As Buck approached, Dan yelled, "Let go of me, you goddam bitch!" She released her grip, but continued to stand over him, her eyes fixed on his hands.

Astonished, Buck gasped, "What are you doing here?"

"I've been looking out for you," Dan blurted. "I figured Jim Owen would show up."

Buck nodded and helped Dan to his feet. "He did show up. He has your brother. He killed two of our security people to get him."

The woman who had thrown Dan tried not to react to the news. "Mr. Faulkner," she said, "what about the people waiting for us in the subway?"

Buck looked toward the entrance and hesitated. "We have nothing for them. I have to call the hotel."

"Use the phone over there," Dan said. "The out-of-order sign is a phony." His anger was growing; if something had happened to Raven, why hadn't Mardigian called?

Buck dialed the Okura, and Jennifer answered on the first ring.

"Buck?"

"Yes. I was told to call you."

"Owen has Raven."

"I know."

"He wants Dan in exchange."

As Jennifer explained Owen's demands, Buck slowly looked around at his son. "Owen thinks Dan and Al Mardigian are here in the hotel," Jennifer said. "In room two-ten."

Buck interrupted. "Dan's here with me. I'll find out the details."

"Buck, what can we do?"

Buck didn't answer for a moment. "Is Babs there?"

"Yes."

"Put her on."

"Hello," she said shakily.

"Hang on, Babs," Buck said. "I'll get him back."

"Thanks. That's what I want—a lot."

"Put Jennifer back on."

"Yes?" Jennifer began.

"Meet me in the lobby in fifteen minutes."

"The lobby?" Jennifer said, surprised.

"Jim's alone. I believe him. There's no need for security any more."

"Fifteen minutes," Jennifer said and hung up.

Buck turned to Dan. "Where's your partner?"

"Damned if I know. Stupid son of a bitch probably got lost again."

"Jim Owen knew your room number."

Dan's mouth opened. "What?"

"How long have you and Mardigian been in Tokyo?"

"He came a couple of days ago. I was here a couple of days before that. Listen, I was going after Owen—"

"Did you see Owen at all?"

"Mardigian did. He followed him and lost him."

"Are you sure?"

Dan stared at his father. "What's that mean?"

"Who takes over Onager Limited if something happens to you? What if Jim Owen didn't blow up your house? What if he found out where you were in Tokyo with a little help from your friend?"

"That little pimp!"

"Listen to me, Dan," Buck said as he began to walk him to the *haiyo* car. "I'm going to get your brother—"

"He's not my goddam brother, so you can forget *that* little act. I've spent my whole goddam life dealing with Raven. Now you have to rescue him again, just like you've done all his life, from California to Vietnam." Dan paused to see if his information had any impact. "Sooner or later, you'll realize who your real son is. You owe me. I've been paying all my life for one dead baby and one stolen son of a bitch!" He turned to the security woman. "Give me my goddam gun."

She only looked at Buck for orders.

"We don't have time to discuss debts," Buck said. "I want you to go with the guard. We have to get out of Japan as quickly and as quietly as possible, *all* of us. Your mother will meet you at the air terminal; there's an Execujet waiting there—"

"Where'll you be?"

"Getting Raven."

"Give me my gun," Dan said. "I'm going with you."

"No, Dan," Buck said. "Then Owen would have everything he wants. Your absence may be the only chance Raven and I will have."

"Of what?"

Buck didn't answer. "I want you to make sure your mother gets out of here."

Enraged, Dan stared at Buck, knowing that he had no choice. "Goddamn you, don't get killed. Tell Mother my passport is in my room, in the top dresser drawer."

Buck nodded. Dan turned and got into the *haiyo* car, followed by the male guard. Buck watched the car edge out into the early morning traffic. He then hailed a taxicab and got in after the security woman. As the cab drove off, Buck glimpsed one of Nogato's men at the subway entrance.

When Buck reached the hotel, he found Jennifer pacing back and forth in the lobby.

"How's Babs taking it?" Buck asked.

"She's holding on."

"And you?"

"I'll let you know when you tell me what our plans are."

"Dan's on the way to the airport. I want you and Babs to join him. I'm going to Ueno Park."

"I was afraid you'd say that."

"I can't send Dan to his death, and Owen doesn't want anyone else, except me. I can't just let him keep Raven; I can't call the police."

"Owen is getting everything," Jennifer said desperately.

"He hasn't yet."

She turned to look at him, her eyes wide with fear. "I don't want to lose you."

"There isn't a choice."

"I know. When Dan was born, you told the doctors that if there were a choice between me and our child, to save me. I wish I could order you to do the same now." She covered her eyes with her hand. "It's as if it were all happening over again. You went for Raven when we needed him. You have to go again now that he needs you. But this time, I may lose you both."

345

"I promise you, we have a good chance. The strange thing is, I know if I save him, he'll leave us."

They sat silently for a moment, holding each other's hand.

Jennifer finally whispered, "Go."

Buck nodded. "When you leave, don't pack anything; Toshiharu's people will send everything later. Go into Dan's room. His passport is in the top dresser drawer. Have Babs bring Raven's, and you get mine. Call the Execujet crew when you get upstairs. At eight o'clock—"

"Eight o'clock," Jennifer said, wincing.

"Yes. You and Babs come down. Don't pay any attention to anybody in the lobby. Nogato may have sent some of his army over. He's not going to be happy with what's happened, but they'll be waiting for me. Go straight to the airport and get on the Execujet. Dan will be there. Have one of the security people wait with our passports in the executive terminal."

"What if our other two men have been found? The police may come."

"Neither of them carried any identification. It'll take longer than that—"

"How long do we wait for you and Raven?" Her voice was emotionless.

"Two hours. At ten o'clock, you take off. If Jim is planning to drive me somewhere else, I'll miss you, in which case, Raven and I will have to find another way out of Japan."

"We'll fly to Manila and send the plane back. If you miss us, the Execujet will be here tomorrow morning."

"All right. But Jim's in as much of a hurry as we are. He'll want to conclude our meeting as quickly as possible, which means he and Raven won't be far from Ueno Park. We should be able to get to the airport by ten. I don't want you and Dan to stay in Tokyo, no matter what happens. Agreed?"

She nodded, then, taking his hand, she raised it to her lips and kissed it. "Don't dare say goodbye." Without another word they stood up. Jennifer hesitated at the elevator. "Owen may be expecting you. He said something like, 'It'll be an interesting choice for Buck to make.' I thought he meant between the two boys, but obviously he knows you would choose to come. He was coughing badly."

Buck nodded. Jennifer tried to smile, but couldn't. She turned and hurried into an elevator.

The clock above the reception desk read 6:05. Buck went over to the security woman, who looked pale and shaken. "I'm so deeply sorry about your colleagues," Buck said. She nodded her appreciation. "I have to ask you to stay with Mrs. Faulkner and get rid of the submachine gun."

Without a word, the woman stood up and went toward the elevator.

Buck left the hotel on foot. The night rain had cleared; the dawn was beautiful and cold. He reviewed what the chauffeur had told him about Jim Owen: a gun with a silencer, a tank of oxygen and a face mask.

For the first time in many years, Buck remembered his old superstition about Connie Manheim's destruction being equalized by his own. Abruptly, he stopped walking and waved down a taxi. He told the driver to take him to the emergency room of St. Luke's Hospital.

36

Jim Owen had an easy time convincing the doorman at the Ueno Keisei Hotel that his friend had drunk too much plum wine. After pocketing a large tip, the doorman helped Owen carry Raven to his room on the second floor. As soon as he was alone, Owen sat down, gasping. He turned a valve on a large oxygen tank in the corner and, hooking the plastic tubing around his ear, he attached the cannula to his nostrils and began breathing deeply.

He had brought the bag of money up with him, but had left the portable oxygen tank in the car. It was empty, but if he had to, he could refill it later. The feeling in his lungs was not only pain but panic and hopelessness, all of which he had to control. Soon, he hoped, it would not matter. He carefully lit a cigarette and absently stacked the money on the floor.

When he finished his cigarette, he took the cannula off and dragged Raven into the small bathroom. Owen lifted the dead-weight body into the tub and turned on the cold water. Then he took two pairs of handcuffs out of the medicine cabinet. With one, he shackled Raven's wrists to the tub's cold water pipe; with the other, he locked Raven's leg to the drain pipe under the sink. Then he turned off the water, packed Raven's mouth with cotton and taped it shut.

Panting slightly from the exertion, he went back into his room and dragged the single chair over to the window and again attached the oxygen cannula to his nostril. He parted the bilious drapes so that he could look across the street to Ueno Park. The Saigo statue was clearly visible through the trees.

As he waited, Owen thought of his daughter lying in the London hospital bed, her face still mottled with bruises, her mouth held shut with wire. He glanced across the room to the dresser on top of which lay an L-shaped tire iron. He hoped Dan would show up.

Hearing a splash, he walked into the bathroom. Raven seemed to be waking up. When he went back to the window a man was approaching the statue. Taking up the binoculars, Jim watched as Buck sat down, reached under the bench for the handcuffs and discovered the note of instructions.

As Buck read them, Owen went back into the bathroom.

"Too bad for you, Raven," Owen said. "I was hoping Dan would join us, but your father insists on being a hero." Carefully avoiding Raven's free leg, he pulled the plug so that the water ran out of the tub. "It would have been easier on you if Dan had come." He watched as Raven thrashed around for a moment and then lay still. Owen hurried back to the window.

Looking around the park, Buck finally gazed in the direction of the Ueno Keisei Hotel and quickly snapped on the handcuffs. With surprise, Owen saw Buck put out a cigarette. He hadn't realized that Buck smoked. Finding his own chest constricted, he picked up the cannula and breathed deeply. He watched Buck cross Chuo-dori Avenue and enter the hotel. The instructions had said to take the elevator to the third floor, make sure no one was behind him, then walk down the stairs to the second floor. As soon as he was sure he was alone in the hallway, he was supposed to put his hands against the wall in front of him and wait.

Drawing the Magnum out of its shoulder holster, Owen took a deep breath of oxygen and put the cannula aside. He went to the door and opened it. Down the hall, he saw Buck leaning against the wall. "Keep your hands where I can see them, and walk toward me."

When Buck reached the room, Owen yanked Buck inside, shut the door and expertly frisked him. Owen pulled out a wallet, a butane lighter, a half-filled pack of American cigarettes, and a money clip. He threw them all on the bed.

"I never knew you smoked, Buck."

"I never did, but in the last few years—"

Inside the bathroom, Raven yelled and smacked his free leg against the bathtub.

"Can I see him?" Buck asked.

"In just a moment." He ran an electronic body wand over Buck to make sure he wasn't concealing a transmitter. "Now drop your coat on the bed and you can take a look."

As Buck went into the bathroom, Owen picked up the oxygen cannula again. "Look. Don't touch."

Buck turned and came back into the room. He stared at the closed drapes, the oxygen tank, and the money that Raven had collected which was now lying on the floor.

"For what it's worth," Owen said, referring to the money, "you can have it back now."

Buck looked at him, and for the first time, Owen saw that he was afraid.

"Jim, I've done everything you said to do. Please—"

"I wanted Dan."

"I couldn't do that."

"You could have. You didn't, because you figured if I didn't have Dan, you and Raven might get more time, but you were wrong."

"Maybe I was. I'm sorry, but Raven has nothing to do with this. I came in exchange for him; let him go."

"I plan to."

"When?"

"As soon as you do to him what Dan did to my daughter." He pointed to the tire iron. "If you hold it with both hands, you can use it with the handcuffs on."

"She fell," Buck pleaded. "It was an accident, Jim."

"That's not what she told me."

"Melanie's been known to lie."

"I'm not here to argue with you," Owen said. "Dan's your son; he disfigured my daughter." He coughed and turned the gauge on the oxygen tank slightly higher. "Now, let's see you use that tire iron."

Buck began to shake. "Jim, I beg you—"

"Don't bother."

Buck stared for a moment, then went to the bureau for the tire iron. He picked it up, but he couldn't hold it steadily, and tried

350

the other hand without success. Turning slowly, Buck walked around the twin beds, past the oxygen tank in the corner. Owen followed him with the muzzle of the gun.

In the bathroom, Buck looked down at Raven. His eyes were on the tire iron, but then he looked up and nodded as if giving permission.

"I can't do this," Buck said.

"You've ruined so many lives. This is only a face," Owen said with a chuckle.

"I can't. I need a cigarette."

"Don't stall, Buck."

"Please."

Owen nodded. Buck laid the tire iron on the bathroom floor, and went to the bed where he fumbled with his cigarettes and lighter. His hands shook and he began to sob quietly.

"Would you have made Dan do this?" he asked.

"No," Jim said. "I would have made Raven watch me. *I* wanted to mess up Dan's face. Then Raven would have called you, and while you were talking to him, I would have shot him."

"Who?" Buck asked, unsure of who Owen meant.

"Raven," Jim said calmly.

"Then you wouldn't have exchanged Raven for Dan."

"No."

"Then how can I believe that you'll let him go."

"You can't, Buck, but it's the only chance Raven has, so you better try it."

"But Dan is still alive."

"I'll find him. That you can be sure of." He watched Buck smoke and wanted a cigarette himself. Reaching in his pocket with his free hand, he pulled out a pack.

"Do you blame me for everything, Jim?" Buck asked with unexpected humility.

"Who else is to blame?"

"I don't know," Buck murmured hopelessly. "Before I ever met you, Llewellyn told me you were very idealistic. When your life didn't hold up to your standards, you blamed me for the failures."

Owen put the cigarette in his mouth and Buck held out his lighter. His hand shook violently.

Owen smiled bitterly. "It won't work, Buck. You've talked

me into setting up your murders, you've lied your way into my wife's bed, you've used me for your convenience, and your son has used my daughter for his."

He leaned forward slightly and Buck lit his cigarette. Then, with a flip of his finger, he turned up the butane which shot a blue flame into Jim Owen's nostrils. In the instant the plastic tube melted, setting his hair on fire, Owen grabbed at the tube. The spark shot up to the oxygen tank. Kicking at Owen's gun, Buck leaped backward over the bed to the floor. The gun went off a split second before the tank blew up. The bullet missed Buck, who was protected by the bed, but the force of the explosion rammed him against the wall and set the back of his clothes on fire as the windows shattered. For a second, Buck couldn't breathe. One arm had been jammed at a bad angle and was broken. Wildly, he rolled over on his back and tried to smother his burning clothes.

Owen had been knocked sideways; his neck and legs were broken and his clothes were on fire. Several pieces of the oxygen tank had torn through his body. The cigarette, however, was still gripped in the side of his mouth. Buck reached down and pried the Magnum out of Jim's hand. "Father!" Raven shouted.

Ignoring the screams in the hallway, Buck yelled, "I'm coming." Outside, the bells and sirens of emergency vehicles were growing louder.

Raven had rubbed the tape over his mouth loose and spat out the cotton. Calculating the angle of ricochet, Buck shot Raven's handcuff links away from the pipes. As Raven stood, Buck handed him the gun and Raven shot off the shackles on Buck's wrist.

In the bedroom they found the money a pile of ashes on the floor.

"Leave the gun. Drop it on him," Buck shouted. Raven did so and saw his father's overcoat on the floor beginning to smolder. He grabbed it.

"I don't need that," Buck said. "Open the door."

"You don't look so good," Raven said, throwing the coat over Buck's shoulders, "and we've got to get past the police."

Buck coughed and they hurried out into the hallway.

The last guests were rushing to the emergency exit. Buck and Raven went down the single flight of stairs and joined the crowd in the lobby as it moved toward the street. Police and firemen rushed in. Buck started to black out. Raven grabbed him and, lifting Buck's good arm around his shoulder, carried him outside to the street. The cold air revived Buck, and slowly they crossed Ueno Park. In front of the Keisei subway station, they hailed a taxi.

Epilogue

Jack Llewellyn clipped off each hair that was out of place. His habit was to have a haircut every other Thursday morning in his Pentagon office, but on special occasions, he took care to trim himself to an even more precise image. The special occasion was his prepared statement to be given that morning before a Senate subcommittee investigating overseas corruption by American business. In the aftermath of Watergate and the President's resignation, the country had developed an insatiable taste for scandal and purging.

Already the Senators had eviscerated the aerospace industry. Northrop, Grumman and Lockheed, among others, had admitted questionable payments abroad of hundreds of millions of dollars. That day, the subcommittee was beginning to hear testimony about Faulkner Aerospace. As he had sworn, Jack Llewellyn had every intention of driving the nails into Buck Faulkner's corporate coffin.

The General put the scissors down and checked the mirror once more. His uniform was tailored perfectly; soon it would include a fourth star. He walked from his dressing room into his study. The window behind his desk overlooked a well-groomed lawn sloping down to a paddock and stables. Usually, he paused at the window, but today he looked down at the neatly bound pages of his prepared statement to the Senate subcommittee. Before his appearance, copies would be made for distribution to the press. What Jack Llewellyn planned to reveal would satisfy them for at least a few days, long enough for Buck Faulkner to be devastated from the public reaction.

The red phone on his desk rang. A direct connection to the Air Force's war room at the Pentagon, it only rang in the case of a national emergency.

"General Llewellyn," he answered.

"Jack, this is Buck. Don't hang up. You have a problem. I have pictures of you meeting Jim Owen at Kennedy Airport." Shocked, the General did not respond, so Buck added, "You should never wear a Homburg, Jack. You look like an undertaker."

"How did you get on this line?"

"I wanted to be sure you'd answer the phone. My people arranged it."

"What do you want?"

"I understand you're supposed to testify today, just after me. I think we should have a meeting first."

"Where?"

"At the Smithsonian. It's on our way to the Capitol. I'll be there at ten. I'm sure you have a prepared statement. Bring it, and don't make copies; you'll just be wasting your time. I'll be waiting under *The Spirit of St. Louis.*"

As he put the red phone down, Llewellyn began to sweat. Not used to being caught at anything, the General was unfamiliar with the accompanying panic. He controlled it with a discipline learned over forty years of military life, but his rage grew. Jack couldn't believe how Buck kept surviving and kept giving the orders. Since Tokyo, the man had dodged and parried every accusation that the ministries of five countries had leveled at him, as well as those put forth by various bureaus of the U.S. government. In the latter, General Llewellyn had either insti-

356

gated them or participated in them. Three conglomerates had attempted a takeover of Faulkner Aerospace; there had been stockholders' suits, and the banks had tried endlessly to force a managerial reorganization. Yet Buck had endured—and had just manipulated the most highly classified communications system the Air Force possessed.

General Llewellyn barely remembered the meeting with Jim Owen. He had managed to blank the details from his mind; but he did remember wearing the Homburg. He also remembered the money. He wondered whether Buck had a picture of that.

A drop of sweat from his upper lip fell and spread on the leather-encased blotter of Air Force blue. He reached for a phone and called for his car. Then he opened the attaché case on his desk and put in the stack of typed papers. Another drop of sweat fell on the desk. He drew from his pocket a key ring and unlocked the bottom right drawer. He took out his service revolver and put it alongside the papers in his attaché case.

On the drive from his home in Virginia, Llewellyn sat rigidly in the back seat of his car. He tried desperately to figure some way to avoid or defuse the obvious results of Buck's photographs. The public was well aware of Jim Owen's activities, not only from the investigations of the Japanese authorities, but also from the series of articles which Melanie Owen Faulkner had published in the London press at the time of her divorce from Dan. One result was the image of Jim Owen as a demented killer. A photograph of him with General Llewellyn would have devastating implications, and Buck could be expected to make the most of them.

Jack had heard that, far from being in any way diminished by all that had happened, Buck seemed to be unaffected. As a result of Melanie's journalism, Dan had been prevented from taking over Faulkner Aerospace, as he had publicly bragged he would do with the help of the banks. The articles had details of Dan's deals with terrorist and revolutionary groups, and seven subpoenas still awaited his entry to the United States. He had gone into hiding, and from what Jack Llewellyn had heard from Defense Intelligence, Dan was still brokering arms sales from Nicaragua.

Jack remembered Jim Owen saying in the Japan Air Lines lobby, "If I don't make it, there's a file in my office safe in Tehran. It's called 'Mannheim, Inc.' If I don't finish Buck

Faulkner, it will." Jim Owen wouldn't tell him more, so Llewellyn immediately ordered the intelligence people at the embassy in Tehran to get into the Onager offices and open the safe. The Mannheim file, however, had been missing. Jack had presumed that Dan had taken it, but there was no time to contact him. The General glanced at the silver-threaded stars on his shoulder.

General Llewellyn thought of his two sons, both graduates of the Air Force Academy, one at S.A.C. headquarters, the other, a pilot, stationed in Germany. He thought of his home, his wife, his stables, his potential shame and dishonor. As he thought about killing Buck Faulkner, he realized that Buck had less to lose, having already lost his sons. Dan had gone into hiding with a final bitter denunciation of his father. Nobody knew where Raven was. After Tokyo, he, with Babs Wheatley, had quietly disappeared. Llewellyn thought of himself as the better father and the better man.

As the car crossed Memorial Bridge and headed up Constitution Avenue, the General considered going straight on to the Capitol and testifying as he had planned. Then he realized he would have to resign from the Air Force, an intolerable act that would not only brand him, but stain his family as well. By the time the car pulled up in front of the old Victorian brick façade of the Smithsonian, he knew what he had to do.

Carrying his attaché case, the General walked briskly into the museum through several rooms of the nation's memorabilia. At the entrance to the great hall, he hesitated, looking at Lindbergh's *Spirit of St. Louis,* which was suspended from the ceiling. He saw Buck across the room studying an old Pitcairn Mailwing. Under his arm was a manila envelope. Jack Llewellyn approached.

"I used to fly one of these carrying the night mail between Richmond and Atlanta," Buck said, as he turned around to face Llewellyn. He offered no further greeting, but opened the envelope and took out the pictures. "I've had a lot of chances to use these, but I didn't. So any debts to you are paid in full. Needless to say, I have copies." He started to hand them to Jack, then drew back. "Just out of curiosity, how much did you pay Jim Owen?"

Jack Llewellyn had already reached out for the pictures. He stared at Buck. "A hundred thousand."

"Yours? Or some unknown account of the Defense Department?"

"Both."

Buck nodded and released the envelope. As Jack put down his attaché case and looked through the pictures, Buck explained, "We did several enlargements, as you can see, to make your face clear; the arrivals board in the background establishes the date. The typed pages in there are your new opening statement to the subcommittee. You'll probably want to go over it before you're called to testify."

As he went through the pictures, Jack Llewellyn began to sweat again. When he saw the enlargement of his own face, he felt nauseous.

"What will you do with—" he began, but he had a difficult time speaking.

"Nothing, unless you make me. But Jack, I expect you to be extremely useful to Faulkner Aerospace in the future. You have a lot to make up for. You've assisted in every attempt to bring us down, but that's over. We're going to make it, with or without your help. With it, you might get your fourth star. Did you bring your opening statement?"

Jack nodded, and reached down for his attaché case. He felt awkward unlocking it on the floor, and hated stooping before Buck Faulkner. As he flipped open the top, Jack hesitated. As he reached inside, he sensed someone behind him.

"Just the papers, Uncle Jack."

It was Raven; he had seen the gun. He was too close for Jack to try to use it. Jack took the papers out, put the envelope inside, and snapped the attaché case shut. Then he stood up and handed his testimony to Buck. He noted that Raven had grown a beard and was wearing glasses, both of which altered his appearance considerably.

"Don't ever expect an apology," the General said.

"We don't," Buck said. "We'll all just have to live with it."

"I paid Jim Owen to stop the contract. That was all. The rest was his idea."

Buck shook his head. "Jack, you knew about him and me. You knew what he might do. Don't try to make yourself more honorable than you are."

The General glared at them, then started to walk away.

As he went, Raven said to Buck, "I read that Uncle Jack's Under Secretary is running for the Senate in Kansas."

"Yes, Kansas," Buck repeated

Raven smiled. "Maybe *Vice*-President at best . . ."

They waited until Llewellyn was safely out of the building before going to their own car for the short drive to the Capitol. As he opened the door, Buck stopped and said, "Before we get up there, I want to thank you for coming back, not just for the testimony today. Your mother and I are just so glad to see you."

Raven shrugged. "As I remember, you've come after me in some pretty hairy circumstances. I don't know how much good I can do, but I'm glad I'm here, too. Besides, Babs and I wanted the kid to see her grandparents. Just don't offer me a job, all right?"

Buck smiled, then turned toward the Capitol. "All right, let's go up there and see if we can bleed enough to satisfy all the sharks."

The two men got in the back seat, and the limousine sped up the Mall.